Crow's Nest

Tales of a Thief: Book 2

ROBIN LYTHGOE

ISBN-13: 978-0-9988219-0-0

First Print Edition
version 1.0

Crow's Nest is a work of fiction. Any similarity
between real names, characters, places and events is
purely coincidental.

Please visit the author's official website:
http://robinlythgoe.com

OTHER BOOKS BY ROBIN LYTHGOE

TALES OF A THIEF:

As the Crow Flies

THE MAGE'S GIFT:

Blood and Shadow
Flesh and Bone

Obscurely Obvious (A Short Story Collection)

CONTENTS

ACKNOWLEDGMENTS

I have to start by thanking my wonderful writing partner, Kristie Kiessling. From reading early drafts to giving me advice on the cover to (virtually) holding my hand through every crisis, she was as important to this book getting done as I was. Thank you so much, my friend.

Special thanks to Alan Mills, who poked, prodded, supplied many impromptu ideas, and tried hard to slap me with jokes.

I am so grateful to everyone who went out of their way to offer encouragement and kept asking, "Are you done yet?"—Mickey, Diana, Tammy, Amy, Paul and Candace, Marshall and Rose, Tania, Vaunda B., Dorkas M., Lana T.

Deepest thanks to my patient, generous, and helpful beta readers: Kristie (again), Alan (yes, him, too), James Lane, Courtney Lynn, Dorkas Michaelis-Iske, and Huw Bran. I confess, I struggled writing this book and I was so afraid to let you read it! Thank you for your lovely remarks, uplifting comments, and typo-reporting. (Those things are hide-and-seek experts!)

—1—
Vermin Is as Vermin Does

"I am called Crow, and I am a thief." A thief, I protested to myself. Not a warrior. Not a 'demon-taker.'

"I know. Shut up." Tanris was the warrior, and an extraordinarily dedicated demon-taker.

Neither of us had signed up for the project. Well, we *had*, but I didn't intend it to be a career choice. For myself, I found a certain appeal in the pardon offered by His Most Exalted Gloriousness Gaziah II, Emperor of Bahsyr. Tanris performed such tasks out of duty and nobility.

A job we'd expected to do in a few weeks now stretched into early autumn. I'm a city man, and all this chasing about the countryside in search of the alleged invaders wore on my patience as severely as it did on my sense of style. We were all in need of a bath—hot and soapy, rather than a mere dip in a convenient stream. Praise all the gods of water, there were plenty of those available and we managed to keep the stench under control.

I cleared my throat and continued my narrative. To preserve Tanris's senses and his temper, I kept my voice low. "I am not just any thief, mind, but the best and most famous in all the glittering empire. Ask anyone." My consideration didn't impress him.

"Are you trying to convince me or the demons?"

The creatures weren't any more demonic than he or his cronies. I could name a good many notables who bore a distinct resemblance to demons in conduct if not in appearance: court officials, military officers, judges, and more.

"Neither, I am committing to memory the introduction to my autobiography. Which I am writing on *your* suggestion."

"Well, write it silently in your head, or you'll give our position away." Braced against a boulder, my companion peered down the length of his loaded crossbow. "Trust me," he muttered, "a demon won't care if you're the best and most famous thief in the whole glittering world."

I didn't like when he called them 'demons.' They weren't. I call them 'foreigners' (which they were), but Tanris resisted.

"Don't say it," he ordered.

I must be growing predictable. With his back to me, he didn't see my theatrical pique, which was a lamentable waste. "Don't say *'Why, thank you, Tanris, your recognition means so much to me'*?"

To my delight, he had to think that through. "Just hush."

Decisions, decisions. I could stay quiet and let the soldiers do their jobs, or I could make noise, spoil the ambush, and instigate a long and dreadful chase. Both choices involved maiming, death— preferably not mine—rampant emotion, briars, brambles, sweat, and inevitable frustration. "Fine," I said, "but no killing."

He only grunted. I said the same thing every time, and he no longer found it worth a reply. This was a recent upgrade from the temper my argument usually sparked. Anger was not a side of him I had known well, but this excursion had obliterated that deficit in my education.

As I studied the sky through the gleaming green leaves overhead, I decided once again that dawn was not my favorite time of day. It did, however, offer a clarity of light that perfectly illuminated the major turn my life had taken. A year ago I'd have still been abed. Still been enjoying the company of a beautiful woman. Still been thanking the gods for my remarkable good fortune.

I meant no disrespect to the gods, for they protected me and taught me valuable lessons. Indeed, they lavished their gifts upon me at every turn. Why then, this redirection from a career of virtual solitude to one linked with *partners?* First, there was the dragon. Who knew baby dragons formed a bond with the first face they beheld? As a baby, he accompanied me nearly everywhere. And, because of his tender age, I frequently confined him to the camp—which he liked not at all.

And then there was Tanris, a fixed part of the gleaming Pardon Package. He was more versatile than one might expect, and full of unexpected talents. Still, I never would have dreamed I'd be crouching in the dubious shelter of the woods, furtively scratching at things I hoped were only imaginary while hunting down *demons.*

Doing such a thing alongside Tanris, a commander in the Emperor's elite Eagles, would once have fallen into the category of a nightmare. Hunting would have been strictly reserved for practical things like research, scapegoats, and supplies. *And silks,* I mused, because women made men giddy like that. Mercifully, I'd escaped the relationship with that particular beautiful woman, and Girl—the other member of our little alliance—didn't fancy silks or inspire giddiness. I quite liked Girl, but Tanris frequently gave me cause to rethink our association. If not for him and That Woman, I wouldn't have been in my current predicament at all, waiting in the woods for a trap to spring.

Not that Tanris didn't have many points to appreciate. Loyalty, brawn, levelheadedness, and extreme packing skills, to name a few. He also had a rare talent for turning obnoxious weeds into tasty tea. However, our perilous adventure previous to this one had left him a widower. I still struggled with the notion of him as a married man. My own doubts aside, his usual tendency toward aloofness had veered straight into brooding, simmering anger.

And me? Keeping up a cheerful attitude took inordinate effort these days. I had my own burden of loss to manage, and the wound of betrayal had scorched me deeper than I wanted to admit. As if that wasn't enough, my unexpected and unwelcome inheritance bedeviled me.

A single, wretched wizard ultimately bore the responsibility for our misery: Baron Duzayan Metin. May a pestilence of fleas infest his robes on his journey through all the hells. He'd used my betrothed to lay a trap for me, poisoned me, then sent me on a foolhardy *quest* to steal a dragon's egg. 'Twas he who'd orchestrated the event that had alien creatures running amok through the empire. He who'd turned my woman into a traitor and sent me slogging over hill and dale with Tanris for company. And he who'd been responsible for countless deaths, both human and otherwise. And fire. Destruction. Disaster. Is it any wonder people find wizards so abhorrent?

Tanris shifting brought me back to the present, but he only squinted down the crossbow's sight in another direction. The epitome of a well-trained warrior, he didn't relax for an instant.

Currently, a half-dozen men hid in the surrounding beech trees. Some had projectile weapons, all had swords and knives. As it happened, I had a knife, too. I used it for cutting meat, and sometimes for slipping latches. Not for poking people. Usually. Tanris's hand-picked fighters remained still as statues, invisible and undetectable—

Unless one was a druid, in which case jagged shards of tension gleamed like fireflies in the dark of night. Evidently, one needn't have polished druidic skills to see such things. That lesson had come to me early after my magical *endowment*. Like any sensible person, I had never liked magic and certainly didn't want to become a magic user of any stripe. After being forced into acquaintance with it, I'd softened my opinion at first.

But *you* try dealing with the nattering, nonsensical, *maddening* Ancestors and see what it does to you.

The Ancestors use magic, and my connection to them had been strictly accidental and—gods willing—it would be short-lived. I had yet to run into anyone in the wilds who knew how to get rid of it. *Them.* While they proved useful now and then, their constant babbling threatened my sanity. They had a penchant for patting and petting me, which would have been less disturbing if they had warmer fingers or kept their affections private. They also had the unattractive habit of transmitting the emotions of others to my senses.

Yet here I was out in the wilds with them. And Tanris. And a small troop of enthusiastic Eagles.

Turning my head, I tried to find the foreigner, KipKap, where he hid in the foliage twenty feet behind me. Did his people have druids among them? I wondered, but communicating with them was even harder than talking to Girl. She at least understood the language. Learning the gestures she used as speech had unexpected benefits. It came in handy, for instance, in situations when one had to maintain silence.

KipKap's polar blue eyes speared me from the depths of a concealing shrub. Yes, I know what you're thinking: snow covers the polar regions, so his eyes must be white, but that is not the case. His absolute blue gaze had the peculiar ability to draw one's attention, even if they weren't looking his way. More unnerving was the way he could freeze a body right where he stood.

That's how we met, but I digress.

Behind his leafy cover, KipKap cocked his leathery head in inquiry.

Do you see us? I signed. *See...* I had to think, trying to frame a complicated concept into limited gestures. *See fear?*

See you, he signed back. A wave of one six-fingered hand encompassed the surrounding area. *See Grimfist and fat one.* He touched his brow, his eyes, then pointed to the ravine. I decided KipKap meant the others had focused their attention on the job at hand, and I should as well.

Grimfist was Tanris's nickname. He didn't like it, but he deserved it, and anyone could sign it. Put fist to forehead and drag the brow down into a glower. The more menacing, the better.

Fat one described Neba, whose size belied his speed. He wasn't easy to conceal.

"Are they coming?" Tanris asked, relying on me to inform him about our intended victims.

"They will."

He let out a noise that was part sigh, part hum, and all irritation. "Are you even paying attention?"

"I'd rather not. I brought you and your assassins here; is that not enough?" From beneath my shirt, I pulled out the talisman the Ancestors had given me. A disk of horn strung on a leather cord, its warmth soothed my nerves.

"Feeling melodramatic today, are we?"

"You know—"

"Shh!" he hissed.

Just then, there came the sound of movement from the ravine and the unmistakable noise of conversation between foreigners— incomprehensible words interspersed with grunts.

"Don't kill them." I kept my voice low as I drew my knife. Habit —and hope—made me flex my left hand before I picked up a rock from a pile I'd stacked nearby. Two fit into my pocket. I needed bigger pockets… "And be careful, will you?"

Everything merely alert about Tanris a second before came together into a knot of intense focus. If—*when*—he loosed that bolt, he would not miss. I had seen him fight, and he possessed impressive skills. I imagine he grabbed a sword the instant he exited his mother's womb.

"Three," he whispered. "Two."

An ear-splitting shriek of shock obliterated the last number as a foreigner stepped into a waiting snare. Whipped off his feet, he would dangle upside down until freed. Howls and shouts immediately resulted. I could see nothing from my concealment, but the gods have blessed me with a vivid imagination.

I winced at the thump of Tanris's crossbow firing.

"Stay here and stay down," he ordered, as if I'd leap up and throw myself into the fray. Without a backward glance, he disappeared around the other side of the boulder.

Wildly disinclined to fight—ever—I happily complied. I hadn't become a good—nay, *great*—thief by being stupid. Need I remind you I am not a warrior?

The usual noises of a melee ensued: thuds, grunts, shouts, and screams. Why do people choose to risk life and limb rather than come to a civilized agreement? It escapes reason. Faced with wild animal attacks, they obviously have no choice. Conniving, no-good wizards also remove one's options. The beings we currently hunted were not wild animals, but the unfortunate victims of a no-good wizard.

A crash and a bellow shook leaves from an alder tree, raining gold and amber. My grip tightened on my paltry weapons. Still new to the art of war, I depended on the knowledge and brawn of my militant companions when I had to. Otherwise, I avoided battles as often as possible. Tanris, I trusted to preserve my person—at least as long as he thought it valuable. I liked him, but he was a practical man, and it simply isn't practical for a high-ranking officer in the emperor's employ to be friends with a thief. I suspected the others would just as gladly see me caught in one of their traps as one of the *demons*.

The bellow turned into pounding and grunting, then the noise retreated down the hill. I squinted through the undergrowth.

[Up up up! Teeth! Jaws! RippingtearingshreddingHIDE!] the Ancestors shrieked.

Praise the gods of quick thinking, I acted first and saved questions for later. Knife between my teeth, I grabbed a low-hanging branch and hoisted myself atop the boulder. None too soon either, for what should come scampering up but three hedge-demons. One of them followed my leap and embedded its pearly choppers in my greave. *Snap!* Teeth broke off, and the fuzzy-faced fiend couldn't unlock his jaw half as quick as he would have liked. It didn't seem a very practical attack plan if one's aim was off as badly as his.

While I beat him unconscious, six more of the things tumbled into my allegedly safe space. Either they'd come through the gate faster than their larger friends, or they bred like bunnies. My beautiful steel greaves had cost me a pretty penny. Long steel plates protected my shins, with bands buckling at knee, ankle, and once between. Smaller plates surrounded the backs and sides, riveted to thick, sturdy leather. No hedge-demon was going to take a bite out of *my* leg again.

And yes, I *will* call this particular breed a demon. Although they resemble hedgehogs, they are vicious little devils. Do not let their fuzziness and cute, flat faces fool you. They have far too many needle-sharp teeth and jaws of iron. Once they sink their fangs into you, they may become a permanent addition. For having such ridiculously short legs, they move with frightful speed, and they can launch themselves a lot higher than they have any right. I suspect they use magic to do it.

They leaped at me repeatedly, and I had to kick the creatures from my perch several times as they scrabbled for purchase. I made good use of both rock and blade. The hedge-demons were eerily silent until they got their teeth set. Then they started chewing and making noises of appreciation for a good meal. Very disconcerting. I pried loose the beast attached to my greave. With him gone, I found myself wishing for a longer weapon.

Or KipKap. Striding through the shrubs into my clearing, he set about knocking hedge-demons every which way with a long-handled mace. The head bore a round ball with sharp spikes poking off the sides and one longer skewer protruding from the end. I'd seen him toting it around and had thought it was some sort of ceremonial token. Now I knew better. In my defense, the band encircling the head had some lovely decorative ornaments carved into it.

Under these strenuous circumstances, the hedge-demons finally made noise. Squealing and screeching fit to wake the dead, they met their gruesome ends. I had to look away.

The job didn't take long. "How do you say bad creature?" KipKap asked in his two octaves too deep voice. He rested the head of his mace on the ground, pushing the little corpses aside with one foot.

"Pest. Vermin. Rodent." I ventured a look at the killing ground and immediately wished I hadn't. Not once had I seen him take the life of anything or anyone before today. Evidence suggested he had plenty of experience.

He nodded solemnly. "Kill pestverminrodent."

"Um… three words. They all mean the same thing."

"Why?"

I shrugged. "I do not know, KipKap." My fine sense of wit and humor would be lost on him, so I saved it for later. For someone like Tanris. "Thank you for your help."

"Yes." He plucked a handful of leaves to clean the blood from his weapon, and I slid gingerly to the ground. My knife needed cleaning as well, so I copied him.

I'd nearly finished when Tanris came tromping up the hill. He stopped at the edge of the tiny clearing, brows drawn together in a frown.

"I thought you said no killing?"

"KipKap says they're vermin."

"Oh, does he?"

I turned to gesture at my rescuer, but he'd disappeared. Swift recovery of my aplomb is one of my many talents. I waved the knife dramatically. "Have you ever tried to talk to one of those things? They eat first and talk during." I made nom-nom-nom noises.

He grunted. He does that often, and it can mean either agreement or disbelief; sometimes frustration. "You didn't kill these yourself with that little knife."

"Wouldn't you be surprised."

"Yes."

So would I, but no sense dwelling on it. "Where's Girl?"

Tanris tipped his shaven head toward the trail where we'd dug a pit large enough to hold one of the emperor's elephants. "Minding the crew. She's fine."

"And you?"

"I'm right here." A wicked gleam of humor shot through his eyes.

"I noticed that," I nodded. "And not even a scratch. Excellent."

"I'm glad you approve." He looked me over.

I *felt* the ripple of his relief as if it belonged to me. Mild gratification that he'd worried about me fell afoul of annoyance. Why did the Ancestors think I wanted to feel what Tanris—or anyone else —felt? I jammed my knife into its sheath. "How many dead?" I asked.

"Four, so far. Theirs."

The news turned my stomach.

"There were a lot more than we expected, Crow." Hands on his hips, Tanris frowned toward the sound of soldiers restoring order. "Another of KipKap's kind is among them, and we've got a problem."

"Is he dead?" Alarm tripped through me.

"Injured. Come with me."

Throughout the woods, foreigners still hung upside down. We'd set several traps in case some of them got through the first line. I didn't expect to see so many sprung. Pairs of soldiers cut them down, one member of the team keeping a weapon aimed at the victim's chest. From there they'd go to the wagons, chained like criminals.

My jaw hurt from grinding my teeth at the injustice.

"Here," Tanris said, and moved to the side.

It looked as if a herd of oxen had run through the place. Shrubs lay flat. Small trees were broken or uprooted. Had I missed a miniature hurricane? Worse, had I missed a wizard? No, the Ancestors would have gone wild with alarm.

And then I saw the... creature.

My first instinct was to turn around and run. I took two staggering steps backwards and saved myself from falling over by grabbing a tree. That is, I casually propped myself against the nearest trunk. "Well, that's different," I managed.

Different being a good ten feet tall and built like an avalanche. Did I want to ask how the soldiers had knocked the creature unconscious? The thing stretched out on the ground, unmoving. Rope bound each of its limbs to separate trees. More or less man-shaped, it had two arms, two legs, and a head like a man. The obscene musculature of its shoulders made the skull look tiny. Tusks jutted from sloppy lips and a series of three horns marched up its face. The thing wore a ragged leather loincloth, which I brought to Tanris's attention.

"Domesticated?" I wondered.

Tanris scratched at the stubble on his chin. "Probably makes a perfect house servant."

Was that a joke or not? "Did it break anyone?"

"What do you think?" He pointed to a knot of men a safe distance away. Green robes marked the pair of Ishramite priests assigned to our merry band. An order of healers, they use magic to do some of their work, but that is a guarded secret. I was uncertain even Tanris knew. "Four down," he said, "and three with minor injuries, thanks to your friend. It's a miracle none are dead, but that's a quarter of my men, Crow. Tell me why we shouldn't kill this thing right now."

Anger and frustration boiled up inside me. "If you do, I'll quit." I'd thought about it often. Understanding the reason behind this venture did not mean I agreed with the methods.

He snorted. "And kiss your pardon goodbye?"

The pardon was conditional upon my services to the realm. It fell to me and Tanris to tidy the problem created by Baron Duzayan, one of the emperor's very own nobles. And I had a sneaking suspicion my involvement with the crown wouldn't end with this. Nobles and wizards bore some strikingly similar characteristics. "I won't need a pardon in the Confederacy." Across the ocean, out of reach of the emperor's long arms.

"You won't leave Bahsyr. You're too fond of your reputation, and forging a new one would take too much work."

I sniffed. "That is unkind." Mostly true, though. I'd spent all my life crafting my sterling character in the Bahsyr Empire. Not long ago, I'd planned to retire into legend, get married, and move to the islands to raise a flock of little Crows.

"What about Not-an-Egg?" he asked, referring to the dragon that kept me company. Still a mere baby, he stayed at the camp during the foray—in a cage, for his own safety as well as that of the soldiers.

"We'd manage."

He grunted again. "With the Emperor's Own hounding every step of your attempt to escape?"

"You'd join the hunt?"

He didn't respond to my question, but asked another of his own. "Who knows what would happen to him when you're caught?"

"I won't be," I answered shortly.

He sent a mocking glance my way. "It already happened once."

Yelling accompanied the cutting loose of another foreigner and distracted us. One of the soldiers thumped their defiant prisoner smartly upside the head with the butt of his spear, and that was that.

"Well?" Tanris pressed. "I can't have this monster going on the rampage when it wakes."

I rubbed my forehead. Here we went again. "None of this is their fault."

"It is if they're going to kill and maim and steal and destroy."

"I know. I *know*, Tanris, but this is wrong!" He knew my opinion well. "What if it were you that had been yanked away from everything you knew and thrust into a strange place? Confused, hungry, in need of shelter. And if that weren't terrifying enough, ugly creatures scream at you, hunt you down, and kill you." I had never put it so baldly before, and I could tell he didn't like it by the way his mouth flattened.

"You're twisting the facts."

"Am I?" I held up one finger. "First, these creatures—"

"Duzayan was summoning demons. Why shouldn't we believe that's what they are? They look like demons, they act like demons."

"First," I started again, "they aren't all savage fiends, as you well know. Second, His Most Evil Worship made three dire miscalculations. Me, you, and that little mathematical error in his star charts." And thank all the gods for Duzayan underestimating my wits, or he'd have had a dragon at his disposal to control the horde. Even missing that critical element, he'd opened a gate. Creatures—a *lot* of creatures—poured through into our world. I didn't even want to contemplate the chaos that would have ensued if his figures had been accurate.

"None of that proves he didn't yank these wretches from his favorite hell."

"Third," I refused to let Tanris shoulder me off course again, "the moment they arrived in our world, people began killing them."

"They attacked us."

"Except the ones that didn't, and they got killed anyway."

Tanris folded brawny arms across his chest, brows bent into a forbidding line. "If I remember correctly, you advised the killing."

I might have done out of sheer panic. "Self-defense is one thing. Killing innocents is quite another."

"How about if I toss you down into the pit? We haven't emptied it yet. Maybe you can work out a quick treaty with your *foreigners*."

The creatures there were likely furious and frightened. Not a conducive combination for muddling through language barriers. "You perceive the predicament, I see. Two opposing forces in emotional stress are in no condition to engage."

"I disagree. *This* force is in prime condition to knock some feathers out of your foolish head." He waved his fist under my nose to emphasize.

"You can't, the map is in there." Not the physical map, of course, but it was I who had access to the Ancestors, and they who could ferret out the foreigners. A peculiar talent, to be sure, but Tanris found it useful.

"I can get by without it."

"Mmhm. And how many will be killed or maimed if you have to do your hunting the usual way?" Dogs, trackers, and scouts took time. The longer we took to find them, the more people *and* creatures would suffer. And traipsing around the countryside gave us little time to figure out how to get them back to their own lands.

"If I did it the usual way," Tanris began, "I wouldn't—"

"You realize our lives haven't been *usual* for months, and there's no sign that they ever will be?" I interrupted. "Well, *you* have a strong possibility of resuming a reasonable routine."

He opened his mouth, then shut it again. "Maybe," he said at last, without conviction. He'd lost too much. We both had.

"Do you want to?"

"I want to figure out what we're going to do with this brute and how we're going to get the rest of these creatures to the camp. This group is a lot bigger than we planned for, and we haven't got enough men to handle them."

"Unless they cooperate." I eyed the horned avalanche while I rubbed my hand. The habit eased the pain and helped restore flexibility after Duzayan's magical dagger had nearly crippled it. Ah, the collection of souvenirs he'd left me. Scars, nightmares, time stolen, torture, and unexpected intangible inheritances... I'd sell them all if I could. The exercise also gave me an outlet for suppressed frustration. The internment camps—two of them thus far—were still new, but the foreigners in them were feared and loathed. Conditions were harsh. Many of the prisoners would die unless someone freed them, and that meant finding someone to open a gate to send them home.

"It's a risk," Tanris mused.

"Can you send for reinforcements?"

He hesitated, then nodded slowly. "Nothing official, but yes. There's a village near here. I can conscript."

I clasped my hands beside my cheek and gave him a simpering smile. "I love when you flex your imperial wings. All that gleaming authority nearly makes me swoon."

"Have I mentioned that you're an idiot?"

"Not today, no."

"You're an idiot. While I'm gone, see if KipKap knows a way to keep that alive—" He waved at the downed monster, "and work on getting your foreigners to cooperate."

"Anything else, Commander?"

"Yes, I want to know why there were so many more than you predicted."

If only he could listen to the yammering Ancestors with their *few, several, scores, countless, some* descriptions. "It's not an exact science, you know."

"We could have all died, you know," he said, copying my intonation exactly.

"You've developed a savagely keen sense of mockery. I'm impressed."

"You have yet to develop a proper regard for the constant danger you're in."

"On the contrary, Friend Tanris, I have an acute awareness of it. I choose not to live in panic, but to face each situation practically and with faith. What I lack in knowledge or skill, the gods make up for, and the gods love me."

Tanris bit back a retort and grimaced. "Don't do anything ridiculous while I'm gone. Don't pester Sergeant Yirik, and don't do anything to endanger my men, Crow."

"I wouldn't think of it."

"Think to *avoid* it." He stabbed a threatening finger in my direction, then left me there with the mountainous beast.

—2—
Leave to Play

Tanris could not like leaving his soldiers while he thought them still vulnerable, yet only his authority would drag village lads away from their plows and cows. And, upon reflection, his decision to leave me behind exhibited a measure of trust in me. While I mused over this revelation, he and Yirik went off with their heads together. A few minutes later, I saw Tanris with a sack. It held something melon-shaped, and did I detect a dark stain on one side?

I shuddered.

The Ancestors rustled and brushed against me. *[Grimfist. Grim, grim, grim...]*

"Yes, well, he does what he must, and as long as we're discussing body parts, you don't complain when he saves my neck. He's done that several times, hasn't he?"

From a short distance away, inquisitive blue eyes studied me, then the surrounding space.

"KipKap, just the man I needed!" I pointed at my assignment. "Tell me about him, please?"

Considering the beast, one finger caressed the length of his broad nose. His oddly-shaped nostrils flared slightly, thoughtfully.

Irregular fleshy slits began at the inward corners of his eyes and continued halfway down his face.

'KipKap' was, of course, not his actual name. When he said it, it was longer. He made the K's more guttural and the P's more spitty—which I found altogether too messy for my mouth.

"Did you name him?" Tanris had asked when I'd introduced the two. He could pack a wagonload of suspicion in his voice. He was, in fact, a master packer. Of everything.

"No!"

"It's a stupid name."

"I completely agree."

"Sounds like something you'd come up with."

"Now you're being insulting." I'd pretended offense. "I assume his parents named him. Apparently people give their children terrible names even in his world." We did not discuss the translation of his own name in Corunn, Bahsyr's northern neighbor.

Waiting for my companion to speak, I shifted from one foot to the other.

KipKap's freezing glare wasn't something you'd expect from a fellow with a face that can only be described as gentle. Mottled, pale skin with vague stripes covered a skull too flat and too long-jawed to be mistaken for a man. And his nose, of course, left no doubt. A wide bridge between doe-like eyes descended gently—and for a considerable distance—before reaching his mouth. Behind fishlike lips hid dozens of small, sharp teeth. He had an admirably square jaw, but his ears looked like his maker forgot what he was doing with them midway through the project. The globs of flesh clung to his head, but the bits that dangled from the backs were difficult to overlook.

Though humanoid shape-wise, he towered over Tanris. His neck was so lengthy he could look all the way behind himself. He had six fingers and toes, each extraordinarily long and knobby.

As KipKap contemplated how to explain the beast to me with his limited vocabulary, I watched its massive chest rise and fall. One hand twitched. I reached for my talisman and cleared my throat. "Faster, my friend. It's waking."

"Ah," he nodded. "Ropes break."

Wrapped around its immense muscles, they looked more like threads than ropes. "I can imagine." But KipKap hadn't yet learned the word 'imagine'. "Yes," I said, waving for him to continue.

"He is *eyanti*. War beast. Quick to anger." Two fingers tap-tapped his skull. "Slow to think."

Blessed by the gods, I did not have that problem. Bowing my head, I squeezed the talisman and petitioned the Ancestors. Let KipKap believe I prayed if he liked. "Honorable Guardians and Protectors, if it is in your power, I ask you to weave a spell of peace and safety over this unconscious *eyanti*, that his life and ours might be preserved." At least its species name was easy to get one's tongue around, not like KipKap's. *Futha*-something. One day I would write it down.

KipKap covered his eyes, bowed his own head, and murmured prayerful-sounding noises.

"Do you speak its language?" I asked.

He nodded and held up his fingers to indicate a small amount.

I hoped it was enough. "Can you convince it not to kill us all?"

"Yes or no."

"The word for that is 'maybe.'"

"Maybe," he repeated, storing it away, and he would not forget. He remembered everything, and had a keen interest in our language, customs, and ourselves as individuals. There were times he made me feel like an interesting bug.

The *eyanti* gave voice to a deep, grating sound. Both hands moved. Unslinging his mace, KipKap strode up to the thing, stepped over its arm, and positioned himself beside its too-small head.

"Hello?" I whispered to the Ancestors. Their lack of response had set my nerves on end. "Are you here?"

[Here. Always near. Present, yes. I am... And I... I... I... We are. Always!]

I would never become comfortable with that idea. Had they no concept of privacy? "Can you calm the beast?" I asked.

[Soothe... appease... We will sing a lullaby...]

"Perfect, if it likes lullabies." They could make people feel false emotions, but the creature didn't fit very well into the mold of a person.

Eagerly, they rushed away. Leaves scattered and grass fluttered in their wake. KipKap paused and cast a glance about. He knew *something* was there. I was fairly certain he attached that something to me. I only waited for him to collect the words he needed to ask for answers.

He didn't have them yet. He did, however, have a prodigiously muscled task to deal with, and he did not so much as twitch at what I'd asked of him. Either he had great confidence in his ability to communicate with the thing, or he possessed some manner of control over it.

I probably should have considered that earlier.

As the *eyanti* stirred, KipKap tapped its skull with his mace none too gently. The murmuring voices of the Ancestors caught it as it lifted its head. The lash of its triple horns became a vague side-to-side motion. What followed was a mostly one-sided conversation interspersed with grunts and strange whuffling noises from the giant beast. Then KipKap pointed. At me.

Finally, he restored his mace to its harness and returned to my side. "It is called Gwurand. I told it you are master now."

"Master? No, no, I already have a pet. A companion, that is." It was insane to call a dragon a pet. The brute stared at me, resentment and doom in his little piggy eyes. "What does it eat?" I asked, envisioning entire larders decimated at every meal.

KipKap folded his neck to bring his face to my level. One long finger waved like a twig in the direction of the pit full of foreigners. "All pets of you."

"What? No." I shook my head. "That is not the right word. You are, ah, this is complicated." It took me awhile to explain to him the difference between pets, prisoners, and slaves. His vocabulary grew. Mine turned into shambles.

At last, he wove his ridiculous fingers together in front of his chest and gave a serious nod. "I am pet slave of Crow."

I nearly shouted in frustration—then I caught the wicked slide of his humor across my senses. Those wide, mellow eyes did not give away the slightest clue, but his strange nostrils widened and his mouth curled inward. "Ha ha," I said. "Will this Gwurand do as he's told?"

KipKap said nothing without considering things first. "You use— What is word?" He spread his fingers and looked skyward. Then he made an abrupt motion and a sound suspiciously like a knife hitting a fleshy target. "Secret wording. Secret moving."

Overcoming the challenges of culture and language barriers had forced me to become a fairly nimble guesser. "Magic?"

His eyes widened the way they did when he'd hit upon the right combination of words and gestures. "Magic. Crow use magic."

"What makes you think that?" I asked, indignation loaning me half an octave.

"KipKap see." He waved his fingers in the air again like an oversized mantis. He did that often. "Wind answers you. Earth, yes? You find others from my world with look and listen. Speak to—ah, what is word? Man after death."

"Spirit," I breathed, resisting the urge to rub my talisman, pull my hair, or do anything else that would betray my dismay. It wouldn't do to have people thinking I was some sort of wizard. I was not alone in mistrusting magic and those who used it.

He nodded.

"Are you a, erm, *magicker?*" I asked.

"No, magic dies in my world." He pointed at Gwurand. "Long past magic made his kind. Hard to stop. Hard to kill. Make many easy and grow fast. Now they are slaves in No End War. They were not in Taketioni."

"Not where?"

"Ah. Place." He struggled. "KipKap in Taketioni. Then KipKap here."

"You and Gwurand came from different places?"

"Yes. And others."

"How many places?"

He lifted his fingers. "Four. Or more."

I still didn't know how Duzayan's Wicked Gate had worked, despite the charts and the pages I'd taken from him before his manor had gone up in flames and magic. The Ancestors helped me shut the one he made, but refused to tell me any details about it.

[Dark, wicked magic,] they proclaimed. *[Ugly magic. Poison, malice, ruuuuuthlessness! Stay away! Stay away!]*

Their refusal to provide information meant I must find another wizard—or druid—who had the skill to open and close gates. How else could we get the foreigners back where they belonged? But the idea of a wizard who could wield that kind of power made me all clammy. I avoided thinking about it too often. I slept better that way.

KipKap's description of multiple origins for the foreigners sounded like an uneven tear across the fabric of his world rather than a simple puncture. "How much distance between the two farthest places?" I asked, holding up my hands to illustrate the concept. "How many days' travel?"

"Six? Ten?"

Farther than I'd expected, though I had nothing on which to base my speculations. I tucked away the information and turned my attention upon Gwurand. The flimsy rope trusses wouldn't last long. "If we loose him, can we trust him not to murder anyone?"

KipKap rubbed three fingers over his bald head. "Maybe."

Huffing an exasperated breath, I stomped over to the creature. I was no doubt risking my own life getting so close, but the gods clearly had other plans for me. If not, I'd have died long ago. Despite gigantic creatures like *eyantis* or angry dragons, I still lived and breathed. "Translate for me. Tell it—him—this country is Bahsyr, not wherever it is you're from. The war there is not here. There is no fight."

"No fight?" KipKap inquired, nostrils wrinkling. "Not in any place?"

"In some places, yes. Far, far away in the east." I pointed, and they both followed my finger with their eyes, as if they might see the distant smoke of battlefields. "*Far,*" I repeated.

He hummed to himself, then began speaking to Gwurand.

"There is a truce among all people from your world," I added. "Those who break it will be killed." Tanris had graciously given me a long and detailed lecture providing the whys and wherefores of such extreme actions. The logistics, security measures, and automatic mistrust of everyone on such a large scale reaffirmed my own career choice. It also explained much about Tanris.

Gwurand thrashed about in his ropes, but without a great deal of effort. Evidently, he didn't like the broad decree.

"Don't fight," I warned him, giving a glower straight from Tanris's stock. "We do not want to kill you. We want to return you to your world."

Faithfully, KipKap rendered my words into Gwurand's tongue, and I paid close attention. Not a breath of a lie did I discern. They spoke for a moment, then he turned to me. "He will do as you say."

Convincing Sergeant Yirik was another challenge altogether. In the end, he detailed his best archer to mind Gwurand. Then, by much arm-waving and mimicry, I set the beast to clearing downed trees so we could move the wagons. Of course, KipKap vanished during all the frustrating bits. And when the alarm of having a mountain of muscle on the loose settled down to a mild simmer, he rejoined us, cool as you please.

Cooperation bought KipKap limited freedom. He had no wish to harm us. He didn't want to harm his compatriots, either. I knew this because I could feel it in him, but feelings and hunches weren't solid evidence to convince the others. Unfortunately, I was the only one who pressed to let any of the foreigners prove themselves. Since the soldiers already had misgivings about me, I wasn't a choice champion. They didn't know me, yet I had their commander's confidence for reasons beyond their understanding. Worse, they suspected I had arcane abilities. Include my 'pet,' and I was the worst kind of human imaginable: a wizard with a miniature dragon familiar.

We had spent weeks on the road together. We'd slogged in and out of countless sticky situations. Through it all, I played the obvious part of tracker, hunter, trap-setter-upper, and occasional savior—and I could not persuade them that Not-an-Egg was a lizard with wings from a foreign land. They were a suspicious lot.

Leaving Gwurand to push and pull trees around like they were toys, I captured KipKap's arm and dragged him to the pit for help in diplomatic relations. "Remind me to request a salary increase when next I see the emperor. Something modest, but appropriate to my new position as ambassador."

"The emperor speaks to you?" KipKap had a marvelous way of swinging his head around on his too-long neck when surprised.

"Not so far, but if he's sneakily going to install me as an emissary, I have a word or twenty to say to him. By the by, Tanris said one of your people was among the injured?"

"Ah. Yes."

"How is he? She?"

"His leg is broken. Maybe he will live."

"Do your kind usually die of broken bones?"

He turned sad eyes down at me from a height I still found disconcerting. "This is not a usual time."

There was no arguing with that. We shifted our arguing talents upon the captured foreigners. Catching my arms waving again, I hugged myself. No, that wasn't manly. I folded my arms and adopted one of Tanris's grim looks. It made Girl laugh. I *felt* it and searched her out where she perched overhead with her crossbow. I hated to think what might have become of her if the horned avalanche had knocked down her tree.

You are angry? she signed.

I shook my head, then changed my mind and nodded. Finally, I shrugged.

Crazy, she decided.

Yes. No. Maybe?

She hooted silently, then rested her weapon on a branch to point at the pit. *Many foreigners. We almost lost control. What happened?*

I shrugged again. *We must learn.*

KipKap and I took the wounded out of the pit for the priests to tend. As usual in these operations, we discovered no children or elderly. Coupled with KipKap's recent information, I suspected Duzayan had torn his hole right through a full-scale war. *Wonderful.* Surrounded by enemies—native and foreign—every one of them was bound to be on edge.

Soldiers escorted the more cooperative (or should I say 'stunned'?) foreigners to the wagons. Diti, KipKap's brother, lent his aid. He was not as tall, nor as trusting, nor as patient, but he accepted KipKap's authority and followed his lead without question. Or at least without questioning him before the others.

Five creatures remained captive in the pit, growling and prowling the perimeter. Two were dog-like animals, only much bigger and with shaggy manes covering their shoulders. I expected they would not be accompanying us to the camp unless someone could put muzzles on them. Their fangs were as long as my fingers. The other three were mostly human-shaped, but had skin of dark gray. Ever patient, KipKap explained their situation to them, but a sour anger smoldered in him.

"They do not accept your terms," he announced. "You should not trust them if they do."

"Your own enemies, or enemies of your people?"

"Yes." One had to admire his faculty to be succinct and vague at the same time.

Girl dropped lightly to the ground and adjusted her crossbow. A sensible young woman, she'd scraped her ash blonde hair into a braid. She wore practical wool and leathers, but hadn't completely been seduced by Tanris's tedious lack of imagination. I liked to think I had some influence on her choice of style. Dark ribbons wove through her braid, and she'd tucked a scarf of green-on-green around the neck of her vest. She had flair without being too extravagant. We were in the woods, after all. Camping. Hunting. Fighting... A small bag at her waist held a collection of pebbles. She used them to get a body's attention—or reprimand them, whichever was required.

Grimfist returns, she signed.

"Already?" I glanced back, and there he was, storming toward us. A dozen peasants armed with farming implements eddied haphazardly behind him. The whirlwind of his purpose drew half, while Sergeant Yirik's shouts claimed the rest.

"Crow!" Tanris's brow set like a thundercloud. "Didn't I tell you not to do anything ridiculous?"

I blinked in confusion. So far, I'd done everything he'd asked of me. I found it astonishing and rather unsettling how often I was innocent these days. Living among a crew of the Emperor's Eagles offered limited opportunities to practice my carefully honed skills. Even the joy of rearranging belongings now and then fell afoul of Commander Tedious. His wrath didn't stop me, of course, it only encouraged better discretion, which was good for me. "What did I do?"

"*That*," he stabbed a finger toward Gwurand.

"He's helping. How is that ridiculous?"

"Pet slave," KipKap offered unhelpfully, nostrils pinching. Was that a snigger? Humor flashed around him.

Girl covered a laugh with her fist, eyes bright.

"You told them they were slaves?" Ire brought Tanris's dark brows even closer together.

"He did not." KipKap made a patting motion at the air as if to soothe his temper.

"I didn't," I agreed.

"You're joking?"

"We need to work on your timing, KipKap." The tall foreigner only looked puzzled. "We had a new word lesson, Tanris. It was fun. You should have been here. I see you didn't have a problem finding substitute guards."

Tanris did not surrender his glower. "No, they're willing enough. They had some trouble with another group of demon foreigners a week ago." How nicely he knit the descriptions. "One man is in grave condition and two more too badly wounded to work. Some of their livestock was stolen, crops ruined, property damaged."

"Are there dead?" KipKap asked, all humor fled.

"Not yet."

He wove his fingers together and bowed his head. "I must offer sorrows." He was not responsible for what his compatriots did. Still, he apologized repeatedly.

"I'll go with you," I volunteered. People didn't always receive his attempted apologies politely. If one foreigner hurt a man or his property, they were all guilty. Bringing Gwurand along might keep them humble, though.

Girl stepped up and put a hand on KipKap's arm in silent support.

Tanris shook his head. "You'll do no—"

"Commander!" The shout came from the hilltop. A soldier waved for Tanris's attention, then pointed at me as well and gestured for us to come.

Apology postponed, we made our way to join him.

"There's something you need to see." Neba, nearly as wide as he was tall, met us partway. From there, he led the way around the hill, circumventing a long thicket. We'd used it in our trap-laying to funnel our subjects into the ambush.

Some distance later, we stood in a rock-strewn clearing. A stream ran along one side, and the path the foreigners had taken bordered it. Several mutilated bodies littered the space. I freed my scarf to shield my nose from the stench of death and charred flesh. I saw no fire pit, and no campfire smoke hung in the air.

"What burned?" I asked.

Neba pointed to a pair of corpses lying next to one another. Or rather, *parts* of corpses. One had its legs missing. The other, a hideous thing like a dog with four eyes and a spiky mane, had lost half its torso diagonally from ribs to tail. Both appeared to have been butchered together by the same giant blade.

Turning on my heel, I headed straight for the stream. Down on my knees and heedless of the way the water soaked my britches, I splashed my face and scrubbed vigorously, but there was no unseeing that horror.

The sound of retching close by nearly undid my questionable control. A tree held Girl up as she emptied her belly.

I sloshed my face again, focusing on the cold, clear water. A long drink helped wash the sour taste from my mouth. Then I profusely thanked the gods of luck and grumpy commanders that I had avoided such a death. I wanted an altar. I had a stream. With another murmur of gratitude, I got up to help Girl move upstream where things smelled less revolting.

When I had her situated on a boulder, I took her scarf and wet it to wash her face. She cried silently the way she was prone to do. Behind us, the others tried to figure out what had happened.

"There's no blood on these two. It's as if they were cauterized," Neba said.

I gagged. Quietly, so as not to upset Girl.

"Where's the rest of them?" Tanris asked, his voice muffled.

"Don't know. Nowhere here. And nothing dragged the bits off or there'd be marks."

I was *not* going to be able to eat my supper.

"These fellows were coming toward the track the first group was on, see?" I could imagine Neba pointing as he described what he'd found. "Looks like a bit of trail here. Lots of standing around there. Talking, not fighting."

"So a second group joined the ones we were trailing." That explained the excessive numbers. "But where did they come from? There should be broken branches. Trampled grass. Like this." Here, Tanris would scrub his bristly chin. More pointing, followed by a scrape and a thump.

Girl abruptly got to her feet. She squeezed her damp scarf so hard her knuckles turned white. The red nose and eyes ruined the brave, rugged look her clothing proclaimed. I wondered how she could shoot someone with her crossbow, but lose her composure at the sight of a corpse killed in a less conventional way.

"Are you all right?" I asked.

Her lips trembled, but she gave a tight nod. *Sorry*, she signed.

"For what? Nearly running me over?"

She made an undignified little snorting sound.

"See leaves. There." KipKap's voice this time.

"Are they burned?"

"That's odd. Crow, come look at this." Tanris assumed a lot.

"Must I?" I would rather leave the savage scene scrutiny to the professionals and stick to my job of hunting the foreigners from a distance.

"Yes, you must. You keep telling me how well read you are. It could be helpful knowing if you've run across anything like this in your vast accumulation of obscure facts."

He had me there. My library is something to be admired. I know, for I have cultivated it from the collections of people who value such things. Private libraries are the most poorly guarded treasures in the empire. From them, I have pilfered books and scrolls and maps and accounts of every kind. I even read them. "Very well, but I can't make any promises."

"You never do."

"Untrue. I merely save them for special occasions." I tied my scarf around my face. Girl mimicked me and trailed behind. When Tanris pointed upward, my gaze followed.

A respectable oak extended its branches over the clearing, providing a fringe of shade. Overhead, its limbs had been shorn off in a straight line. I glanced down at the cleaved bodies, wished I hadn't, then immediately glanced up again. "At the risk of stating the obvious, this echoes the, er, cut line."

"Yes," Tanris agreed with a coaxing tone.

"Are the rest of those branches anywhere about?" I pointed at charred stubs thicker than my wrist. They looked as if they had been neatly sawn.

"Um… No," Neba supplied after a moment. "But there are leaves everywhere. Blackened and not."

"There's no corresponding slash on the ground." Tanris tucked his thumbs in his belt and rocked back and forth. The scarf covering the lower half of his face hid expression.

I dared to stand next to the dog creature, aligning the strokes above and below. "There's… a good cubit missing." Picking up a stick, I poked at a leaf by my foot. It broke into pieces.

With a longer branch, KipKap did the same to the leaves overhead. "*Dilayik*," he said, puzzled.

I didn't know the word, but I knew the feeling. "Not burnt. More like frozen, but that's not right, either."

"Have you ever read of such a thing?" Tanris asked.

"Not that I recall, but let me think about it." The Ancestors might know…

"You do that." He clapped my shoulder and moved off. "Neba, KipKap, collect the weapons, then burn the bodies."

That was a stench I could live without, but Tanris said it would prevent local wildlife from sickening if it ate the flesh, and stop disease from spreading. There was the extra caution of nipping magic in the bud. The last thing we needed was some crazy wizard reanimating the corpses or draining them for blood magic.

Neba saluted and went about his business. He was one of the few who didn't mind the company of KipKap or Diti. As a result, they often accompanied him on assignments. He added color and flavor to their vocabulary, too.

We returned to the trap site to find that Gwurand had felled the trees clear to the wagons we'd hidden nearby. In fact, he was well on his way to taking his new road to the village Tanris had visited for his reinforcements.

"Well," I observed, "look at all that firewood. I didn't expect him to stack entire trees."

Girl put her tongue in her cheek. *Very tidy*, she signed.

Tanris grunted. "Can you make him stop?"

"Possibly, but why? He's busy. He's happy." I waved at the new road that went nowhere. "We should name it. The Tanris Highway sounds auspicious."

"Fine, but only if you pave it first."

Oh, he was getting quick and sharp! I loved these moments when his sorrow retreated and let him be himself.

The clatter of a rider approaching drew everyone's attention. Still on edge from our encounter, the Eagles had weapons out and leveled in the blink of an eye. Tanris, too, suddenly held an ax.

Always a practical man, I slipped behind him.

"Commander Tanris," the fellow greeted, drawing his mount up and leaping to the ground. From a worn leather satchel he withdrew a folded and sealed letter. He raised his free hand to the square in a salute I'd only rarely seen, then unfastened the top of his tunic. On the inside lining, the symbol of a flaming brazier was embroidered.

A messenger from the *emperor?* Delivered covertly, no less.

He said he was no wizard, but Tanris had a way of making that ax come and go as if he conjured it from thin air. He magically stowed it on his belt as he accepted the missive. With another motion, he sent his men back to their tasks. I was still learning *that* language.

I tried to read the letter over his shoulder, but he was having none of that. I made out a small version of the emperor's seal affixed over the elaborate tail of the man's signature before he turned away.

"What is it?" I asked after a suitable interval of at least ten seconds.

"We're wanted in the city."

Real beds? A bath? Girl's eyes lit.

"Aren't we busy?" Not that I objected to beds or baths at all. I much preferred them to living in the woods, and it had been too long since I'd enjoyed either. "We haven't finished this job yet."

"Thank you. Please inform him we come at once," Tanris murmured to the messenger, then turned on his heel, already striding away. "Yirik!" he shouted.

The sergeant broke away from a group near the healers and trotted over. Girl and I hurried to keep up. Tanris on a mission moved at thrice the speed of regular Tanris.

"You are now in charge," Tanris told his man.

"Y-Yes, sir."

"Wait, what?" I asked.

He ignored me. "I need to return to the capital. Crow and Girl will come with me. Take this bunch to the camp at Sken Aymar. I'll try to see you get reinforcements." A sharp sideways glance sliced my way. "And some hunting dogs. KipKap and Diti or some of their lot might help you out, if you're willing?"

Yirik hesitated, then nodded. "They've been useful. I'm pleased to have them if they're agreeable."

Mild surprise filled me. Regular people cooperating with *demons*? What was the world coming to?

"What should I do with the, ah… the big fellow? He won't fit in the wagons."

"Ask KipKap what he thinks. Otherwise, I leave it to your judgment. Be careful."

"Don't kill him," I remonstrated.

"Do what you have to do," Tanris overrode me. "You are familiar with the situation, and my previous orders stand, sergeant."

"Of course, sir. When will you be leaving?"

"Now."

"I'll see to your horses." Yirik saluted and dashed off like a good little soldier.

Why does the emperor want us? Girl asked.

"Actually, he wants Crow."

"Me? Why?" Alarm rippled through me. In most cases, being wanted by monarchs or mages involves life-or-death situations. Or a lot of pain. In predictable reaction to my apprehension, the Ancestors gasped and moaned—a sound only I could hear. Usually. The leaves trembled.

Tanris cast a suspicious glance upward, then turned an intense gaze upon me. "He seems to think you can recover an important relic."

Girl's mouth made an exaggerated *oh*.

Relic-hunting would be a pleasant break from the hunting and camping activities. I grinned. "Finally, someone who appreciates my talents. What are we idling about here for?"

—3—
Road Games

I'd done a lot of riding since making the unpleasant acquaintance of Baron Metin Duzayan. In fact, I had ridden horseback more in the past few months than in my entire life. Tanris took it upon himself to correct my lack of equine education. I learned about riveting things such as frogs (not the hopping variety), hocks (not the ham variety), pressure-and-release (if only Tanris would respond to such cues), colic (I wondered at his experience with babies), filing teeth (a task I had no intention of undertaking; have you seen a horse's teeth?), and cherries. Why cherries? It appeared our horsey friends prefer them to apples. I experimented once when Tanris was otherwise occupied, and stab me if it wasn't true!

And speaking of questionable things, I wondered if 'Tanris' was his first name or his last, or if he only had the one. If he had another, why go to such lengths to conceal it?

When we had left camp, he set us to a pace that meant business. The emperor called, and prudence answered with all speed. Or at least Tanris did. I was less inclined to rush. As much as I longed for a respite—and a familiar thrill or two—we had an important task to finish. Leaving it half done made me uneasy. The longer it took to round up all the foreigners, the longer until I got my pardon and the more chances I wouldn't get it at all. But the gods loved me, didn't they? However mysterious their ways, they would help accomplish the job. They had, for instance, already turned me into a capable horseman.

Not-an-Egg had his own method of travel. A cage on horseback had long ago proven unwieldy. So the little dragon alternated between riding with me, snoozing in the sun aboard the packhorse, or jogging a course parallel to the road. The packhorse—and thank the gods for making him such an amenable creature—was the clear favorite.

Walking and trotting hour after hour is exhausting, if you ask me, which Tanris did not. Luckily, we'd got started late, and the setting sun dictated that we put an end to such absurdity. He ordered a quick meal of jerky, bread, and cheese. Girl gave him a look that froze his mouth solid on the words 'early start,' and pulled a pot out of our gear. I have become a devotee of packhorses and all the extra luxuries they provide. In this case, it resulted in a tasty soup, thanks to Girl's foresight. Her cooking skills have saved us from many horrendous meals, for which I am grateful. So grateful, in fact, that she has discovered how to blackmail me into doing all sorts of things.

We won't talk about how she forced me to teach her how to pick pockets. Tanris would discover it, rest assured.

Darkness and quiet settled oh-so-comfortably. The Eagles, bless their crusty hearts, tended to chatter into the wee hours, snore, and grunt a lot. We often had the dubious pleasure of guarding numbers of foreigners, who made their own noises. All night long. Every night.

Filled with contentment, I listened to the burble of a nearby stream and the song of crickets—

Until some clod shook my arm and demanded that I get my lazy backside up and moving. The bulk hovering over me impeded my view of gray sky. Was it cloudy or not yet dawn? I bestowed a narrow-eyed glare that affected the bulk not at all. Not-an-Egg, nestled against my side, hissed a warning. Tanris ignored that, too.

"C'mon," he said, all sweetness and cheer.

Girl, already busy by the fire, lifted a mug in my direction. Trying to tempt me out of my morning grumble, no doubt.

"Is that kaffa? And do I smell bacon?"

She nodded and speared her pan with the knife in her free hand. A lovely, thick slice of cured pork appeared, immediately setting my mouth to watering.

"In that case," I decided, "good morning."

She'd availed herself of eggs from the cook's stores, and there was leftover bread. Regrettably, no jam.

I noticed Tanris didn't complain about the meal and even helped clean up. He gave me the task of saddling our mounts, an assignment that might prove he actually trusted me with such a thing after all our lessons. I had never been very fond of animals, except as meals. I do love a good steak, thick as my wrist and bright pink in the middle. Yet here I was with Not-an-Egg and two horses, aptly named Horse and Horse Too.

Well, they had once gotten by quite nicely with such simple epithets. Tanris objected and claimed their names were too confusing. Girl took sides—his—and bestowed my dear little mare the moniker 'Sunblossom.' I immediately shortened it to 'Sunny.' That had happened in the first weeks of our new engagement chasing foreigners.

I'd acquired Horse Too when I fled the devastation of Hasiq jum'a Sahefal after finding Not-an-Egg (before he hatched, mind). He was an enormous animal with a steady pace and a mild disposition. I couldn't say whether he was a good-looking horse, and Tanris never offered an opinion past his performance. A blotchy gray, he sported a black nose, mane, tail, and feet. Usually corralled in camp with others like him and thus out from under Tanris's eagle eye, he had escaped Sunny's fate. Until now.

The commander had slowed our pace to give the animals a break. Unimpressed by all the farms and cottages we passed, and sleepy from the warmth of the afternoon sun, I dozed. It had taken forever to learn how to nap without falling out of the saddle —or tying myself in. My accomplishment not only filled me with pride, but offered miles and miles of opportunity. Not-an-Egg perched on my bedroll, slumped against my back.

"You're calling your mare 'Sunny,' aren't you." Tanris had a fine talent for stating questions.

I refused to open my eyes. "Mm-hm."

"What about the other one?"

"Too?" I asked, just because I knew the excuse for a name annoyed him. And because it was *my* horse, and I'd call him whatever I pleased.

Tanris grunted as he often does.

Sunny's easy pace rocked me back to the edge of a doze. I resisted the urge to speak until I felt Tanris tensing. "I'm thinking about calling him 'Mouse.'"

"That's terrible."

"Why? He has the character of one."

"It's a ridiculous name. He's too rugged and handsome to be named after a rodent." Aha! He *was* good-looking.

I sent a glance toward Horse Too plodding along behind Girl. He displayed all the enthusiasm of a sack of grain, barely picking up his feet. "How about 'Bolt'?"

"I've never seen him do that. Can he?"

"He did once. Back in Hasiq when the, er *beast* appeared," I recalled. It didn't seem proper to bring up the tale of Not-an-Egg's mother—or father—while he was in hearing range. The adult dragon had torched a temple and half the village. An exciting story, certainly, but in the end poor little Not-an-Egg had been left orphaned. And Horse Too had dumped me and run away.

Tanris grunted again. "I was there. He wasn't very fast. If there hadn't been another target, he'd have been dinner."

I'd been that target. Better roast Horse than roast Crow. Remembrance made me shudder. "Is this going to be a game like naming Girl?"

"Could be. I'll let you know when you give me the right one."

"Ha," I said.

Girl snickered. She'd urged her mount a little closer to listen. The three of us bunched up with Too trailing behind on a long lead.

"Very well, 'Farmer.' He came from a farm. I imagine." I had no way of knowing. The temple brothers might have used him for a carriage horse for all I knew.

"Dull," Tanris complained.

"Fine, fine. How about Twinkletoes?"

He leveled a severe glare at me. "You jest. How about mercy and compassion?"

I made a face. "If you say so, but it's kind of long."

"I was talking about *you*, feather-brain."

I chose to mistake his meaning. "Oh, I already have a name, thank you, and I've been using it for years. I don't think I could get used to a new one." A bald-faced lie. I've utilized aliases my entire career and never had trouble responding to them.

A funny noise came from behind us, and I turned to see Girl clinging sideways to her saddle to keep from falling off. Waves of laughter did something to the space around her, making it uneven and… bright. That was interesting.

"Are you all right?" I asked.

She waved one hand and pulled herself upright again. Plucking a kerchief from a pocket, she wiped her face.

"You are impossible." Tanris shook his head.

"Usually, but now I have Mercy and Compassion." I waggled my brows.

"Very little."

"Huge, actually."

The horses walked along, ears and tails twitching. Girl's giggles turned into hiccups. Tanris kept doing strange things with his lips, as if he couldn't decide on an expression.

Finally, he asked, "Were you dropped on your head when you were a baby?"

"That's entirely possible." I mused for a little while. "I don't recall, but my skull is perfectly shaped. Not flat anywhere."

"Gods protect me."

"They do, Tanris, they do." I meant it, too, for he'd led a dangerous life prior to the forming of our partnership, and I'd witnessed many improbable escapes from death since. If the gods didn't watch over him, who did? Well, I did, of course, and the gods had watched over and protected me my entire existence. "Speaking of which, you might want to know we're being followed."

Tanris stiffened, but he was too canny to turn around and look, giving away any advantage his pretend ignorance gained. "How long?"

"Mmmnot sure. A few hours, at least."

"Why didn't you say something?"

"I just did."

He loosened the ax on one side of his belt and checked the sword hanging from the other. "Did you see them? How many are there?"

"I caught glimpses. Two or three. They're catching up."

He relaxed a fraction. *Two or three* constituted little threat. Not to him, anyway. I preferred avoiding threats altogether.

"They might simply be traveling the same road we are," I pointed out, exercising logic and broad-mindedness.

"Maybe." A man of few words. "You could ask."

"Do what, now?" I straightened in alarm. Surely, he didn't mean to send me on a scouting mission.

"Ask your Ancestors." Tanris made a loose, flappy circle near his head. He and the Eagles under his command had their hand-talk, and Girl had hers. His gesture didn't *quite* label the Ancestors 'insane,' but it came close. Either he couldn't come up with a better sign, or he wanted to insult me. Probably the latter.

"I could," I drawled. It always felt silly making requests aloud to personages no one could see—including myself. Their response to my thoughts was random at best.

"You've done it before."

Whether or not I had, it didn't make the doing any more comfortable.

"Shall we give you some privacy?" Tanris inquired, voice dripping with condescension.

Girl threw a stone at him, and it clacked off his leather brigandine. The bag of pebbles was never empty. She could hit his head as easily as his back any time she desired, especially at that distance.

Tanris lifted a hand in surrender, then pulled his mount to a stop and slid to the ground. Checking the saddle's girth made a fine excuse for surveying the trail behind us. Girl tugged the newly dubbed Mercy and Compassion—a cumbersome name sure to vex Tanris—past to give him an unobstructed view.

I brought Sunny up a dozen steps away. Still and quiet, I *listened* to the world. This focus had served me well all my life, but it was different now. Better. The experience in the Ghost Walk where I'd been attacked by magic had dramatically increased an innate ability to feel, hear, and *sense* things. I did like that...

"It's KipKap and Diti," I said, astonished.

Tanris's gaze went from the road to me, then back again. He squinted. "Why?"

"I can't read minds. You'll have to ask them." While we waited, I dug out an apple to snack on and sat on a grassy hummock.

Not-an-Egg glided from the saddle to land at my feet. When our company was a dozen yards away, he leaped up, spitting and hissing like he'd never seen them before and must give challenge.

I rolled my eyes and took another bite of my apple.

The pair stopped abruptly.

"Hullo, KipKap," I greeted. "Diti. How are you?"

"Pleased," KipKap answered for both of them, provoking an unintelligible grunt from Tanris.

"Why are you and your brother here?" Tanris cut in, fingering the hilt of his sword.

KipKap drew himself up to his considerable height, touched his fingertips together, then bowed. "We are pet slaves of Crow."

"Oh, please," I snorted.

"We follow master," Diti affirmed, too-big eyes unreadable. To clarify, he pointed at me.

Tanris turned to me, jaw knotted in obvious displeasure. "Explain."

"Me? I had nothing to do with this."

His arms folded across his chest.

"I didn't, I swear."

"Is true," KipKap agreed. "We did not know of leaving until long. We follow. We help."

"You just walked away from the camp?"

"Yes."

This did not bode well for the Eagles given the responsibility of tending the foreigners. *All* the foreigners...

"Alas," I said, getting to my feet and dusting my backside. "We can't do anything about it now."

Tanris ignored me. "You'll have to go back."

"Why?" I asked.

"This is not their assignment." A roundabout way of saying they weren't welcome. "The emperor did not ask for them."

"Did he ask for you and Girl?" I do not know what overcame me. Certainly nothing related to good sense. Most likely, it was a momentary leave-taking of sanity and the persistent desire to tweak Tanris's nose.

He ground his teeth.

"We can't send them back alone, Tanris, it's too dangerous. They're our responsibility. Either we take them, or they come with us."

Tanris gave me a long look, as if he'd like to punch me, then swung into his saddle. "We'd best not keep the emperor waiting."

—4—
New Assignment

The emperor's waiting hall had been fashioned to awe and intimidate. It worked well. Ninety-seven steps descended into it. Tanris did not know the reason behind this number. Luck? Bodies sacrificed? The kings who had died or surrendered to create the empire?

Despite the stairs, the upper half of the chamber remained above ground level. Light poured through great arched windows, illuminating imperial splendor. The hall was so vast it took forever to traverse. While I trudged along, I imagined a secret passage that ran alongside or underneath. Only for the emperor. And he rode in a chariot. No trudging for him.

Marble statues twenty feet tall depicted former monarchs, leaders, and heroes. They formed two neat rows all the way from one end to the other. Magnificent murals illustrating centuries of Bahsyri history covered the ceiling. A person could take injury gawking up at the glorious detail and color. Potted trees and giant baskets full of greenery softened the space and soothed the senses. Fountains appeared here and there, gently splashing their placid melodies.

Hushed conversations came from dozens of courtiers and petitioners. Some of the arrivals cheated, arriving through occasional doorways marking the long walls. At the opposite end of the hall, a pair of doors towered. Black enamel frames inlaid with brass vines and flowers surrounded sapphire blue panels.

Unless one counted the individual plants, not a single item in the entire chamber could fit in one's pocket. Such a shame...

As if I might figure out a way to claim a souvenir, Tanris kept me between himself and Girl until we found a place to sit. I immediately concluded that the stone benches were part of the intimidation process. "You'd think a man as rich as an emperor could afford cushions," I said, getting up to pace. "Oh, wait! He *is* the emperor! Aren't either of you cold?"

Girl shook her head. Tanris merely grimaced. The Ancestors didn't respond at all, though a little comfort from that direction wouldn't have gone amiss. I much preferred visiting the palace— properly called the Kumeti Palace, named after the ancient clan—in disguise. Rich, important people were prone to suspicion and violence with an expert thief in their midst. That I'd been invited rather than arrested should have eased my restlessness. If Tanris still harbored nefarious plans for my person, he would walk me into a room full of men with swords and no way out. This room had dozens of ways out. Also a lot of swords. And pikes.

Beneath my shirt, I fingered the reassuring shape of my talisman. I hadn't noticed the Ancestors since we'd arrived. I also hadn't noticed any prickling that would give away the presence of magic wards.

As I returned from a tour around a statue of Qahan Nijamar, a man so heroic I had thought him fictitious, I spied Girl gaping at the ceiling. Tanris put a finger under her chin to close her mouth and said something that made her smile. He would have been a good father—*was* —though I knew he would deny it if accused. Why Girl had abandoned a safe, reasonable life to follow us into danger, she never said. And she flatly refused invitations and strong hints to remain in my apartment in Marketh. So we praised her handiness with a crossbow and waxed lyrical about her stew. Tanris taught her about honor, hard work, and self-defense. I gave her lessons in reading, writing, and dancing. She taught us her sign language, and I had to keep my promise, didn't I? When Tanris wasn't looking, I instructed her in thieving.

"You're sure the cage is secure?" Tanris asked, watching my approach.
"Yes, Tanris."

"And there's nothing flammable close to it?"

I offered him a worried frown. "I might have left your clean shirts on top."

Despite the dangerous narrowing of his eyes, he was very fine in his official uniform of imperial blue with gold and white. He looked... *dashing*, perhaps. He also looked as comfortable in uniform as he did in his usual garb of drab colors, leather, and steel. Definitely as deadly.

Girl giggled at my comment. She cleaned up nicely, too. An embroidered short-sleeved tunic in a rich shade of plum lent color to her pale features. A broad white sash gave her a waistline and matched loose pants tucked into soft gray boots. She'd done something artful and impossible with her hair, braiding it in a manner that surely required four or five hands. She even wore earrings. Modest, but purple and sparkly.

"I'd rather not burn the building down while we're gone," Tanris said, interrupting my admiration of the pair. "One camp tent was enough."

"It was an ugly tent, anyway. Stop worrying. He's sleeping."

"You poisoned him?"

Girl's eyes widened, then her face creased immediately into a threatening expression. Clearly, she'd been taking lessons from Tanris. *You had better not hurt Not-an-Egg!* she scolded.

"No, I didn't poison him, I gave him a little Adamanta Dust, and a lovely big bone to chew on if he should wake before we get home." Dragons, as it happened, enjoyed gnawing on bones. I couldn't see the appeal.

"You're going to kill him one of these days," Tanris muttered. He turned his finely honed glare on an approaching secretary.

"Your confidence in me is overwhelming."

"Did you poison KipKap and Diti, too?"

I pressed a hand to my chest and feigned an expression of horror. "What do you take me for?" We ensconced the brothers in a safe house I owned on the outskirts of the city. We'd brought them to it in the dead of night so as not to draw unwanted attention. They had strict (and strictly unnecessary) orders to stay inside.

The secretary's arrival prevented any answer. "Commander Tanris and Master Crow?" he inquired with all the warmth and cordiality of a spoon.

Coolly, easily, Tanris took Girl's elbow to help her up as he rose. Faced with such poise, his uniform dared not crease or wrinkle.

"This way, if you please."

Behind their backs, Girl poked me and mouthed, *Master Crow.*

I puffed out my chest.

She clapped a hand over her mouth to trap her laughter.

The pompous secretary led us not to the vast blue doors, but to a small chamber nearby. Or rather, a chamber not as large as what I imagined lay beyond those tantalizing portals. Even so, my entire apartment would have fit into it with room to spare. Four guards with spears also fit. I hesitated on the threshold, expecting magic, but nothing happened.

Tanris stopped, saluted smartly, then bowed. Beyond him, a silhouette peeled away from the window to face us.

"Bow," Tanris hissed out the side of his mouth.

Girl had not forgotten his etiquette instructions. I hadn't, either. I was just not as eager to show them off. For six seconds, I would be Crow: bold, independent, and capricious. Six seconds could be insolence, or it might be awe. Who could say?

With admirable grace, I offered the prettiest bow any emperor could ever desire.

And he ignored me. "Commander Tanris!" He came forward with outstretched hands to raise the object of his attention. "How good to see you. You look well."

A slender man of indeterminate years, His Revered Majesty, Gaziah the Shepherd, the Lawgiver, the Radiant, Emperor of Bahsyr, King and Ruler and Prince of Ninety-Seven realms and principalities, Custodian of some scepter or other, Protector of three or four Knightly Orders no one but his clerks remember, was disappointingly average. Dark hair framed a sharp face, a small mouth with too-generous lips, and a beaklike nose. For all that, he was not unpleasant to look upon, and he knew exactly how to pitch his voice. Still, Tanris's sheer presence dwarfed Gaziah. I had not expected that.

"Come, sit." He gestured to a group of chairs arranged in a circle before a modest but artistic throne on a dais. He and Tanris made brief small talk while Girl and I followed. As I passed him, Gaziah stopped me with a hand on my arm.

Then a prickling sensation went over me. Instinct prompted me to jerk away, but the gods have blessed me with a superb ability to control my reflexes. They have protected me through circumstances far more dire than a warding spell on a monarch.

"So you are Crow. Tanris has told me about you."

I had a dozen witty rejoinders in my repertoire and, judging by the fist he held curled at his side, Tanris fully expected me to use them. How amusing that my desire to preserve my existence coincided with dumbfounding him. I merely inclined my head and murmured, "Most Illustrious Highness…"

"That's all you have to say? You told me he was outspoken," Gaziah complained to Tanris. "He's not shy, is he?"

"Not in a million years."

"Overcome by the grandeur of court and the experience of being in my presence?" Gaziah looked me over as he might a three-legged goose.

"Mildly insulted," I put in, "but willing to overlook the slight and speak for myself."

"Gods, Crow," Tanris warned, "mind your tongue."

"Be careful what you wish for." I winked at him.

He rolled his eyes and shook his head.

"That's more what I was expecting," Gaziah nodded. "And the gods—I understand you're a religious man."

"The gods have earned my devotion."

"How curious."

I wondered how a three-legged goose walked. Like a centipede, or always leading with that middle leg?

Gaziah's gaze shifted to Girl, who inched her way out of the direct line of fire until concealed behind Tanris. "And who is this?"

Tanris stepped aside, brutally exposing her. "This is, ah… Girl."

"I can see it is a girl. Has she a name?"

It was, you will have to admit, a delightful snare of words. I had to bite my lip to keep from snickering.

"I'm sure she does, Majesty, but she is mute. She communicates by way of sign language, and our understanding is limited."

"Do you read and write, young lady?" Gaziah asked her.

Girl wobbled her hand back and forth, then pointed at me.

"Crow is teaching her," Tanris filled in.

"Do you have the skill to print your name?"

She hesitated, pressed her lips together, then nodded.

"Why have you not?"

Her hands moved in a blur.

"She won't before—" Tanris's brow furrowed as he turned to me. "Crow can translate better than I."

"Cheeky," I murmured in response to her declaration.

"I beg your pardon?" Gaziah looked puzzled and possibly insulted.

"She will not tell her name until I ask her properly." It was exactly the deal I'd made her when she conveyed her desire to learn the art of strategic relocation of items.

"You yourself?" He looked askance.

She pursed her lips and gave a firm nod.

"Well, get on with it, man. We have business to attend to. I've pen and paper here for her to write on," he offered, waving toward the larger of two desks set in a corner of the room.

"Unnecessary, Magnanimous One."

Tanris grabbed my arm. "What is this?" he hissed under his breath.

"I did not realize." I turned up an apologetic palm. What else could I do?

Gaziah waited beside a chair, annoyance writ clear on his brow. "How long have you known her? Begging your pardon, miss."

"Oh, months."

"And you couldn't come up with anything more suitable than 'Girl'?"

"We tried," I explained. "We spent many hours trying to guess. It was an amusing game."

Girl's eyes sparkled and she nodded. She had often laughed herself to tears at our suggestions. Her secretiveness about her name had spawned another game, in which we tried to fathom what dire circumstance or criminal behavior necessitated her anonymity. As you can imagine, Tanris made for a grudging playmate, but every now and then, he'd surprise us with his wit and imagination.

You are a sneaky one, I signed.

She grinned and shrugged.

Will you please tell me your name?

The emperor received a long, not altogether happy inspection. Finally, she sighed and nodded.

"Is it a secret?" he demanded.

She shook her head. Taking my hand, she spelled her name out on my palm. Her finger tracing out each letter tickled at first. Warmth followed in the wake of each small motion. A moment later, a tingling sensation lifted the hairs on my arms and made me shiver. Little motes of orange drifted over us.

A woman kneaded bread on a thick, flat stone by the fire.

The rubbing of a dog's silky ears soothed a heartache.

Gleaming silver, a knife blade peeled bark from a new bolt shaft while a man's low voice pointed out how to—

"Crow?" I heard Tanris ask as though from the other side of the empire.

The images evaporated in a mist. Girl's brow tented in uncertainty. No, not *'Girl.'* I wrote her name across her palm to confirm I'd got it right.

She nodded and her smile chased away the oddness of the moment.

I made another extravagant bow to Gaziah. "Your Most Imperial Highness. Commander Tanris. May I present to you the lovely and talented Miss Senza Darmen?"

"It has been most interesting to make your acquaintance," Gaziah allowed. He took her hand, turning it so that she might kiss his fingers as she curtsied.

She'd practiced for at least an hour and didn't miss a beat.

"Senza…" Tanris experimented in a low voice. "You couldn't tell me?"

Appropriate or not, she deserted the emperor to grasp Tanris's hand in both of hers. Then she pointed to him, to me, to herself, and signed, *Not ready.*

Gaziah cleared his throat and made a show of going to his throne and taking a seat. "Now that the introductions are finished, shall we discuss business?" As if anyone could gainsay an emperor with impunity. "How soon can you begin looking for my uncle?"

I immediately reconsidered disagreeing with emperors. "A moment, Your Omnipotence." I caught Tanris's sleeve before he could sit. He wore a smirk like he'd just pulled one over on me in the grandest style. "You said 'relic,'" I reminded in a whisper.

"So I did."

"It had better be a priceless artifact, not a virtual cadaver."

His face was deadpan. "Careful who you're insulting, bird-brain."

"Is there a problem?" Gaziah inquired.

"No, sir," Tanris pulled free and sat next to Girl.

"Possibly," I disagreed. "You want me to find your *uncle?*"

"Yes. He's been kidnapped, and I want you to steal him back."

—5—
Attitude Adjustment

S hock and dismay stabbed me so hard I had to struggle to breathe. A glance at Tanris showed his complete composure, but he wasn't the one with his freedom being threatened...

"I beg your pardon?" An annoying tremble in my voice gave away my apprehension.

"A situation has arisen that requires changing the conditions of your pardon. You will bring my uncle home—alive and unharmed— by any means necessary, or you will be imprisoned." He tipped his head the barest fraction, challenging.

Only the gods know why the motion reminded me of Tanris cocking a crossbow.

Flight was premature, however tempting. I would not be imprisoned. It would require agreeing with him now and fleeing later, so I let him think he had me pinned in place with his icy stare while I mustered my poise. Self-respect kept me from agreeing immediately. Contemptible, *loathsome* arrogance... Anger tightened my mouth and lifted my chin. "I do not steal people. Rule number five."

"Your rules are irrelevant."

"Not to me. My life depends on them. It's difficult to make plans to abduct *people*, and the goods are liable to become complications. If they don't wish to be stolen, they scream and fight back. If they want to be rescued, they think they can help." Experience was a harsh tutor. I hid my clenched fists at my sides. "Send someone else after him." Doubtless he had hundreds of minions at his beck and call, and I was *not* anyone's minion.

"Crow…" Tanris growled oh-so-softly.

Gaziah silenced him with a flick of his hand. Leaning back in his seat, he stroked the head of one of the winged lions that made the arms of his throne. I couldn't read a thing from his expression, nor could I discern his emotions. What else did that little warding spell of his do? "It's possible that you believe sentiment is impeding clear thinking. However, let me point out that I have a nice, shiny army to hunt down demons. What I don't want is for my uncle to be accidentally killed, particularly in sensitive territory. This is delicate work. Work for a thief, not a negotiator. I have heard rumors you are the best thief in all the Bahsyr Empire. Are you telling me you are not up to the task?"

"My abilities are not the issue. The target is. Your word is. How do I know you won't come up with another job to prevent me from fulfilling my part of the bargain? And another after that? What assurance do I have that you intend to keep your promise?"

Senza covered her mouth, eyes like saucers.

Tanris lost three shades of complexion. "Your majesty, what he means—"

"What I mean," I snarled, rounding on him, "is that I don't trust him as far as I can throw him."

He closed his eyes, took a deliberate breath, then said in a perfectly calm and rational voice, "You cannot talk to or about the emperor like that." I expect he wished to strangle me.

"Why? Is he so delicate he'll fracture if he hears a truth he mislikes?"

"I am not delicate," Gaziah put in with surprising mildness, "and I don't crack easily." He kept stroking the lion-head armrest as he watched me.

I speculated whether it and its mate might come to life and leap at my throat, wings thundering, talons and teeth rending. A powerful musky smell and a sense of warm, moist breath made the image *too* vivid. I resisted pulling out my talisman. Instead, I continued to clench my fists, reining in my temper.

Finally, *finally*, I heard the dry rustling whispers of the Ancestors and the faint stir of air around me. I wanted to shout at them. What good were they, anyway?

Girl fiddled with her sash as she chewed on her lip. She kept her eyes glued to the emperor and her feet set for imminent action.

The silence grew brittle and thin.

"Well?" I urged before it broke and cut someone.

Gaziah lifted a brow. "Humor me. Hypothetically, could you do such a job without getting Enikar killed?"

I rudely answered his question with my own. "Is one old man really worth putting scores of people in jeopardy?"

Tanris cleared his throat softly, as if struggling to keep it a secret. He needed background noise for that, and he had none.

I rubbed my forehead. "Imagining the possibility that he'll cooperate with me rather than the reality of him having his own ideas for doing things? Also imagining that whoever kidnapped him doesn't have an army arrayed to prevent such an event? Yes, I could do it." I'd never disabled an army before. How intriguing…

"There's an army involved, though not in the conventional sense." Gaziah gave another flick of his hand, as if by doing so he could dismiss an unknown number of soldiers.

I folded my arms. "It sounds like quite the challenge."

"You'll do it, then."

Probably better not to voice my opinion about his own bad hearing. "As I said, I don't steal people. And I don't take on armies, conventional or otherwise."

"Mmm… Guards, take Crow out, and be careful. I've heard he's slippery. Put him in a cage he can't wriggle out of."

Things had escalated fast. The guards started toward me, lowering their shiny spears. Girl leaped to her feet with a funny sound. Tanris caught her arm as he stood, preventing her from doing anything rash. "Blast you, Crow," he growled, and had the decency to look indecisive.

I ignored him—for his own health. "Well, that's a bit extreme," I objected, considering my escape options.

"I don't have time to play games with you, thief. My uncle is more fragile than he admits. He is in a dangerous situation that only worsens while we bandy words. You come highly recommended. You can either do the job or rot." He offered his pronouncement as if presenting a choice between fruit or cakes.

I backed toward the possibility of exit via the windows. I had little doubt I could get myself up and out of them, but what would happen to my companions? The glittering, resolute spears pursued me. Behind them, Girl—That is to say, *Senza*—waved her hand and signed something about *goats* that I didn't quite catch.

"You drive a hard bargain, Your Almightiness, though making me a deal for one job then yanking that job away seems underhanded."

"Great shades, will you keep your mouth shut?" Tanris implored. "You can't talk to the Emperor of Bahsyr like that!"

"He doesn't seem to have any difficulty at all," Gaziah noted drily. "If you enjoy your *job* so much, Crow, I expect the business with the demons will still need your attention when you've returned Uncle Enikar."

Two spear tips pressed against my chest. "Careful," I scolded. "This tunic is new."

Use your head, Crow, Senza signed, mouth pinched and eyes worried. *You can't help your people if you are dead or behind goats*. No, she must mean *bars*.

Trying to ignore her, I placed a fingertip against one spear to push it aside. It didn't budge. The guard didn't even blink. I tried the other weapon with the same result. I huffed a reluctant breath. "Very well, but I cannot guarantee what condition he'll be in."

"You'll do your utmost to keep him safe," Gaziah declared. Although he didn't say it, the promise of dungeon rot was clear in his voice.

I gave him a practiced smile. "Naturally."

"You have *my* word, Highness," Tanris the Incredibly Noble swore.

"Where did you say your uncle was taken?" I asked before he could put me in the same foolish position of swearing or giving away other valuable words.

"He's gone to Masni to acquire an artifact." With another gesture from the emperor, the guards stepped back.

"Masni's nice." I love the islands. I had long dreamed of retiring to the beautiful beaches of Pelipa. Even my unfortunate romance had not soured that ambition, though I'd exchanged my goal. Instead of a picket fence, I now fantasized about a villa on the other side of the island. South of Pelipa, Masni's white sands and gentle breezes offered the same appeal.

Gaziah went back to stroking the lion's head. "It's claimed by Basi Serhat, who styles himself a prince. There is no love lost between his house and mine, and Enikar has fallen into his hands."

"Ah, complications." I proffered a fake smile and turned a stoney look upon my partners.

Tanris shrugged.

Girl had recovered some of her composure, but she looked worried. And I was clearly going to have a difficult time adjusting to calling her Senza.

Senza, *Senza, Senzaaaaa,* I repeated to myself. A nice name. Strong and sharp. She would grow into it. Happily, she no longer dissolved into tears every other minute as she had once done, although one could never predict when she'd cry. Or why.

"The islands, though…" Sweeping past the guards as if they didn't exist, I deposited myself nonchalantly in a chair. Elbow propped on the back, I dragged my fingers through my hair as I thought. "Aren't there pirates on Masni?"

"Why send Enikar for this antique?" Tanris interrupted.

"I didn't send him, he went of his own accord." Disinclined to answer the pirate question, Gaziah pushed himself up to pace in front of his chair. One fist rested on his hip and the other scrubbed his jaw. "Retirement apparently doesn't suit him."

Folks tended to like Enikar. Relinquishing his claim to the throne in favor of true love had turned him into a romantic hero.

He'd spent decades as an ambassador for his brother, Emperor Akmahn, Gaziah's father. His poorly pedigreed wife died childless and he had never wed again. He'd left the military game-playing to his cousins to pursue education in the guise of diplomacy. Several universities bore his name, one located in the islands, which I applauded and occasionally visited. It had a marvelous library. Though detractors criticized him for it, he focused his monies and efforts on the Karahan School (creatively named after its island home). He succeeded in turning it into an institution independent of either empire or confederacy. His travels as emissary had given him access to places and people—and libraries and histories—all across the country.

"What's the relic he's after?" For an old man to brave pirates *and* a family enemy, it must be quite valuable. I wondered how hard it would be to pry from Basi Serhat's greedy paws.

"The Masni Idol, and I understand it is ancient. It's said the thing attracts the blessings of the gods." He lied.

I mulled over that fact and came to no useful conclusion. "A statue, then. Does it work? Has Serhat drawn any particularly wondrous gifts?"

Ice lining the edges of the Zenn river in winter was warmer than the smile twisting Gaziah's narrow features. "Is it a blessing to incur the wrath of an emperor?"

"Probably not, but is it wise for an emperor to vent that wrath on neutral territory? If you attack Masni, the Confederacy's likely to send a fleet in reply. I think there's a tiny truce?" I held up thumb and forefinger a scant distance apart.

"I am not planning to attack anything today." Gaziah's mouth turned down. "I am sending the empire's greatest thief to Masni to reclaim that which was stolen from me. Two can play this game, but I can play it better."

How could I not appreciate that line of thinking?

"I want my uncle back—and I want that stupid little idol Serhat loves so much." Gaziah returned to his throne and sat. The carved beast on his right purred as he stroked its head.

That was alarming.

"Can I have some time to think about it?" I wanted to consult with the conspicuously silent Ancestors, and talking out loud to invisible spirits was never a popular thing to do in mixed company.

"There is nothing to think about. You sail to the sunny islands, or you go curl up in a dark cell for the rest of your life."

I did not need to see to know Senza put her hand over her mouth the way any other woman would to prevent crying out.

"I suppose you'll want us to leave this afternoon." Was it likely he detected the sour note in my tone?

"You can do that?" His brows lifted.

"No!" Tanris put in hastily. "I'm sorry, Highness, but there are plans to work out and arrangements to make. We will sail as soon as possible. Three days at least."

Gaziah frowned. "I have a ship, supplies, and a squad at your disposal."

"Oh, that won't do at all," I objected. Emotion clearly clouded his senses.

"Crow." Tanris had such a nice growl. It made lesser men shiver.

"Highness," I tacked on, perhaps soothing his ruffled feelings. "If we're sailing to a pirate's island, we need a pirate ship. And if we have soldiers tagging along, the pirates will turn into hedge-demons. They'll eat us first and ask questions after."

Gaziah narrowed his eyes at me, but he had too pleasant a face to achieve Tanris's ability to strike fear into the hearts of men with a mere glance. "You'll need guards. I won't have Enikar unprotected."

I opened my mouth to argue, but Tanris cut in. "Of course, Highness. Do you have a map of the island? And it might help to look at whatever information you have about the area—Serhat and his people, contacts, enemies."

"Dear gods, save me," I grumbled, folding my arms again. "This is ridiculous."

Gaziah turned to Tanris. "Do I have to employ insurance for his cooperation?"

That *really* singed my tail feathers. "You're exactly like Metin Duzayan. You high and mighty lot are all the same. You take what you want, when you want—and if that doesn't work, you threaten, abuse, or kill whoever gets in your way." Oh, what I wouldn't have done to throw some druid magic at him! A good wind, ground heaving, and a little lightning were precisely what he needed. The callous, unthinking wretch. If only I knew how.

"I am so sorry, sir," Tanris murmured like a mortified mother with an outspoken child.

"For what?!" My voice went up an unattractive octave.

He didn't answer, and an uncomfortable silence fell, pricked only by the sharp points of the guards' spears aimed in my direction. Tanris wore a resigned expression. Senza perched on the edge of her seat, ready to flee.

"Do you agree with his assessment, Commander?" Gaziah asked at last. "Am I like the late, unlamented baron?"

Tanris's jaw worked. "At this moment, my liege, I am afraid so."

Gaziah's brows lifted. "Mmm…" he said and tapped his fingers on his lions' heads. Their lips curled in snarls. "And you, my lady, what do you think?" He gave Senza a flinty gaze.

She flinched.

"Feel free to speak. Or sign, as it were." He smiled. "I insist."

I heard her swallow. We all did. Finally, her hands moved and I translated. "Commander Tanris is less than himself in this room. Crow is caged, whatever choice he makes. Something was taken that was only mine to give. I do not think I wish to know you better. Sir."

Beside us, Tanris sucked in a breath.

"Mmm…" Gaziah said again, then pursed his lips. "If only more of my subjects were as forthright, and that includes you, Commander."

"You make that impossible." Taking the seat next to Girl—Senza! —I crossed my arms and propped an ankle over the opposite knee. "Who will say what they're thinking, truth or not, if the attachment of their head depends upon your mood?"

Both chair-arm lions continued to receive his attention. Their menacing gazes fixed on me. Did he know they were spelled? Had he set them on any guests? And wouldn't *that* give the servants assigned to clean the room something to talk about… *Blood on their teeth, Myrtle! And them just chairs; did you ever see such a thing?*

"A piece of advice," I dared to go on. A perverse part of me wanted to watch how the Ancestors would handle an attack from the chair-lions. "Look down on my profession if that makes you sleep better, but *you're* the one who wants my services. You ask. We discuss. We come to an agreement."

"Payment. A reward." The emperor nodded.

"I adore rewards—" I was not sure Tanris would survive this encounter, even if the emperor let us leave. He ground his teeth so hard they might explode in his head. But the goddess of opportunity opened her arms before me like a lover, and I would not refuse her. "Unrestricted access to the imperial libraries would be acceptable. Emphasis on the plural. Also on the lack of restriction."

Tanris's expression shifted, brows wrinkling. I loved confusing him. It was a bonus to my request, which I'd had days to consider, for surely the emperor wouldn't send me—*us*, that is—on a mission without reward.

Gaziah stared at me, as nonplussed as my strapping partner. "Not a house in the city?"

"I would be pleased to accept that, likewise, Your Magnanimousness."

"Crow." Tanris's constricting throat strangled my name. His high color probably baked it into the bargain.

"Not for myself." Hands pressed together, I offered an entreating smile, then inclined my head. "The commander—"

"Is quite happy with his quarters by the barracks," Tanris interrupted. If he had quarters by the barracks, why did he bunk at my apartment? What had happened to the apartment he'd shared with his late wife?

"—deserves something comfortable for his eventual retirement. After many more years of tireless, selfless service to your most Wondrous Majesty, of course."

"I do not need a house."

From the corner of my eye, I glimpsed Senza. With one arm wrapped around her middle, she chewed furiously on the thumbnail of the opposite hand. Humor and alarm gleamed from her in equal measure.

"I see." Gaziah regarded me with an unrecognizable expression. Disbelief, perhaps, or possibly indigestion. "I did not invite your lady friend to take part in this undertaking, but I presume you'll want something for her, too?"

I turned a palm up. "Whatever your conscience prescribes."

Senza waved both hands and shook her head, trying to decline her unnamed reward. *I don't want anything!*

"Very well. Will a purse of silver satisfy her?"

"That depends on the size of the purse, Most Exalted One." Palms together, I bowed.

"Mm. You'll fulfill your task first."

"It goes without saying."

A hiss of air announced Tanris expelling the breath he'd held. Were there whalebone stays in his uniform to keep him from collapsing? That might account for the excellent posture of soldiers...

Gaziah's regard turned to his commander. "Tanris, Secretary Jebba will provide you with the details of your men. Make whatever other arrangements you need through him. Crow, the secretary will also show you to my uncle's office. I hope you can find the information you require there."

Tanris stood and bowed. "Thank you, Highness." His relief was palpable.

Senza rose, too, bobbing a stiff little curtsy.

Without any orders at all, the guards approached with their pointy spears to prod us out. The secretary with the spoon-like disposition took us under his wing and promptly turned into a fork.

"Commander Baran is expecting you, Commander Tanris," he said sharply, then stabbed me with an undeserved glare. "You will follow me. Mind your fingers, or the guards will take them. Once we arrive at Duke Enikar's office, the guards will remain to monitor your actions. You will take nothing, do you understand?"

"I've already taken offense, but carry on." I gave a generous, nose-in-the-air wave.

Tanris produced a thin, put upon smile. "Senza, how would you like to have a look at the Eagle Armory?"

"Oh, not fair," I protested. "I could use her help."

"You'll work faster alone."

Senza interrupted. *I want to see the emperor's animal park.*

I should have known better than to tell her about that. Her campfire tale was made real—and for a moment I was jealous, but a challenge had been issued. I had riddles to reveal, trifles to transport, and imperial noses to tweak

—6—
Well, That Changes Things...

The journey to Duke Enikar's office offered the opportunity to see parts of the Kumeti Palace off limits to casual visitors. I admired the striking style. Unfortunately, Gaziah and the former occupants were prone to decorating with huge statement objects. Statues, carved columns, giant vases, trees, and fountains filled every nook and cranny. What man puts trees *inside* his residence? The sheer boldness appealed to me. I would have to get one or two for myself. I might also need a bigger house...

Secretary Spoon—er, Jebba—forbore speaking at all as we made the lengthy trek. And after he delivered a quelling glare on par with Tanris's best, my escorts, too, declined answering my questions—at least until he left us on our own. With him gone, they opened up a shade about life at the palace. I learned where they were from, how they'd come to be guards, and other such thrilling information. It interested me not in the least, but encouraged them to act like regular people. Soften them. Like clay.

Enikar's clerk, a man of middling age with a receding hairline and copious pockets, provided all kinds of information. He also offered a valuable exit strategy for the things I wasn't supposed to take. While anyone would sound chatty compared to Secretary Spoon, the clerk soon filled my ears to overflowing. He knew *everything* about his true love: the extinct indigenous peoples of the lower islands. Even better, he produced sketches of the Masni idol, maps, and customs that had been passed down to the mixed breed offspring of the natives and their conquerors.

Fairly crackling with glee, he opened a small jar and he held it out for my examination. "Red ochre," he gloated.

"Of what significance is that?"

He launched into an explanation of how the Masni clans used the stuff to mark their bodies, houses, weapons, boats, and a hundred other things. They did this extensive decorating during an annual celebration that lasted for days. Particular designs or characters represented identity, while others symbolized blessings—or curses.

While the fellow lectured, he waved his arms with wonderful exuberance. On the one hand, it was a challenge to dodge them. On the other, no one noticed when I slipped interesting documents and trinkets into his pockets.

We spent several educational hours together. When we left Enikar's office, the guards dutifully patted me down to look for contraband, cracking jokes the while. I was happy to comply and offered my own jests in return. They had orders to see me to the gates. I asked the clerk to come along, wondering if he would tell me something about the history of the palace?

It was as easy as luring a child with sweets. During the long walk, I had plenty of time to transfer the purloined items from his pockets to more comfortable positions in my own. The clerk happily fulfilled the role of instructor, and the guards were delightfully distractible. The unfettered freedom to work my craft lifted my spirits. Once free of the palace, I sold a few of Enikar's things in the market and increased the weight of my coin purse. Another cause for joy.

I took the steps to my apartment two at a time. My status as best thief in all the empire allowed for such luxuries as accommodations in the Sunhar District. I'd purchased it years ago, and protected its existence dearly. Before my encounter with Baron Metin Duzayan and the subsequent adventure with Tanris, I hadn't actually lived there. I kept things there—most notably my library and reserve resources—and used it for sabbaticals from time to time. Over time, the place had assumed a delightful eclectic comfort.

Girl—By all the gods who favored me! How long before the use of her name came as easily as styling her 'Girl'? *Senza's* first reaction had been wide-eyed wonder. Then she'd settled in like she might stay there forever—which was alarming. In typical Tanris-style, my erstwhile hunter often picked up items to examine with suspicion. I feared he would chew his cheek through in an effort to restrain himself from asking how I'd come by them. Occasionally, I tossed him a bone and gave out splinters and shreds of explanation. He'd study me, purse his lips, and nod. Whether he believed me was another story.

On the threshold, I paused, letting the Ancestors go before me. It was a habit now, and effective—for they would give warning if intruders had broken in. If only I could trust their (sometimes horrifying) promise to be with me always… Now and then their silence suggested otherwise.

Today they flowed past me and into the apartment with nary a sound. Nothing to alarm them meant nothing to alarm me (though the reverse was not necessarily true).

I found the little dragon sitting in his cage. Talons wrapped around the bars and snout protruding, he was the very image of dejection. Upon seeing me, he loosed an enormous tear. Drama at its finest.

"Pitiful, but a bit much," I advised, crouching to fill his dish with my purchase from the butcher. The market provided an excellent opportunity to shop for goods as well as information about the goings-on in the city at street level. And I was sorely behind on the news. I'd spent hours there and had expected the others to have returned already. The notion of a few precious moments alone hurt me not at all. It would give me a chance to begin working on my plan.

Not-an-Egg wilted against the cage bars and whimpered, pretending not to notice the food. A dribble of drool gave him away.

"Where are you learning this kind of behavior? Are you sneaking out to attend acting school?"

He sat up with a huff heated enough to turn my knuckles red and snatched a chunk of meat. Sharp teeth tore at his meal.

"Ouch! You ungrateful little snake with wings!"

He bared his teeth at me and hissed.

The bone I'd left him this morning, a huge thing any brawny ox would have been proud to own, was conspicuously missing. I checked beneath and behind the furniture.

"Tanris keeps pestering me to give you a real name. What do you think of 'Bottomless Pit'?"

With a pronounced expression of skepticism on his craggy little face, he swallowed the next bit of meat whole.

"I could call you 'Pit' for short. No? 'Gobbler'."

A chunk as big as my hand didn't deter him at all. He sank claws and teeth into it and ripped it into manageable pieces.

I would very much hate for him to do that to me, but I could fantasize about him dealing so handily with some nameless enemy. "How about 'Brute' or 'Shredder'?"

A sharp knock at the door interrupted my hunt for the Perfect Name. Tanris and Senza (Look at me, remembering!) were the only people who knew where I lived, and they had very strict orders not to divulge the address to anyone. Ever. It didn't matter how important the emperor thought he was, he did *not* need to know the location of my favorite apartment. I would be livid if I had to move. Also, Tanris and Senza would not be invited to visit my new quarters.

Opening the door jogged my memory. "Oh. I forgot about you." A blatant lie. That Woman was too exquisite and had caused far too much damage for me to easily put her out of my mind. I did have days, though, when I didn't think about her. I took my victories where I could.

Nonplussed, she stared at me for an entire minute, then glanced away. "Of course you have," she said, her mouth tightening. Her visage hinted at 'angry' and 'disbelieving,' but her emotions proclaimed 'hurt.' Any of them looked marvelous on Tarsha of Vidarya. Everything did; it always had. Her skills were not limited to looking good and dancing. She could perform with all the finesse of a trained actor.

Was Not-an-Egg taking lessons from *her?* If that were true, I knew a spice sauce that would be tasty on grilled dragon.

"I've brought you something," she continued. A few beguiling tendrils escaped the knot in which she wore her thick, dark hair. "May I come in?"

Refusing to stare like a dazzled boy on the cusp of manhood, I folded my arms and blocked the doorway. I'd no idea why my lungs were doing unfathomable things in my chest, but they had better behave. "I don't want anything from you, and no, you may not."

"This is yours." She fished inside her embroidered purse anyway. What should she offer on her upturned palm—right there on the balcony for anyone to see—but the Great Gandil.

That beautiful, magical, *wretched* pearl was to have been my wedding gift to her. I'd gotten it especially for her. Went through several hells for *her.* For *nothing.* I'd taken it from Baron Duzayan, given it to Tarsha, lost everything, killed the baron, then been turned —temporarily, I assure you—into a hunting dog. Technicalities of ownership and betrayal wove a web of confusion about my senses. I glared them away and didn't touch that damnable pearl. "What do you want, Tarsha?"

Moving as if she might startle me into flight, she reached out and slipped the Gandil into my pocket. I let her. I was resentful, not stupid.

"You cannot buy back my affections."

"I know." Her small smile was understanding. Her smiles always turned my knees to jelly. Stoic, I resisted the effect. "That is—Well, it's yours," she said with a firm nod, and folded her graceful hands at her waist. "Whatever happens next."

Next? One brow curled in dubious question. "There is no 'next' for us. There is no *us.*"

"I need to hire you."

That was unexpected. It took three entire blinks to recover from the surprise. "No."

"Will you—"

"First," I held up my fingers one at a time as I calmly counted the reasons I wouldn't take her on as a client. "The last time I acquired something for you, you betrayed me. Second, you can't afford me. Third, I have a previous engagement. Fourth, I don't trust you. Fifth, I am going to be out of the city for the foreseeable future. Sixth, if you need help, ask your darling Jackal." Her husband's name was actually Jashel. "Seventh, I don't care. Whatever it is you've gotten yourself into no longer matters to me. Eighth—"

"Crow." She lowered her head and let out a short sigh. Thumb and fingers rubbed her forehead.

I got the distinct sense of *loss* and *pain*, senses I did not feel inclined to share or relieve. She'd chosen to betray me, not the other way around. Of course she'd lost me. Anger knotted my belly, then resentment tightened the muscles in my jaw. She should not still have this power over me, *any* power over me.

The Ancestors brushed my cheek and feathered my hair, their curiosity and protectiveness eddying close. They'd learned a little discretion in the months we'd spent together. Sometimes they remembered it. I could imagine three or four of them peering over my shoulder at our visitor. Too bad she couldn't see them. Deliberately, I kept any kind of emotion out of my voice. "I can't help you. Goodbye, Tarsha." I stepped back and reached for the edge of the door.

"This isn't about me. It isn't *for* me." Her hands tightened into fists. She didn't meet my gaze. Sincere determination imposed an aura of strength. "Please let me explain."

"You don't seem to understand. I don't want to see you again. Ever." It took a serious effort not to growl.

She lifted her face then. I closed the door on eyes glittering with unshed tears, gratified that I hadn't yelled at her or been unforgivably rude. Tanris and Senza had lectured me about that. Tanris elected the noble route, and blathered about rising above my enemies (as if he didn't put a sword through his regularly). Senza warned me against becoming a monster.

That one had wounded.

Had I been a monster just now? I might have been mean about her husband, but that situation rankled. It really did. Was it cruel to tell her I didn't care? It was the truth. I hadn't said it to be cruel, but to—what, exactly?

Behind me, I heard Tarsha sag against the door, felt her silent despair. Tendrils of hopelessness drifted through the wood, threatening to entangle me. Uncertain if the notion was magical, real, or my imagination, I made my escape to the other side of the apartment and opened a window. With any luck, the ventilation would protect me.

The Gandil was a weight in my pocket and on my heart. It shocked me when I pulled it out, green sparks glittering and biting my skin. I dropped the jewel with an impolite exclamation and it rolled across the carpet. This time, I used a kerchief to pick it up. In the light of day, its pearlescent blue perfection could steal breath away, and I found myself holding mine. The thing was not just wildly rare, but magical, too. I'd known the rumors. Now I knew the truth. Rare things and magic went together, didn't they? What might it do, besides ruin lives and break hearts?

"That's melodramatic, Crow," I said aloud. "This beautiful jewel didn't wreck anything. *She* did." And Tanris, too, had played a part in the disaster. To be sure, I hadn't been in love with him. I'd rather enjoyed our roles, his cat to my bird. A thief should expect a lawman would use all the tools at his disposal to do his job. Oh, I had blamed him, cursed him, and had him save my life on several occasions. And now look at us. Friends.

"Maudlin." I pursed my lips in a reproving sneer.

Not-an-Egg licked the remains of his meal from his claws, watching me as if I might do something crazy.

"What are you looking at? You don't know her. She's—Oh, shades and ashes." I thumped the heel of my hand against my forehead. "That woman knows where I live."

The dragon caught hold of the bars and straightened.

I paced, the Gandil wrapped in its cloth in a fist on one hip, the other hand scrubbing my head as I thought. "She's known all along." The realization brought me up short. She could have told Metin Duzayan any time, but the baron had never crossed the threshold.

No guards or assassins had come here. Prompted by suspicion and uneasiness, I stalked through the entire apartment, examining everything with a critical eye.

"Help me," I bid the Ancestors. "Has anyone visited this place besides myself, Grimfist, and Girl?"

Not-an-Egg hissed.

"And the dragon." I cast my gaze ceiling-ward in exasperation.

The spirits whisked about. They ruffled my hair and clothing and scattered the papers on a nearby table. I let Not-an-Egg out, and the two of us tracked their progress through the apartment. They made broad sweeps through each room, then focused their attention on the doors and windows. Draperies flapped. I caught a vase before it crashed to the floor and picked up a tumbled stack of books to return to Tanris's nightstand. *Petri's Rules of Combat. Fortresses and Defensive Structures of the Kuldyri. Qronq's Guide to Small Game on the Izam Peninsula. Stalked and Chalked: Bounty Hunting for Fun and Profit.*

What was this? I couldn't decide which was more outrageous—the fact that there was a book about pursuing lawbreakers, or that Tanris used it. I picked it up to have a look.

[Not here! Nor here!] the Ancestors interrupted. *[Unscathed! Secure. Whole. Perfect! Safe safe safe...]*

They danced around me, flapping the pages of the amusingly slim volume detailing criminal pursuit. Within the first few paragraphs, I discovered that 'chalked' referred to tallying the number of necks stretched and rewards collected. How appalling. I clapped it shut and tidied the mess my invisible companions had created. More important things demanded my immediate attention. Like food.

Booklet in hand, I returned to the apartment's common area. First came the construction of a few *nakari'an*—satisfying portable meals made of flatbread, smoked meat, fruit or vegetables, and a sweet, spicy sauce. Not-an-Egg sat beside me as he always did. Without Tanris here to scold us, I fed him a half while I looked over the notes I'd absconded with. The dragon tried to sneak another bite and got a swat on the nose for his efforts. Unruffled, he laid his head on my knee and pretended to study the squiggling characters. In the last few months, he'd grown from the size of a large cat to the size of the bronze foxes we'd seen in the wilderness—though rather less nimble.

When I finished my meal, I massaged my stiff hand. A note in a margin caught my attention. *"Investigation into regular arrivals of supplies suggests mining. (Iron, grinding stones, tools, bellows, picks, hammers, and so on.) Labor force not imported or local. Natives moving away from southern end of island. Rumors of sea monsters—or monsters from the sea. Related, coincidental, or unnatural?"*

A key in the lock brought Not-an-Egg upright from his slouch against my leg. Tanris came into view with Girl—no, *Senza*—peering past him. She smiled when she saw me.

"Did you have any luck?" Tanris asked without embellishment.

"Oh, yes. It turns out your clean shirts weren't on top of the cage after all."

He cuffed me as he passed. I'd learned how to tip my head to avoid actual injury while still allowing him to believe he'd chastened me. Or given me a brotherly swat of affection. One never knew.

"Aren't you pleased?" I asked as he divested himself of his splendid uniform jacket and pulled up a chair. He was conventionally wrinkled underneath.

Senza giggled as she plopped a bag down on the table. From within she withdrew a bright golden-yellow peach to toss to me. *Grimfist is worried,* she signed. *Bad news, I think.*

Tanris unfastened a leather satchel bursting with papers. "Gaziah has our trip planned out in every detail."

Not pleased, then. I felt no compunction about following someone else's ill-advised strategy, and if Tanris didn't like the plans, there was no chance at all that I would. "So?" I took a good-sized bite of the peach.

"So all we have to do is board the ship and sail off into the sunset."

"How romantic. How many Eagles?"

"A dozen."

"Ah." I thought it might be fifty or so. A dozen couldn't be too hard to get rid of, though dumping them overboard in their armor would be impractical, not to mention it would earn Tanris's wrath.

"That's all? You're fine with that?"

"I already made my opinion clear. How soon does the plan say we're leaving?"

"A few days." He sighed and sat back in his chair, scrubbing his shaved pate.

"Or we could go earlier. Without the extra baggage."

He shook his head. "We've got a ship—the *Silver Hind*—and a crew."

I stared. "Who names a ship after a backside? Is it the emperor's? Is that why it's silver? It doesn't have a figurehead, does it? Or I suppose that would be a figurebottom…"

"A hind is a deer, idiot." Still, a smile tugged at the corner of his mouth.

"Then why not call it a deer?"

"The common folk do."

"Oh, I see. If that's the case, a ship with a name like that screams nobility and imperial superiority. And with the company of soldiers he's ordered, we'll be as obvious as a crown in a stack of hats."

Chewing on her lip, Senza nodded agreement.

"It's the emperor's uncle. He wants him safe, and he insists on a squad of Eagles and the ship."

"He requested that *I* fetch the old man." I could think of other, less charitable words than *requested*. "I can't do my job wearing the emperor's colorful and obvious livery or with a bunch of clods— no disrespect to your friends intended—drawing attention." Another bite of fruit had juice dribbling down my chin.

Not-an-Egg straightened to lick it and gave me a mournful look when I pushed him away.

"We don't have a choice."

"You don't. I do. You go, and I'll stay." Or rather, I wouldn't sail off to the islands. Neither would I wait around in Marketh for a spiteful emperor to collect me and lock me up. "I'm sure you and your trusty Eagles can swoop in and out with little trouble."

Studiously, Senza unpacked her bag and put things away, not looking at either of us.

Robin Lythgoe

Tanris shook his head again. If he wasn't careful, it might come loose. "Crow." His voice was determined, and his brows drawn in a serious line.

I waved a dismissive hand. "I don't need a lecture, and I don't need your lofty nobility making my choices for me. I'm not you. We've discussed our differences of opinion before and—"

"The north side of Pelipa is gone."

As a way to bring a mounting tirade to an end, that worked splendidly. My usually nimble mind could not fathom such a thing, nor formulate the words for a witty reply. Knowing that Tanris didn't lie made the announcement more awful. *My* island was ruined? It took several tries to get my mouth to work. "What do you mean, it's gone? Half an island can't just disappear."

Tanris's jaw muscles worked. "The message arrived after you left the palace. The islands have been experiencing earthquakes, and this one—Well." One fist clenched.

"How many quakes?"

He shrugged. "Multiple."

"More than, say, five?"

"Yes."

That was a lot, particularly since they did not have a history of earthquakes. "And Gaziah expects us to sail to probable suicide to save his uncle."

A nod.

I nodded back, solemn as a priest. "Perhaps you need to work on your persuasive arguments. I would rather face pirates than earthquakes, and I wasn't at all convinced to do that much. My answer is still no." I discarded the peach pit on a plate that yet held a crust of bread Not-an-Egg hadn't found, and licked my fingers.

"You could stop them."

"Stop the earthquakes?" I laughed. He didn't. "How do you propose I do that?"

He glanced sideways at Senza, who squeezed the living daylights out of the bag she'd emptied, gaze fixed on the floor. "Gates are causing the upheavals. You closed Duzayan's."

68

What a mess Baron Stinkhead Duzayan had left behind. It's funny how many emotions can cram themselves into a handful of seconds. Shock. Horror. Anger. *Comprehension.* "By Kashar's Crusty Cudgel," I muttered. "Is that what happened to the dead foreigners we found?"

"Maybe." Speculation slid to likeliness. "Probably."

The awfulness of gates winking in and out of existence made my stomach turn. Had there been a quake in the wilds? I couldn't be certain. If so, it hadn't been big enough to notice. Did the gate have to touch the ground to produce a quake? Perhaps manifest *partway* into the earth?

Crusty cudgel? Senza signed. *Disgusting!*

"Kashar was Gaziah's great-grandfather," Tanris supplied for Senza's benefit. He turned the papers I'd been perusing so that he could see them better. "A big, bold man with a big, bold—"

"Sense of self worth," I inserted. "It's a family trait."

"—strategy for expansion. He was successful and liked to remind people of that. So he commissioned a new emblem of office." His brows drew down as he paused, skimming over the page. "It was an enormous cudgel fashioned of glass and encrusted with jewels."

Because he was rich and boastful? Senza asked.

Reading, Tanris missed her question, so I answered for him. "Yes. The original story was that it showed how he wielded his power with delicacy and generosity."

"Did you take these from the Duke's office?" Tanris's accusing glare was a marvel to behold. It was a wonder my skin didn't sizzle under the heat of it.

"Secretary Spoon warned me not to," I sniffed. "So I didn't."

"Who did?"

"Enikar's clerk. He is a very well-informed and generous fellow."

The chair creaking as he leaned back, Tanris folded his well-muscled arms across his broad chest. He could look very intimidating when he chose. He drummed his fingers upon the opposite elbow, considering me with one of those long, unblinking stares of his. "There are," he said at last, "three known gates in or near the islands. Currently, that is. You dealt with Duzayan's; you can deal with these."

The Ancestors whispered up one side of me, then down the other. I couldn't quite hear them, which I found annoying and unhelpful. One hand rubbed my head, and there went another of those split-second, irrelevant thoughts. *I needed a haircut.*

Because *that* would solve so many problems…

"I don't know how." I enunciated each word. It was not a new discussion. I could not change the facts. "Circumstances and pure luck—"

"And the love of the gods," he reminded with all the solemnity of a grave. His jaw inched forward as if tempting me to contradict him.

Mouth open, I stared at him. He was developing an uncanny talent for leaving me speechless. Fortunately, it didn't last. "Yes, that, naturally. And do you have any idea how *excruciating* it was, Tanris? I cannot close one portal, never mind several."

"How did you do it before?"

"The Ancestors did it." Seeing another question open his mouth, I guessed what shape it would take. "Through me, yes, but they refuse to give me any information about what the gate was, how they closed it, or what is needed for me to do it on my own."

Again, he speared me with a long, uncomfortable examination as he decided how much I was lying. At last, he gave a curt nod. "The duke may be able to help. He's studied the lives and teachings of the druids."

Paint me astounded. "The Mazhar druids?"

"I don't know, maybe. Does it matter?"

"I don't know, maybe," I echoed, sarcasm dripping all over the place. "I have a Mazhar legacy. There are at least three druidic schools within the empire alone, and you might have noticed that the Mazhar don't exist anymore."

"They all deal with the same sort of magic, don't they?"

I bit my tongue on the urge to argue with him. "Two do." I could not deny a swell of hope, however hazy. While I'd found a few books on the subject, I'd yet to find a druid—or someone who knew about druids—to talk to. Demon hunting with Tanris and the Eagles had rather cut into my research time and my ability to visit the schools.

"Well?"

Tanris and Senza both ogling me did nothing to ease a whirlpool of emotion. I loved the islands, and the thought of losing them ran an unhappy parallel to losing Tarsha. And the foreigners falling through the gates had exactly one champion: me. Poor saps. "You're the hero, Tanris, not I." The soft, wistful declaration surprised and annoyed me. I pushed up from my chair to go pour myself a drink. The setting sun winked from the palace dome, painting it amber. I let the sight pull my gaze away from my companions, yet it failed to capture my entire attention.

"You underestimate yourself, even after all you've done." His voice held a note of gruffness.

I kept my focus on the glittering city spread out below. Hero or not, my conscience squirmed under the idea of leaving those infernal gates open. What destruction they would wreak, dumping more unwitting foreigners into a strange place to be hunted and cursed. Anxiety spurred distressing memories from my distant past. Memories I thought I had buried long ago. "How are there more gates?" I whined.

Tanris couldn't say, so he didn't.

Senza came to lay her hand on my arm in a show of sympathy and support.

I hated being in this position. Regret for what I was about to do loomed like doom on my horizon. "One of these days I'm actually going to retire to some private, cozy little nest of my own."

Silence.

I sighed. "We need KipKap."

"All right."

I'd expected him to argue. When he didn't even ask why, I was forced to continue my line of thought. I wouldn't go so far as to call it a plan yet. My next question broke at least four of my personal rules. "Can you get me Duzayan's magic dagger?"

—7—
Integrity

Port Master Sidu, for reasons of safety and snobbery, did not frequent the public houses in the district where he worked. A man of habit, I found him in the Red Pigeon. I'd done some business with him—or to him, some might say—on several occasions. The proper clothing, hair, make-up, and accent prevented recognition. Truthfully, he dealt with so many men and women every day that only those faces he saw often made an impression. Though I could not fault him for his stern work ethic, his people skills were second rate at best.

So was his ability to hold his liquor, but that provided so many opportunities to a clever person such as myself. On my own, I had the freedom to move unrestricted and unreproved. It had been months since I'd had the opportunity to sow the seeds of chaos among the innocent and unsuspecting. It was a game that never failed to lift my spirits.

I had a goal in mind, though, and didn't simply stir things up on a lark. This time. That said, I enjoyed myself. A drink here, a shared laugh there, several card games I lost severely…. Along the way, I relocated the belongings of a handful of men, including the port master. Then it was time to feign my own robbery, gain the commiseration and support of my fellow victims, and fortuitously 'find' Sidu's missing locket. In my debt, he would help me locate transportation for the upcoming trip.

At least, that was the original plan.

A heavy hand fell on my shoulder and shook me with unpleasant familiarity. "By all the stars above, if it isn't *Blackfeather*!"

I suppressed a groan and thanked whichever gods watched over me today that Raza Qimeh had the decency not to use my real name. It was an old courtesy, which usually meant he wanted in on whatever I was doing. We shared a long-standing and colorful acquaintance. I'd first met him years ago when he stayed for a short time with the Family—the people who had raised me. It wasn't a good fit, and he'd left to pursue other opportunities. Before he'd changed his line of work to 'protection services,' he'd practiced thievery. Despite the amount of practice he put in, he'd never matched my skill nor attracted the favor of the gods. Through no fault of his own, they ignored him and showered me with blessings that saw me through all manner of obstacles, including Raza Qimeh.

"Ah," I said, mustering a smile. "Look who's here. How are you?" *Been in any good gaol cells lately?*

"What are you up to?" No polite chit-chat for him.

"Playing a friendly game or so, and you?"

"Shopping." Vernacular for looking for some action or, given the circumstances, selling out a friend. Acquaintance. Despite the lack of introduction—a sure sign he was unwelcome—he pulled out a chair and sat. My companions regarded him with mixed curiosity, irritation, and alarm. Sentiments I shared, except for the alarm, although I could well understand theirs. The demon I'd thrown in Raza's face the last time we connected hadn't done him any favors. His original scars hid under a new arrangement of knotted tissue that tugged at one eye and bunched across his cheek. Purse and vanity must be worse for the wear, or he'd have found himself a magic-wielding healer, or at least a priest of Ishram.

"Oh? What are you in the market for?" one of my companions inquired in an attempt at politeness.

"A new face, from the look of things." I goggled rudely and with enthusiasm.

The curl of his lip pulled at his scars. "You gentlemen know you have a ruffian tern in your midst, I hope? Your best bet would be to call for the constable and have him arrested."

Ruffian terns were the bullies of the seaboard, bird-wise, and if anyone fit the description, it was Raza, not I. "I beg your pardon..." I gasped, sticking to the mild-mannered and easily astonished persona I'd adopted for the evening.

Sidu came to my defense. "He can barely keep himself in the game." He patted his waist. "I'm nine silver *jukati* richer now, thanks to him."

Raza nodded. "He's very good at luring a man in, then snapping the trap closed when you least expect it."

I considered my cards, assuming a sad expression. "These fellows are much sharper players than you."

He leaned forward, folded arms on the edge of the table, and studied me for a long, uncomfortable time. "No," he said at last. "They're not, and you're fleecing them."

His decision not to join the game suggested he meant to try to turn me in to the law. I waggled my brows, knowing full well how that would end. "You do hold a grudge, don't you?"

"You have no idea." He motioned to someone behind me. "Veli, go fetch the guards."

"That's inadvisable." I put my cards face down.

"Why's that?" he sneered.

Sidu and the others shifted warily in their seats. "What's he saying? Who are you?"

"He's a slick, lying thief, is who he is," Raza explained, victory gleaming in his blue eyes. "Not too bright, though, or he wouldn't have come back to the city. Where *have* you been, Featherhead?"

"Working for the emperor, actually." I smiled at him, fingers drumming.

"Right. And I'm Gaziah's maiden aunt."

"Why don't you ask him?"

He laughed. His men laughed. Only two extras this time; Raza never went anywhere alone. "You want me to get arrested or something?"

"Truly," I pressed my hand over my heart—over the reassuring shape of the amulet, "I would love it if you got yourself arrested. Again."

An ugly look contorted his face. Both hands slammed the tabletop. "You're one to talk!"

"Oh?" Up my brows went. "How many times have I ever been arrested?"

One of my card game comrades stood, hands held out to either side. "It's time I got home to the missus."

More chairs scraped the floor as the others, with the unexpected exception of Port Master Sidu, took their leave. Raza ignored them, glowering at me instead. He had an admirable scowl, perhaps equal to Tanris's. I wondered if I could get them together for comparison —preferably angry at each other rather than me.

"How many?" I repeated mildly.

Raza stabbed the air between us with his forefinger. "Don't tell me you weren't in prison last winter."

I shrugged and gave him a commiserating expression. "Yet here I am, free as a bird. Two hands, two feet, and no brands." I waved my fingers to illustrate.

"How?" he demanded. "I know blasted well that you took the Great Gandil."

"Is that the rumor? If it were true, then why would the emperor employ a convicted thief?"

Wisely silent, Sidu pursed his lips and nodded agreement.

"My point exactly." The table got stabbed this time. "You lie. I don't know how you're walking the streets, but it won't be for long."

Cold steel touched the side of my neck. Lackey Number Two put a hand on my opposite shoulder to discourage action.

The Ancestors hissed their displeasure. *[Stop him! Fright him! Show him ghosts of his dead. He will scream, scream, scream.]*

Vengeful, weren't they? "Easy," I warned them. They roiled around me, more energy than motion.

"Ha. How big is the bounty on your head?" Raza asked, oblivious.

"There isn't one, but I'm sure there will be consequences for interfering with the emperor's business." How strange—and how delightful—to throw that title around. I didn't usually. The association had some disagreeable details tied to it. Remaining calm wasn't as easy as I'd like with the Ancestors whispering all around me, worried, yet eager. A card flipped over. The flames in the nearest lamps flickered.

So intent was he on the victory in his grasp that Raza didn't notice. Sidu did, but only glanced at the card. To those who engaged in divination, an ace of suns was the sign of a rising star, fame, and glory. Or possibly a fiery death. I'd yet to burst into all-consuming flames, so clearly I was meant for fame and glory.

"You and the emperor? Do you honestly think I'll fall for a tale like that?"

The lamp flickered repeatedly, and the door slammed.

"Don't," I murmured to the Ancestors.

"Come again?"

"Boss." The man holding me shifted, and a moment later three uniformed constables came into view. One wore a drooping mustache and a dented, triangle-on-a-circle badge denoting the office of sergeant. The others had only the triangles, shiny and newly minted by the looks of them.

"This is him?" The sergeant's voice was deep and scratchy. He was of a height and had hair the same fiery red as Raza's. "He don't look like much."

"No, but he's worth a lot."

"Worth more if you let me go," I countered. "Unless you don't like your freedom. You seem to keep losing it."

"Is he worth more dead or alive?" the sergeant asked.

Raza's thug moved away and the two badgers—so called for the emblems they wore—took me by the arms. When they lifted me out of my chair, they knocked it over backward.

Sidu finally slid from the table at that, alarmed. "Now, now, boys, there's no need for violence. He's cooperating."

"I am," I agreed, and got a fist in the belly for the effort. I had to admire the muscle behind that punch, even as I wheezed for air. "You—should go, Master Sssss—"

There went my breath again. Badger Two had to show himself equally well muscled. They had no trouble holding me up while I sagged between them.

Raza placed two gentle fingers under my chin and lifted. He examined one eye, then the other, which I thought strange. "I don't think we want to risk killing him, but there are no rules against having a bit of fun."

He patted my head as he straightened. The badgers hoisted me upright, giving my arms a painful twist.

The Ancestors wound themselves up for some retaliation that would be lovely to see, but bring me a wagonload of trouble. "Still, still!" I begged them. I didn't need rumors of my "'arcane' abilities running loose in the streets of my favorite city.

Raza flipped my nose hard enough to make my eyes water. Was that a common form of torture? "Still what, Feather Boy?"

"Still—stupid," I got out.

Bam! He socked me in the eye. Stars spangled my vision—and I might have lost consciousness for a moment. When I pried open the eye that still worked, I found myself on my back. Half the lamps had gone out, their glass strewn over the floor. Chairs lay every which way. One badger sported an oozing gash across his forehead. The other sat nearby with his head in his hands. One of Raza's thugs was stretched out and not moving. His companion had disappeared. The tall sergeant crouched under a table, gripping his sword, face white.

Raza himself stared around the room with wide eyes. Bits of glass shone in his hair and clothes. Blood streaked his cheek. He spun toward me. Dropping to one knee, he grabbed my shirt front in both hands and shook me like a rag doll.

"What was that? What—by all the glittering stars—*was that??*"

I caught his wrists. "I don't know." My teeth knocked together. "I didn't see anything." My grip on him kept his punch from carrying much weight.

"Don't you lie to me! What did you do?"

"Stop it. Just stop. You clobbered me. I laid here on the floor, unconscious like any proper victim. What happened?" As if I didn't know.

[Hit you! Struck you! Attack! Attack!] the Ancestors cried. *[Come away! We will help you. Aid you. Protect you!]*

"Wind," Raza spat, looking around as if that wind might take shape and do him actual damage.

I waited a breath or two. "Right," I nodded sagely. "Wind."

He shook me again. "If it wasn't you, where'd it come from? The door is still closed. So are the windows. The others saw it, too, so don't tell me I imagined it!"

I rather liked the panic edging his voice. One didn't see Raza Qimeh reduced to fear often—which likely wouldn't go well for me. "As you say. Can I get up now?"

"I'm not done with you," he growled, dragging me along as he stood. "Are you hurt, Andyr?"

The sergeant gave up his hiding place, but not his sword. "Fine." He went to check on his companions.

"Friends, are you?" I inquired. A tap against Raza's knuckles freed me from his grasp. I'd thought he'd need more convincing, but didn't press the matter. With a crooked brow, I brushed glass from my shirt. It had little tears in it. Ruined. Hopefully, my skin hadn't suffered the same fate.

"Cousins. Get moving."

Everyone else had apparently deserted, including the public house's employees. To my astonishment, Port Master Sidu crept from hiding, though only far enough to view the goings-on.

"C'mon, boys," ordered Sergeant Andyr. "Let's get him out of here."

Stubborn, weren't they? "I'll make you a deal, Raza."

"Not interested." He bent and slapped his friend's face to bring him round. The fellow groaned and staggered to his feet, holding his head.

"Since when? Oh, wait." With one finger, I indicated the shambles surrounding us. "You've lost your nerve. Your luck? Your—"

"What kind of deal?" He'd recovered the icy glare, but apprehension left high color in his cheeks.

"My freedom against your—Hmm. What have you got?"

"A fist to your face if you give me any more trouble."

He'd already done that once, and the throb in my eye tried to obstruct my clear thinking. "Have you forgotten how a transaction like this works? You're supposed to offer me something of equal value."

"I've a pair of pit dogs." A sneer curled across his face.

I withdrew a kerchief from my pocket, dipped it into a drink someone had abandoned, and pressed the cool, wet cloth against my eye. It stung. "You needn't be insulting."

His mouth pursed. Little sparks of irritation flickered over him. "How about an Ashlock relic? A thumb."

Some might find that compelling, but the idea of carrying around a desiccated thumb turned my stomach. It didn't matter if it had belonged to the man who had nearly overcome heroic Qahan Nijamar—the fellow immortalized with a twenty-foot statue in the Kumeti Palace. "Mmm, no. Not interested."

"It's worth a fortune."

"If you can prove it's his. Can you?"

Raza glowered.

"There's the boat, boss," the remaining thug suggested.

"Shut up."

"A boat? What would *you* do with a boat? Last I heard, you get seasick in a bathtub."

"I won it." Gloating triumph was one of his favorite accessories.

"What is it, a rowboat?"

"No!" He bristled. "It's a 75-foot caravel."

"What tonnage?"

Ignorance drove his temperature up another notch.

"Fifty," his companion supplied, as if that made it quite a catch.

"Ah." I affected indifference as I leaned against the table. Dipping the cloth again, I wrung it out and pressed it back to my eye. "Leaky as a sieve?"

"As good as new. Ask the port master."

I put on a show of consideration. Offering Sidu as a reference guaranteed its condition. Sidu wouldn't lie, and he wouldn't stoop to doing any shady business with the likes of Raza Qimeh. The gods indeed smiled upon me. I gave a nonchalant shrug. "What would I do with such a boat?"

"Brag, I imagine," he said, startling a laugh out of me.

Cousin Andyr lifted his sword and took a step closer, confused suspicion all over his sharp features.

Raza waved him off. "Or you could sell it."

"Maybe. I doubt it's worth as much as my freedom."

"Take it or leave it. I'm still fine with hauling you off to the nearest gaol."

"That's the best you can do?"

"It's all you'll get out of me."

I heaved a not-too-dramatic sigh. "Very well."

"What now?"

I righted a chair and sat down. "You send your man for proof. You've three choices: Commanders Tanris or Baran of the Emperor's Eagles, or Secretary Spoon—no, his name is…" I had to think about it. "Jebba."

"At the palace?"

I don't know why he looked so incredulous. "I imagine so, being the emperor's men and all."

"If you're lying to me, I'll take your tongue before I turn you over to the emperor's men. You go." He pointed at the constable nursing the gash on his head. "You're only to speak to one of the three he named. Tell him that the thief Crow is being held here, your companions were wounded, and to send reinforcements."

"You make me sound delightfully dangerous," I beamed.

Raza yanked out the chair opposite me and settled in. The others ranged around us with various weapons in hand.

Smiling, I picked up the cup and tipped it in a silent toast, then drained the contents. I should have started with a sip—the stuff was toxic. It took several hard swallows to keep from choking. "You," I pointed to the one thug still standing, mimicking Raza's demeanor, if not his commanding voice. "Go get the title and legal documents pertaining to the—What was the name of your little boat, Friend Raza?"

"The *Integrity*." If looks could flay, he'd have taken a swath of my hide.

"That's... rather perfect." Utterly, delightfully ironic. "Shoo! Shoo!" I flapped at the man.

Mouth tight, Raza nodded, and the fellow hurried away.

"Are you up to a game of cards to pass the time while we wait?"

"No. You cheat."

"No more than you." I cast about, looking for inspiration, and found it in a bowl of soup. "I'll tell you what: we'll use spoons for currency."

"That's it?" Suspicious as ever.

I bobbed a nod.

"You're on."

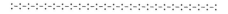

He did cheat. I cheated better, and soundly trounced Raza no fewer than four times before Tanris and a twosome of sturdy Eagles appeared on the scene with the sergeant in tow. By then the Red Pigeon's owner and employees had come out of hiding. They supplied us with cakes, drinks, and spoons, but otherwise kept their distance. They dared not even clean up the mess the Ancestors had made.

"Ah, there you are," I greeted cheerfully. "Care to join us in a round? Alcohol or cards. Your choice."

The two Eagles fanned out to Tanris's left and right. Good Sergeant Andyr and his friend faded into the background, though whether prompted by intelligence or cowardice, I couldn't say.

Tanris wore a strained expression that melted away as he looked me up and down. "How badly are you hurt?"

"Nothing fatal," Raza supplied. "You brought the reward, I assume?"

"A couple punches to my belly and this." I whispered, so as not to interrupt, and pointed at my purpling eye.

Tanris nodded at me, then speared Raza with a withering gaze. "The reward for interfering in the emperor's business and assaulting his agent is a lashing."

"Agent? He's a *thief.*"

"Soldiers, take this man into custody," my trusty protector said, giving a tip of his head in Raza's direction.

"What?" As usual, seeing my rival's surprise was a thing of joy.

"Wait a moment," I interrupted. It didn't look like he would go anywhere, cornered as he was by three Eagles. It's rumored that there is only one group of soldiers in all the empire who might equal their skill, and they are a religious order. Familiar with the Eagles' proficiency, I had my doubts about the others. "You have something that belongs to me." I held my hand out.

Raza had a problem with his anger manifesting in a distinct rosy flush from the neck up. It clashed hideously with his hair. "You scabrous little cheat," he hissed, and fished the documents for the *Integrity* from where he'd tucked them into his vest.

"I told you the truth. Is it my fault you never believe me?"

"I trust you as far as I can spit you." He slapped the leather-bound packet down and backed away. "You won't get far."

"Stay where you are. We're not done yet. Master Sidu, can we call upon you to witness the transfer of ownership?"

Sidu straightened from where he'd hidden, sporting a sour expression.

"I'll just need your written statement and signature." I unfolded the documents and spread them out across the table.

"Gods," he grumbled, and retreated behind the counter to fetch pen and ink.

"I could have done that without jeopardizing the port master," Tanris murmured under his breath.

"And have you face accusations of collaboration?" I stared at him in manufactured astonishment. "I would never do such a thing to you, my friend."

"So what is it?"

"The fruits of a small wager."

We watched as the port master wrote out his witness and signed, then blew on the ink to dry it. When I shook his hand, I pressed a gold *dural* into it for his troubles. He gave Raza a hard look, then took his leave with more dignity than I'd have imagined he could muster.

"Thank you, Raza," I said with a charming smile. "May your hands always shake, and may you never see straight again."

"This doesn't end here." Definitely not charming.

"Come with us," Tanris ordered.

Instead, Raza picked up a cup and a candle. Before even the most excellent Eagles could react, he tossed the contents across the tabletop and tossed the flame onto it. *Whoosh!*

I yelped. Thank the god of quick reflexes, I caught the papers up and beat out the fire that lit one edge. Someone shouted. The chairs went crashing in every direction.

It was an opportune time to seek shelter. On the way, I had to dodge a flaming Eagle. My conscience pricked at me, forcing me to pause. An apron came to the rescue. I snatched it from the counter and attempted to wrap it around the soldier's burning arm. His panicked flailing nearly blacked my other eye, and the blow sent me stumbling away.

"Smother it!" I hollered at him.

That worked. Eagles are such sensible fellows. He twisted the cloth around his arm and tucked in the loose ends. Still smoking, he drew his sword and leaped into the fray. Chairs flying through the air barely slowed Tanris and the other soldier, yet somehow Raza lit the drapes on fire. That induced screams from the vicinity of the kitchen and more shouting. Raza cleverly used a piece of wood to toss the burning fabric toward his assailants. The shattering of glass announced his departure. While the Eagles chased after him, I helped myself to a pile of towels on the bar. After wetting them, I set to putting out the flames before the entire neighborhood went up in smoke. Thankfully, the keep and his wife pitched in, then a few passersby.

By the time Tanris and Friends returned, we had saved the day. The master of the house offered us a free round of drinks to celebrate our heroism. The master was less inclined to reward the soldiers who had instigated the conflagration, so I handed Tanris my cup.

"What's this?" he asked, prickly with annoyance at losing Raza. No doubt his usual suspicion about my motives added to his mood.

"Ale."

"Yes, but why?"

"To thank you for vouching for me. I shouldn't have let myself get into such a position."

He grunted his agreement. "You know our orders very well. Getting yourself arrested might have landed you in far worse trouble than a night in gaol."

"Don't I know it." Fickle emperors. Who could trust them? "Luckily, I've already finished most of my errands." Raza had an uncanny ability to show up when he was least wanted. How delightful to know that the Ancestors had nearly made him faint. I'd have to remember that.

He sniffed at his drink, then took a swallow. Eyes closed in appreciation, a sigh lifted his chest. Evidently, he hadn't recognized Raza from an unfortunate encounter we'd had before leaving on Duzayan's errand. Perfect.

"Thank you."

His expression narrowed. "Why?"

"I do have *some* integrity…" I smiled, all innocence. "And I know how to use it."

After my aborted plan to put Port Master Sidu in my debt and all the ruckus with Raza, I still had opportunity in my pocket. Sidu was not much pleased to see me until I showed him the locket I had swiped.

"Is this yours?" I asked, concern wrinkling my brow. "I thought I saw you wearing it last night."

"Sweet Dumera!" he cried, calling on the goddess of prosperity with unfeigned relief. "I feared I'd lost it. It's been in my family for generations, and always brought us good fortune. Already this morning I've had ink spill over an entire page of records, two *durals* fall through a crack in the floor, and my clerk is late. Dead, for all I know. Thank the goddess you found it!"

I dropped it in his trembling hands and watched him don it. I'd never heard him string so many words together all at once. "You must have lost it during the, er—"

"Disturbance," he rushed to fill in. Evidently he didn't believe in random destructive indoor wind any more than anyone else did.

A serious nod and pursed lips convinced him I shared his doubt. "You have the luck of the gods. After you left, a fire broke out. What a night, eh?" I pointed at the locket. "That was near the counter," if *near the counter* included my pocket while I stood next to said counter.

"*Thank you*, young man." He took my hand in both of his. "The reward I was going to post is yours by rights."

"Oh, that's not necessary! I'm glad to have found it. Family heirlooms," I murmured, shaking my head as if I knew. "Priceless."

We spoke for a few minutes about inheritances. It wasn't long before Sidu asked if I'd looked over my new acquisition. I confessed I didn't know where to find it—and before you could say 'Qahan Nijamar,' he escorted me to where the *Integrity* was docked. With uncharacteristic cheer, he described all the best points of her construction. Then he introduced me to her captain and mate, and told me about her last voyage. Compared to the *Silver Hind*, the *Integrity* was solemn as a monk.

The former vessel, all gleaming white and imperial blue, looked a lot like a certain house of ill repute in Jewel Lane. Suspecting that Gaziah hadn't made the actual assignment himself, I wondered who would so boldly place targets on our backs—and on Duke Enikar's, too.

My conversation with Captain Raymid Zakkis didn't go as well as I wished. News of a new owner surprised him. The announcement that we must be ready to sail at a moment's notice vexed him outright. He didn't much like the idea of a voyage to the islands, either. He called it 'certain death,' and I couldn't deny the possibility, which led to promising bonus pay. With Emperor Gaziah financing the mission, how could I object?

My chat with the captain of the *Silver Hind* went even less well. He'd received no orders about the change of transportation! Who was I to think I had such authority?

I considered a bash-and-stash, but that would likely draw all the wrong attention. Not to mention wrath. No, I wanted to do this quietly. So I called his bluff. "Fine. I will make sure the supplies are loaded properly. You report to your master, and he'll report to his, and so on. In a few hours, our quiet trip for the emperor will be known all over the city. But you do what you think is best." I stalked away, leaving him slack-jawed and worried.

The *Integrity's* first day under my proprietorship saw her receive a slight makeover. One couldn't venture among pirates looking like they'd just left the shipmaster's wharf, no matter how somber the ship. "You have two days to refine the *Integrity*," I informed the captain. "Knock off the spit and polish, make her less desirable. A lot less desirable."

"Excuse me? You want me to *wreck* her?" Zakkis asked in a shocked voice. For such a serious-looking fellow, he wore surprise well. Gray sprinkled neat dark hair, and a very short circle beard decorated his chin. Easily as tall as Tanris, but narrower, he reminded me of a clerk, but more weathered.

"Starry nightshirts, no. I want her to look like a doddering old lady, but have the speed and agility of an Asonian dancer." They were well known for their bright beribboned skirts, fast footwork, and mesmerizing hip swings. The modest upper classes of Marketh pretended outwardly that they did not exist. Secretly, they sought them out in the lower districts or hired them for private performances.

The captain's brows scraped his forehead. "I... see. You want to fool the eye of passersby, and surprise them if they try to make contact."

"Exactly!" Beaming, I clapped him on the back.

"That won't be easy to do in two days."

"I am sure," I commiserated, bobbing my head. "Do your best."

"You're an odd bird." His lips pursed as he juggled the excitement of challenge with the horror of defacing his precious ship.

A grin tugged at my mouth. "And wanting to protect my little flock. The uglier the *Integrity* is, the safer we will all be."

He scratched his neck, then nodded. "There's wisdom in that, but I can't say I ever imagined taking such advice."

"You've never sailed to the islands?"

"I have." He hemmed and hawed, then shrugged. "Not much in the last handful of years. Those pirates are worse than crows. One is as likely as the other to peck your eyes out."

Never in my life have I pecked anyone's eyes out. What an appalling notion. He couldn't know he was insulting me, as the name on the ship's documents—and by which I'd introduced myself—was Bayram Blackfeather. "Crows are quite smart," I asserted modestly.

"If you say so." He scratched his neck again. Did the man have fleas? "Work would go faster if I could hire extra hands."

Calculating the emperor's expenses came so much more easily than doing my own. "Five men. Make sure you trust them implicitly."

"Or else?" He crooked a brow.

I gave him another beam. "Exactly!"

The crew was none too pleased with the proposal of alterations to their lovely vessel. I couldn't blame them. She cut a fine appearance; every line promised speed and efficiency.

"We're going into pirate territory," I reminded them. "There's no sense inviting disaster. Do you chase after the homely girls or the pretty ones?"

My speech inspired them, and the captain, too. He suggested we give the figurehead a little update. The stalwart defender of righteousness wielding a torch and symbolic holy flame got an eye patch (honoring my shiner) and an oversized morning star pointed dead ahead. I had no doubt it could do some serious damage. After that, the crew swiftly got into the spirit of re-characterizing the ship.

When they finished as much of their preparations as time allowed, the *Integrity's* sails were no longer pristine, but a haggard off-white. They'd sanded off most of the gleaming paint, replaced striped awnings with patched canvas, and stove in a selective rail or three.

The pirates of the strait didn't fly national flags, but tribal streamers, so I purchased several options. For now, we ran up the flag of the impartial and ambiguous Marketh City. There was safety in obscurity

—8—
Send-Off Party

Two days after meeting with His Most Radiant Highness, I sat on the balcony of a public house nursing a cup of spiced kaffa. What better way to spend my time while waiting for the inevitable arrival of Tanris's Eagles? Much to my lack of surprise, the quartet was all decked out in their splendid uniforms and armor.

I hastened to catch the Shining Examples of Imperial Justice. "Hoy!" I called out, waving as I got within shouting distance. "Did Commander Tanris send you boys?"

"Yes, sir," a tall blond answered.

"Oh, good. I'm the commander's partner, Crow. There's been a slight change of plans, and we'll be aboard the *Integrity* here instead of the other ship." By design, I intercepted them near the *Integrity's* mooring.

"Who?" A soldier with a nasty scar across his jaw frowned.

"I know of him," another volunteered. Curly hair. I'd never seen him before. "Is there a problem, sir?"

I gave them a cheerful smile. "Oh, no. We were blessed to find something more—"

"Sleek."

"Swift."

"Ordinary."

They sounded uncomfortably like the Ancestors. "Indeed. You recognize the *Silver Hind*, then?"

"Mmm," was the consensus, with one "lovely ship" thrown in for good measure.

"She's a little too, ah, *striking* for our needs." That seemed a safe assessment to offer the Emperor's Own. I peered past them. "I thought there would be more of you."

"The others will arrive tomorrow," the tall blond fellow said. "We're here with the bulk of our gear and supplies. The wagons are right behind us."

Bulk sounded ominous. The *Integrity* didn't have the storage space of her bigger, uglier sister, but I was more than happy to let them figure that out.

"Will that be a problem, sir?" Scar-face asked, as if he were hoping to inconvenience me.

He was out of luck, but I paused to relish the honorific. Months spent with the demon-taking Eagles, and none of them had ever called me *sir*. I rather liked it, though it gave me an overwhelming desire to call him *boy*. Oh, wait. I had. He was only four or five years younger than I. "No, no." With a wave of my hand toward the *Integrity*, I stepped aside. "Carry on!"

My heart swelled when they all *saluted* and clattered off.

Getting Not-an-Egg from my apartment to the *Integrity* required moving his cage. We wrapped it in canvas to protect him from view. He protested with little growls, whines, and the scrape of talons on metal as he tried to keep his balance.

"Hush!" I warned him as we levered our burden into the bed of wagon. "Or I'll throw you and your cage into the river!"

Senza punched me in the arm.

"Ow!" She'd gained real strength over the last months. "Watch it, I'm fragile!"

She snorted and handed a rope to Tanris.

"You will not hurt him," he declared. Competent hands tied the cage down securely. "Never make a threat you're not prepared to carry out, Crow. Not with him, not with anyone."

"Thank you, Oh Fount of Knowledge." You'd think me twelve springs instead of an actual adult.

"Makes you look weak if you back out of death and dismemberment," he said in a mild voice, and patted the top of the cage. "All set. See you at the dock in a couple of hours."

Senza climbed onto the seat, arms folded primly, and gaze straight ahead.

I clambered up next to her. "You're mad." With a click of my tongue, I gave the reins a shake. The old nag we'd rented set out at a sedate plod, and I sighed for having to leave my own dear Horse— and even Horse Too—behind.

You don't need to be mean to him. He's a baby, she signed.

"He's a very smart, very clever baby. Someone has to keep him in line, or he'll be tearing up the neighborhood and ruining my reputation."

She donned an exaggerated expression of disgust, and for the length of several blocks said nothing at all. Then, *What will you do with him? Later.*

I chewed my lip pensively. The dragon was growing fast. How long before he reached full size? His parents had been huge. Though deprived of the opportunity to measure, three or five times as big as a plow horse wouldn't be an exaggeration.

Logic suggested I take him back where I'd found him. So did guilt, but guilt also recommended I stay far, far away. Maybe his other parent had survived. Maybe it would roast me in a giant, searing ball of flame for my sins. And when Not-an-Egg learned what I'd done, maybe he'd help.

Senza squeezed my arm and put her head on my shoulder. A moment later, she gestured between the two of us. *Me and Tanris and you. We are in this together.*

I wasn't sure what it meant that I didn't argue. A lot had changed in the last half year; more than I found comfortable. I soothed a surge of restlessness with the knowledge that I could leave whenever it suited me.

Wrapped up in my own musings, I didn't give a second thought to our destination. When I pulled the nag to a halt beside the *Integrity*, Senza plucked my sleeve.

Wrong ship.

"No, this is the right ship. That one will only get us killed." I pointed out the gleaming, gaudy *Silver Hind*.

Her eyes widened and her mouth formed an "oh" of surprise. She had a curious way of exaggerating her expressions, but usually only with Tanris and me. Around strangers she tended to adopt a stoic, neutral countenance occasionally betrayed by a flush of anger or embarrassment.

Does Tanris know? she asked, crooking her brow the way she did when she thought I'd done something devious.

I scratched my ear. "He ought to by now." Unless he hadn't yet talked to the men assigned to him for this little jaunt.

Senza stuck out her tongue and swatted my belly with the back of her hand. *You must like goats.*

No, not 'goats,' bars. "I like goats better than bars."

Her expression shifted to one of confusion. *You are strange.*

"And still you insist on keeping company with me. Shall we get the beast aboard?"

Not-an-Egg growled his indignation, which sparked a grin from Senza. She made an expansive gesture. *After you!*

At midday, Girl and I leaned against the bulwark on the deck, enjoying grapes and meat pies. All our things were properly stowed, including Not-an-Egg. He currently sat in the corner of his cage in our quarters, pouting despite the leg of lamb I'd left him. The supplies that had fallen to me to gather sat together (much more cooperative than he) in the hold: equipment for getting into and out of places, tools for sabotage, bribery options, a barrel of Taharri Red wine (because Tanris would forget such luxuries, probably on purpose), and a little reading material.

The autumn sun shone with a weight that coaxed people to sleep despite a frisky breeze laden with the scent of brine and fish. A few crew members and Eagles had done just that, sprawled wherever they pleased while they waited to set sail. Some had sought shade, others basked in the sun's rays. My companion tossed occasional grapes to the ever-begging seagulls.

"Such a waste of good food," I complained, lazy with warmth.

I could toss coins.

"Carry on."

Her cheeks dimpled.

A glance toward the *Silver Hind* brought me upright. "Tanris is here at last."

Hands on his hips, he stared at the showy vessel. Nary a soul stirred on board, even when he shouted. He had one of those voices that carried a long way when he wanted it to. With no gangway in sight, he'd have a tough time boarding. How fun to watch.

He had with him another quartet of men—soldiers, presumably, though they'd wisely doffed their smart uniforms. He, of course, wore his usual uninspired attire of neutral colorlessness. Trailing them came a green-garbed Ishramite. Two other figures—concealed in long, hooded gray robes—stood close together nearby, impossible to miss for their great height.

People on the pier gave them a wide berth. Understandably. Only a few short months ago, I'd have done the same.

A commotion farther down the docks caught my attention. A knot of men pushed their way through the throng, brandishing all manner of weapons. I climbed up on the rail to see better. "Oh, blazes. Cast off!" I hollered and jumped right back down. "Cast off!"

Like magic, the captain appeared at my elbow. "Take a breath. What's the trouble?"

"If we don't get out of here at once, there's going to be a fight."

The tall redhead leading the bristling gang was impossible to mistake. Raza Qimeh had a hard time losing, especially to me. As often as it happened, he should have learned better by now. Hands cupped to my mouth, I bellowed as loud as I could. *"Tanris!"*

He spun around, another sort of trouble clear in his glower.

"*Run!*" I pointed in Raza's direction, then waved for him to hurry.

"We can't just hoist the anchor and skip out of port," Captain Zakkis objected. "There's the wind to mind and—"

"*They're* managing quite well." He couldn't miss the lofty coaster moving past us.

"They've had time to—"

"Get the canvas up, captain. We'll catch a ride with her."

"What? How?"

I tossed him a tight grin. "Where are your boarding hooks?"

His mouth opened and stayed that way for the space of several apprehensive breaths. Finally, he relented. "Ask Evrane. But what about the commander?"

"He's coming. Hurry," I urged and sprinted aft.

Evrane caught on to the purpose of my request at once. He cast an imploring look toward Captain Zakkis, only to get a shrug and a nod in return. May the gods bless the man.

Shortly, we had hooks lodged over the taffrail of the passing coaster. The stern jerked our direction in concert with a handful of shouts from the crew. Our own deck lurched beneath me. Thank the gods of quick reflexes, I hooked my arm over the wood before I fell overboard headfirst.

Behind us, the *Integrity's* crew swarmed like ants, dashing about in practiced chaos. The noise of chains clanging, canvas flapping, and men shouting drowned out everything else. I cast a look toward Tanris, only to find him still standing by the *Silver Hind*, speaking to his cohorts and shaking his head.

"Blazes," I repeated, with feeling. He couldn't see what was coming our way. "Tanris, *run!*" I yelled again. One of the towering, hooded figures caught Tanris's arm and pointed.

"CROW!" He was too far away for me to actually hear him, but I'd seen that furious expression before and my imagination filled in the obvious word and volume. *What is happening?* he signed.

In my alarm, I'd evidently lost a few of my wits, else I would have thought to use our hand language to instruct him.

Senza must have read my mind, for she signed back swiftly. *Hurry. Red Hair and army coming fast....*

Tanris shook his fist at me.

I shrugged, palm up. How was this my fault? At least he started running. Such a sensible fellow. His companions followed his lead. The hoods fell free of the tall fellows, revealing KipKap and Diti. Their appearance inspired shouts of alarm.

After the initial heave, the *Integrity's* forward movement slackened to a crawl.

The thump of boat hooks on wood accompanied the *Integrity's* progress as men pushed us away from the pier. The coaster's crew broke out axes to hack at the grapplers. No surprise there, but they'd already done their work, tugging us away from the dock.

Raza and his pack charged through the crowd, bouncing off of people, carts, and horses alike. Some of the victims struck back. I cheered when a fight erupted between the thugs and a gang of dock workers. Thugs went down in a knot of heaving bodies. The rest crashed through the tangle of men and raced down the street. Or tried to, anyway. The dock folk didn't take kindly to a mob of toughs making waves in their territory.

[Foe! Enemy! Antaaaagonist?!] The spirits quivered. Uncertain or eager, I wasn't sure. *[Not ours. No, not. Angry! Vengeful! Hurt Friend!]*

"Hush," I murmured. One wrong word—or right word, depending on one's outlook—would have my invisible companions swarming Raza. Sometimes, if they got worked up enough, I couldn't stop them. Maintaining my own calm helped and, thank the gods of serenity, I was not a man prone to hysterics. That didn't mean my heart wasn't pounding like the gavel of a berserk magistrate.

Breathe, Crow. Breathe...

The port was laid out like a comb, short teeth pointing into the estuary. The *Silver Hind's* berth lay two piers from our own. As Raza closed the distance between us, I bounced on the balls of my feet. Would Tanris make it in time? He and his companions leaped the corner a hairsbreadth ahead of the mob and didn't slow.

"Ropes!" I cried. "Help get Tanris and the others on board!"

When someone thrust a coil at me, I hurried to tie it off and tossed a noose dockward. Along the bulwark, more cables hissed outward. Tanris missed catching mine by a whisker, spun in mid-step, and launched himself toward the dragging line. For a split second, I hovered between dismay and astonishment. Then his weight yanked the rope through my hands. The injured one spasmed. With a hasty half twist, I anchored the line against my torso and braced.

Tanris struck the water, went under, and came right back up, hauling himself hand over hand. For a miracle, he didn't smash against the hull, but pulled his legs up as he swung. Both feet planted, he gave a nod. I started pulling.

KipKap tossed his cloak aside with a deliberate flick. One, two leather parcels soared upward and over our heads. Diti mimicked him, tossing baggage aboard as he ran. A soldier tried to do the same thing and lost his pack with a splash. Sailors and soldiers on either side quickly parted to make way.

A pair Eagles caught ropes and dragged through the water, while a third plunked into the river like an awkward pelican. The fourth—I scanned the pier and found him thumping ruffian noggins. Then he whirled, dove, and came up swimming strongly.

KipKap landed nearby, pretty as you please. Behind him, Diti's long fingers wrapped around the rail, then he vaulted over. Add *incredibly athletic* to their talents.

I didn't see the healer, and I could do nothing to help the pelican, occupied as I was with getting Tanris aboard. My shoulders strained as I heaved him up, up, up. Senza caught the back of his jerkin and tumbled him over and onto the deck.

The burden gone, I propped my hands on my knees to catch my breath, but that only lasted a heartbeat or two. My hands screamed in protest. Rope-burned both of them. Lips pressed tight, I flexed them slowly and tried to calm a new panic.

"Crow!" Raza shouted from below. He and several men broke clear of the clot of humanity to thunder down the pier alongside us. "I want my ship back, you filthy little cheat!" he shouted.

"A deal's a deal," I returned, just as loud.

KipKap caught a spear as it hurtled past and swiftly reversed it. "Do we kill these?" he inquired.

"Nah, they're not worth the trouble."

"You lied!" Raza refused to give up, though what he expected to happen now eluded me.

I clapped a hand to my chest in mock offense—and immediately regretted it. The wince was real. "How could you *say* such a thing? I've told the truth more often in the last six months than I have in my entire life." Oh. Had I said that out loud? Ahem. "Word's going to get out that your promises mean nothing." *There* was a threat to make a man tremble in his boots. I had better skill than that. "You are a feckless swindler! A slime-addled double-dealer!"

I didn't quite have Tanris's impressive volume, but I made enough noise to draw attention.

And missiles.

Raza threw a knife. It *thunked* into the rail next to my hand, quivering.

My heart tripped, but I didn't move an inch. "Aww, you missed. My turn."

Working it free, I hefted it briefly, testing my smarting grip more than its weight. Then I sent it flying back. To my satisfaction, it elicited an oath from Raza when it sliced through his upper arm, veered away, and splashed into the drink. "Graceless as a cow!" I taunted.

The crew still worked their poles to push us free. A thug grabbed one, and his mates copied him. My boys turned their tools into weapons, cheerfully smacking the thugs over the head or across the shoulders, shouting curses at them. Whether they approved of their ship's new owner or not, the previous one had just given away a sizable chunk of his reputation.

Two enterprising thrill-seekers shimmied up dangling ropes. Senza came to stand beside me. The dear girl had her crossbow and aimed it at the closest. When he surrendered and let go, she loosed her bolt at Raza. It caught his shirt and pinned him to a barrel. There might have been blood. She made a rude gesture. Astounding.

One sailor went overboard, joining the flailing Eagle. Meanwhile, Tanris's remaining companions flopped to the deck like fish, gasping and panting. I recognized portly Neba, soaked and sorry-looking.

While I engaged in exchanging insults, Tanris checked on his men. The swimmer had wisely chosen to head for the opposite pier, away from Raza's rabble. The sailor, more experienced with unexpected dives, caught hold of another dangling rope and let his mates pull him back aboard. He seemed none the worse for the wear.

"This isn't over!" Raza shouted, clutching his wounded arm. I just smiled and waved.

"You've got some explaining to do." Tanris appeared next to me, stripping off his jerkin, splashing water everywhere. He had a marvelous way of injecting dire threat into every word.

"For saving your life?"

Wet leather slapped to the boards. "For switching transport. For doing it without telling me. Because of you, we're short a third of our company."

"How unfortunate." I tried to sound contrite.

It brought a severe glare. "You've put the mission in jeopardy, and—"

I interrupted him. "I beg your pardon? *Jeopardy* would have been taking that sailing brothel into the islands."

He held up one finger. Paused. Then said, "True. That doesn't excuse the mess you made. And who did you steal this tub from?"

"It's not a tub, and I didn't steal it."

He snorted. "You expect me to believe that?"

"You witnessed the transaction." I started to fold my arms, then changed my mind. One wrist propped on my hip, I swept the other hand to the side dismissively.

"Did you trick him into it?"

"I am shocked—*shocked*, Tanris, that you think so poorly of me."

"Because you have such a sterling reputation," he retorted, deadpan.

"Which you have been trying your utmost to ruin." I sniffed in disdain.

"Successfully?"

"Enh…"

Meanwhile, the crew dealt with getting the sails up and the ship underway. I'd been to sea before, and I marveled at the skill of the sailors every time.

Nearby, Senza leaned against the ballista, her crossbow beside her as she gawked at the view of the estuary opening to the sea. KipKap watched our exchange with keen interest while Diti hung back. Minus the robes, both of them.

Tanris gave a grunt that didn't translate to anything. "We have been in town for exactly three days. *Three days*, and you couldn't stay out of trouble."

"I did nothing to instigate such brutish actions."

He narrowed his eyes. "Who is he?"

"I met him at the Red Pigeon." I shrugged. I didn't lie, exactly. I'd met him *this time* at the tavern. "Playing cards."

"His reaction suggests something more than losing a bet."

"He thought he was collecting a bounty. And you did try to arrest him," I reminded.

"And that somehow led to an attack on you? How long have you really known him?"

Cornered like a child with blueberry juice all over his hands, I pursed my mouth in displeasure. I didn't even have to fake it. "Three days into our new *assignment*, and you are already treating me as a criminal. Again."

He drew back a little, and I could tell my words stung. "You're right," he said, nodding tersely. "Sorry."

There was more to his temper than Raza. "I mess this up and it's your head on the block, isn't it?"

One shoulder lifted and fell. "Not that fatal, but it won't be good. For either of us."

I grunted and dropped down beside Girl. Senza. Frowning, she set aside her crossbow and crouched to take one of my hands. A frown marred her features. *Needs balm*, she signed, and sprang up to go fetch some.

I watched her retreating back. "Have I mentioned lately how much I loathe the ignoble nobility?"

"You're an idiot."

"For disliking the upper crustiness?"

"No, I just recalled that I hadn't told you today."

I mangled a smile.

"I'm not letting you off yet. You want to explain about the ship switch?"

I'd like to hear him say that last phrase three times fast. "I chose not to argue with you. And you'd have told the emperor. And there may be a traitor—or someone merely trying to make trouble."

"Oh? Do tell…"

"Morning," Tanris pointed out as I came up the ladder from belowdecks. He'd propped himself against the bulwark, arms folded and aspect tranquil.

After the crew's first fiery fuss over the presence of the *inhuman beasts* directly after we'd put to sea, Tanris had taken things in hand. The sailors could sail and be paid, they could volunteer to fight said beasts and accept the consequences, or they could swim back to port.

Diti dangled one brawny challenger over the bulwark, and that ended that debate. From there, some of the crew condescended to converse with the foreigners. This endeavor involved a lot of hand-waving and the two brothers learning new swear words. *Uncivilized sailors.*

"Morning, yes," I agreed with a yawn, rubbing a hand over my head. The sun rose in the east, where it always did. Peach-colored clouds drifted across an otherwise azure sky. The surrounding sea was a lovely, deep gray-blue. Off our side of the ship, cheeky crested terns skimmed the waves. The ship creaked and groaned the way ships did, singing its way to the next destination. The temperature was a little brisk, but the season promised heat as the day progressed. Altogether, those characteristics made for an enchanting beginning.

"Girl up yet?" I inquired. At my feet, Not-an-Egg's talons scraped the deck as he paused and stretched.

"You mean Senza?"

"Habit." I gave him a lopsided smile.

"She's still sleeping. Had any visions lately?"

"Me? I don't have visions." Even as I said it, I recalled the strange images I'd glimpsed when Girl—Senza!—had written her name on my hand.

Tanris grunted. "Really? What about when we were on the moors? The old man's cottage? The tree? And that fellow that stole the map?" he reminded.

"Oh." I'd made too much of a fuss about it then to deny it now.

"Yes, *oh*," he mocked.

I fetched up next to him at the bulwark and leaned my elbows against it, bandaged hands dangling. "Why do you ask?"

Among his many talents was the art of pointing with his chin. Like a backwards nod. He gestured across the deck. Naturally, I looked.

Naturally, I squawked and swore. "Shades and ashes! What in all the colorful hells is *she* doing here?"

Tarsha stood with her hands against the rail. Her head turned so the wind streamed her long, dark hair away from her face. She'd chosen a loose blouse and baggy pants for the day, and the breeze pressed the fabric against her body. A brightly embroidered sash emphasized her narrow waist. In the early morning sun, she looked outrageously alluring.

"I was hoping you could tell me."

"Did you see her before we left?" I asked, bristly with sudden suspicion. "Did you bring her?"

"Hardly." He shook his head. "I haven't seen her since the Duzayan mess. Found her in the galley this morning. She said she's here to talk to you."

"Me? No. Uh-uh." Sunrise on the sea had suddenly lost its appeal. "We've got to take her back."

"Too late."

"Then throw her overboard."

Skepticism wrinkled his brow. "That might be a bit harsh."

Vexed, I waved my arm in her general direction. "I don't want anything to do with her, now or ever. I made that quite clear. If she can't take no for an answer, she has to accept the results. Is it my fault she followed me onto a boat in the middle of the strait?"

"When and what did you say no to?" Completely unperturbed.

"A job. After we saw Gaziah." The recollection made me seethe.

"Mmm... I suppose she wanted you to steal something."

"How would I know?" My hackles were up, let me tell you. Bad enough to have her drop in on me at my home—now she was following me?

"What if the job's an excuse for her to talk to you? Just *talk*."

"Then she is doomed to disappointment. We should put her on a passing ship." I searched the horizon in vain.

Sharp humor glinted about him, competing with the rising sun. "I knew she'd tweaked your tail feathers, but I didn't expect she'd plucked them and stuffed them in your ears."

Stabbing him with a glare made no impression at all.

"Since when did you let aversion to a client stop you from taking a job? Are you sulking?"

"I don't sulk." My conscience took that moment to prick me. *Was I?* "How long until we reach Masni?"

He scratched his bristly jaw. "We're sailing across the wind. Three days if we're lucky, more likely four."

Four days on this dinghy with that woman? Renewed resentment twisted my gut. My hands curled into—well, claws. I couldn't make fists. I glowered in Tarsha's direction, but my best black look did not reduce her to ashes. She appeared oblivious to my presence.

Tanris caught one arm. "Crow."

For a moment or twenty, I let my hostility circle my good sense —or Tanris's good sense, because I suspected he might be right.

A scraping sound drew my attention downward. Traitor that he was, the little dragon rubbed his head back and forth across Tanris's booted shin. Did that mean he agreed?

I freed a pent up breath. "Fine, I'll talk to her." And I promptly headed for the ladder leading belowdecks. I couldn't put it off forever, but I could drag my feet like any good victim.

It didn't take long to shave or break my fast. Still disinclined to confront Tarsha, I sat down with the sheaf of Duke Enikar's papers. On a fresh sheet, I copied some of his notations and added some of my own—including the news of Wycked Gates in the islands, hundreds of miles from the location of the original.

How was that possible? And was the thing we'd encountered in the Wilds connected?

"How did I get into this mess, Chicken Legs?"

The dragon, sitting on Tanris's bunk, drew his lips back from fangs twice as long as a dog's. Another name rejected. A piece of jerky eased his outrage, then he decamped to the window, hanging halfway out with his face to the wind, mouth open, and eyes closed. I envied the lack of responsibility.

Not, I reminded myself, that I was responsible for any of the current circumstances. *I could leave whenever I chose.* So why didn't I, if I were so put out?

Disgruntled, I knelt beside my makeshift work table (the bed) and stared at my scribblings until they blurred. *Something* shifted a notch. Awareness? Perspective? But the whole of it hovered beyond my grasp.

While I puzzled, a figure filled the doorway to my left. "Ah, Tanris. There you are."

"Did you call for me?"

"Not yet." I blinked, expecting the sensation to disappear, but it persisted. "I'm right on the edge of figuring something out."

"And here I thought you were hiding. From a woman."

"Besides that. Did Gaziah tell you about any other gates?"

"He didn't tell me about any of them. Baran did. Eagle commander," he reminded helpfully.

"That answers one question and raises more. Did you know the monsters are foreigners?"

"What monsters?"

"The duke thinks Basi Serhat is using monsters to do mining. Here." I tapped the pertinent notation, then handed him my paper. *Labor force not imported or local. Rumors of sea monsters—or monsters from the sea.*

Tanris's brows creased as he read.

"He's enslaved foreigners." Spoken aloud, the words triggered memories of frightened creatures tumbling into a nightmare. Memories of my childhood surfaced to tangle with them. And more, so much *more*… Darkness. Burning. Screaming. Blood. It struck with unexpected force, literally knocking me backward. All the blinking in the world didn't banish images of pain, terror, confusion, anger… Of Fate or Death or *something* watching me, waiting for me to fail.

Crow?

Something hit my cheek once, then again, harder.

"Crow."

Tanris's worried face swam into view. His grip on my shoulder eased, but the impression of bruises hung like a promise. Wide-eyed, the dragon peered at me from where he clung to my other arm.

"I'm fine," I croaked. Echoes remained, murky clouds tattered by the wind of Tanris's concern.

He nodded, but doubt lingered in his expression, in his… aura. *Is that what it's called?* I wondered, and the Ancestors rustled around me, affirming my guess. From the cabinet between the beds, he withdrew something and I heard the splash of liquid. "Drink." He pushed a cup at me.

A lemony pine scent warned me to brace myself for the effervescent sharpness of gin. My eyes watered. "Thank you."

"Mm. What happened?"

There was a funny sound somewhere between a grunt and a whimper. It took a moment to realize it came from me. I took another swallow of the alcohol. I didn't care for hard liquor, but it cleared the remaining fog like a northern breeze. *Far* northern.

"Magic," I told him. I could say that much without divulging anything… sensitive.

"Explain."

"No."

He didn't budge.

I could leave whenever I wanted. Even with Tanris more or less pinning me in place.

Or I could just tell him the bald truth. He would roll his eyes. Possibly make a cutting remark. Lock me up for my own safety. Deliver a scathing report to the man who held my physical freedom in his hands…

Inconvenient, but not catastrophic, I told myself. "I have to free the slaves."

—9—
Tarsha's Troubles

The intense expression on Tanris's rugged features only increased. "I'm not surprised."

"You're not?"

He eased back to sit on my bunk. The one with the papers all over it. He moved some of them aside, putting them in a tidy pile. In order, I noted. "You've defended them from the beginning, and now you say magic is involved in this defense. Is this some kind of… compulsion?"

I hesitated. "I suppose that's possible."

"Who would have laid it on you?"

My mouth opened and closed twice. "Me, I think." And why was I telling him this? Why would I tell anyone? I sounded like a crazy man, but the words marched right out. "The Ancestors. I wanted—*want* to keep the foreigners from going through what I did. And that is overlaid with memories from the Ghost Walk." My people had died there. Horribly.

"What did you go through, Crow?" he asked, voice soft. Careful, but inviting.

It was not an invitation I cared—*dared*—to accept. I rubbed my arm, not meeting his eyes.

Elbows to knees, he rubbed his hands together. "What happens if you can't save them?"

"Besides their torture and death?" More guilt on my shoulders. The weight of the priests I'd killed was already too much.

"What happens to *you*?"

The memories rushed me again. Closing my eyes made them sharper and more real, so I looked away. At the wall. The window. Tanris... Dread and terror clogged my throat. Was this some new manner of vision? I hated it. Hated the disaster laid out before me. Opening my mouth to speak hurt as much as clenching my jaws. "I might die, but it's more likely I'll go insane."

Everything about him grew still. Silence stretched out between us until I thought it must snap. "Well," he whispered, then went on a little louder. "That's completely unacceptable."

I could only nod.

"We probably won't be able to save them all. Will that be a problem?"

I laughed without humor. It sounded like one of Not-an-Egg's creaks. "Let us pray sincere effort counts."

"The gods love you," he reminded.

He was right. I could not let an enormous task and unwelcome *responsibility* erode my faith. The gods would see me through this. And Tanris, too, apparently.

"You need help with any of this?" He gestured at the paper landscape. *Would you like me to stay awhile?*

What made him so willing to save me time after time? I didn't understand. Every time he did, I stayed a while longer. "Not yet."

He squeezed my shoulder as he got to his feet and headed for the door. "You know where to find me."

I rubbed my chest. Rubbed the strange warmth that grew there. I didn't understand that, either, so I distracted myself with the first thing I thought of and unwrapped my burned hands. "Hey, Sparky."

The dragon lifted his head from my shoulder to give me a long, considering look, but he didn't hiss or lash his tail. Perhaps we were getting somewhere...

I held my hands up. "Can you help me with these?"

I didn't talk to Tarsha that day.

She knew I was avoiding her. After all, the ship was only so big. She didn't press the matter, but her downcast looks raked like nails across my senses. I preferred hating her from a distance. Out of sight, out of mind, and all that.

KipKap, curious as always, had all kinds of questions about her. *Who is she? Where did she come from?* And, more pointedly, *What did she do to you? Do you not wish to know the reason for her betrayal? You must be important to her if she snuck aboard and risked punishment. What could have driven her to such a thing if she knew you hated her?*

I wanted to toss him overboard. KipKap, however, was safe from such a fate. Agile and strong as he was, he wouldn't go willingly. And getting rid of him—literally or figuratively—would not dislodge his questions. I found myself wondering if I really, truly hated Tarsha.

As it happened, I missed her introduction to Not-an-Egg, though I did hear the high-pitched scream and the panicked cries. *It's a dragon! Why have you got a dragon?? It'll kill us all!* A fox-sized dragon killing every man on board would be a sight.

A man's voice soothed her. Tanris or a crew member. Won over with her serene smile, sultry eyes, and graceful hips. I punched the wall. It gave me scraped knuckles and a sliver the size of a post.

Gods save me…

These violent feelings were foreign to me. Unwelcome. They colored everything. They churned in my gut and made my head hurt. I hadn't even known such fury until Tarsha double-crossed me.

No… That wasn't true, but I knew that unbridled fury destroyed good sense. I'd seen it. Felt it. Determined never to walk that path.

There was the rub. Tarsha might have pried open that door, but instead of slamming it shut, I'd stood back and let in an entire horde of dark things. It was up to me to drive them out and close that door again.

While Tanris's indomitable strength propped me up, Senza's high spirits shone like a beacon. She loved the ship, the wind, the banners, the dolphins, the sense of speed, the spray of salty water. She bounced and beamed and asked a thousand questions.

And it was Senza who happily filled me in on our stowaway's surprise and confusion concerning the demons. She also reported Tarsha's awkward attempts to treat them politely. I almost regretted missing the interactions, which included Not-an-Egg eating a chunk out of Tarsha's shirt sleeve. KipKap studied her. Often. From mere inches away. Senza found that hilarious.

With calculated deliberation, I focused on the humor of the situation. After all, humor had once been my principal weapon. Little by little, the iron grip cinched around my chest eased.

As the sun set that evening, Tarsha found me on the forecastle deck feeding Not-an-Egg from a bucket of fish. Bones, fins, and all, he demolished them with relish. Like a winged, scaly cat, he licked his chops and swished the tip of his tail as if he'd discovered the most delicious delicacy in all the known world.

"You like it, don't you?" Tarsha's figure cast a brief shadow over us, then she sat down next to me. The forecastle boasted an open rail rather than the solid bulwarks down on the main deck. Though she'd bound her luxurious locks into a braid, the breeze still played with wisps it teased free.

Not-an-Egg hissed at her, then returned to devouring his fish.

"Like what? The sea? The ship? Fish?" I asked in the most neutral tone possible. The scar she bore on one cheek held my attention. She'd received it in a nearly fatal scuffle with Duzayan. I remembered the blood on her face reflecting the lurid light of the Wycked Gate. Not a memory I enjoyed revisiting. I looked aside.

"The dragon."

"It's a he."

"I see." She looped her arms around drawn-up knees. "You're looking well. Thinner, though."

"Am I." Not a question.

"Yes." Her dark eyes took in every visible inch of me. "How'd you get the black eye?" As if she actually cared.

"Ran into a fist. I'm fine."

"More tense, too."

"I'm fine," I repeated, choosing a quiet, neutral tone.

She took my hand in hers, unruffled by the fishy smell, and turned it palm up. Months after the injury, the skin remained pink with irregular jagged lines. *Tear* lines. "What happened?"

I reclaimed my hand and used it to offer the dragon another fish. "Metin Duzayan."

She touched her scarred cheek with a fingertip. "He was a monster."

And yet she'd chosen to work for him... I bit back the accusation.

"Is it healing well?" Tender concern laced her voice.

"Why are you here, Tarsha? I said I didn't want to see you again." I didn't yell or growl, but anger burned along every word, incinerating my attempt to remain calm.

"I would like to tell you what happened." She sat up, cross-legged, rubbing the fingers of one hand.

Deep breaths, in through the nose, out through the mouth. *Calm.* "I am not interested. If that's why you came, you've wasted your time."

How was it possible to feel *her* tears threatening to spill? Actual tears, not dramatic, false emotion.

She just swallowed and nodded. "I understand. I thought you deserved to know why things happened as they did. Regardless, I need to hire the best thief in the empire. You're the only one I trust."

I snorted. Too bad I couldn't say the same. "Would you care for some fish?" I held one up by its tail.

Not-an-Egg snatched it, sharp teeth clashing and bones crunching.

Tarsha tried to suppress a shudder. "What I want is to help my sister."

"Does everyone have a sister?" I complained. She'd never mentioned this sister when we'd been together. Never mentioned much about her family at all, come to think of it, except to inform me she did not have a brother. Disinclination to share my past had kept me from asking about hers.

"I don't." Tanris's voice came from the steep steps leading to the deck below.

"Well, good," I grumbled, sounding waspish. I hadn't heard or sensed his approach. That fact did nothing for my humor. The magic foisted on me endowed me with the ability to perceive any presence—or approach. I'd begun to take it for granted. How had I missed him?

He propped himself against the rail, arms folded as usual. "What's that supposed to mean?"

"Nothing. Don't try to change the subject." My attention returned to Tarsha while Not-an-Egg draped himself across my lap and set to licking the fishiness from my fingers. Tarsha watched him with a strange air of revulsion and despair eddying around her. "What deadly trouble can the sister of a dancer get into? What is she, a seamstress? A chandler?"

"Prejudiced against women much?" Tanris asked mildly.

"Only one. And I don't steal people."

Tarsha's thin, bitter smile didn't melt my knees. That was new. And a welcome change. "Of course not, Crow. I only need you to acquire a ledger."

"Why?"

"To fortify your accounts and your reputation." She shut the door on whatever emotion she'd experienced a moment ago. Her words took on an edge, though her hands rested quietly in her lap.

I scratched my nose. My hand bore the distinct odor of fish. "My reputation is excellent."

"How long have you been out of the city?"

Long enough for vicious rumors to spread, apparently.

"What's the ledger got to do with your sister?" Tanris cut in. Bless his knobby little heart.

"The less you know, the better."

"You're asking Crow to commit a crime."

She looked at him quizzically. "Committing crimes didn't bother you when you came to enlist my help."

"I believe the word you're looking for is *blackmail*." See? I could be helpful.

Not-an-Egg bent his neck in half so he could give me an appealing look. His tongue slithered around his snout. I showed him the empty bucket, and he heaved a sigh.

"I felt bad for you," Tanris continued conversationally, one shoulder lifting in a shrug. "For about five minutes. You were awfully quick to accept the offer. I felt bad for you, too, Crow, but I had bigger fish to fry."

"I'm not a fish." I only *smelled* fishy currently. With my foot, I tipped the bucket on its side. Not-an-Egg crawled in to lick the bottom.

"And you never once…" Her voice trailed off as she pursed her lips, stillness overcoming her. She did that when she got caught up mentally chewing a notion into bite-size pieces. "You were setting the baron up."

"Yes."

"But he set *you* up instead."

"Yes." Tanris gave a slow, rueful nod. Noticeably, he did not ask Tarsha why she'd been so swift to throw me to the wolves. Not that I actually wanted to know.

"Set us both up," I said, getting off the mental seesaw. The baron's duplicity still rankled. "We turned the tables on him, though, didn't we, Tanris?"

A small smile bent one side of his mouth. "We surely did."

"Why did you go after a wizard, of all things?" Tarsha asked. "Wait. You're with the Watch. No, the Watch doesn't go after wizards. It would have to be something bigger than that. Oh." She caught her breath for the barest second. "*That's* why I heard you called commander! It's the army."

Tanris's gaze didn't shift. He didn't so much as flinch. He neither confirmed nor denied. I admired his cool self-possession in the face of trouble.

"What about them? What are they here for?" Tarsha's gaze shot down the deck to where KipKap and Diti peered over the railing, talking and pointing. This would be the first time they saw dolphins. Or maybe sharks. And I was missing out on another convoluted language lesson. How unfortunate.

It seemed an opportune time for a change of subject. "I'm not convinced Duzayan didn't fling those tables right back at us from the grave." What with the foreigners and gates and all…

"He was too busy trying to stay alive to summon a deathbed curse." Tanris didn't have any problem following my lead, but Tarsha clung to her theory.

"How long have you been working together? You were both there the night he died, and now you're here."

"Oh, the joy." I bent to peer into the bucket. Not-an-Egg dozed inside with only his tail hanging out.

"You're assuming Crow knows what the word 'work' means."

"I did that once," I nodded, reclining against the bulwark again. "Didn't like it at all. Now I'm more of an advisor."

"He's excellent at that—"

"See?" I interrupted, turning my palm up. "Skills."

"—if you want a quick trip to madness."

My hand went to my chest. "*Ow.*"

Tarsha let out a surprised laugh and shook her head. "You two are actually friends... How in the world did that happen? I *really* want to hear that story."

"Unlikely."

"Maybe one day," Tanris countered.

I rolled my eyes and looked out at the water.

"Why don't you tell us about the ledger instead." He had a talent for turning questions into statements. "How will it help your sister?"

She studied him for long enough that KipKap and Diti had transferred their attention to a game of knife throwing.

"I would like to involve the law. You, Commander. But people of rank rarely believe people of common status."

"The really rank." I smirked and held my nose.

"Try me," Tanris prodded.

"And have my plans foiled, my sister lost, and myself in gaol? I don't think so, Commander." She tucked a loose strand of hair behind one ear. The wind promptly dislodged it.

The commander tipped his head my way. "I work with him, don't I?"

"I am neither rank *nor* common. You're going out of your way to insult me today, Friend Tanris." Irritation flared, sending my partially revived humor into the bucket with Not-an-Egg.

And just like that, the Ancestors flew to my defense. They attacked Tanris in a miniature whirlwind. It lost effectiveness without dust and leaves for weapons, but still made him duck and cover his face with an arm. At that velocity, salty mist likely stung exposed skin.

He squinted at me with one eye. "Sorry."

The Ancestors battered him for another moment before relenting.

One must appreciate his restraint in not hollering at me as he might have done had Senza been our companion instead of Tarsha. I lowered my vexation a notch or two. "I accept your apology. Carry on, Commander."

"Whatever was that?" Tarsha's brow wrinkled in bemusement.

"The wind?" Tanris didn't even give me an accusing glance.

Tarsha turned away to see if anyone else had noticed the miniature hurricane. "Yes, but it—" An uncertain smile formed. "I don't suppose it attacked you. That's silly."

He gave a characteristic grunt and smoothed one hand over his head as if straightening his nonexistent hair. Then he folded his arms again in resolute patience. When the mood struck him, he could be as immovable as a statue.

With my back to the bulwark, I lifted my face skyward, searching for the first stars. Despite professional curiosity about the job on the table—er, *deck*—I kept my mouth shut. A summary of the particulars wouldn't change my answer.

"My sister is in trouble," Tarsha announced after a lengthy, silence. "I'll spare you the details, but I need the ledger to—what was it you did to Duzayan? Turn the tables."

"And the ledger?" Tanris pressed.

"Safer not to know," I muttered, eyes still closed.

"Because that's a rule you always follow." Any more dry and he'd have started soaking up seawater.

I grinned. "Sometimes."

"Extortion, I assume?"

"Nnno… Proof."

"Was Duzayan involved?" It was a random thought, or maybe the Ancestors whispered it to me. Did his connection to Tarsha go beyond Tanris's involvement?

"I—" Tarsha hesitated. "I'm not sure."

"Duzayan is dead. I saw it happen." Helped accomplish the deed, even. Did being killed three times at once make a man any more dead, whether or not he was a wizard?

"He didn't work alone in all matters." Tanris should know. "His sister might well have picked up the reins where he dropped them."

I straightened. "He had a sister, too?" Everyone had relatives but me. "Please tell me her name isn't Duzayana."

"Ferah."

I slumped back into my position of lazy indifference. "How utterly reasonable and pronounceable. Somehow it seems anticlimactic." I've often had reason to lament the fact that so many people choose to give their children unpronounceable names. Who, for instance, thinks up names like 'Ammeluanakar'? The man had been another wizard. (May the gods help him figure out whether he belonged on the path to doom or veneration.) Unfortunately for him, he had figured heavily in the quest Duzayan had sent us on. And look at *his* name. Awkward at best. At least he didn't need to use it anymore. Not in this world, anyway. While Tanris's name might be easy to pronounce, in the language of one of Bahsyr's neighbors, it meant 'flatulence.' I was not allowed to bring that up.

"What's in it?" Tanris prodded, admirably implacable.

Tarsha folded her hands and lifted her chin, at once demure and stubborn. "I can't—no, I *won't* tell you until we reach an accord."

"Then we're through here."

"Fine. Conspiracy."

Tarsha must be quite desperate to surrender so easily. Fingers laced together and propped on the top of my head, I watched the scene play out, spectator to Tanris's interrogation.

"Yours, your sister's, or someone else?"

"No, unwillingly, and definitely."

Nothing about Tanris's posture or expression changed. Like a statue. "On what level?"

"State."

"To what end?"

"Power. Isn't it always about power?" Her mouth flattened. Red-orange irritation colored the space around her like ripples around a stone tossed into a pond.

Tanris revealed nothing at all. How did he do that? And when had he started? "You are not doing anything to persuade us to help you."

Her attitude shifted as quickly as the wind. "I beg your pardon, Commander." Her voice took on that smooth, throaty quality that had so often led me to forget good sense. "I wasn't aware that you had become Crow's keeper."

"Partner," I tossed out before inconvenient facts came to light. It earned only a sideways look from Tanris.

"Crow works alone." Her velvet gaze swung back to me. "He always has."

"Yes, well, now he's not." I gave her my best imitation of a shark's smile, full of sharpness to shred the enchantment of her lovely eyes.

"Why?" she asked.

"Why not?" I countered with a careless shrug. "I do as I please."

She sighed, a long, deep sound that was annoyance and desperation all at once. I felt it. Tanris felt it. I could tell by the down-turning of his mouth. "What will it take to... *encourage* you to help me, Crow?"

"A few facts." In the twinkling of an eye, Tanris softened. "Help us help you, Tarsha."

"And by *us,* he means himself." I pointed at him. Dangerous finger-waving. Everyone should fear and tremble.

He breathed in hard through his nose. Hard enough to inhale bugs, had there been any in this wind. "Can I have a word, Crow?"

"No?" I ventured. I couldn't exactly get away from him within the cramped confines of a ship.

"Now," he said over his shoulder, using the tone that made his men jump and run. As he descended the stair, he disappeared briefly, then his shaven head popped back into view.

I resisted the order on principle and dawdled, but eventually caught up with him at the other end of the ship. My leisurely pace gave me a few minutes for thinking.

Feet braced against the pitching of the deck, arms crossed, and jaw set, Tanris had clearly made up his mind about the help we were going to give Tarsha.

"You're angry," I surmised, then changed my mind. Whatever he'd done to suppress his aura, he wasn't doing it now. "No… guilty."

His brows bent in a wicked frown. "Why would I feel guilty?"

"Her." I gestured toward the bow. "Just because you carry out orders doesn't mean you like all of them. You're noble like that."

Genuine anger shimmered abruptly around him, outlining his figure. His fists bunched, and I turned away instinctively, knowing I couldn't move quick enough to avoid a blow.

"You think because you can use magic you've got me all figured out?"

[Hush! Hush! Grimfist is angry! Vexed! Cross!] The Ancestors, mostly silent until now, dashed around in fits and bursts, tugging at my clothes and hair. For a wonder, they didn't attack him.

[Easy,] I cautioned.

My skull didn't explode, and I didn't suddenly end up in the strait, so I ventured a look out of the corner of my eye. His features were still curled in a snarl, his hands were still fists. "No," I said. Now wasn't a good time to admit how much the magic helped. "I think I know you fairly well after spending the last—how long?—eating, sleeping, fighting, and slogging alongside you."

"And you think you're innocent?" he growled, a defensive bear. But he still didn't clobber me.

The Ancestors didn't exactly relax.

Tanris's glance flickered around at the spirits he could not see, then settled on me again. He *chose* not to fear. They didn't frighten him, and I realized how often we were alike in strange, unexpected ways. Namely, an admirable sense of determination.

"You put her in danger," he pressed. "You—a criminal. A man hunted up and down the empire. You attract trouble like a lodestone. Did you honestly think none of it would rub off on her?"

"It didn't!" For someone who preferred to avoid confrontation, getting right in Tanris's face struck me as a poor plan, but there we stood, nose to nose. "I kept her safe."

"Did you." He stretched his neck this way and the other, like he did when he was warming up for a fight. Joints crackled. "I found her, didn't I?"

He had me there.

His step forward prompted me to take one back. "And if I found her, do you think it impossible for someone else to find her? Threaten her? *Hurt* her?"

My eyes narrowed as I considered the several paths his words suggested. "You think her sister's trouble has something to do with me?" I couldn't help a bark of laughter. "What, I outwitted Duzayan, so now this sister—this Ferah—I've never even heard of has set up an elaborate conspiracy amongst the blue-blooded incrustation to get revenge?"

He grunted. Standard Tanris-speak for, *'You might have a point.'* At least he'd relaxed his fists. "Talk to her. See what you can find out."

"I'll think about it." For perhaps ten seconds. "We have a more pressing problem. We should consider the possibility that Tarsha is a wizard."

"Great shades." He rubbed his forehead. "And how did you come to that conclusion?"

"You are not your usual logical, no-nonsense self. You're all—" I waved my hand up and down to indicate his stalwart self. "*Moody.*"

"I'm not moody," he sighed and closed his eyes to conceal their roll.

"No? You went from stoic to mushy to furious fast enough to make me dizzy."

He turned to brace both arms against the rail, silent.

"It's been a crazy few days—months—and she pinched your nose with her talk of a situation you can do nothing about today. We need to focus on the idol and the gate, then see if we can coax more information about this insurgency out of Tarsha."

"Don't forget Enikar," he reminded, brows lowering.

"Right, Enikar. Didn't I say that?"

"Idiot."

"I'm just watching out for your sanity. That woman will take it before you even notice." A glance over my shoulder revealed the object of my suspicion standing atop a crate. Not-an-Egg circled around and around. Oh, dear.

As I watched, Senza bounded up the ladder, lips pursed in a whistle as she tossed something to the little beast. He leaped up to catch it easily, wings spread for balance. To my amusement, he made a great show of chomping his treat to bits, gaze trained on Tarsha. Then he turned his back on her to sit with his nose to the wind and eyes closed.

"You realize she still loves you," Tanris said bluntly.

"I don't care if she does." I pointed island-ward. "We have a job to do. Two jobs, since we're not finished finding all the *demons* yet."

"Mm. Did you pick up any suggestion that she might be lying?"

"I wasn't paying attention."

"Yes, you were. You always do. This new talent of yours is just another weapon in your armory."

Like a sixth sense, feeling the emotions of others just *happened*—like breathing or smelling. The Ancestors sometimes buffered it, but I couldn't control it on my own. Drawing my teeth over my lower lip, I sought the medallion under my shirt and rubbed the familiar outline. Eyes closed, I sorted through the emotions I'd picked up on. Mine were easy: the constant prick of betrayal, anger, and resentment of losing something precious.

Tarsha, Tarsha... It was fuzzy behind my own feelings, but I recalled sincerity and urgent hope. "No," I said at last. "She left things out, but she didn't lie."

I don't know why that dug at me. Leaving Tanris abruptly, I joined Not-an-Egg and the others on the forward deck. Our foreign friends, too, had drifted that way. KipKap sat on the crate Tarsha had abandoned; she was nowhere in sight. He polished his great mace while Senza tried to wrestle a well-chewed ballista bolt from the dragon.

Rather than focusing on the mess Tarsha had served up, I nibbled on fragments of the journey that had brought me to this point. Things like the avalanche creature, KipKap and his brother following me, the meeting with his Most Capricious Majesty.

Abruptly, I turned to Senza. *How do I sign your name?* I asked.

She made the symbol for *girl*.

"No, your real name."

After a thoughtful look, she nodded and signed again. It was graceful—a swooping motion with one cupped hand into the other palm, held upright, fingers waggling, then lifting to point downward like beams of light. Or so I imagined.

The Ancestors whisked past me, teasing Senza's hair. She blinked in surprise. That she'd shared her name—both written and signed— seemed an important thing. An expression of trust. And it directly opposed Tanris's simmering doubt.

Thank you, I told her. *I am going to go rob sailors.*

I'll help.

No. Thank you. I drew a hand down my face. *I need some time.*

Is something wrong?

A shrug lifted one shoulder. "Maybe."

Your woman?

Gods preserve me. *She's not my woman.*

I'm sorry. I did not mean it that way. She showed me a new sign, then wrote the word on my palm. D-a-n-c-e-r.

I summoned a smile. "That will work."

KipKap watched us with his usual big-eyed curiosity. Diti ignored us, engrossed in a cord-tying project. Now and then he leaned over the rail and retched miserably. Seasick, poor fellow.

With a sympathetic pat on his shoulder, I went to exorcise my thorny temper by relocating the coins of my crew from their pockets to mine.

—10—
Dog Bait

There is nothing quite like shouts of alarm to hoist one out of the comfortable realms of dreams. Footsteps thundered on the ladder and across the deck. Then came thumping and creaking and groaning enough to give a man a heart attack.

Curled against my side and snoring ever-so-gently, Not-an-Egg leaped ceiling-ward with a rusty shriek and startled flapping. Leather slapped my face, ensuring that not even a fragile vestige of hope for sleep remained. Within seconds, he was glued to the wood overhead, wings outstretched to keep him as inconspicuous as possible. The door crashing open ruined the humor of the moment.

"Master Blackfeather!" The first mate, a fellow calling himself Rego, had a bellow to rival Tanris's.

I'd hardly got to my feet before the ship heeled so hard I crashed into the wall. Another stagger brought me upright. I rubbed my abused noggin. "What in all the starry depths…?"

"Comp'ny, sor. Forest to starboard and peacock to port."

Wouldn't it be something if sailors could call the sides of a ship *right* and *left* like everyone else? As to the symbols, the forest represented the confederacy's strength in union, while the peacock boasted Bahsyr's immortality.

"Are we under attack?" I inquired. "And where's Tanris?" Not in his bed. It was so tidy, I wondered if he'd slept at all. Hadn't he had a book in hand and a lamp lit, keeping me awake half the night?

"It's hard t'say. And th'commander's topside."

The ship jolted. The mate hesitated, several shades of unhappiness oozing from him. I dragged on pants and a shirt. My hands still stung from the rope burn and bore a blush of heat, but they functioned, thank the gods—At least the right one did. The left, as always, needed the stiffness worked out.

Rego shifted uncomfortably. "They said to tell you to stay put. Th'commander an' th'captain, that is."

"Oh, did they. Wonderful." The next sway brought the bed up to meet my backside, and I yielded to the movement. I had to sit to put my boots on, didn't I?

"Eyah. Sorry, sor." And with that, the door banged shut. How rude.

I snorted. Surely, Tanris knew a message like that wouldn't keep me out of the way. I paused only long enough to finish dressing and strap on my belt with its handy pouches. "Are you coming, my acrobatic friend?" I asked of the dragon on the ceiling.

He made a whiny, creaky sound of protest. I rolled my eyes. Between him and Tanris, I did that a lot. Which of my dozen aunties had told me they'd stick that way one day?

"Stay if you like, but at least if you're up on the deck you can fly to safety." Wherever *safety* might be in the case of a pitched battle.

Out the door I went, and the whoosh of wings and scrabble of claws followed. Actual flight was still tricky. The principle seemed instinctive, but now and then he struggled—usually when going through a growth spurt. Or after a huge meal. Even so, those wings did a marvelous job of propelling him, and with weight, teeth, and talons, he could cause considerable damage.

Controlled chaos reigned on deck. The captain and the first mate shouted orders. Sailors dashed this way and that. Brawny men loaded and cranked the ballistas—four of them ranked along the sides. More men, including the trusty Eagles, prepared for battle. They had hand weapons, metal tubs full of leather bags, and a flaming brazier on a wide, solid base.

I clambered to the aftercastle to get a better view of the situation. Sure enough, representatives from each country had positioned themselves nearby. The *Integrity's* sharp turn had doubtless rearranged the playing pool. The ships loomed on our stern, turning to follow us. Scrambling aboard each resulted in the sheets keeping the wind, more's the pity. The maneuvering put two of the ships further away, and the Bahsyri crew aimed squarely for the lagging Asonian ship. It looked like they meant to take it out of the fight entirely.

"What are you doing up here?"

Tanris's voice startled me. I gave him a brief glance, then pointed. "Four ships? That seems excessive."

He hauled himself up next to me. "They patrol in twos and threes, usually. Sometimes larger packs. We're lucky there's only two of each."

"Yes, but they appear to be chasing us."

He grunted. "I'm guessing one side caught sight of us and decided we were worth investigating or claiming. The other side saw *them* and you know how the story goes from there."

"Only one winner. Too bad we aren't a plague ship."

"I haven't heard of any sailing the strait lately."

"But you aren't a sea captain." I could have kicked myself. "We should have flown those banners right out of the port."

"Plan wrecked already?"

"Of course not. I always have a plan. My plans have plans." Not necessarily good ones, not always the *right* ones, but the gods have blessed me with flexibility and a sharp wit. And the gods see me through, one way or another.

Tanris rubbed his ear and screwed his face up in disgust. "So it was your *plan* for us to be the bone for this bunch to fight over?"

"I didn't even know about them, but you did. You should have told me. Look at it this way—if the Bahsyri win, you can flap your magnificent imperial wings at them and send them packing."

"And if the Asonians win?"

"We're shark bait." I tried one of Tanris's grunts on for size. Freeing, but uncomfortably uncivilized. "Does Captain Zakkis have plague banners?"

"It's too late for that. They'll know it's a ploy."

"They very well may," I agreed, then gave him my best smile. "Be a good fellow and check with him?"

"I'd rather you told me your actual strategy."

"What, and take away the element of surprise?"

"Fill me in. Surprise them." He thumbed over his shoulder.

"I'll think about it." Jumping down from our perch, I made my way forward, mentally tossing ideas around. Not-an-Egg flap-trotted at my heels, creaking his worry at me. The little beast had an uncanny ability to decipher emotions, words, and even guess what we'd do next. Or what *I'd* do next, anyway. He viewed Girl as safe, and Tanris as someone to respect—though he didn't always treat him politely. Likely a side effect of my attitude toward him. Either way, Tanris didn't understand the full extent of the dragon's skills.

"He's a beast, Crow," he'd say. *"Smart, but still a beast."*

"But dragons are magical beasts," I'd reply, and never tell him what Duzayan had said. He'd intended for Not-an-Egg to be bonded to him, not me. Even before those fateful words, I'd felt more of a connection to that scaly little thing than I'd ever felt to anyone. Or almost anyone…

Nothing was the same anymore.

The magic awakened in me by the Ancestors changed me.

This *bond* changed me.

I didn't like spending too much time thinking about that drastic turn of events. "So," I said to the dragon, fetching up against one of the forward ballistas. "Got any ideas?"

The sailors and soldiers nearby ignored us, focused on the impending dogfight. Er… battle between ships. Not-an-Egg hopped up beside me, wings spread and tail stretched out to find balance against the force of the wind. Talons dug into wood. He chirped—not like a bird, but a deeper and more metallic sound. I got an impression of rocks falling down. Burying? He'd figured out enough about ships already to know they floated. Clever, as I've said.

"I'm not carrying any rocks. How about you?"

He chortled and shook his head and neck.

"The crew can use the ballista to punch holes in the sides of the ships, but not until they are beside us."

Fire!

"Same problem. They have to be close." Close was dangerous. Wrapping one arm around my middle, I cradled the opposite elbow and chewed on my thumb.

"This ship more fast than those ship?" KipKap asked with his terrible grammar from behind me.

I'd appreciate it if he quit sneaking up on me. "It's lighter and has a narrower frame, but they've got more cloth. Sails." I shrugged. "It could be a long chase."

"Better to not, yes?"

"Yes."

KipKap nodded and blew through his lips thoughtfully. "And if they have magickers?"

"Wizards. That would give them an easy advantage." What was the likelihood of two magical competitors pursuing us at the same time?

"Ah. We have same advantage."

"We do?"

"We have you. You have wind. Spirit. What more?"

With his gaze on the ships, he didn't see my mouth opening and closing like a stunned tuna tossed up on the beach. "I—"

[Might. Could. Should. Can. Can! Listenlistenlissssten!] The Ancestors exclaimed on every side.

"No! Stop it. I am not a wizard!"

Heads turned our way. Not-an-Egg creaked and bared his teeth, as threatening as one small dragon could get.

KipKap glanced at him, then back at me, perplexed. "It is another word?"

I squeezed my eyes shut and shook my head. "I have—the voices of spirits. The Ancestors. They help me sometimes. I can't *do* anything."

"Why?"

[Why? Why? Why?] they echoed like a flock of insane parrots.

"Because," I said, enunciating pointedly, "I am not a wizard."

The little dragon's tail lashed and he spun in a circle, snapping at the ethereal, aggravating Ancestors. How intriguing that he could sense them, too. Did he see them?

"Is bad to be wizard in your world?"

"It isn't good." I sent a glower toward the general vicinity of the crew, and one at the predators on our tail for good measure. None of them seemed cowed, though the sailors had drifted a little away from KipKap.

[Magic is bad? Wrong? Dishonest? Wicked? Why? Why? WhywhyWHY?]

"You *said* so," I replied, disgruntled at their vacillation.

[Not true! Correct… Fact… Misunderstand!]

"Misunderstood what, exactly?"

KipKap lowered his head to my level, fascination in his frosty blue eyes. "You are speak to them. The Ancestors."

The voices stilled, if only for a moment. *[He can hear? He can see? Who is this? Who? Who? Not one of us. Not Mazhar!]*

"Hush."

"I am hushed." KipKap nodded. And waited.

The unintimidated sailors waited, too, still keeping their distance. They milled around a bit as Tanris made his way through them.

"How's that plan coming?" he asked as he joined us. He let a large canvas bag slide from his shoulder to thump to the deck.

"Hush," KipKap instructed in a whisper, as if trying—rather too late, in my opinion—to protect a secret.

"I beg your pardon?"

"He is speak with spirits."

Tanris looked from him to me and back again. "He told you about his magic?" he asked.

"I see him use it." Still whispering.

The remark elicited a grunt. "He's not very subtle."

"Some people have very good imaginations." I tried the glower again.

KipKap nodded. "Is needed for magicker. Wizard," he corrected himself. "Imagination makes thinking burn."

"He definitely has an imagination."

"Hey." I waved my hand between them. "You're not helping the situation, Friend Tanris." Emphasis on the word *friend* to remind him whose side he was supposed to be on. "And for the record, I haven't used any magic."

"Call it whatever you like, anything that gets those ships off our backs qualifies as *help*."

"Why are you looking at me? Surely the captain has experience dodging patrols and pirates alike."

"That's your plan?" Disgust dripped from Tanris's voice.

My reputation and prowess found themselves in sudden jeopardy. "Only the first part of it," I lied.

"And your friends? Can they help?" Tanris knew a little about them; they'd helped me find his wife—for all the good that had done. They'd helped the three of us evade a gang, and they tracked down foreigners. The rest, well… He took my denial with a grain of salt, dubious looks, and his signature shrug. A mere verbal distinction separated me from the wretch, Duzayan. The Ancestors had given me the label 'druid,' and Duzayan 'evil mage.' The first was natural, the other… not.

"I don't see how."

[We can help help. Aid! Give service. To Friend Crow. Kin to Kalinamsin. One of us. Ours… Counselors, we are. Friends. Guardians. Protectors. Advisors.]

"I'll see what I can do," I assured Tanris.

Out upon the windy sea, no one could tell when the Ancestors did strange things to my hair and clothes as they liked to do. I felt them, though, running cool fingers over my scalp, plucking at my shirt, stroking my back and shoulders. All I had to do was resist the urge to slap them away, which looked foolish and accomplished nothing at all. It disturbed me less now than it once had. I had the distinct impression that the Ancestors needed reassurance that I was real. Maybe that worked both ways.

Tanris pursed his lips the way he often did, nodded, and started off. He hadn't gone three steps before he turned back. "I got the banners you wanted," he said, pointing to the canvas sack.

"Thank you."

[Banners. Flags. Pennants. Standards. For what are these? Fly in the wind… signal… warn… flock… herd… tribe…]

My teeth ground together so hard it was a miracle no one heard them, even over the sound of wind and wave.

Tanris gave another nod and went on his way, barking orders at the dawdling soldiers, redirecting their attention away from me. KipKap remained, as did Not-an-Egg. I welcomed the latter, but the foreigner's intense curiosity unsettled me.

"I'll need some time to myself," I informed him. "Unless you think you can help?"

"Help with spirits? They be your kin, not mine."

I pondered that for a moment. "You cannot see or hear them?"

"Only see *of* them. When they pass, or when they… touch. That is not word I am needing." One long finger rubbed slowly up and down his nose as if he might discover the elusive word there.

"Affect? Influence?"

Satisfaction swept over his face. "Yes. *Affect.*"

"What do you know about spirits and magic?" May as well ask him as anyone else, especially since he didn't find the subject objectionable. "I'm curious."

"Ah." The nose-stroking continued as he worked on organizing his thoughts. "That is story for future time. Now we is prey."

"Ah," I echoed, doomed to disappointment in both magical and grammatical matters. "You are right. Would you see that they leave me alone?" I illustrated my request with a wave of the hand at the bustling soldiers and sailors. As I did, I glimpsed Girl with Tanris. No Tarsha, though. Had she followed instructions, or was she hiding? And what was that twinge of emotion I suffered? "She knew the risks."

I thought I'd muttered that under my breath, but KipKap wrinkled his brows at me. "Say more?"

"It doesn't matter." A quick glance around didn't turn up anyplace where I could both talk to the Ancestors and keep an eye on the following ships. I had no desire to be observed during our… chat.

The cramped quarters of a sailing ship were inconvenient that way. "Look, I need some time to myself. To be alone. I need quiet to work out the rest of the plan."

KipKap nodded sagely and waited.

May the gods of patience guide me.

"I will watch," he clarified.

"Fine. You watch those ships." I pointed to our pursuers. "Don't let them out of your sight." Slipping past him, I headed to the stairs. Not-an-Egg followed close behind. The Ancestors prickled and glared. And it worked—The crew made way for me without a word; KipKap didn't follow.

In the cramped quarters I shared with Tanris, I paced back and forth in a huff of my own. Four steps one way, four steps the other. A man could go mad confined in such a space. Not-an-Egg creaked at me from the safety of my bed. The Ancestors had elected to stay on deck.

"They've got their nerve, leaving me on my own at a time like this. What am I supposed to do? Eh, Squeaky?"

Not-an-Egg, objecting to the epithet, flared his wings and hissed at me. With flames.

"Stop that." Risking a finger, I pointed sharply at him.

To my surprise, he did. He drew back, arched his neck in indignation, then turned his back on me and sat down.

"You, too?" I snorted. Twice, to make sure my own indignation was properly appreciated. Then I dropped onto the bed beside him and proceeded to think.

"Ancestors?" They said they were always with me, so where were they? Or why didn't they answer? "Mesuk? Keshava?" I'd learned the names of some of them on the way back to Marketh with the dragon. Sometimes they responded when I called to them specifically.

Not today.

What did I need to learn from this situation? The gods had put me in an interesting place where I'd discovered something about my hidden past. It had come at a price. Magic had awakened within me. I hated magic. But the gods had blessed me with talent and wits as well.

They had been with me at every turn of my life—almost every turn, anyway—and I had faith they would not desert me now.

A tap came at the door, and it opened as Tarsha peeked inside.

"Oh, for the love of all the gracious gods!" I exclaimed. "Can't I have more than a minute to myself? Go away! Leave me alone!"

She looked stricken, curse her lovely eyes. No, no, I didn't want that. I adored her eyes and didn't want anything to happen to them, despite my vexation.

"I—I'm sorry," she stammered, which was unlike her. "I was worried about you, but I see you're fine. Of course you are."

I swatted at the air. "Yes, thank you." Look at me being all polite. "I'm trying to work through a problem, and it's impossible to think with all the noise and stares. Worse, I may be developing an allergy to cramped spaces."

"Can I help?" She spoke meekly. Again, unlike her.

"No." I scratched my head. "Are you feeling well?"

"Certainly," she lied and lifted her chin, daring me to contradict her. "Can you tell me what's going on up there?" She waved her hand, as elegant as always.

"We're a nice tasty steak, and there are two pairs of dogs racing to gobble us up."

"Oh, I see." She gave a bright smile, but her cheeks paled.

"While the captain is working on out-distancing them, I need to sort out an alternate plan or three." I'd no doubt I could bargain, lie, or cheat my way to freedom from either victor. Doing the same for my companions—and possibly the crew—was another story altogether. It underscored all the reasons I preferred to work alone. And yet...

I wondered if Tanris knew as certainly as I did that I would not leave him to his own devices. And if I worried about someone perfectly capable of taking care of himself, the others received double the consternation. What was happening to me?

"I'll just be across the passage." She nodded that direction, hesitated, then stepped out, closing the door behind her.

Agitation set me to pacing the small space again, and I dragged the talisman out from under my shirt. It was a polished slice of horn or antler strung on a plain leather cord. Dark-colored beads bracketed it. They looked black until held up to the light, and then they burned like dying embers. Two narrow, vertical rectangles with another lying across the top etched one side of the amulet. Faint lines in a ray pattern marked the lower part. *A portal. A pathway. Power.*

I didn't know what good holding it did me, besides providing vague comfort. Warmth threaded through my body. As I focused on it, I felt *lighter.* My feet stilled. I stood for some time, listening, trying to stretch out my senses, as foolish as that sounded.

"Where are you?" I whispered. "Where are you, my friends? I need your counsel."

Nothing happened. Frustration and discouragement filled me in equal measure. "Is there a proper way to call you I have not yet learned? An... an incantation to summon you?"

The ship rocked smoothly under my feet. Timbers creaked. I could almost feel the sensation of the wood sliding through the waves. Hear the soft gurgle of water. Smell the wind.

Obviously, I could not smell the wind, closed into the cabin as I was. How ridiculous!

"Are you there, friends?" It never hurt to be polite to them.

[Here... Here... We are here, always here, near, close, so close!]

I could hardly make out the tumble of voices. "Are you whispering?"

[Would not disturb. Do not wish to worry... trouble... upset... Sorry, we are sorry... sorry... sorry...]

My brow creased. "I'm not upset. Not at you."

[Angry!]

"If that's true, please tell me why I am angry." I didn't associate my uncertainty that they'd deserted me with anger.

[Hate magic. Hate us. Hate Friends. Counselors. Brothers. Cannot work magic. Will not! It is wrong... foul...]

"I do not hate you."

[Hate magic. We are magic... We are! We be! We are enchanters... druids. Hate magic, hate us. Hate heritage. Abhor us... looooaaaaathe...] Their voices rose to wailing shrieks, and I clapped my hands over my ears.

"Stop it! I don't hate you. Stop. Please."

Silence descended like a falling rock. I half expected a hole to open in the floor. I heard my heart slamming in my chest—I did *not* hear the sound of the ship. *Where was I?* Maybe the better question would be *when* was I? I didn't move. Couldn't. My mouth turned to cotton, my brain floundered about in search of a reaction.

Feather-light, a chill stroked me. My arm. My back. Then my cheek. The Ancestors waited. They eddied about me in a loose circle, somehow blurring the details of the cabin—all but Not-an-Egg's eyes glinting a dark, lustrous yellow-orange. *So precise, so intent.*

Screaming, I mused, was an option, though not something I did often, if at all. I licked dry lips, proving to myself that I could actually move. "So you're saying I'm magic?"

[Yes... Mostly... Indeed... Completely... Practically...]

"Wait." Closing my eyes, I held up a hand. The other stretched and balled at my side. My wounded hand. Good, it needed the exercise, and the motion helped me focus. I drew a breath and spoke with as much patience as I could muster. "I cannot understand when you are all speaking at once. It's confusing and it gives me a headache."

[Cannot understand us? Feel us? Know us? He is pained! Distressed!] Their dry, leafy voices twisted around me. Each held its own individual measure of shock and dismay. *[We must tell... pass on information! Advise! How will he know? What is this misfortune? What has befallen him? Us? What of us? What of ussss?]*

I cleared my throat to get their attention. It didn't work, so I simply spoke into the muffled panic. "Can one of you speak for the others?"

[One? Only one? What of me? And me... me... me...?]

[Can it be done? How will we choose?]

[There are many... scores... countless... abundant...]

"You could take turns," I suggested.

[Channel... flow... merge... yes. Yes. Perhaps. We will try. Help Friend Crow, son of sons, hope, legacy...]

No pressure there, right? "Tell me what you mean, that I'm mostly magic. Am I like Baron Duzayan?" Would power corrupt me as it had him? As it did so many wizards in the empire and beyond? The thought sent a shudder through me, but I remembered Tanris had promised to kill me if such a dreadful thing happened. And I believed him.

The spirits whispered and hissed as if at a distance. It was as if they'd gone into another room so they could talk about me without me hearing. Not-an-Egg flowed off the bed and crept across the floor to wind around my ankles. He settled close, talons lightly clutching my booted calf.

That worked as long as the Ancestors didn't frighten him. If he startled, I'd be punctured.

"Hey."

He looked up, wide-eyed.

"Mind you don't poke me, eh?"

The little beast grinned at me, then patted my shin apologetically.

Sometime during our discussion, the cabin had come back into focus. The usual noises of the ship reasserted themselves, along with thumping and clattering. With no warning whatsoever, the door burst open.

Tanris lurched in. "What in blazes—?"

"There's a fire?" I inquired, looking for smoke to fill the corridor.

Straightening, he checked behind the door. "How did you do that?"

"Do what?"

"Keep the door closed. The latch worked fine, and I could see light around the edges." A swift glower covered his confusion, and he had the temerity to growl at me.

"I don't know what you're talking about."

"Never mind. You need to come up top. We're going to be boarded in a few minutes."

My brows shot skyward. "What? How is that possible? Both ships were *hours* behind us."

He waved his hand for me to follow and disappeared back into the dark reaches of the corridor. "That was this morning," he informed me over his shoulder, "and they've got wizards."

"What time is it?"

"Mid-afternoon. Quit your dawdling!" he shouted.

Noon? What had the Ancestors done to me? And there were *wizards?* I hated wizards. Alarm flooded my senses, and I dashed out. The Ancestors followed uncertainly. They whispered among themselves, a sound as grating as a rasp across iron. I wanted—no, *needed*—to be up on deck. Tanris's bulk slowed me, but finally I broke free and ran aft.

[Wizards... Wizards... Wizards...] the Ancestors hissed and whistled from every direction. The crew of the *Integrity*, silent as a library, ranged along the side of the ship. Weapons in hand, every figure was tense as they waited for the boarding party. Spying the captain on the aftcastle, I altered my course. I wasn't sure why, except for the incessant whispering of my alleged protectors.

"Zakkis!" I called out as I approached him, and slowed my steps from a run to a more subdued... trot. He shot me a brief sideways look, his expression grim. "How have they caught up with us so fast?"

His chin jutted toward our pursuer. "Windskinner."

I blinked. I'd forgotten that seafarers sometimes hired wizards who specialized in harnessing the wind. "Where's ours?"

The next glance came with a crooked eyebrow. "Can't afford one. Or I suppose you might, but you didn't hire one."

"Why didn't you say so?" The rotten scoundrel. Not that I'd have been pleased about hiring a wizard. While decent ones probably exist, I'd yet to run into any.

"It's your ship. Figured you knew what you were doing."

"*Brilliant.* I hope your petty vengeance makes you happy." Putting his life and the lives of his crew at risk that way wasn't the least bit logical, but I'd take it up with him another day. If we should live so long. Instead of venting my ire with a fist in his face, I merely stalked away. The gods, in their wisdom, would either get me out of this prickly plight or alter the course of my life. Again. Somehow, my faith in them did nothing to ease the sense of anxiety that had struck me at the mention of the existence of a wizard nearby. Or *wizards*, Tanris had announced.

I shouldered my way to the bulwark, fetching up next to Tanris. I hadn't sought him out on purpose, but his calm, solid presence reassured me. His collection of weapons promising mayhem to all enemies didn't hurt, either. Knowing he had not jested about the nearness of the enemy ship and seeing with my own eyes were two different things. We were near enough to pick out the faces of the sailors aboard the Asonian ship. Some grinned, some focused intently. All brandished sharp, pointy things.

Behind them and some distance off, the Bahsyri vessel limped. Battered and torn, it still gave chase. I couldn't see the purpose. They were a stubborn lot, I'll give them that, but it would take a miracle for them to provide rescue. I saw nothing of the second Asonian ship.

My glance swung back to our pursuer. The *Gallant*, if I read the name right. Marketh traded with the Confederacy, and I'd picked up a smattering of the language. A tall, imposing figure with black hair stood near the mainmast. One hand braced against the wood. His tattooed features were tight with concentration. The wind pushing our sails worked double for the *Gallant*. She closed the space between us at a staggering speed.

[Danger! Danger! Perrrril!] the Ancestors shrieked needlessly.

"I know! I *know!*" The memory of my capture and torture by other wizards haunted my dreams on a regular basis. I had no inclination to repeat the experience. A part of me clung to the idea that the Asonian wizard knew nothing about my magical inheritance. I could talk my way out of severe harm without the magic *or* the spirits. Another part of me screamed bloody murder and sent panic clawing from my gut to my throat. In that moment, I hated magic with every fiber of my being.

At the very same instant, the Ancestors fled from me.

—11—
Ripping, Tearing, Cracking, Breaking

"What are we going to do?" For the proclaimed leader of our expedition, Tanris wasn't providing a lot of direction. In an hour less wrought with terror, I might appreciate him looking to me for guidance.

"Give me a minute." I rubbed my throat, certain the strangled voice issuing those words hadn't belonged to me. Where was my vaunted composure now? Likely throttled by that cursed wizard aboard the *Gallant*. Resentment and fear of him and his ilk made my hands turn to ice. Nevertheless, I would not let him beat me. *Could* not.

"This would be a great time for some of those impressive skills you said you used at Hasiq, Wizard Bane," Tanris drawled.

I shot him a dirty look. "This is different."

"How? You want him closer, like before?" Was that mockery?

"No, *thank you*."

The Asonian wizard chose that moment to send a punch in our direction. A hazy globe of air plowed through soldier and sailor alike, sending them reeling and floundering. Thank the gods of convenience that the pair of us weren't in its path.

"Crow..." Tanris growled, knuckles whitening where he clutched the rail.

Panic gripped me anew. Without knowing why—or if the Ancestors would return—I brought the talisman up to my mouth, pressed hard against my lips. *Help me. Help. Me... Shred their sails. Break their masts. Ruin them. Ruin them...* I couldn't speak the words aloud. Dared not. Instead, it was as if I pushed them through the disk of horn and magic. Fueled by fear and anger, they burst through in a cold, dark, violent shape that sent me staggering backward.

Tanris's hand wrapped around my upper arm kept me upright. "Is that yours?"

The screech of wind and *voices* all but drowned him out. The Ancestors reappeared as if from a void, howling like mad things, careering this way and that. Icy fingers scraped through my hair and tore at my clothes. They plucked at Tanris, too, and he swore but didn't let go. I clutched him and tried to see through squinted, burning eyes.

"*Wait! Stop!*" I shouted, terrified at the precipitous, staggering power the Ancestors displayed as they gathered themselves. Early in our acquaintance, they'd used a whirlwind to frighten a gang of boys. Compared to this, that was nothing more than a playful zephyr.

Crewmen and soldiers on the back half of the ship staggered and cried out. Beyond them, the others watched in bewilderment. First Mate Rego stomped through, hollering and shoving men into action. A bellow preceded the swing of the boom. Like ants swarming from their nest when attacked, sailors scampered into the shrouds to adjust the canvas. It didn't keep the *Integrity* from lurching.

Tanris and I hurtled into the bulwark and tumbled into a heap. He still kept his hold on me as one brawny arm hooked over the top and held us fast. I managed to pull myself up to my knees. The two of us hunkered down, out of the way as much as possible.

"You good?" Tanris demanded over the racket.

I nodded and felt for the talisman. Fingers slid down the braided leather strap and I gripped the smooth surface. Its faint warmth reassured me. I brought it back up to my lips, half hoping and half dreading it would carry my words to the Ancestors.

"Are you *praying?*"

"With all my heart," I said fervently. *[You're going to break this ship. You will drown us!]*

[Hurt them? Drown them? Finish them?]

"Stop them," I hissed. "Just stop them. Don't kill them!"

The sails overhead snapped and cracked, then abruptly fell limp.

A heartbeat later, the *Gallant's* sails flapped insanely. Their wizard grabbed the mast with both arms, his attention jerking skyward. The impossible wind blew from two different directions. Cloth stretched. Timbers groaned. The ship bucked and jolted. *Ripping, tearing, cracking, breaking...* Men screamed as the masts came down, battered by wood and rope and chain. Some fell into the sea.

"Don't kill them!" I cried again. No one heard me.

Wind encircled the *Gallant's* bow and pushed her around, then sped toward the lagging Bahsyri vessel. Water cleaved as if swept by a giant hand, sending up great sheets behind each digit. Wild waves crashed into the ship. The fingers dug into the rigging, and the canvas shredded. The mizzen mast gave a tremendous *clap!* as it exploded into splinters.

I stared at the instant destruction.

"By Onuial's awful ax," Tanris murmured. It was the first time I'd ever heard him use the name of any of the gods. It figured that he'd choose the god of war, the default god of most soldiers. "Did you do that?"

"No. Yes. I don't know." My heart and gut both fought for space in my throat.

A new pitch in the screams from the *Gallant* demanded my attention. Flames burned on the forecastle. Fire pots knocked over. Fuel spilled. I squeezed my eyes shut, then leapt to my feet, pulling away from Tanris. The *Integrity* rocked as the captain brought her nose to port, and the mate shouted orders to fix the sails.

My planned escape didn't keep Tanris from catching my shoulder, and his chin gestured towards my forehead. "You're bleeding."

Instinctively, I lifted my hand. My face must have struck the rail or the deck. I had no memory of it. Warm stickiness bathed my brow. "I'm fine."

He examined me intently, brows knit in a familiar frown. "What was that, besides a little extreme?" He thumbed toward the floundering ships, master of understatement as always. Accusation glimmered in his eyes. I didn't like that any more than I liked the wounded, drowning, or dead men. I was not a murderer. Was I?

"Their wizard may still be active. I can't—" Words failed me, and I looked down at my hands. It seemed as if they belonged to someone else.

"Looks as if you did a cracking job to me."

Trying to breathe normally only resulted in a horrible sense of lightheadedness.

Tanris pressed his lips together into a tight line and his gaze slid to the side. "KipKap, will you watch him?"

"I'm *fine*." Shrugging his hand off me, I shoved past him. Past KipKap and his huge, worried eyes. Past sailors and soldiers going about their jobs, intent on keeping the ship sailing and the people on it safe.

The Ancestors roiled as I retreated belowdecks to the cabin I shared with Tanris. Not-an-Egg kept close to my heels, making a clicking sound in his throat. *Worry*. It did nothing to impress the spirits one way or another.

"What have we done?" I demanded, banging the door shut behind us.

[What you asked. Requested. What is needed. Protected. What we are...]

"Would it be asking too much for you to make sense for once in your lives? Surely you can talk in complete sentences."

[Lives... we do not have lives. We are gone, not gone. You have life. Energy. Existence. It is ours. One of us. Rare. So rare! Rare and precious! We must protect. Guide. Nurture.]

"Why? Why me? And why do I matter so much?" When had I ever mattered to anyone? Anger twined with the horror of watching the ships wrecked to splinters.

Not-an-Egg whined and slunk off under the bed.

[Ours, you are... Son of sons... Our legacy. You have a birthright... It is ours. It is yours. Through us. A past. A future. Duty... Authority... Leadership... Heritage...]

"You want me to be a leader? That's a terrible idea. What heritage? And didn't we agree to only one of you speaking at a time?"

They hissed and churned around me. It raised gooseflesh on my skin. Worse, they started talking to each other about me, as if I weren't even in the room.

[He is angry... vexed, so vexed. Burdened. Frightened! Frightened by us. Like a child. Hasn't knowledge. Cannot know! Who is he? Kalinamsin's. Where, oh, where is Kalinamsin? What has become of him?]

"What happened? Did you lose him?"

[Lost... so lost... What shall we do? Help him. He hates us. Looooaathes us.]

"I do not," I insisted, though I very well might in a moment. They *were* magic.

[Fear, fear, fear! How can he fear us? We protect him. Guide him. Guard him. Always... always... He is ours! Ours! Must tell him! Must teach him!]

They sped through the little cabin, jumbling the blankets, tossing shirts, ruffling Tanris's book. The more they jabbered at each other, the more agitated they became. Worse, they paid no attention to me at all, though I shouted at them to stop. Pressure built around me. Green sparks pricked and danced over my skin, waking in me a deep sense of foreboding. Suddenly, I wanted out. I *needed* to get away from the magic. Away from them. Out of this cramped, pocket-sized closet and into the air again.

I yanked on the door, only to find it impossible to open. Oh, the latch worked, and the wood shuddered, but the disquieted Ancestors kept slamming it closed. "Let me go!"

If they heard me, they gave no sign. They battered at the walls. The door. Me...

Tarsha found me later. Much later, I thought. Silence held me down on the bed, though I'd somehow propped myself against the wall. The weight of the air had changed, as if made heavy by the setting of the sun. Or by my guilt. Suspicion and wariness kept Not-an-Egg in hiding, but after a while he'd come out to curl up beside me. When the door opened, the dragon slithered to the floor and out of sight again.

"Tanris send you to check on me?" My voice was a rasp.

"No." She sat beside me, hands folded in her lap. The only light came from a lantern in the corridor, slicing across the gloom in a wedge of amber. "Others talked."

"Oh?" I didn't have the energy to move away from her.

"They're saying the Asonian wizard lost control."

I barked a rough laugh.

"Tanris and your tall friend are worried, but they won't say why."

The near-darkness veiled her face. I could make out little more than a silhouette. Couldn't see the scars she bore, though the memory of them scraped at me. "What does Girl say?"

Her clothes rustled as she shifted. She could not speak the hand language, and Girl had made no effort to teach her. Girl's province, not mine. "Something else happened, didn't it?" she asked softly, gently. "Are you hurt? It's not like you to hide."

I thought it exactly like me. That's what I did. I hid—in closets, corners, cisterns, behind drapes, under stairs, in shadows.

"Do you want to talk about it?"

"No." Not to her. Not to anyone. Who could possibly understand who I was? Or that everything I'd known about myself had changed with the coming of the Ancestors? "There's nothing to talk about." A bald lie, but the truth was impossible.

She fell silent, considering. "What were you like as a boy?"

I might have gaped, the change of subject was so unexpected. "What?"

"Tell me about when you were small."

"It was a long time ago; I don't live there anymore." The past deserved to stay in the past. "I have nothing to connect what *was* to what *is*."

"Your life."

"Petty." How did a man—the son of the son of some stranger—go from being part of a tribal community to being a single unidentifiable mote in a city far from home?

"That's not true. What about your parents? Your brothers and sisters?"

"I didn't have any, but I had many uncles and aunts. Lots of cousins, or at least that's what we called them." Why did I let her pull me along this path? It was ugly. Painful. It brought keen shards of memory certain to cut me to the quick. "There was one girl…" Wide green eyes. Freckles. Choppy dark hair. Small hands.

"A cousin?"

"They were all cousins. Completely unrelated." A hodgepodge collection of nobodies and nothings.

"A chosen sister, then. What was her name?"

No, not that. Too sharp, even after all these years. "I don't recall," I lied, my voice razor-edged with bitterness.

It did not deter her. "How old were you? Both of you."

I lifted one shoulder in a shrug. "Eight? Ten?"

"What made her special?"

"She was nice to me."

"What about your aunts and uncles? Were they nice, too?"

"Now and then." One could call a cuff upside the head *nice* compared to a beating.

Another rustle and a soft, muffled sound. *Sympathy* soothed my nerves. I didn't want her sympathy, but I had no way to ward against it.

"What happened to her?"

"She went away." Died, for all I knew. "Why are you asking me all this?"

Tarsha was quiet for so long it became uncomfortable. Then she brushed my hair back and cupped my cheek. The warmth of her skin against mine was a balm. I turned away, but it didn't break our contact. We were too close. Her hand fell to my shoulder and rested there.

"Because," she murmured, "the strongest, bravest man I know is sitting alone in the dark. You won't talk about why, so perhaps talking about something else will ease the pain. Or distract you until you can cope with it." She turned to me, and the amber light—faint as gossamer—lit her face and made deep pools of her eyes.

It was beautiful and seductive in a way I did not recognize. I refused to let my attention wander down that path. What was she trying to do? What did she want? We both knew men stronger and braver than I. Tanris, for a perfect example. It was common knowledge she didn't care about me one whit—she'd already proven her opinion. I nearly asked. Instead, I said, "I'm not hiding."

She swallowed. A strange, melancholy sound. "I see. What *are* you doing here? Alone?"

"I'm not alone. Not-an-Egg is here. Below us."

She squeaked and yanked her feet up to safety.

In another situation, it would have been funny. "If he were going to nibble on your ankles, he'd have done it already."

"He doesn't like me."

"He's a little reserved with his affections." An understatement. To be honest, he wasn't familiar with anyone besides Tanris, Senza, and me. The Eagles we'd spent the summer with pretended to ignore him. Sometimes they discussed what he'd be like in a stew, or if they could train him to hunt rats or, even better, rabbits. At least they could count on those to taste good. KipKap and Diti kept their distance, more reverent than ravenous. And if Not-an-Egg remembered Tarsha at all from their first brief meeting, the memory would be clouded with anger: mine and Senza's.

"He's the egg Duzayan wanted, isn't he?"

"You're overflowing with questions. And he is obviously not an egg."

"Are you—" She paused to reconsider. To rephrase. "His name is awful. So… lacking character."

"I suppose you have something better picked out," I grumbled.

"No." She turned her head away. Amber outlined her profile and gleamed in her dark hair. Would she—the shape, color, scent, expressions, moods, movement—ever stop enticing me? "I could help, if you like."

"You've helped enough."

Her swallow was audible. "I want to. However I can," she murmured.

I wanted her to go away, but saying so would be rude. "Thank you," I said instead, though it didn't sound terribly sincere, even to me.

To my relief, she got up to leave, only to pause at the door. "The cook is making octopus stew."

"Oh, joy."

"I knew that would tempt you out of your cabin." Flashing me a knee-melting smile, she disappeared.

Needless to say, I did not rush to dinner. When I fetched my bowl of savory-smelling stew at last, I took it to the deck to watch the descent of twilight. Tanris joined me. He had a loaf of days-old bread—one of the rewards of brief sea journeys—clamped between elbow and ribs. Without so much as a by-your-leave, he sat down on a crate next to me. Tearing the loaf in half, he handed one piece to me, then tucked into his meal. When he continued wordlessly for several mouthfuls, I ventured to finish my own food.

Silent, we watched the waves turn black as the sky faded from rose to iris purple to deepest blue. The sounds of laughter and camaraderie drifted from below. Someone sang, and soon a woman's voice joined in. I turned from the view to find Tanris watching me.

"You're not—" I waved a hand in his direction. "Anything."

His mouth crimped in exasperation. "Thanks."

"I mean, you're just quiet and not... simmering." That sounded feeble.

"I did. Simmer, that is." He stacked our bowls together, then drew his legs up, arms draped over his knees and hands clasped. His gaze returned to the sea. After a dozen heartbeats, he spoke again. "I went to see you. The door was locked."

Except there were no locks on the cabin doors.

"Did you hear anything inside?" I asked hesitantly.

"Moaning. I called out, but you didn't answer. The Ancestors?"

"Yes." I scrubbed both hands up and down my face.

Tanris chewed on his lip for a moment, then let out a sigh. "I'd help if I knew how."

"You would?"

He nodded. "This magic doesn't sit easy on you."

A half-dozen attempts to swallow didn't make the sudden lump disappear. "I never asked for this."

Another nod. "If these spirits that came with you out of the Ghost Walk are ancestors, is that literal? Are they ancient relatives of yours?"

"That's what they claim."

"So they know your bloodline."

"They say I am descended from someone called Kalinamsin, but there appears to be a gap between him and me."

"How many generations?"

I scratched the back of my neck. "I wish you could listen to them. Many. A few. Scores. Maybe they'll figure it out some day. They said I was lost. Or the *Friend* was lost." Senses rather than eyes told me his brow wrinkled in question. "As I understand it, some of the Mazhar escaped the Ghost Walk. Some never went in at all. A few of the survivors served as... as agents. Spokesmen. Champions of a sort. They called them *friends*. They are the Ancestors. Their purpose is to protect their people and preserve the tribe's heritage."

"And this role is passed down from generation to generation?"

"Apparently. Somehow the magic changed those who were chosen. That change is inherited."

"Interesting." Tanris nodded thoughtfully. "If some were spared from the destruction, there are still Mazhar people in the empire."

Interesting as a three-legged goose? As an idle curiosity? "I suppose so. Are you acquainted with any?"

"You." His teeth were pale in the dim light as he grinned.

"True... Do you have an idea where we might find others?"

"Not yet."

Those words implied a lot. I pursed my lips and rubbed my head. "You plan on looking?"

"Why not?"

"Why?" I countered. "You have no reason to look for my long-lost relatives."

"If I didn't, I wouldn't offer." Getting to his feet with a grunt, he collected the bowls and stalked away.

What did he have to gain from searching for my people? I puzzled over that for awhile, and over his lack of anger at the destruction of the ships. And crew. I still felt queasy thinking about it, and the Ancestors had provided no useful information. None that I could recall, anyway. Maybe some details from the barrage they'd launched at me would surface, but I couldn't be sure they'd said anything instructive. Perhaps they were only whining and shouting at each other. Or me.

Full dark had not yet blanketed us when I heard Tanris call out. "Crow? You'd best come look at this."

—12—
Sharks and Hard Places

Nothing came to mind that would make me want to get up. I was comfortable, pensive, and disinclined to move. But Tanris was not prone to foolishness or practical jokes, so I gave up my moody thoughts to join him.

'This' turned out to be a tall, sparkling slash of amethyst light floating over the water. The distance was difficult to judge. Tendrils like liquid fire bowed and weaved over the surface. Sparks jumped off it, and it produced an ominous, shuddering whine. The hairs on my arms and neck rose.

"You feel that?" Tanris asked.

"It can't be good."

Crew and soldiers alike came to see. Murmurs and signs against evil passed among them. The captain shouted orders to adjust the sails, keeping the *Integrity* as far away from the thing as possible. We were still too close for my liking.

"This bears a distinct resem—"

A high-pitched hiss obliterated my words. Right on its tail came an ear-splitting *crack!* Bolts of violet lightning stabbed the sea's surface so hard it sent up geysers taller than the ship's masts. I clutched the rail as water rained down on the deck. Captain Zakkis achieved the impossible, pitching his voice over the uproar to shout the crew to their stations. The mate didn't lose an ounce of volume as he echoed the orders. Sailors bolted to their tasks. Men screamed and shouted, scrambling to get to their posts.

Despite the mayhem, my attention remained transfixed on the slash as it widened into the shape of a dragon's pupil. Purple light seeped into a center as black as pitch. "It's a gate!" I grabbed Tanris's arm and pointed. As if he might completely forget what one looked like.

The roiling middle bulged outward, first in an even swell, then as if pounded by a multitude of fists. Inevitably, it burst, rending the air with screams. The din overwhelmed the shouts of sailors, clanking chains, and creaking wood.

Tanris spun away from me.

"Where are you going?" I shouted.

"For weapons."

A good plan, if the foreigners could swim at all well. And what did I have? Nothing but a small knife.

Usually, the Ancestors took offense to such 'bad' magic. They would seethe around me in a blend of worry and bloodthirstiness. But I hadn't felt them at all since regaining my senses right before Tarsha's appearance. I pressed the talisman against my skin. "Are you deserting me now?" I asked aloud.

The rip in the fabric of the gate widened, spilling out creatures of every shape, size, and lung capacity. No longer muffled by the gate, they rushed through in a frenzy of shrieks and howls. To my astonishment, some of them clawed and tore at each other on the way through. Striking water dampened their ferocity not at all.

"Starry nightshirts!" I exclaimed. "What has come over them?"

"Magic." Diti had a voice every bit as deep as KipKap's. He lurched against the railing beside me, gripping a wicked ax. "Hate magic." He spat the words—followed by a great gobbet of saliva—over the side. Certain habits of soldiers and sailors were perhaps not things worthy of emulation.

"Do you mean you hate the magic, or that the magic is made of... of hate?" I could not pull my attention from the seething ocean. All that blood promised trouble.

His head bobbed on his long neck. "Magic is not alone bad." He hadn't his brother's talent for learning language.

Several responses leaped to my tongue—none of them useful. "Can you feel it?" I nodded toward the gate.

Diti's odd lips thinned and he and stood motionless. "Yes. Is different. Bad still. Like drink in eyes burn." His six-fingered hand tightened on the rail. Watching *people* fall into the ocean tearing each other apart troubled him as it did me. "Like—ripping. Tearing. Pulling. We are useless against it."

"Shades and ashes," I murmured. "That's terrible."

"Bad magicker use bad magic for bad thing."

"Have you ever seen someone use magic for good?"

"Yes. Healing. Building. Protecting." With the last word, he looked pointedly at me.

I ignored him. It was easy. I had a horrific scene to stare at. "Shouldn't we try to rescue them?"

"Captain will not." KipKap's voice came from directly behind me. He put one hand on my shoulder and pointed at the gate with his mace. "They are dangerous."

"They might be friends, or relatives!"

"Maybe. But the magic they pass through makes them... wrong."

"Crazy? Not right in the head?"

"Not right, yes." Worry and sadness rolled off him in waves. "They do not know what they do. I do not believe we can stop them."

They did, however, recognize a ship when they saw it. Some of those on the outskirts of the stew began making their way toward us. Most of them, though, flailed and flapped and floundered as if they didn't know how to swim. Their frenzied screams turned to cries of distress. The noise dragged along my nerves like a fork sliding along glass.

"We can't just leave them," I protested. "They're strangers here, frightened and confused. If they don't drown, the sharks will get them."

The jackal sharks of the Rahiya Strait are the sort of creatures that parents living on the coast use to threaten disobedient children. Most are not longer than a man is tall, but they are blisteringly swift, agile, and vicious. Swimming in packs like dogs, they will attack prey many times their own weight. Drawn to scraps thrown overboard, they often follow ships, quarreling over the spoils, and even setting upon each other.

"This new conscience you've been developing lately takes some getting used to." Tanris cocked his crossbow and leveled it at the floundering foreigners. I hadn't noticed his return. "Look—if we go closer, they could board and kill us all. Or the gate could shift and wreck the ship. If we manage to bring some of them aboard safely, the sailors may mutiny. Fights will break out either way. And if none of that happens, what do we do with them? We haven't supplies to care for them, and we've no place to take them, except to Masni." He speared me with a hard glance. Taking them to the island wouldn't be safe, sane, or at all helpful.

"Can we lower the dinghy?"

"There are too many of them."

"Some would live." KipKap nodded gravely.

"Do you see any of your people out there, KipKap?" Desperation clawed at my throat.

"It is no good. I can do nothing for them."

"Is true," Diti agreed, legs braced against the pitch of the deck as he slapped his ax against one palm. It was hard to recall he'd ever been seasick.

All three of them waited for me to choose.

In unfamiliar, uncomfortable anguish, I gripped the talisman. It had come free from my shirt, and the polished bone fitted neatly into my hand.

[Hush… hush… Quiet. This is not yours…]

"What?" What were they talking about?

Tanris and KipKap exchanged a glance.

Indistinct voices murmured around me, easing the mounting distress over the fate of the foreigners. The Ancestors brushed their cool hands over my hair, face, and shoulders. Their whispering nonsense soothed me. The grief and wretchedness didn't belong to me—but to the foreigners in the sea and those on board.

"Your boat, your captain." Tanris gave an encouraging nod.

"Mine, right." I took a deep breath in and let it out, striving to regain my scattered composure. "Throw the dinghy over. I'll deal with the captain."

Zakkis did some yelling about that, let me tell you. Tanris with his sword and the combination of KipKap and Diti kept him and his sailors at bay until after the deed was done. The Eagles might not have liked their orders, but they obeyed swiftly. Then I asked the captain if he had any empty barrels or crates.

"You are crazy as a starling drunk on last year's berries," the captain pronounced.

"Let me ask you something, Captain Zakkis. Imagine yourself being dragged against your will into their world, suddenly flailing about in an ocean. It's dark. You're surrounded by a lot of scared people possibly trying to kill you, and you don't know how far it is to land. But lo! There's a ship passing by. Would you prefer the ship to leave you on your own, or would you appreciate help from some thoughtful soul watching you drown?"

"You don't know if we'll need that boat." He pointed to where it bobbed around like a lost cork.

"Answer the question."

His mouth bent in frustration. "I'd want help."

I thumped his shoulder. "Good man. Do what you can for them."

"They're not people."

There was a snort for that. "Tell that to them." With a thumb, I gestured to KipKap and Diti. "What characterizes a living creature as a person? No, never mind." I massaged my brow. "We haven't got time for this. Please do as I've requested."

"The boat will have to be replaced."

"Remind me to think about philosophy and calculate the cost of equipment if I'm ever on hand when you need saving."

"Here now," he growled. "That's not—"

Shouts interrupted his self-righteous defense. It wasn't tricky to figure out which direction the uproar came from, and we pushed our way through the crowd to the bulwark. The jackal sharks had found a veritable feast free for the taking. Black shapes reflected the gate's purple light as they sliced through the water. Overlong dorsal fins resembled knives, but it was the teeth a swimmer needed to worry about. As they rushed to their meals, they twisted and turned, revealing tawny bellies. Water and bodies alike heaved in their wake.

The pitch of screaming escalated. I had to close my eyes, but it did little to ease the thrumming emotion and the sickening wrongness. The sensations scraped my nerves and churned in my belly. I tasted bile.

From nearby came a *thump* and *thwish*. Then another, and another. I opened my eyes to see a grim-faced Senza leaning against the rail, loosing quarrels at the sharks. Two Eagles and a sailor had bows as well. I could only hope they aimed at sharks and not foreigners.

Captain Zakkis might disapprove of his orders, but he followed them anyway. A small group of men tipped empty barrels over the ship's side. Meanwhile, Rego hollered instructions that kept us from sailing into the frothing, flickering disaster.

"Hoy!" Someone shouted, pointing at a towering, shadowy figure slipping past the far edge of the gate. Purple light bathed it, revealing another ship. A trio of long banners fluttered from the mainmast, though it was impossible to make out the colors.

Pirates...

"Take us out of here!" Captain Zakkis renewed his bellowing, and the sailors did whatever mundane magic sailors usually do to coax the ship to greater speed.

Those of us still at the rail watched the new vessel suddenly slow. Ropes were lowered and foreigners hauled out of the kettle and into the serving dish. Truly, what was the likelihood their rescuers would take them to safety rather than to slavery? As we pulled away, I wondered at the convenience of their arrival. They carried out their task efficiently, no strangers to the situation. No, they'd arrived just in time to pluck a good crop of foreigners from certain death. They weren't afraid to bring their ship close to the gate, either. I pondered on that, and none of the ideas that crossed my mind brought comfort.

My glance shifted to the infernal portal. Where it had throbbed at first, it now flickered and crackled. With no more warning than that shift, the gateway closed with a formidable *crack!* that stiffened my spine and made my ears ring. For one brief moment, the purple gleam remained, encircling a center blacker than pitch. Parts of bodies fell into the water, severed in transit. Some of them sparked as if they'd caught fire. Then it was gone.

"Did you see that?" My voice sounded strange. Muffled shouting penetrated the jangle in my ears.

Beside me, Senza grabbed my arm to get my attention. Crossbow slung over one shoulder, she moved her hands so swiftly it was a challenge to keep up. Flash blindness didn't help. *By the creek. Burned tree. Chopped bodies.* She pointed repeatedly, frantically to where the gate had been. The wind carried the scent of charred flesh. Vision ruined, I couldn't see the struggles of the survivors and the feasting of the sharks. Thank the gods.

Senza thumped my chest. *Did you see me?*

I grimaced and nodded. "You're right. That thing back there in the woods had to be another gate. Up high, like this one." And it, too, had snapped closed on the poor saps coming through. My imagination made me light-headed and nauseous. "Well, now we have proof."

She gave a brisk nod.

"They open and close themselves," I realized out loud. That was the only explanation for the widespread, random appearances. Kneading my forehead didn't make it any easier to comprehend. "How is that possible? And how can it be stopped? I know nothing about magic, Girl."

Senza made a face of disbelief. *Not true.*

"Nothing useful, then. My knowledge might not fill a thimble." And yet Tanris expected me simply to close the dreadful things. *Multiple* things. "This is madness."

Duzayan's madness, she agreed, then signed something I didn't understand, but I thought I could follow. Something about the task being up to me.

"There is no guarantee I won't make worse mistakes."

She shrugged. *I believe in you. Tanris believes in you.*

"On what grounds?" Truly, this magic affliction had only recently struck me. I was a druid of a few months' experience—months filled with the attempt to avoid using it at all. I'd spent a lifetime of steering clear of magic. Duzayan had studied his craft for *decades*, and he'd still got it wrong. Druids dealt with... nature, from what I understood.

Senza signed something and tapped her temple with a forefinger.

"I have—brains?"

A sharp nod. *Ancestors.* She signed another word, then pointed at her ears, drawing her fingers upward from the top of her head.

"Strong... rabbit?" I tried to decide whether I was insulted.

Senza frowned, jabbed my chest again, then my head. *You want to do a thing, you do it,* she signed.

I worked through her meaning while I rubbed my abused noggin. Not a rabbit; a mule? Mule-headed! "Oh, strong-willed."

She flipped one hand palm up, shrugged, and gave me an exaggerated expression that said 'Of course, idiot,' without a single word.

Brains and a strong will combined with the Ancestors and ignorance didn't sound like a recipe for success. "I would as soon look for someone who actually knows what they're doing," I grumbled.

Senza waved at our surroundings. *Here?*

"Well, no, I—" I squinted as I looked out at the ocean. "Say, is that—"

"*Sail ho!*" came an answer from the rigging. "Abeam to port and closing!"

Three long banners rippled overhead. *More pirates.*

"Naturally, they didn't come alone," I muttered. *Now what?*

"Now what?" echoed Tanris, coming to stand nearby and propping his hands on his hips. "They'll give chase. Can you—?" He made a circular motion in the air with one finger and went right back to his heroic stance.

"No. *No,* by Nijamar's ghost." If he thought I would try to repeat the death and destruction from earlier, he was sadly mistaken.

"Can't or won't?"

"Yes. Both."

He scratched his nose. "Odds are they have a windskinner," he announced as if he were discussing the likelihood of supplies on board.

"Do not threaten me." My eyes narrowed severely.

Tanris only crooked a brow. "You have another idea?"

I turned in a circle, surveying the ship, the crew, the deck... *There!* "Yes." I snapped my fingers. "The plague banners."

"It's too late for that, Crow."

"Not if we're trying to hide our plaguey-ness."

His expression lit with comprehension. He spun on one heel and started barking orders as only Tanris can. Pennants and banners swapped places. The headsail was changed out for the gray plague sail (the only canvas change required of plague ships). Weapons got stowed close against the bulwarks and out of sight. The men and women aboard ship rearranged themselves—not to hide their numbers, but to give the illusion of doubt and despair. The darkness covered much of our activity, thank the gods of mystery.

Girl—Senza!—helped me apply ash to cheeks and under eyes. The cosmetic trickery wouldn't stand inspection in daylight, but we had some hours until then. Vermilion ochre (was it a coincidence to have some of the stuff after what Enikar's clerk had told me?) mixed with fat reddened noses and created passable blotchiness. In the wavering torch light, we looked as unsavory as anyone could ask of plague victims. The cook came up with the brilliant idea of burning what he called *incense*. He said the strong, acrid aroma was a potent force for driving away evil spirits and foul air. The brazier full of fire I'd first seen now put off a cloying, gag-inducing smoke. The wind blew the stench ahead of us, which seemed counter-productive. Many of us covered our faces with scarves and strips of cloth. It didn't hurt the atmosphere of doom at all.

After giving what help they could, KipKap and Diti went belowdecks. With pirates scooping their compatriots out of the ocean, there was no sense stirring up an extra helping of trouble. Not-an-Egg sheltered safely in our cabin, though uneasiness made him prickly against my senses. There had to be some way to quiet that... *itch*.

"You look like rubbish," Tanris said, quite pleased for no discernible reason.

"Why thank you, you look—" I surveyed him from head to foot. "Astonishingly like a hairball. How did you do that?"

"Unexpected depths of talent." He rocked back on his heels.

I snorted a laugh and was glad to see his mouth twitch in a short-lived smile.

"If this doesn't work, you get somewhere safe," he ordered.

I gave a sage nod. "Yes, all sorts of places to hide on a boat in the middle of the sea. I appreciate the thought, though." Had he told Senza the same?

As the sleek, dark shape slipped closer, we heard the men aboard her talking. Someone bit out low, crisp orders. Quiet voices responded. Silvery light from the scythe blade of the moon reflected on drawn weapons.

"This must be the muscle," Tanris murmured. "The guard dogs. One more body on that vessel will sink the thing."

"Would it be that easy?"

"Are you volunteering?"

"Don't be ridiculous. It's my goal in life to avoid risking life and limb, and flinging myself onto a sinking ship sounds particularly risky. I was merely considering sinking it in the literal sense."

From the corner of my eye, I saw his smirk.

"Did it hurt much? Thinking?"

"This is a fine time for your decrepit humor to surface," I grumbled, and pointed at the pirate ship. "I hate to say this, but can you focus on them for a minute?"

"Right. What's the plan?"

"Warn them off."

He swung a sharp look my way. "Me?"

"Of course. It's got to be you or the captain's mate." I made a sweeping motion up my chest with my palm extended. "You have the lungs of—"

"Fine." He scrubbed his bristly chin.

"How *are* your acting skills? Should I call for—"

"Shut up."

"Touchy, touchy." Talk about a mood swing.

He grunted and twisted his head one way, then the other. It crackled ominously. "I'm getting into character."

"Very well, carry on." Hand to chest, I silently thanked whichever gods had put Noble Tanris into this cooperative and uncharacteristically dramatic mood. "Slouch," I reminded in a whisper. The straightening of his shoulders to meet the oncoming challenge immediately reversed. Amazing how adopting disease can take six inches off a man's height...

"Hullo, the *Integrity!*" The spokesman for the pirates rivaled Tanris in volume. "Prepare—"

Some clever soul amongst the crew chose that moment to let out a hideous moan. The sound transformed into hacking and gasping— and robbed the pirate of momentum and motivation.

He tried again. "Prepare to be boarded!"

"Nice of him to warn us, don't you think?"

"Praise the glorious gods!" Tanris shouted back. "Thank you! Thank you, good sirs!"

My brow wrinkled. *Thank you?*

But he hadn't finished. After an admirably timed pause, he called out over his shoulder in a lower voice—but one that still carried very well, "My friends! Look! Help has arrived."

As if we'd rehearsed it, our companions offered their own greetings—and questions...

"They've brought food?"

"Is there medicine?"

"Water!"

"My son is dying. Is there a healer?"

By ones and twos, the group advanced toward the bulwark. Nary a weapon in sight, the scant moonlight shone down on a pathetic lot. Some were in rags, some with lanterns slowly unshuttered, all with features pale, haggard, or frighteningly mottled.

"Help us... please help us..."

Someone vomited—which I sincerely hoped didn't signify either abject terror *or* actual illness.

"Are you sick?" came the suspicious question from the pirates.

"Do dogs have fleas?" I muttered not-very-quietly.

A chorus of murmurs arose on the *Integrity*.

"Surely they'd know... Supplies were promised! Where are the supplies? Are they going to kill us? Disease... I'll share... Sickness... Kill them... Sickness..."

They sounded too much like the Ancestors, and for an instant I stood stock still, strangely and instantly quiet *inside* myself somehow.

[We are here. Always here. Wary. Watchful. Shields. We will be shields... shields... shields...]

"Wait," I said to them, but beside me, Tanris shook his head.

"We need to put a serious scare into them. The sooner, the better."

I shook my head, too, banishing the odd sense of being in two places at the same time.

Violent light shot at us, which would have been an excellent diversion for them to employ under normal circumstances. Men and women cried out and staggered away from the brilliance. Many went to their knees, cursing and swearing fit to curl a body's ears.

As always, the gods watch out for me. Tanris's brawny shoulder blocked most of the infernal light. While he jerked his head to the side with eyes squeezed shut, I lifted my hand for further protection and peered between my fingers.

"Ah," I murmured in appreciation. "It's a lantern, I think, but with mirrors. Clever."

"Plague ship," a member of the other ship hissed much too loud to go unnoticed by anyone. Like wildfire, the terrible word swept from stem to stern.

"*Plague ship!*" a man screamed, and chaos erupted.

"Oars out! Get us out of here! Ready all! One and—back water!"

"What about our food?" Tanris thundered, crabbing along the rail. "You can't leave us like this!"

An order to trim sails led to a swift change of direction and the tangling and snapping of oars. Men, too, I imagined.

"I don't know if they should—Ah. Well. Maybe they've never seen a plague ship before?" I wondered aloud.

A good deal more shouting accompanied the panicked bungling. Someone on the *Integrity* shouted curses and tossed a lamp after the slowly departing ship. It broke against the side, spilling oil and flames. Hardly enough to do any serious damage, it still helped add to the mayhem.

Our crew continued their yelling, shrieking, and fist-waving until the pirate ship was well away. A few of the more boisterous Eagles were hushed by the first mate. "Pipe down! Sound carries uncanny-like on the water."

Tanris returned, wiping the disguise off his face with a kerchief.

Untying my scarf, I followed suit. "It almost worries me how easily we pulled that off."

Darkness swallowed the pirates, but overhead a watch with a spyglass kept a close lookout. He, apparently, could see them still.

"A little plague'll do that. Plague *and* a magical portal spewing demons?" Tucking the kerchief away, Tanris leaned against the bulwark. For a long moment or two, he just looked at me. "That was a brilliant idea," he acknowledged at last, that trace of a smile back again and this time lingering.

I bumped him with my elbow. "Brilliantly executed."

"Is that a compliment?"

"One good turn deserves another?"

"Mm. Did you get your Ancestors to help persuade the pirates to leave a bit quicker?"

Ah, there was the suspicion behind his first question. "No."

"Did they volunteer?"

My heart stuttered. My tongue stayed calm. "Not that I noticed."

He drew a breath, then exhaled inch by inch. As if I might not notice. "Is there something going on between you and them?"

"Besides magic?" I asked sharply, my good mood evaporating like smoke.

"No need to get defensive." His soft tone was surely meant to soothe me. It had the opposite effect.

"No need to patronize."

He didn't respond at once, but when he spoke again, his voice maintained its mildness. "I'm going to be blunt—"

"Oh, there's a surprise."

"If you don't come to terms with this, it will destroy you. It might destroy me, Senza, and the dragon as well, not to mention everyone and everything around you. You keep telling me you're no murderer—"

"Until now."

His jaw worked. Irritation burned, then eased. He had remarkable self-control. "Do you remember how I was standing right beside you during the Ancestors' attack? You screamed yourself sick trying to call them off. You did not *choose* for those sailors to die." He turned and gripped my shoulder. "If there is a way I can help you, please let me."

"Why would you want to help me figure out how to use disgusting magic?"

"You appear to be stuck with it, and instead of reconciling yourself to it and learning what it is—what it means to *you*— you're letting it drive you mad."

"What?" Mad? Angry, yes, but I was not teetering on the brink of insanity.

Tanris pushed himself off the railing. "You've lost your edge, Crow."

And with that dire pronouncement, he stalked away and left me staring at his broad back, straight and true as a mast.

—13—
Facing Temptations

B right Bay didn't *quite* live up to its alluring name. Seven tall ships filled the harbor, wind ruffling their banners. In the space between them was a bizarre assortment of vessels: fishing boats, merchantmen, an Asonian runner, and the local *tumarams*—large rafts with canoes attached to either side and a triangular sail to guide them. Two piers extended out into the bay; hardly enough to handle the straggling traffic. They were rather long, with a tendency to drift and sway like drunkards linked arm in arm.

Rego, our first mate, had some familiarity with the port operations. We'd ditched the plague banners the moment land came into view. Since we had nothing to unload, we did not rate a berth at the floating bundle of sticks, which suited me just fine. It had all the appearance of a disaster waiting to happen. The absence of the ship's dinghy threatened to make disembarking a chore. Captain Zakkis complained until I shouted down a passing fisherman and bargained for transportation. While we waited for them to dock and transfer their catch, I examined the town from the quarterdeck.

Lit by the morning sun, it sat in a wide bowl surrounded by low, rugged mountains. Trees descended the slopes: pines, beeches, oak, cork and more. A small river zigzagged from the heights to the bay, with a bridge spanning the sparkling ribbon. To the river's right, the buildings were picturesque cob houses. Some bore fanciful curving roofs. Others sprouted wooden towers. Still more sported grassy green roofs with goats grazing on them. Curiously, there were much fewer people on the right side of the town than the left.

The thought sparked a memory. Enikar had noted that the locals were moving away from the southern part of Masni. *This* part…

The left bank of the river provided a study in clashing architecture. Half-timbered structures stood shoulder to shoulder with elegantly domed and columned buildings. Here was a construction with the top story nearly twice as wide as the lower. There, a squat domicile of stone. Next to that, a flat-roofed plaster house painted brilliant blue and white. Occasionally, one could make out a simple cob building. A remnant, perhaps, still standing despite the encroaching styles of either continent.

Marketh City, melting pot of civilization that she was, organized various cultural designs into their own districts. The powers that oversaw such things did so with a sense of artistry. Well, mostly. The fringes of the metropolis might tend toward the chaotic.

"There's Serhat's stronghold," Tanris announced. He pointed over my shoulder to an outcropping above the town and to the south, past the architectural nightmare. From this distance, the fortress bore an unexpected appearance of elegance. "Do you see the road?"

"No, I was looking for the temple."

"The—No. You cannot mean to throw away coin and time now. I thought we agreed to get in and straight out again." He checked his person for missing valuables.

"I have some thinking to do."

"If you can save it for a day or two, I will personally escort you to whatever temple in Marketh you wish to visit. *All* of them, if it makes you happy."

"Would you?" I pressed a hand over my heart. "How touching."

"I'm serious, Crow. I don't want to spend one minute longer here than we must." His frown pushed his brows down and illustrated an unexpected uneasiness.

"You're afraid. Of Basi Serhat? The pirates?"

"Not afraid, cautious," he corrected.

"Really." I studied the rickety wharf, the variety of ships with their multi-national passengers, and the shocking fusion of culture. There was nothing more intimidating than a street entertainer juggling fireballs. I'd have to learn how to do that; it could be a useful—and deadly—distraction.

"It's a trait that's kept me alive for a long time."

"You're not that old. Are you?" A more careful study of the left side of the town revealed a pattern of Men With Swords. Pirates and mercenaries by their looks, with a smattering of impartial children to act as lookouts and informers.

"What do you see?" Tanris asked.

"A web of security. Serhat's either hiding something or he's really insecure. And foreigners." I gestured with my chin, and Tanris's eyes narrowed as he scoured the streets. "Look at that, on the pirate side by that place with the gold-plated columns. Have you ever beheld anything so garish and blatant?"

He just nodded, which could mean that he'd seen the foreigners or that the garishness did not surprise him.

The clothing worn by the more numerous Lefters differed from the Righters. There was more to it—more layers, more ornamentation, longer coats and tunics. The Righters stopped what they were doing to watch the foreigners pass. I straightened abruptly. "They're chained together."

"We can't concern ourselves with them, Crow. Not now."

"Not yet," I agreed reluctantly, already mentally teasing out an idea to put KipKap and Diti to good use. "I thought there'd be more of them after reading Enikar's notes."

"Aren't they in a mine?"

Underground. Invisible. *In the dark.* A motion toward the pier successfully vanquished my involuntary shudder. "There. The new crop's arrived."

A man with a spear herded the foreigners off the ship. Some went in chains, others behind bars. None went gently. In the few hours since we'd seen the pirates reeling in their catch, they'd intimidated the foreigners into submission or stuffed them into cages. The wind carried the sound of their moaning and bawling inland, or I'd have heard them straightaway. A whip flashed out and its victim screamed.

Fury seared the back of my throat, and my hands clenched into fists.

"Easy," Tanris warned, gripping my shoulder.

"I could help them." My voice shook. "Or the Ancestors could."

"Would you risk the foreigners that way? You need better control." Blunt as usual. "And a plan. What if you did free them? This entire area would run red with blood."

He was right. Pirate and villager, young and old—it wouldn't matter to the rightfully terrified and confused newcomers. They would attack their enemies without mercy. The knowledge only made my rage burn hotter. Is this what we—what the *empire*—did to the creatures we'd rounded up? Was stuffing them into a holding camp any better than putting them to work in a mine?

"You need to come up with a plan, Crow. What've you got so far?"

"Nothing."

"Then wait," he nodded sharply. "An undertaking of this size is going to need more than a little house in the country as a center of operations."

I speared him with a glare. Did he know about my secret home away from home? Not possible.

"We don't have the resources," he continued, "and you've yet to win your freedom from Gaziah."

Teeth grinding, I returned to studying the town, looking for options. "Shut up."

The pressure on my shoulder increased until it hurt. With a snarl, I yanked myself free.

"Stop it. Breathe," he ordered in a voice of steel. "You need a strategy or you're going to get them killed. All of them."

I rounded on him. "In the meantime, I'm supposed to let this happen." I jabbed a finger shoreward. "Do you know how it feels to be treated worse than livestock? To be voiceless and invisible?"

"I don't, Crow, but you evidently do. I'm sorry for that." His assessment, however sympathetic, only fueled my anger. He mentally shuffled his opinion of me like a deck of cards. I could *see* it.

"I do not want your pity."

"My friend suffered something I can only imagine, and I'm not supposed to feel anything about that?" he growled, stepping closer, challenging, dark eyes narrowed. "Trust me, little bird, I can feel sympathy for your pain without holding your hand and coddling you."

He hadn't called me that in a long while. I didn't move, didn't surrender any ground. Shorter than he, I was forced to look up at him. It put me at a disadvantage I disliked. "You try holding my hand and you'll lose more than your purse."

Disgust curled his mouth. "You whine about your sad and sorry upbringing, and you'll get more than a friendly cuff upside the head."

"Then we're in accord," I snarled right back. "Shall we go fetch Duke Feckless?"

"Certainly." He withdrew slightly, propping his hands on his hips. "As soon as we get ashore, we'll ask around town."

I retreated a step, too, and folded my arms. "Good idea, except we don't want to warn Basi Serhat what we're about."

Tanris chewed on his lip. "Something about this doesn't feel right."

"All the more reason to sneak in and steal the old man before we lose the advantage of surprise. You may recall that Gaziah insisted Enikar not be harmed. If he's being held hostage, letting Serhat know we're here to get him—without the price he's demanding—will only put Dear Uncle in danger."

Tanris turned his gaze to the busy harbor and mulled over that notion for a while.

Meanwhile, Senza joined us, looking from one to the other. She'd donned a wonderfully nondescript outfit in unremarkable blues and grays. A loose blouse, a skirt—of all things—with a belt from which hung a pair of pouches and a knife. A scarf covered her hair and she'd done something to her face that made her appear wan and undernourished. She tapped Tanris's elbow to get his attention, then asked, *Is there a problem between you?*

"No," I replied and smiled.

Tanris glowered. "Not at all."

Senza crooked a questioning brow. *I saw you fighting. Everyone saw.*

I flicked the idea away. "We merely had a difference of opinion. It's hardly the first time."

Anger with each other will (something) *our job.* Her hands moved swiftly, gracefully.

"It'll do what?" One day I would understand all the words of that peculiar language.

She grabbed my wrist and spelled it out on my palm while Tanris looked on. T-H-R-E-A-T-E-N. She paused, then wrote R-U-I-N. Sheer determination flowed from her and washed up against me. It was a remarkable sensation, for it bolstered my resolve and made me stand straighter.

"Are we good?" Tanris asked me.

I nodded. "Of course."

Senza beamed. *Let's go.*

"So what's your plan?" The anger bursting from him a moment ago had completely disappeared. It left not even a trace of resentment. How curious…

I confess, I did not recover so quickly. Perhaps Tanris was right, and I *was* losing my edge. Now was not the moment to figure it out. "We'll go into town. To do otherwise will raise suspicions. I'm going to the temple—" I raised a hand to soothe Tanris's displeasure, "where I will pray piously and loudly. I'll also be scouting so I can figure out the best approach for storming the castle."

"I thought we were sneaking in?"

With one fingertip, I tapped Tanris's chest. "Your grasp of humor is slipping."

He grunted. "And what is our assignment?"

"Shopping."

Senza clapped her hands and bounced, which was foolish but endearing.

"And what, pray tell, are we shopping for?"

"Information, my good man. You've done that before, haven't you?" At his nod, I gestured at his gear and went on. "It's impossible to take you for anything less than a warrior. You will appraise weapons and such, adopt an air of disaffection for your employer, and seriously consider the options of going to work for Prince Basi."

The frown melted away into a look of sheepishness embroidered with irritation. He might as well have said, *I knew that.* "And learn about his army, numbers, placement, and so on."

His head bobbed in approval, but the moment gave me pause. Since losing his wife, he applied himself to his job with doggedness, but every once in a while, he missed a step.

"Senza, you can be the employer's daughter—"

No. I want to do some shopping.

I let out a sigh. "You can't go shopping alone."

"I'll go with her," Tarsha announced from the steep steps, coming to join us.

"She needs a translator, and you don't know how to sign."

Senza frowned and signed swiftly.

When she finished, I snorted and shrugged. "She says you can come, but you need to blend in." Tarsha's full crimson silk skirt and white, colorfully embroidered blouse would draw attention. Much as it annoyed me, it drew mine. "You'll be freelancers looking for a new job."

"Freelance what, exactly?" Tarsha's delicate brows knit.

"Hunters."

At that, Senza unsheathed her knife and dragged it slowly down her cheek. The nefarious look in her eyes was something I hoped never to see again. Where had it come from?

Tarsha breathed an *oh* of surprise, then laughed. "I love it. Checking out the setting, I assume?"

"That's right." She'd always been a quick study. I'd never let her play an actual part in the strategic transportation of goods, but she had a good eye for detail and made a stellar distraction.

"Take one of the Eagles," Tanris instructed, the frown back.

Tarsha gave him a coy look. "Whatever for?"

"Your safety."

In a move I had to admire for its audacity, she stroked his cheek. "You're darling." Then she spun around. "I think I've got just the thing. Come with me, Senza, and give me a hand?" She didn't wait, but sailed off to plot and connive—two things at which she excelled.

I tried to hide my smirk. "I almost feel sorry for Bright Bay."

"She is... something," he allowed, rubbing his jaw.

"Do you need to change your dress, dear?"

He backhanded me in the chest and started away. "Your boat's on the way. You've got the others settled?"

"Everybody stays belowdecks while it's light out, yessir."

"You didn't poison the dragon, did you?"

"Not at all. I promised him an outing."

"You'll get us all killed," he grumbled. Forward progression was halted by crew members and eager Eagles crowding the rail. Sailors lowered a ladder, and soon our merry troupe had set out for the shore—and far from the miserable excuse for a pier. To my great pleasure, we hadn't been forced to wait long for Tarsha and Senza to change clothes and make themselves beautiful. Rego and a few of his mates joined us with the purpose of purchasing a new dinghy and supplies for the return trip to Marketh.

"No wind wizard?" I inquired and was met with a snort.

"You payin' for one?"

"I could, yes." I had no trouble availing myself of the emperor's treasury.

"Huh. I'll ask about, then."

"You do that." I gave Rego's shoulder a companionable clap and turned to see Tanris glaring at me. "What?"

We don't have coin for that, he signed, *and your talent with wind is*
—He waggled one hand back and forth.

"I can't believe you doubt me," I sniffed.

Happily, Girl—Senza!—appeared at my side. Weather picked out a blush of color in her cheeks beneath the makeup she wore. She closed her eyes and smiled into the wind.

I nudged her. *You stealing my supplies?*

She nodded and closed her eyes again.

"Did I give you permission?"

Practicing, she signed.

This changed things. I was proud of her initiative and natural talent, but if I wanted to keep anything safe from her, I'd need to devise something better than a simple lock.

[Magic,] two or three of the Ancestors whispered.

"You heard me?"

Senza opened her eyes to give me a questioning look.

"Not you, *Them*."

[Feel worry…] they replied. [See images… Pieces… Ideas…]

Giving Senza's arm a brief squeeze, I retreated to the relatively empty prow of the ship. "That means things are changing. *Have* changed."

[Yes… Improving… Bettering…]

"How?"

[We learn one another…]

"By all that's good and grand, you are remarkably easy to understand today."

[We listen… We sorrow…]

"Sorrow? Why?"

[Frighten the Friend… our kin… Overwhelm… Exhaust…]

"Yes, yes." I rubbed the bridge of my nose. "I appreciate your concern and the effort you're making. But you haven't explained how we went from me needing to voice my requests to you hearing me think them." And what did that do to my alleged privacy if I didn't even have the space of my own head? A fishing boat offered little opportunity for running away—and the Ancestors would simply follow me.

[We took time…]

Realization struck me like a beam over the head. The incident they referred to had been aboard the *Integrity* after destroying the *Gallant*.

When Tanris had claimed the cabin door had been locked. Sudden dizziness and nausea made me grip the rail tightly.

"You stole time from me."

[Necessary to help... teach... instruct... balance...]

"Is this—You can't just—Blessed gods," I groaned, and bent to press my forehead against the cool wood.

Unnatural fingers stroked my hair, patted my back, and attempted to soothe me. I could refuse them, or I could let it happen. What were the advantages or disadvantages of either choice?

Tanris claimed—what, exactly? The magic distracted me. Truly, I could not make up my mind about it. Although I'd accepted the title of *druid*, I didn't act the part. If there was magic that needed doing, I left it to the Ancestors. It was a curse I didn't want, but I could *use* it. There was no way to rid myself of it, and—

"The spell that brought us together," I forced out in a strangled whisper. "Pretend we've never spoken about it. Explain it to me again."

The sense of motion around and against me continued, calm, cool, earthy. I heard none of the usual exchange of opinions and questions, but perceived they still communicated with one another somehow. I decided I preferred them silently talking about me rather than burying me in an avalanche of unintelligible words and emotions. It came with a profound relief.

[Magic is in you, Friend... Always in you... The spell was a key... an awakening... crucial foundation...]

"To what? What am I supposed to do? Be?" I'd already asked that. I don't know why I hoped the answer would change.

The hesitation was slight, but I caught it. *[Bridge... connection...]*

"Doorway?"

Assent swirled around me.

"Crow?" Tarsha paused a short distance away. "Who are you talking to?"

"The Ancestors." I put my back to the water and leaned my elbows against the rail, adopting a casual, unconcerned stance. See? I hadn't lost my edge. Yet.

"Spirits?" She glanced about as if she might catch sight of them, drifting closer as she did.

"Mmhmm."

"Whose?" She'd traded her earlier vivid costume for one similar to Senza's. Disappointing on the eyes, but far more practical for this excursion.

"Mine."

She studied me, her lovely dark eyes suddenly worried and sad. Then she bowed her head and folded her arms. The stance lacked Tanris's air of self-confidence, suggesting uncertainty instead. "Have you found your parents, then?"

I opted to sidestep. "Is it necessary to have parents in order to talk to whatever spirits accompany me?"

"You see... ghosts?" Genuine alarm shook her voice and widened her eyes.

See them? No. Feel them? Often. "Of course not." A further evasion offered itself. "Do you suppose gods are the only ones who listen to our prayers? I imagine that would keep them very busy. It's possible they use messengers. Don't you think? Or maybe I *am* just talking to the gods."

"You didn't used to."

"Mmm... I've always prayed to the gods. *Always*."

"Yes." She relaxed a fraction. "Do they answer?"

"In one way or another, yes. The gods love me."

A bright smile lightened her features and the strange mood. "They always have."

We soon reached the shore and our motley party disembarked.

"We meet back here at midday," Rego announced. "We'll have the dinghy then." He marched off toward a medley of cob and brick buildings between the two floating docks.

"I thought I was in charge," I complained without rancor.

"Oh, you are." Tanris fell in beside me as I started up the beach and the waiting marketplace. "You're in charge of chaos, confusion, missing personal belongings, and utter nonsense."

Right behind me, Senza giggled.

"Your sense of humor is out of tune."

"It sounds right on key to me," Tarsha offered. "You have an exceptional talent in all those areas."

"Yes, exceptional," Tanris agreed, simmering with something that felt a lot like laughter.

"Then we are opposite sides of the same coin."

"Complementary." Tarsha drew her wind-blown hair over one shoulder and wove it into a messy braid. It looked far more appealing than it ought.

I lengthened my stride, moving ahead while she and Tanris played their silly word game. My self-imposed peace lasted all of two minutes. Senza trotted up to join me. As long as she remained quiet, I could forgive her.

You are going to a temple? she inquired, bursting my little bubble of equanimity.

"Yes."

Why?

Sand and pebbles crunched under my boots. "Because I have been remiss in my worship."

That kept her silent for several steps. *Can I come with you?*

"No."

Disappointment radiated from her.

I relented a fraction. "Not this time."

She tucked her hand into my arm and said nothing more.

"You'll be all right on your own?" I asked her as we came to the outskirts of the market.

Yes. You?

I squeezed her fingers. She stood on her toes to kiss my cheek.

I'll find you a pretty, she teased. *You pray for me.*

"I'll pray for us all," I murmured as she and Tarsha slipped off into the crowd.

"I suppose it's a waste of breath to tell you to avoid temptation here and don't give all our coin to your greedy priests."

I chuckled. "Rather, tell me to keep myself safe."

"Aye, do that." Hitching his belt straight, he made for the grass-roofed hut where knives and swords were sold. A brace of handsome, bare-chested entertainers played before it, pretending to fight, showing off the deadly wares.

I watched as he approached and hailed the dealer, and in a moment the two of them had their heads bent together, haggling, quizzing, battling with words. What a strange place I found myself in. Not the islands, no, but amongst people who called themselves my friends. Which of us were fooling ourselves?

On my own—more or less, and only temporarily—I bought myself a skewer of freshly grilled seafood and proceeded to grill the merchant. I came away with directions, a recommendation for a drink, and a handful of the man's coin. Unhurried, I made my way through the market, listening here, questioning there. Never staying long enough to make my targets uneasy, nor delving too deep into affairs. Skimming off the top. Skimming out of their pockets.

I came at last to the Temple of Doves, which seemed completely dove-less. It sat some distance back from the hustle and bustle of commerce in a picturesque grove at the edge of a pond. Not surprisingly, it was on the south—or right—side of town, which served my purposes well. Locals and natives had a better sense for these things.

It was a beautiful place. A curved, double row of columnar evergreens muffled the noise and filtered the briny smell of the sea, creating a pocket for the temple itself. It was smaller than those I knew on the mainland, but of a similar pattern. Circular, the usual thirty-two pillars surrounding the building were necessarily more... slim. Nevertheless, they bore the traditional carvings and supported an elaborate dome—this one modestly covered in plain tiles. Within, I would find small shrines to each of the Greater Gods. A *traveling* temple, people called it; meant for pious travelers such as myself.

"Ancestors," I spoke softly. "I need some time without you. Wait for me outside until I am finished with my task."

They didn't answer.

I didn't care.

Like a familiar cloak, comfort settled over me.

As I had done hundreds of times before, I climbed the stairs, then stopped to remove my boots. This temple had no vestibule with shelves for the footwear of visitors, so I set them under one of the benches arranged in a ring around the outside the pillars. It showed respect to bare one's head and feet in the temples of the gods, whether they honored a single deity or many.

A movement caught my eye. An old man stood half a dozen yards away, clothed in a colorfully striped robe. The style represented the diversity and plentitude of the gods. It also indicated that he was a member of the holy brotherhood who oversaw the traveling temples and ministered to pilgrims, wanderers, and local worshipers.

The man put his fingertips together at his lips, then bowed a slightly. "Can I be of service to you, blessed brother?" he asked.

"No, but I thank you. I've come to pay my respects and make offerings."

"Blessings on your head, your hands, your heart," he murmured, bowing again and backing away, creaking like a weathered old tree.

"And upon you, sir."

Barefoot and bareheaded as was proper, I entered eagerly. Light streamed through clever little eyebrow windows around the roof, lighting every niche. Kneeling at each, I confessed my gratitude for the many gifts the gods so generously showered on me: safety, direction, comfort, and succor. And, as always, I remained longest on my knees at the altar of Qarshan, patron god of merchants and thieves. It was there I left the best of the items I'd procured, and there that I gave my offering of herbs and fragrant incense.

Last of all, I approached the stone altar at the center of the temple—a simple thing, round and unadorned. A deep, hollow bowl carved into the rock received offerings to the lesser gods, who had no shrines of their own in this place. I left a fistful of coins there and thanked all those gods who continued to help keep me safe and well.

Hesitation dragged at my feet as I turned to leave. I did not feel I had finished…

Instinct drew me back to Qarshan's altar, uncertainty about my purpose filling me. I brushed the cold white stone, then absently traced the braided design chiseled around the top edge. "Why," I blurted, not meaning to, "have you afflicted me with magic?"

Everything had been so easy before that. I knew who I was—despite the lack of a father and mother. I knew my place in life and reveled in the gifts the gods gave me. To waste the talents I'd been given was a serious affront to them. They loved me, and I had known it, even through the long, terrible journey north with Tanris and the impossible task we had been set. I could accomplish it because of that love. Wary of taking their favors for granted, I thanked them every day—every hour. I worshiped at their temples. I gave them lavish offerings. *Why,* then, had they burdened their servant with this curse?

The Ancestors aggravated me more than they helped, and if I were to be honest, they frightened me not a little. Who were they? What could they do? *What were they doing to me?*

What I wouldn't give for things to return to the way they had once been…

I could.

The thought floated through the darkness of my mind like a distant star. The closer it came, the brighter it grew. I could go home and pick up the threads of my life. I would have to sacrifice much of what I had won over the years, but financial support was never an issue, not for the greatest thief in all the empire.

I lifted one of the tiny figurines I'd brought for Qarshan. Its wooden curves, highly polished, allowed my fingers to slide over the surface without resistance.

I could leave these unwanted ties and responsibilities. Go *home.*

Tanris would, of course, attempt to catch me again. I had the Ancestors now, with their promise they would never let anything happen to me. I would evade him. It would mean losing my home and becoming someone else—and what of it? I had the ways and means, and if things got too hot, why I could skip across the strait. There was no need to wait upon the emperor's ever-changing pleasure, nor answer Tanris's assumptions about my magic and the gates. No reason to figure out how to do the truly impossible and get the foreigners back to their own world. How had that become my responsibility?

Somewhere, there was a secure little nest for me to go to ground in. I had the funds to lay low for awhile. Be safe *and* smart.

Giving the figurine a toss and grasping it out of the air, I tucked it into a pocket and strode across the floor. Masni had boats and ships aplenty; no one knew me here. Passage to Marketh was a wish away.

—14—
It Figures

Dusty old pine needles softened the path leading back to the town proper. I'd gone halfway before thinking to check the sun. Past midday. Had I spent so long in prayer? It seemed unbelievable, but the sun had definitely moved beyond its zenith. Tanris would search for me, no doubt.

I reversed my course and headed away from Bright Bay toward the interior of the island. Taking the long way—and staying out of town completely—would hurt my fledgling plan not at all. Perhaps I would even stay in the woods for a few days. Tanris had taught me all about sleeping in the wilderness, bless his lumpy heart. If I was unable to find a secluded house and food, going short for a day would do me no harm. I patted my belly in warning. "Don't go getting your hopes up, you hear?"

It would hardly be the first time I went without a meal or two, though it had been a while. Had I grown fat since? Pinching myself, I was satisfied to discover only my sinewy self. All that tromping around the countryside with the Emperor's Eagles had not been an entire waste.

Now what? Sunlight provided beams for dancing dust motes. Cheerful birds sang in the trees. Lazy flies buzzed. The afternoon heat could not dull my sense of purpose, and I considered the details of the easiest path to escape. I immediately discarded it, because Tanris would think of it, too. Technically, I could leave from either of the island's two main harbors. Or I could avail myself of any of the little fishing villages scattered along the coast. A dozen Eagles wouldn't be able to scour the entire island, even with such a doughty commander.

Dallying in rustic hamlets held little appeal, but it beat the alternatives. On the bright side, I liked fish and most other varieties of seafood. When I arrived in Marketh, though, I would most certainly pay a visit to the Yasmin Gardens and buy myself a fine dinner. Steak. Roasted peppers smothered in white cheese. An enormous dish of greens fried up with garlic and nuts. Perhaps a little Taharri red wine.

And a bath.

Not a dunk in a wooden barrel, but in a tiled pool so large a man might practically swim. There would be a long massage after. With oils and incense. Mmm, perfect…

I'd have to give up my delightful—and expensive—apartment. Needless to say, I would have to steal back my favorite possessions. It would be too bad about the Aiobi carpet, but it was not irreplaceable. Nothing was.

Further down the pathway, a shadow separated itself from a tree. It gave me a start until the shape materialized into Tanris. In his dark clothing, he'd blended in too well.

"I so wanted to be disappointed," he announced. As he moved out onto the track, sunlight gleamed on his shaven dome and on his diverse collection of buckles and weapons.

With a hefty sigh, I stopped a healthy twenty paces from him, cocked one hip in the most jaunty manner I could contrive, and planted my hands on my belt. "Is that what you look forward to each day? No wonder you're always so cross."

"I suspected you'd decide to leave. I wanted to be wrong, Crow."

One slow step at a time, he approached. Could I run faster than he? I wasn't weighted down with a miniature armory, but he had an impressive aim, and those sharp, pointy things he wore would easily turn me into a pincushion.

"You always suspect me of something, Friend Tanris."

"Are we? Friends?"

"I'd like to think so." Friends didn't kill one another. Usually.

He gestured to the surrounding trees. "Friends don't leave without saying goodbye."

I was sure there were some appropriate instances when they did, but nothing particular offered itself.

Little by little, he closed the distance. "Did it upset you that much when I told you what I see happening with you and your magic?"

"No," I answered, too quickly.

He nodded and kept coming. "Then what's got you on the trail away from our job? Away from me."

"It's nothing to do with you. I—fancied a walk. By myself. You'd never have agreed, so I didn't ask."

"Don't lie to me. Please. Give me that much."

It amazed me he was not boiling mad. I would have accepted that, but this... this *sorrow* cut me to the quick. Why? *Why?* Was it more to do with the wretched magic? Why should I care what he thought or how he felt? When push came to shove—well, he would win, but let's consider this figuratively. It's safer. Tanris was in the way of what I wanted, which didn't seem very friendly to me. What did one do with a friend who had a contrasting opinion of a situation?

My jaw knotted. "You can join me if you like. If you can be quiet."

He halted an arm's length away, and it was all I could do to hold my place when remaining out of reach seemed the more practical choice. "Can we talk?" he asked. *Talking* wasn't *quiet,* but when I didn't answer, he went on anyway. "You want to be free, I know. What's happening to you is hard, but running won't help. Not because you'll be caught, but because you've crossed a bridge in your life. You can't go back. I'm sorry this happened to you—"

"Don't be," I snapped.

"No one should be poisoned once, let alone twice. First it was the baron, then the magic. And I'm glad for the magic—"

"That's a fine thing," I grumbled, turning away and crossing my arms. That was an obvious indication of self-protection, so I went back to the more aggressive hands-on-hips stance. I thought about these things. I *always* thought about these things. Right alongside the thinking came the opinion that folding my arms helped keep my irritation in check.

"If it hadn't happened, you'd be dead now. Have you forgotten it saved your life?"

"It *ruined* my life."

"Would you really rather be dead?"

"*Yes!*" I shouted at him, anger finally boiling free. Faced with his sudden grief, it didn't last long. "No…"

"Which is it?" he whispered, voice rough.

"I can't be—*this!* Whatever this is. Whatever the Ancestors, or you, or Girl think I have become. Or could be." Moving away, I gripped my hair. Tanris was right about one thing: running away was no cure for magic. The Ancestors, cautious now, eddied nearby. They didn't touch me, but I sensed their presence.

"Crow."

"Magic is a curse. Do you hear me? Even if I wanted to learn what to do with it, I can't because there's *nobody like me*. I've never known a druid, have you? Ask anyone in the market if they've seen or heard tell of one, and you'll get blank looks. Wizards, now, they're a *sentin* a score."

"Stop." Tanris wound his fists in my shirt, turned me around, and shook me. Anger flickered off him like sparks leaping up from a fallen log on the fire. "*Stop* it. Why can't you accept who and what you are? It doesn't matter what you call it; it matters what you do with what you've got."

"Oh, like the emperor or his malicious majesty, Prince Basi? Because they're so high-minded and decent."

If his brows lowered any further, they'd push his nose down his face. "Think about it. What if you'd found out you were a king? Or the Marketh Prince of Thieves?"

"I'd have walked away, Tanris. People in power have the biggest targets painted on them. I don't want power. I *don't want magic*." I enunciated every word as if that would somehow pound my feelings into his dull brain.

He shook me again, harder. "And what are you going to do about it, eh? You can't change it any more than you can change the color of your eyes. Magic runs in your veins, my friend, and you use it as unconsciously as you breathe."

"I do not."

"Not all the time," he allowed, voice gentling a fraction. "But there are parts of it that slip into your everyday life. Tell me that's not true."

I couldn't, and he knew it. His sturdy common sense deflated my rage. With a groan, I pushed at him. I might as well have tried to push the mast off a ship by myself.

"Look at me," Tanris ordered, and caught my jaw. "The magic awakened in you doesn't change who you are, it only changes what you're able to do. You are wicked as the day is long, Crow—thieving, arrogant, selfish, reckless, and habitually thoughtless—but you are not evil."

I would take offense at all that if I knew what to do with it. "What if it changes me, taints me? What if I get so used to it that I—"

"Stop," he repeated. "The fact that you worry about it so much ought to tell you something. I promised once, and I'll promise again, if you ever become anything like the late and unlamented Baron Duzayan, I will kill you."

A laugh threatened to choke me. "Have I mentioned that your way with crazy magic-wielders is dreadful, not to mention likely suicidal?"

"Have I reminded you today that you're an idiot?" Tanris gave my shoulder another little shake, then let me go. "Duzayan was a piece of work, and I gather the brothers in Hasiq were not a far shade from him—but tell me why you hate magic so much. You've had a worm up your nose about it since before you landed in that cage under the baron's mansion."

I bit the inside of my cheek to restrain my irritation, and started back to the temple. I needed to move, and it clearly wouldn't be toward the first ship sailing for the mainland. Tanris fell in beside me. "Wizards are not logical. They don't play by the same rules. They're temperamental, contradictory, and irrational." I may have stomped.

"Uh-huh," he said, earning a glower.

"Have you no experience with them outside of Duzayan?"

"Now and then. Their power makes them a real challenge to oppose, but in the end—at the most basic level—they're still men and women."

"That's a generous assessment." I kicked a pinecone. "I have hated wizards and magic my entire life."

"But why? Have you never known a good, kind magic-user? Think about it before you answer."

I thought. While I did, I played with the figurine I'd taken—stolen, I realized now—from Qarshan's altar. The idea put a knot in my throat. I'd never even thought of doing such a thing before. How insane was filching from the god that protected and directed me? What would the consequences be?

"Well?" Tanris probed.

There'd been the old man, Jelal, who'd expected our arrival out in the middle of nowhere during our egg-gathering adventure. He'd read the bones for me, and I had to admit his reading had been true, and he had been helpful. Brother Oman, an Ishramite priest, also came to mind. He was a decent sort. And I supposed that all the Ishramites qualified as 'good' magic-users. In theory, anyway. "One or two, I suppose."

"So be one of the good ones."

Easy as making a pie. Was pie-making easy? I'd never tried it. "That seems self-contradictory. As you just informed me, I am 'wicked as the day is long.'"

"There's a difference between wicked and evil."

I snorted. "Enlighten me. This is a philosophical lesson I *must* hear from you."

When we passed the temple, I slipped inside to return the figurine to the altar. Tanris refrained from commenting. He said not a word about the gods he didn't believe in. He let lie one of his favorite lectures—what the Temple Custodians actually did with all the riches that passed through their hands. When he put his mind to it, he had extraordinary self-restraint. At the edge of town, Senza leaned against a low cob wall and munched on crackers and cheese. A glance about showed no sign of Tarsha.

"Tarsha is still in town, doing more shopping. Rego and his friends are with the boat. Senza and I found you in the temple," Tanris said before I could ask. "I asked her to wait here while *I* took a walk."

"You *lied* to her?"

"No, I took a walk. I didn't tell her why."

"Look at you, being all clever."

Senza smiled and waved, and when we came abreast of her, she fished something out of her pocket and held it out in her fist. *For you,* she signed, pointing at me. Dumping her find into my hand, she bounced on her toes.

What should greet my eyes but the same little figurine I'd inadvertently stolen from Qarshan. So great was my shock, I almost dropped it

Senza froze. *Is it bad?*

"No. No, not at all." I smiled at her, forcing as much good cheer into it as I could. "It reminds me of something I never thought to see again. Thank you." A kiss on the cheek soothed her worries. I waxed poetic admiring the skill that had gone into the gift, the beauty of the woodgrain, how it felt smooth as a polished stone.

Tanris wore an arch expression, but what could he know? He hadn't seen what I'd done, nor the item in question. He didn't know how the gods watched over me.

Senza took my fingers in hers and walked with me to where the others waited. I let her do it, just as I'd let Tanris shepherd me back down the trail. If I hadn't recognized the subtle hand of deity in Tanris's appearance, the figurine struck like a club to my skull. I misliked the notion that they would clobber me into submission. It sounded painful on many counts, however well deserved.

Rego was put out at my tardiness. Tarsha welcomed me with a smile. Then, all the way to the ship, she drilled worry and compassion into the back of my head.

Ensconced once again aboard the *Integrity*, the four of us squeezed together into one tiny cabin to discuss what we'd discovered during our little foray. Even Rego had been useful, sharing small talk with Tanris while the group waited on the beach for me.

While they talked, I sat in a corner making notes, a map, and a list. Situated as I was, no one could see what I'd written and I kept it that way. The conversation eventually drifted to trivialities. I folded my papers and put them in the pouch on my belt.

"Do you have a plan?" Tanris asked. I looked up from fiddling with the figurine to discover him watching me. Not a hint of doubt or suspicion clouded his aura.

"I'm working on it." Getting up, I made my way out of the room's stuffy confines and up on deck where I could breathe again.

Naturally, Tanris came right behind me.

"Problem?" he asked, low voice for my ears alone.

For safety's sake, we had not discussed our plans with the captain, the crew, the Eagles—and assuredly not with Tarsha. They knew only that we had come to Masni to find something for an anonymous *client*.

"Tarsha stays here on the *Integrity*," I said.

"Agreed."

I'd not expected that. "If I keep her busy for a while, will you pack what we need?"

"Are you sure you don't want to do it the other way around?"

"No, you are a packing fool. I mean genius. Here's the list."

He snorted. "Always full of compliments."

I'd scarce passed the list to Tanris before Tarsha ran out of yes-or-no questions and the women came up out of the hold. Conversations with Senza tended to be short.

"I don't know if I can sleep down there tonight!" Tarsha exclaimed. "It's so hot!"

"It'll get cooler," Tanris assured her, "or you can sleep on deck."

"Is it safe?" she worried, glancing toward the shore.

I slipped away to the galley. The two were still talking about the weather when I returned a moment later, brandishing a pair of wine bottles and four mugs.

"Drinks, anyone? You might need them to manage dinner tonight. Cook has decided on some sort of stew made from last night's meal and today's lunch."

While I repaired to the quarterdeck with the ladies, Tanris begged off. His excuse? He had a new set of throwing knives to sharpen. Behind Senza and Tarsha, I lifted gaze and hands skyward at his choice of explanation.

"Bring them up here and sit with us," Tarsha implored.

"I'd like that." He glanced down at his boots, looking for all the world like an addled teenager. Was he falling for her? Gods protect us. "Give me a bit. I'll be back," he promised.

"You've got to admire his dedication to his blades," I said, lifting a bottle to toast his departure.

Tarsha held her mug out. "It's possible I could like him. In another time and place." She took a deep drink. Calm, devious, I refilled it… several times.

:-:

"They're meeting us at the Craggy Pocket cove, like we planned?"

"Oh, no." I clapped a hand over my mouth and stopped in the very center of the sun-washed road. In the rushes nearby, a thrush warbled a song much too cheerful for so early in the day. Or for Tanris's nagging. "I might have left that bit off the captain's instructions…"

Tanris took two stalking steps toward me with his face arranged in that horribly neutral mask he wore when things were about to get ugly. I could decipher nothing of his feelings. This was becoming a habit.

Senza flinched and took a hurried step back.

"Except I'm not actually an idiot." I rolled my eyes. They'd been getting plenty of exercise lately.

At my feet, Not-an-Egg's chortle lit a patch of grass on fire. I stamped it out, hitched up my pack, and continued along the road that ran next to the river.

Tanris sucked in a breath. I was half a dozen steps away when he let it out in a gusty sigh. "Must you do that?"

"At every opportunity," I tossed back over my shoulder.

Senza and I had assumed the guise of pilgrims. Inquiries about the temple yesterday had turned up a nugget of information that served us well: Masni boasted a holy place only twelve miles inland—the Sanctuary of Henitra. We weren't going there, of course, but it got us headed in the right direction and provided us suitable cover. I suspected that Tanris secretly objected to what was tantamount to a lie, but I was more clever than he. I named him my bodyguard so he didn't have to pretend to be something he wasn't. He'd never pass as a humble pilgrim, anyway.

It hadn't been difficult to leave Tarsha on the *Integrity*. She'd had too much wine, and we didn't. She might also have had a tiny sleeping draft. Despite that precaution, we took care to be quiet when we left. Captain Zakkis's instructions included tarrying at Bright Bay for the day, then sailing with the tide—with or without Tarsha. He would meet us on the north side of Serhat's fortress. A simple diversion, and simplicity made any heist go more smoothly.

'Simplicity' had meant leaving the stalwart Eagles behind. Tanris had dithered over that decision, but I'd persuaded him that KipKap and Diti would stand out less than the soldiers. That, and a few of us could get in and out of Serhat's stronghold more quickly and easily than the entire troop.

To avoid too many questions about the dragon, we passed through town before dawn. We'd met a stream of farmers and tradesmen on their way to market, but that, too, had been taken into account. We withdrew into the cloaking woods until the traffic died down. KipKap and Diti wouldn't pass as pilgrims at all, so they had to masquerade as slaves—which required collars or chains. Diti had balked savagely, but KipKap stared for a long, long time into my eyes, then eventually nodded consent.

"Pet slaves of Crow," he said. Equal amounts of humor and ferocity glinted around him.

"Don't be a clown. Here." I'd given him the key to the ugly, heavy collar, then held the second out to his brother.

"What is clown?" KipKap inquired, tucking the key away into his clothing.

"A performer. Someone who does things to make others laugh."

"A clown I will not be." He stretched his too-long neck and settled the collar more comfortably.

I winced. "I'm sorry..."

"Is safer, yes?"

An understanding nod seemed insufficient. Impulsively, I pulled back my sleeves and showed the marks on my wrists—gifts from my stay with Duzayan. "I've worn chains. I know what it's like."

KipKap bent his head and brushed one long finger over the scars, which had begun to fade. Then he made a clucking noise. Diti came to peer at my arms, at my face, then my arms again. Eventually, he grunted acceptance of his own collar.

"You say free soon?"

"I promise, Diti," I said, and gave him his key.

He stroked the knife at his waist. His own silent promise and the look in his strange eyes sent a shiver up my spine.

"You'd best hide that. You're not allowed weapons in this place. We don't want to make anyone so suspicious that they kill us first and ask questions later, eh?" I tried a humorous tone.

It fell flat.

KipKap, though, presented his marvelous mace to Tanris. "Carry this, please."

"I'd be honored," Tanris replied, accepting the weapon as KipKap laid it across his hands. While I pondered the word choice, the two figured a way to add the staff to our guardian's harness in such a manner that KipKap could pluck it free if needed. Then we were off. Sullen still, Diti trailed behind. Senza fell back beside him, kindly keeping him silent company.

Months of chasing down foreigners up hill and down dale made this trek easy. Or easier, I suppose, than it might otherwise have been. Basi Serhat's not-very-humble abode stood atop a tall bluff, which required us to labor uphill the whole way. The bit on the road winding between craggy hills was not difficult, but too short to provide much respite.

An hour after we'd left the main road, we came upon a narrow path that restricted us to walking single file. It went the direction we needed to go, so we took it. Rambling back and forth across the rocky hillside, there were places where the trail had fallen away or disappeared entirely. Tanris had no trouble finding where it resumed, and 'back-and-forth' was more practical than straight up. Twice, we had to crawl up the hill to bypass a slide. Trees and enthusiastic shrubs sometimes blocked the way, or sometimes offered hand- and foot-holds.

Shoving through the undergrowth didn't make our passage particularly discreet. Branches cracked and snapped, loose stones tumbled free, and there were the frequent grunts of effort. Humidity —Did I mention we were on an island?—and perspiration had us all drenched. One of the plants we plowed through didn't agree with Diti; he kept sneezing. Like a dainty kitten. To our great good fortune, dainty kittens sneeze quietly. I feared, however, that Senza would wear her lip through, biting it to keep from laughing.

While we struggled past a particularly noxious tangle, Tanris stopped dead in his tracks. KipKap nearly crashed into him. I stumbled right into the big foreigner's back. Like a tree himself, he hardly even swayed under the impact. The others were far enough behind not to be involved in the muddle. Except Not-an-Egg. Where had he got off to?

"What is it?" I asked, peering under KipKap's arm.

Hand close to his side, Tanris made one of the signs the Eagles used. Fortunately, it was one I recognized: *trouble.*

"Are you lost?" someone with a loud, rasping voice inquired.

"So it would seem," Tanris replied, unruffled. "We're looking for the Sanctuary of Henitra. We were told it was hereabouts."

Someone—not the raspy fellow, for it was in a higher pitch— laughed. "Haven't heard that'un before."

"Who's that with you?" Rasper demanded. "Come out of there. Slow like. Hands up where I can see them."

The five of us oozed out of the bushes into a glade barely big enough to hold everyone. On the uphill side, they had a natural advantage. Rasper posed on a wide, flat boulder and trained a spear on us. Four other men brandished swords and loaded crossbows. By their lack of uniform and general appearance of hostility, I assumed they were pirates.

"Who are you?"

"Pilgrims," I offered, meek and mild as a maid. "My brother has told me I am wicked as can be, and I fear he is right. I don't mean to be. I've come to ask the goddess for forgiveness and guidance."

"Wicked? You, little mouse?" The fellow closest to me poked my side with his sword.

I gave an exaggerated wince and forbore to tell him it was *bird*, not *mouse*.

Diti hissed a warning at the man. Ignoring him, KipKap solicitously patted my shoulder and murmured: "Hurt, Master? Bleeding? I fix."

"Stand down," the guard ordered, waving his weapon at KipKap.

"Sorry. So sorry." KipKap pressed his hands together in front of his face and made himself as small as possible, which is a wondrous feat for someone his size. At the same time, he edged closer to me. He plucked at the white pilgrimage scarf I had donned in town—as if begging me for protection from these fierce assailants. I expected he could flatten them like bugs, even without his mace..

"You'll have to go back," Rasper said.

"Why? Where are we?"

"You're trespassing on the estate of Prince Basi Serhat."

"The prince? I didn't know we were so close. I was hoping to see him after we visited the sanctuary. There's this misunderstanding about a small piece of property, you understand." I patted my clothes, ostensibly searching for a nonexistent document.

"Go to the mayor's in Bright Bay. Y'get no passage without an appointment."

"Oh, is he accepting visitors today?" I swiveled an earnest look at Tanris. "Can we make it back by, say, this evening?"

"Prince Basi is a busy man," Rasper cut in. "There's a long wait."

"That is unfortunate. How long, do you suppose?" I inquired, leaning heavily into wistfulness.

Rasper glared at me. "A month, if you're lucky."

"Oh." I glanced around at my companions. "Oh, but—But…"

"Hie your buts outta here." The guard took a step forward. He shifted the aim of his crossbow at my chest—which effectively stoppered my snicker at his play on words.

"Wait. Where did you get these?" Rasper asked, pointing at KipKap and Diti with his spear.

"Near Marketh, in Bahsyr." Tanris was as unintimidated as always. "Where they're free for the taking." When he set his mind to it, he could drum up the most wolfish smile.

Diti, of course, took exception to the availability of himself and his kinsman. Unlawful knife in hand, he surged forward with a deep growl—whether to skewer Tanris or Rasper, I knew not. I—Well, reason clearly fled, for I spun to block him. As if time slowed and my senses leaped to new heights, I felt a little tug as the blade pierced my shirt. Its continued motion immediately did the same thing to my skin, jerked to an exquisitely painful stop, then veered to the side, opening me up as it went.

—15—
The Craggy Pocket Problem

I fell into what was clearly an alternate reality. The altercation continued, but as if time had slowed. Diti shouldered me aside, only to have Senza catch his free arm, throwing him off balance.

As my body swung around, Tanris came back into view. He clocked Rasper with the mace, continuing the motion to hand the weapon off to KipKap—while drawing his sword and lunging at the next attacker.

It was a lovely thing to see. Not a motion or a moment wasted. Something—the Ancestors, I don't doubt—caught me and gently lowered me to the ground. Just as slowly as the scene played out, the fire of pain spread outward, promising to consume me.

KipKap rattled the third pirate's gourd—with his fist—and sent the business end of the mace swinging at another.

Senza, bless her, dragged Diti completely around and the pair of them collapsed in a heap. She followed up with a punch squarely in the mouth, which, because the two orifices were so close together, meant she punched his nose, too. I flinched, for it must have hurt terribly, but at the same time I was glad for her fearlessness. Diti deserved that.

One pirate guard remained on his feet.

Tanris threw himself between him and our party, and time resumed flowing as it ought. Bloody sword up, he glanced at us, pausing for the slightest fraction of a moment on me. "Get out of here. *NOW!*"

The shout galvanized everyone.

Senza leaped up and yanked on Diti's hand to urge him upright. When he swatted at her, KipKap barked something foreign and jabbed a finger back the way we'd come. Diti froze for the merest instant, then scrambled down through the little shrubby tunnel we'd forged. Senza disappeared after him. KipKap gestured for me to follow. When I moved too slowly to suit him, he seized my shoulder, hoisted me up, and hurled me down the hill.

Bump! Bang! Skid! Crash!

Fetching up against the trunk of a tree knocked the shout right out of me. Hail-like needles showered down everywhere. I couldn't move. Agony lacerated me like a white-hot spear. While I was still gasping in shock, KipKap lifted me like a toddler and set me on my feet. The entire world keeled over sideways.

"Go. Follow Diti."

"The fellow who just tried to get us killed?" I squawked, grabbing hold of him to keep myself upright. "What about Tanris? What about *me?*" But one does not argue with KipKap when he is full of purpose.

"Tanris comes," he informed me.

All I heard was lots of shouting—and not by Tanris.

"How do you—"

"*Come*," he insisted and helped me on my way with a six-fingered hand firm on my shoulder.

Stumbling, sweating, *bleeding*, I staggered after the others. Then, with no warning whatsoever, Diti and Senza disappeared. I rounded the corner and they were *gone*.

KipKap, still behind me, shoved me to my knees. On that level, I discovered the gap in the bushes my companions had dived into. I wriggled in, the motion promising to tear Diti's hole open the rest of the way. KipKap pushed.

As soon as she saw me, Senza grabbed my arm and pulled. After I slithered to a stop, I crawled forward to give KipKap room, then rolled onto my side, breathing hard. My teeth squeaked from grinding them in a useless attempt to keep from groaning.

Senza put a finger to my lips.

With a nod, I attempted to quiet the complaints my abused body wanted to make. Not that it made any difference—I couldn't possibly be heard over the sounds of crashing and breaking as the pirates chased Tanris. I had an instant to inspect our refuge. Trees, shrubs, and vines covered the space above us, blotting out the sky. It looked for all the world like a humongous, overturned bird nest. Diti crouched against the far wall, still gripping the knife, rage on his strange face.

Then KipKap plunged in and slammed into me, eliciting a drawn-out grunt on the verge of tears. Quick to silence the sound, Senza pressed her hand over my mouth. I peered toward the entrance, waiting for Tanris to arrive. The cacophony of the chase plunged down the hillside, then passed us by. More crashing, punctuated by swearing, heaved down the hill. Then, with a scrape and a jingle of gear, Tanris slid into view, evidently none the worse for the wear. He rolled to his feet without the slightest pause. The nest roof forced him to crouch, but he moved so fast Diti had no time to assume a defensive posture before the sword point touched his throat. Tanris loomed over him, quivering in anger of his own.

"Friend Tanris…" KipKap whispered, imploring mercy.

No one breathed. A tiny blossom of crimson at the sword's tip appeared.

Senza let go of my mouth to cover her own.

KipKap closed his eyes and bowed his head. "My blame," he murmured. "Take me in his place."

"Why," Tanris gritted out, "would I trade an intelligent life for an idiot's?"

"He is dear to me."

"Crow and Senza are dear to *me*, and your fool brother almost got them killed." He leaned lower, blazing with fury. "Are you so delicate you cannot play a simple role to help us, Diti? To help your brother? Your people? All you had to do was *stand* there."

KipKap whispered a translation.

Diti didn't move, didn't speak. His anger mutated into something unreadable, and I could only describe the space around him as *murky*.

"This is the only chance you will get." Tanris flipped out a cloth he wore at his waist as he straightened and wiped his blade. The *hiss* and *crack* when he re-sheathed it made everyone flinch. "You put any of us in danger again, and I will plant this steel in you."

I raised one brow in astonishment. "Really? That's not usu—"

"Quiet." His brows dove downward in reprimand. An instant later, he knelt beside me. "How bad is it?" he asked, suddenly gentle as he pulled my hand from my chest.

I shook my head. How was I supposed to tell him if I wasn't allowed to speak? I struggled into a sitting position, my pack pressed awkwardly against a small tree that supported the nest wall.

He divested me of the belts, packs, and gear, then sliced through my shirt ties without so much as a by-your-leave. The blade sheared through the fabric all the way to my britches. My alarmed gasp went tragically unnoticed.

"I need to check it. It's going to hurt. Be still. Be silent." He met my eyes, allowed me a moment to brace myself, then probed at the wound with two fingers. Gently, I'm sure, but it blazed with agony. The injury was high near my armpit—and it dawned on me that my heart was perilously close to the same place. Without a doubt, the gods loved me. The knowledge didn't keep me from moaning, lips clenched so tight I tasted blood.

Girl made a hissing, shushing noise as she held my hand hard against her chest. While Tanris explored the damage, I banged my skull against the tree—little movements, so as not to cause the leaves to shake and reveal our hidey-hole.

Eventually, he drew his wrist across his forehead as he decided what must be done. "It's deep." His jaw worked. "Not a puncture wound, though, so there's that." He shrugged his pack off and dug through one pocket to produce a snowy square of folded cloth, which he pushed against the wound.

Agony.

"Senza, hold this."

While she did that, Tanris took my pilgrimage scarf and tied it around my chest over the bandage. "You need stitches, but not here. Not now. We need to go before the guards return. Hold your arm still."

The journey up and down the mountain had thus far been a two-arm task. "You're joking." I shrugged my shoulder (the uninjured one), trying to restore a modicum of dignity.

"No. If you can keep it pressed tight, it should slow the flow of blood."

"My hero," I murmured, attempting a sweet smile. Lightheadedness made it a challenge. "Can we rest here a moment?"

He nodded, curt. I nodded back, grateful. I didn't like the promised pain of stitches, but it beat being dead. The problem thereafter lay with how this injury would affect my ability to do the job ahead.

In the meantime, KipKap had knelt beside his brother. With their heads together, they carried on a hissing conversation. None of us understood a word.

Tanris frowned at them for the briefest of moments, then turned away. Efficient and practical, he examined all sides of our upside-down nest for another exit. When he found none, he made one, but not until he'd peered through crooks and crannies at what lay beyond.

Not-an-Egg was nowhere in sight.

I closed my eyes and tried to remember when I'd seen him last. Failing that, I spent a panicky moment imagining him running through the woods in terror. Lost. Or skewered. *Stop it, fool,* I chided myself, and worked on blocking out the admittedly hushed noise my companions made. It was somewhat harder to ignore the hole in my chest through which my lifeblood leaked...

On the bright side, I had more than the moment's rest I'd requested. Tanris disappeared for several minutes, and when he returned, we squirmed out, one at a time. I hung back until only Diti and I remained. Nose to nose, I looked him right in the eye. "I trusted you," I said. The entirety of my disappointment weighted every word. I didn't wait for a response, but brushed past him and hitched myself out the too-small opening. Thank the watchful gods, KipKap was there to help.

Still no dragon.

The four of us stood under the arms of a sheltering tree. I searched uselessly for my scaly little companion and wished we could stay hidden in the strange nest. The idea of traversing the island with my chest on fire and blood seeping out of me made my mouth dry as cotton.

I should have looked at the damage myself. I've been wounded before. Perspective might have eased my fear.

When Diti finally emerged, we followed Tanris across the hillside to a scant opening among the trees that might be named a clearing if one were in a generous mood. He told us to sit tight, then disappeared again for what felt like forever. Which was fine with me. The lack of motion lowered the bonfire of pain to a mere sear.

KipKap assumed watch. A glowering Diti crouched near him. Senza gave me a drink of water and fretted, and I mentally talked myself through the agony. The red-hot poker scorching my skin was not actually the size of a dinner plate, but only the length of my hand. The blade had not cut through tendons or sinews. I could still move my arm, though I very ardently wished not to. How, I asked myself, did it compare to having my arm chomped by a demon? The rich used them to protect their treasures, and I'd dealt with a few. On reflection, I decided I preferred the single stroke of the knife to lacerating talons and jagged teeth. And how badly would this injury compromise our undertaking?

The wary, uncomfortable silence was broken by Not-an-Egg creeping up on us—in plain sight—belly low to the ground and tail held straight out. As if that might somehow conceal him. Relief made me light-headed all over again. The beast crawled into my lap and his nose went without deviation to the bloodied, makeshift bandage. He creaked softly and sat up higher to examine my face.

"I'm all right," I whispered, running my free hand over him to check for any wounds *he* might have received. "Sshhh… We're just resting for a bit."

Knobby brows furrowed, illustrating his doubt, but he leaned his head against my undamaged shoulder and waited patiently.

When Tanris returned, we resumed our journey, which was more horizontal than vertical, thank the gods.

"What now?" I asked him when the undergrowth opened up enough for me to walk alongside. Not-an-Egg loped at our heels, as close as he could get without tripping me.

"We'll get you someplace I can wash that wound out and sew it up. What were you thinking, Crow?" He didn't look at me, but I didn't miss his fierce glower. "You could have been killed."

"And *that* would have ruined the mission." Funny how things could go from heart-pounding to agonizing to sour in so swift a time.

"I didn't say that."

"Not in so many words. Forget it. Apparently I wasn't thinking at all." I slowed my steps to let him move ahead and, more importantly, buy myself some space.

Tanris stopped, jaw working, and waited for me. Grabbing my arm —which was turning into an appalling habit, all around—he made sure I kept moving. "You're no fighter, Crow. If you've said it once, you've said it a hundred times."

"Quite right. I'll never do it again," I promised.

"Idiot."

"Ingrate."

"Stop talking," he growled.

"You first." Out of the corner of my eye, I could see the smile threatening his mouth. That pleased me.

"Like old times, eh?"

"Not quite. I haven't stolen anything from you today."

He laughed. He *actually* laughed. I likely would have stumbled in shock if he hadn't been holding onto me.

"Do you know where we're going?" I asked, covering the brief loss of composure.

"To storm the castle, but from around to the north."

"Excellent." I hoped. "Will you tell me what you did back there when you hid us?"

"I created a false trail and disguised ours."

"Oh, you *are* clever!" I leaned against him, looking up and batting my lashes. Immediately, he pushed me off, leaving me to trudge on my own again rather than being hauled along like a contrary donkey.

"Yes, and don't you forget it." He paused for a beat, a sideways squint underscoring his concern. "Are you going to be able to do this?"

"I have to, don't I?"

"Can the Ancestors help you? They healed you before."

Intriguing, horrifying idea...

He wasn't finished. "Where were they during the attack?"

"I haven't heard them since—" I had to think about it. "Since our secret meeting aboard the *Integrity*."

"Did you chase them away?" His head swiveled so he could spear me with one of Those Looks. "Are you blocking them somehow?"

My mouth opened and closed like a fish out of water. *Blocking them? Could that be done?* "N-not to my knowledge. To both questions."

He grunted. What he meant was, *You need to work this out, and the sooner, the better.*

"I don't know how to do—anything. With the magic." Must clarify. I was not a completely useless lump.

"They still babble at you all at once?"

"Nnnooo... I got them to refrain themselves to two or... five or so. Mostly. It's an improvement."

He bared his teeth. That was new. And unsettling. "Have you asked them for help? Can they give you a few lessons or something?"

Resistance grabbed my throat. I walked along a little further without replying. "Why is my magic important to you?" I was careful not to make the question an accusation.

"I care about what I see it doing to you." His voice was gruff. "It's another reason for me to come after Enikar. Even if he doesn't know about your variety of druids, he may point us in the right direction."

What was I to think of this... solicitude? As we moved, I kept my arm pressed against my side, which shortly had my hand cramping. My *left* hand. Surreptitiously, I rubbed it. Already, the joints felt knotted and halfway useless. No doubt, my imagination was working extra hard.

"Are we making camp tonight?"

"Yes, of course," Tanris threw a startled look my way. "No fire, though I wish I could cauterize that wound. Keep infection from setting in."

"Shades and ashes!" My stomach dropped into my boots. "Is it that bad?"

"I want to stop it from *getting* bad."

"What if we sacrifice some wine instead of charring me?"

"I would if we had any."

"We do. Why wouldn't we?"

"Of course we would." He made a noise like a strangled chuckle and shook his head.

"It's only a little flask. I haven't even touched it yet, though it has severely tempted me about forty times today."

He just snorted.

As it happened, there was more *uphill* to traverse on the north side of Basi Serhat's stronghold. We arrived shortly after the sun set, and Tanris located a place where we could spend the night. A jumble of boulders surrounded us, and trees grew through them in strange, unnatural shapes. As I stared at them, I prayed they weren't haunted.

"Have you got anything in your packet of herbs that will relax you?" Tanris asked. He had his own, and dropped it and himself down beside me. We hadn't even broken out our dinner of bread, cheese, and apples. No sizzling steaks or roasted fish. Or bird.

I chewed on the inside of my cheek. *Relaxed* meant *vulnerable*.

"We've got to take care of that wound. It's deep, Crow. I suspect your rib might be cracked too."

Still, I hesitated.

He tugged at my shirt to pull it off. "I will keep you safe, I swear it," he murmured.

Our eyes met. His word was as good as—no, better than—gold. Not a conclusion I was willing to share with him. I managed a nod and fished a small brass tube out of my pouch.

"Adamanta dust." Expensive stuff, but awfully useful. The pretty, delicate flower it came from was native to the eastern parts of the Asonian Confederacy. Its inability to be cultivated led to a steep price. A breath of it would cause unconsciousness; more than that could induce a comatose state or even death.

Tanris crooked a brow as I uncorked it and spilled a trace onto my index finger, then handed the tube to him. He closed it and returned it to my pouch without comment.

I, however, had words. "If I die, the Ancestors and I will make the remainder of your life utterly, wretchedly miserable."

"More miserable than you already do?" he shot back, mouth quirking ever so faintly.

I sniffed. Prematurely, but it hardly mattered. The careful pinch I administered to myself wouldn't render me insensible, but it would make me as pliable as a half empty wineskin. I'd be dopey into the bargain. Tanris caught me as I tipped over sideways, and lowered me to the ground.

I remember the taste of leather. I remember wild, trauma-inducing pain. Girl gripping one arm, Tanris kneeling on the other. Dragon tongue dragging across my face and the incongruous odors of fish, flowers, and wine... More, I recalled the sound of strange voices. Some were deep, vibrating my bones. The others whispered like the crackle of autumn leaves underfoot. The Ancestors, I realized. Were they bargaining? With who?

An uncomfortable sleep was disturbed in the middle of the night when an unholy *scream* brought us all up out of our skins about ten inches—even me. That kind of heart-pounding is a rude way to awaken, especially when injured. Tanris went to investigate. Not-an-Egg trotted in a few minutes later, the perpetrator of the scream dangling from his jaws. He approached to offer me the nice, fat rabbit he'd caught. I scratched his scaly chin and declined. He didn't seem to mind, and set to crunching away a few feet from my head.

"Is fierce flying lizard," KipKap commented, tension easing from his broad shoulders.

"Indeed," I agreed, and settled back down in my blanket. Adrenaline had chased the effects of the Adamanta dust straight out to sea. I'd be awake for the rest of the week.

"Where from are flying lizards? Are there many?"

"He's from the north, and no, not many."

"Flying lizards be precious." He paused and lowered his voice. "Magic."

"Oh? That's interesting. Good night, KipKap." I turned on my side and chased dreamland, where I'd been caught in a pelting rain. Not an ideal fantasy to return to, except the raindrops had transformed into clear, glittering chunks of stone. The problem then shifted from getting wet to lamenting the lack of space in my pockets. One couldn't just leave diamonds lying about on the ground.

Tanris returned shortly. From beneath the edge of my blanket, I watched Not-an-Egg generously share a bit of his kill with him. That came as a surprise. The dragon was not particularly fond of Tanris. Or maybe he was, and he thought I was asleep and wouldn't see.

"You eat it," Tanris murmured. He gave the little beast's head a rub. "You need it more than I."

If there was anything further to their exchange, I missed it. I also missed everything else until a determined ray of sunlight attempted to scorch my eyelids. With a groan, I rolled away. As luck would have it, Tanris was right there on his knee beside me, a flask of water in hand.

"Thirsty?" he asked.

I frowned at the flask, then propped myself up to take a drink. The stuff tasted like the wine sacrificed to the god of unfortunate holes. Things were already looking up.

"How are you feeling?"

I considered my condition as I sat up, every movement ginger. "Astonishingly well, but for the sludge coating my mouth."

"The Dust?"

"Mmm..."

He looked at my chest, brows wrinkling.

I glanced down. Bare skin and stained dressing met my eye. "I have another shirt in my pack."

"Did you loosen this last night?" With one finger, he flicked at the drooping bandage he'd wrapped around my ribs. One layer had been raggedly torn, and the rest sagged.

I pressed my fingers to my forehead. "Was I in the throes of a raging fever?" That would account for the voices I thought I'd heard. For the life of me, I couldn't recall so much as a phrase.

"Mmm..." He wore skepticism so very well. "I tied this up over your shoulder to keep it in place."

I tucked my chin to see for myself. The shoulder bit was all askew, and the remnant sagged noticeably. "I can't think of a single reason I'd choose to expose more of my inners to the outers."

Tanris tugged again, pulling the bandage down. The cut beneath it was a fierce shade of... pink. The edges had knit together, nicely decorated by my companion's neat stitches. Or some of them, anyway. At least half were gone entirely.

"Well, I'll be a Prince of Pasina!" I exclaimed.

"I thought you didn't want to be a prince."

"Pasina is not a real place." I probed the vicinity of the injury with a cautious finger. It hurt outrageously but, all things considered, I preferred wrinkly-and-closed to gaping-and-oozing. Whether it was actual pain or the memory of a knife slicing into me, cold sweat dampened my forehead. I feared dwelling on it would decimate my poise. "And if I really were one of their plethora of princes, no one would notice if I left the country."

"If you've never been there, how can you say with absolute certainty that it doesn't exist?" Tanris inquired, harking back to a debate we'd had about the existence of the fabled Amber City. The discussion had ended in a draw.

Its reappearance startled a glance out of me, but he didn't give me time to respond.

"The dragon slept by you most of the night."

"Yes...?"

"Lift your arm. Easy, now. Does it hurt?"

I nodded. "It burns a bit, or rather it tingles. And it's stiff."

"Stiffness you can work out."

"And a burn I can ignore." I grinned. "I may have to keep the little beast around."

"Because he's magic?" Shrewdness narrowed his gaze.

I opened my mouth to retort, but my usual flair for words deserted me in the face of my own hypocrisy.

With a grunt of disgust, Tanris got to his feet. "You slept through a patrol from the stronghold last night. The dragon warned me. I distracted and misled them until they gave up. They decided I was a fox." By the gleam in his eyes and aura, that pleased him well.

"What's going on? First you're blushing at Tarsha and now you're friends with the dragon?"

He pursed his lips. "It's too bad you're still an idiot." From a flat rock next to me, he picked up a plate and handed me breakfast—a repeat of dinner.

"Tanris?"

"What?"

"Thank you."

He nodded and began packing things up. "There's a place nearby with a good view of the stronghold. You ready?"

"Always. Soon as I bathe, put on a shirt, and pay a visit to the bushes. Don't say it—" I pointed at him threateningly. "You're the one that let me sleep so long."

"Don't make me regret it. Start moving, birdbrain."

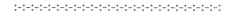

The outcropping Tanris had chosen provided an exquisite place to look over the fortress—and the sea, the beaches skirting the bluff, the town, and nearly half the island looking north. With his spyglass, I studied every inch of the building. Satisfied, I examined the paths around it, the patrols coming and going, the roads leading away…

"Two roads," I muttered.

"Is that a problem?" he inquired, stretched out on his belly beside me beneath the concealing branches of a floppy pine.

The easternmost wound down to Bright Bay. The other descended seaward in a series of sharp switchbacks heading west. "Where does that go? Has Serhat got his own harbor? A dock?"

"Not on any of the maps, but that makes sense."

I handed the spyglass to him and scooted back, staying out of sight. From my pack I fished out a tube as long as my forearm, and from it I pulled out the papers I'd taken from Enikar's office.

"Handcarts on that one. Supplies, I imagine." Tanris kept the glass trained on the small section of visible road. "There are foreigners pulling them."

KipKap immediately left his lean against the tree-trunk and sank to his belly next to Tanris. Curiously, Diti followed him partway, then hunched at his feet. I noticed he no longer had his knife. Without a word, Tanris handed KipKap the glass.

It wasn't five seconds before the tall foreigner started clicking his teeth in agitation. "We go there. Look better?"

"We can't spare the time," Tanris objected. "In and out."

Finding the map the duke had sketched, I turned it until it aligned with the view. I gave a small grunt of satisfaction. "We'll make time. The trail we'll use to get to Craggy Pocket runs that way. We need to scout it out and avoid any surprises." If all went well, we'd be dashing along that path right about the time the sun came up. And if Enikar was too old and creaky to dash, why I'd have KipKap throw him over one shoulder and do the dashing for him.

Tanris's reluctance was obvious, so I showed him the map. Maybe one of these days he'd trust me.

"Very well. Senza and I will go take a look. We'll be right back."

"Best we all come." I got to my feet and dusted my backside. "I want to see what we'll be dealing with in the dark."

"Are you up to it?"

The simple exercise of getting ready for the day had set my wound to throbbing and burning. Experience suggested that without the intervention of the good Brothers of Ishram, I should have a fever right now. "I'm fine."

"If you're not, this rescue is doomed."

"No, it's not." I swung my pack over my left shoulder, opposite the cut. "I'm sure you'll manage very well without me." A wave of bitterness fueled my jump down to the game path running alongside the rocks. It jarred my wound, which was a stupid thing to do.

"What are you—"

I was already walking. Not-an-Egg followed with flapping wings and took the lead as if he knew where we were going. It would take time to sneak into the stronghold to discover where the old man was being held. A hiding spot for one within Serhat's walls wouldn't be too much trouble, but for five? That meant we had to stay outside. Or at least they did. I could go ahead, find Enikar, and bring him to Tanris. Yet the longer we stayed in the vicinity, the more likelihood of discovery, chase, or capture. None of that would do Enikar any good, and I couldn't imagine our health would improve in captivity. And the longer Serhat had the duke, the faster his patience would wear down. How long would he wait for an answer to his demand for ransom?

The only solution? Magic.

Tanris expected me to use it—or the Ancestors—to do this job. Magic was the only way we'd find Enikar quickly in that pile of pirate-riddled rock. It shouldn't be hard. It was how I'd found my way out of the dragon's cave in Hasiq. How I'd found Tanris's wife. And how I continued to find the foreigners outside Marketh.

And... it was how I smashed two ships with full companies to kindling, setting one on fire in the process. Could I trust the Ancestors not to turn the fortress into rubble with Enikar stuck inside? Or *us?*

Before the Ancestors had come into my life, I'd done the finding and transporting of goods on my own. I could do it now, without them. Gods knew it would be safer that way.

Twice, Tanris called out for me to wait up. I ignored him and walked faster. Thinking about using the magic made my palms sweaty and my lips dry. I needed time to learn it, and I had none.

It took an hour to get from our first lookout point to another above the twisting road. I'd already tucked myself into a hiding place beneath a shaggy evergreen by the time the others caught up. The trail hugged the hillside below and disappeared from view beyond a pile of rocks. Below that gaped a hole as tall as one of Gaziah's marble statues and perhaps as wide as my outstretched arms.

Movement by the opening held my attention. A steady train of shackled foreigners pushed and pulled handcarts stacked with rocks out and empty ones in. A handful of men enthusiastically wielded spears and whips. Corpses filled a ravine below the road. A quartet of men swung a limp body between them and heaved it over the edge and into the pile. The impact made corpses further down the slope tumble out of view, presumably into the sea. The men laughed. Behind them, the foreigners remained disturbingly quiet, gazes trained on their feet.

My companions crawled up beside me. I heard Senza gasp and Diti let out a long, shuddering growl.

Below, a whip lashed out and its victim staggered and fell. My sense of utter outrage shot up and kept climbing. There was *no* reason or excuse for such inhumane treatment. Not gold or jewels, not vengeance, not war, not... *anything*.

"Great, shivering shades," Tanris muttered.

KipKap froze. Shock and horror rolled off him in sheets that did nothing at all to calm my swiftly rising fury.

"I will kill him," I said, and the frost in my voice surprised even me. Ice and rage seemed so contradictory.

Tanris sent me a sideways look. "We have one—"

Senza squeaked and pointed. A jangling sliver of violet split the air in front of us with a searing hiss. Like the other we'd seen in the strait, the energy sparking and crackling from it lifted the hairs on my arms and up my neck. Maybe even my head. With a high-pitched whine, blackness flooded the center in a long, irregular gash, opening much faster than the other. Lightning leaped out of it. *Crack! Crack!* *BANG!* Chunks of rock exploded and tumbled in every direction.

My companions ducked and covered their heads. I didn't. I sat still as a bug trapped in honey while pandemonium heaved around me.

Boulders the size of cottages wiped out figures on the road, human and foreigner alike. Something fell out of the blackness of the gate—*several* somethings—smoking and smoldering as they tumbled to the earth and sea below.

Violence shook the ground. Trees toppled, and the living below us ran screaming in utter chaos. They ran into each other. Shoved *each other* down to save themselves. With a tearing sound, another ravine opened near the first. Half a dozen smaller fissures followed. The hillside shifted downward, and the bodies rolled away.

I squeezed my eyes shut. Why did this sight bother me more than seeing people bombarded, knocked down, and killed?

Tanris swore, and I *felt* him drag Girl close to protect her.

Diti howled.

KipKap wept.

Not-an-Egg did his best to shove himself underneath me. I hugged him tight and waited for the world to right itself.

—16—
Diverse Discoveries

The incident lasted only seconds, leaving a surreal, ponderous silence. People shouted. They must have, for their mouths were open though I didn't hear them. Boulders bounced seaward, every contact with the earth damped to a mere *thud*. One passed scant feet from us, churning the air in its wake. Behind it came an entourage of smaller rocks, shrubs, sticks, and forest detritus. The voice of their passage was muted as though by the thickest of wool.

My companions scrambled away from the edge where we perched. Tanris shook my shoulder. He may have hollered. I dragged my gaze upward to his face. A bloody scrape reddened one cheek and I frowned. Where had that come from? I couldn't hear what he said, but he still had his wits about him—he signed. *Move. Now. Danger.*

He pulled at my arm and I went with him, though gods knew why. Habit? Trust? Instinct? I wanted—needed—some vague thing that eluded me.

Tanris led the way, and I brought up the rear with the dragon. The others strung out between us like beads, hollowed by what they'd seen. Girl kept crying. The two foreigners barely shambled, shoulders drooping, grief turning them gray.

I cannot even describe my own condition. A strange silence spread throughout me, made more complete by the deafness caused by the explosion. It was cold there inside, but ringed by searing anger. The silence was not still. Ribbon-like fingers rippled outward, though that didn't seem logical. It was as if they—as if *I*—searched for something. When one tendril encountered an amorphous shape, I jerked aside and stumbled.

Not-an-Egg pushed against my knee. The motion kept me up. Steadied me.

What was that?

I stopped and looked for it again. "Xuchai? Cimara?" I named two of the Ancestors and a moment later felt the reassuring touch of invisible hands on me.

[Here… Here, dear one… we are here…]

The ability to hear them left me dizzy with relief. "What is happening to me?" I asked.

[Misery… Imbalance… Fragments…]

"I'm in pieces? Because of the gate?"

[No… Yes…]

"Don't be exasperating," I complained, rubbing my forehead between thumb and fingers.

The spirits eddied around me and I realized I saw glimmering strands of… of *energy*. They drifted so peacefully, it was mesmerizing. Calming.

[Gate is magic… Crow is magic… Different magics… Gate magic and heart magic happened together… together… at once…]

Had any of them ever used that many words in one sentence before? *Irrelevant, Crow, focus!* "What do you mean, heart magic?"

[Obvious…]

"I—cared about what I saw happening at the mine."

[Yesss… Sympathy.]

"Sympathy will only get me in trouble and make my job harder." I glowered. I certainly didn't need to start feeling sorrow and regret for every little coin and knickknack I relocated, or the marks that would miss them.

[Sympathy will make you strong... We will show you...] Their voices—two of them, I thought—wound around me, overlapping and echoing as they revealed what this confluence of *gate* and *heart* magic had wrought in me. One, as I understood it, had crashed right into the other and shaken loose parts inside me. Mazhar parts. It was astounding and—

"Crow?"

I blinked. Tanris stood in front of me, Senza behind him, and the foreigners—Why did I keep calling them that? I needed another word, a better word. Their people name. KipKap and Diti hovered several paces off, melancholy lumps. "What?"

"Are you well?"

"Yes. No..." I scrunched my brows together as some of the weight of what I'd learned pushed down on me. "Yes."

Tanris looked me over, peered into my eyes, then lifted his hands to examine my skull.

I leaned away sharply. "What on earth are you doing?"

"I'm checking your head. I don't see any blood, but we shouldn't take chances."

One brow up, one brow down. "You've lost your mind, haven't you? I'm fine, Tanris." Drained and tired beyond belief, but fine.

"*Fine* people don't stand in the middle of nowhere gawking at nothing and twitching."

"I was twitching?" How unsettling.

He let out a noisy breath through his nose. "Have you got a fever?" He pressed his hand against my forehead, and I allowed it. It was slightly less invasive and far more brief than the head-rubbing.

"Satisfied?" I asked when he stood back and put both hands on his hips.

"No. How's your wound?"

"Stiff and sore," I admitted. "I don't think carrying a pack is doing it any favors."

"Hot?"

To appease him, I opened my shirt and stuck my hand inside to check the temperature of my skin. "No hotter than the rest of me. All this trekking about in the heat of the day is toasty business."

Without warning, he loosed my shirt ties. With a forefinger, he tugged it open and looked for himself. "It looks all right..." He sounded almost disappointed.

"Thank you." I tied myself back up. "Can we go now?"

"I wasn't the one holding us up," he remarked drily as he moved off.

A surreptitious glance at our surroundings revealed nothing familiar. There'd been a long meadow after we left the overlook. At the moment, we wended through a thick stand of cork trees, most recognizable for their leathery skins. Or bark, rather. None of the trees had been harvested, which I found peculiar. Were they protected as part of the prince's estate? Curious, but hardly relevant to the current matter.

It struck me that I could hear now. Very well, in fact. How long since the gate had opened? "How's your hearing?" I asked Tanris, working my hand as I walked—and the opposite shoulder, as well. I couldn't afford to lose the use of either.

"Fine," he said slowly, suspiciously. "Why?"

"The noise of the gate. Did it not bother you?"

"Some."

I followed him down a little path—a path I hadn't even realized we trod.

Tanris circumvented a clump of trees to the right, I chose the left. "After it closed it felt like I was under water, but only for a while. I take it you're still having trouble?"

"No..." But I couldn't remember when the sensation had faded.

[Magic... magic...] The Ancestors whispered.

"Did it affect me differently than anyone else?" I asked them.

"How would I know that?"

"Sorry. I forget you can't hear the spirits."

"Ah, so you're talking to them again. Can they find us a way into the keep?"

"Are we there?"

He moved a low-hanging branch aside. The high stone walls stood a good three hundred paces away, bordered on one side by a ravine. The remaining space was completely cleared of vegetation that might screen the approach of an invading army… Or a small troop of thieves. Anyone crossing would be in plain view of the guards, who patrolled the wall in desultory fashion. Bored, likely. Who would come to attack the pirate prince in his pirate home with all his pirate guards?

"Plan?" Tanris asked.

Crouched down on my heels, I studied the layout from our vantage higher up the hillside. After a few minutes, I set my pack down to fetch out my spyglass. Walls staggered up the incline as though built by a drunk. "Let me go look." I snapped the glass shut and tucked it away.

"I'll come with you."

"No, you won't." I transferred a few tools into the custom-made pouch I used for such tasks.

"I don't want you going alone. It's too dangerous."

"I am touched, Tanris." It was the work of a moment to thread the pouch onto one of my belts. I offered him a sunny smile. "I've been doing this sort of thing in my spare time. You know, between all the reading and fishing I engage in."

His jaw inched out, but he nodded reluctantly.

"I'll be back in a few hours." With a cheery wave, I trotted off into the forest surrounding the heart of Basi Serhat's little kingdom. I'd gone all of two dozen yards when I became aware of being followed. Tanris made for an annoying nursemaid. With a gusty sigh, I stopped. "What?"

Not-an-Egg bounded up and wound himself around my legs, creaking happily.

"Oh, it's you." No need to snap my patience and turn it into something sharp, after all. "What are you doing here?"

He gave a toothy grin and pranced about, flapping his wings.

"You cannot come."

In the space of one breath, he melted into the image of pure dejection. I stared. He somehow looked more crestfallen by the second. He was very good at this, I'd have to admit. If he sank any lower, he'd have to lie down.

"Unless…"

He perked, golden eyes lifted, hopeful and adoring.

I felt my decision swaying toward allowing him to come, then caught myself. He was still only a baby. Was it safe? "Unless," I said slowly, uncertain of the workings of the gods, "you can be absolutely quiet. No talking, hooting, hissing, flapping, or any other noise-making. No twig- or leaf-crunching. *No* noise." I snapped thumb and flat fingers together like jaws closing on prey.

Not-an-Egg startled backward, then gave me a considering study. After a moment, he got up and walked again, each step curiously cat-like. Not a sound did he make.

"Bless the gods of clever dragons." I chuckled and rubbed his knobby head.

Pride arched his neck, though he remained quite still and stealthy otherwise. I crouched down to his level and explained to him what I meant to do—as if he perfectly understood every word. Did he? I knew not. He often seemed to. And who was I to question the gods that had brought the two of us together?

Well… best not go there. I'd been tallying up questions and doubts by the score lately. Had my earlier prayers and sacrifices been sufficient? I cast a glance up at the sky visible through leaves and needles overhead. "Protect me on this venture, and I promise I will return to the temple with proper thanks." I paused. "Twice. At least."

Not-an-Egg nudged my leg, but didn't make a sound. He was taking this very seriously. As should I.

Starting off again, I began my exploration on the west face of the stronghold. It would give me the advantage of the setting sun shining in the eyes of any onlookers. This required a quick dash across the empty road at a strategic point, and I slid behind a stubby evergreen to make sure I'd gone unseen. Not-an-Egg glided up beside me like a whisper. Satisfied, I moved on.

It was deliciously freeing, this slinking about in the descending twilight. My earlier exhaustion vanished. How easy to fall into the habit of noting every detail: doors, windows, guards, guard stations, vines growing up the walls, the very stones themselves, lights, sound, smell, motion of any kind. Not-an-Egg solemnly copied me for a while, then ventured out a little to investigate on his own, although he was never out of sight for more than a minute or two. I wondered if he could sense my concern...

Serhat's fortress, situated as it was atop a steep hill, boasted three walls altogether, though not concentric. The first, with a trio of small guard towers, barricaded a formidable ravine. The second enclosed the bailey, and the third wrapped snugly around the keep proper. I bypassed the chasm and a few gaping holes in the rock, ignoring questions offered by my active imagination. If they housed another dragon or a den of demons, I would know soon enough.

The second wall would have been more challenging had Basi Serhat taken the time to polish the granite. The particularly mistrustful were prone to the habit. As it happened, the only snag I experienced was when my newly acquired puncture protested in the most inconvenient way. Well, not the *most* inconvenient, praise the gods of the afflicted. I gave myself a stern warning about forgetting divine patience and mercy. Taking the gods for granted could have calamitous consequences, and I would be devastated without their continued goodwill.

I was frequently devastated *with* it.

Yet every obstruction I had ever faced had been overcome by the gifts of the gods. True, some of them had come at a pace so slow and plodding that progress was hard to mark. Others had sped in through the back door by way of convoluted alleys, but things had always worked out for the best. I had learned to trust the wisdom of the gods.

So... *who was I to question the gift of magic...?*

And yet I did. Time after time. The thought of the stuff running through my veins made my throat tighten and my brain turn to sludge. *Could I not simply go back to the old way of accomplishing things by agility, skill, and astonishingly keen wit?*

The scrape of boot on stone snagged my attention. Crouched in the shadows against the middle wall, I twisted my head to look straight up. I'd chosen to enter on the northern side of the structure where the wall abutted a bell tower. The steep layout must have required some clever engineering, and it had resulted in an assortment of rock walls and cliff sides. This route still involved plenty of climbing, but in stages.

The guard overhead glanced down the crag, then out over the water. Unconcerned with the likelihood of marauding crabs from the sea, he lingered for a while. I thought I caught a whiff of pipe smoke. Beside me, Not-an-Egg bumped his head against my knee, no doubt wondering at the delay. The wait seemed an appropriate time to stretch my shoulder and massage my hand. In due course, the fellow wandered away, and we made our ascent. Soon we were slinking through the shadows again—my favorite sport next to shimmying up invincible walls and through unassailable openings. It had been a long time since I'd had such freedom.

Up and down, this way and that, my companion and I glided. In a whisper, I reminded him of the wretched demons the rich on the mainland kept to protect their goods. He'd had his own encounter with them and seemed in no hurry to repeat the performance. Much to my surprise and pleasure, he proved an able scout. Twice he warned me of someone approaching, and several times he climbed the walls to peer into windows for me in the hopes Enikar would be easy to find. He returned without success.

From the roof of the bell tower, I plotted out three favorable courses for getting into and out of buildings. As I did, I pondered the information Enikar had sketched out in his notes. Incomplete as it was, my knowledge of other castles provided reasonable assumptions about the layout. Since we'd already investigated the smaller towers, that left the main hall. A tower itself, it was much larger than the others. And then there were the dungeons. Mulling over that reminded me of a pair of possibilities for entrance seaward, on the bluff, where deep shadows had marked the otherwise granite surface.

The first and easiest cleft in the cliff wall proved itself a useless chink. It extended inward only a half dozen paces. The second required removing a small pile of rubble and squeezing through a narrow space. It was uncomfortably reminiscent of the Ghost Walk. The lean opening dropped us out into a sizable chamber—or so Not-an-Egg informed me. Thanks be to the gods who so auspiciously blessed me, the dragon could see in the dark.

I took out my witch light and held it high. I hadn't expected to find the remains of civilization, but this area was clearly a part of the fortress above, though it appeared deserted. The place had been ripped asunder. The broken tiles upon which I stood were a good ten paces lower than the rest of the room. A jagged, irregular crevasse separated the two levels. With Not-an-Egg as my eyes, we discovered that the little canyon broke through one wall. Its floor rose upward, bypassing halls, stairs, and any other manmade design. Was this recent? That would explain the lack of guards. I couldn't help but wonder at the damage it had caused further up within the fortress.

As I considered how best to proceed, the sound of voices, cries, and groans drifted to my ears. Basi's prisoner cells, I imagined. Hopefully, Enikar was not there, but in some princely, civilized apartment. Though, on second thought, the latter would be harder for me to break into unnoticed.

I daren't explore any further, for dawn was not far off. I set out to rejoin my companions. Creeping about the city is a different exercise altogether than skulking about in the woods, but under Tanris's meticulous tutelage, I'd learned a great deal. To sneak up on him was delightful. Behind Tanris, I said conversationally, "Did you save any breakfast for me?" It came as no surprise that Tanris had chosen to go without a fire. There would be no bacon, not even a cup of kaffa. So disappointing. What was *not* disappointing was Tanris's reaction.

He shot up so fast and so high I thought he might take flight. He landed with his ax in his hand.

Senza, sitting nearby on a fallen log, tumbled backwards with a squeak and came up with her crossbow pointing at me. KipKap and Diti, too, dove to either side, taking up shelter behind the trunks of trees.

"*Crow!*" Tanris growled. "Do you have a death wish?"

I crooked a brow. "What, you didn't hear me coming?"

He hefted the ax as if he might cleave my skull, glared, then stowed it away. "Well? Did you find a way in?"

As the others returned to their places, I took a seat on Senza's log. "A few, though sadly I saw no place that screamed *Here's where the Duke is being kept*. The best entrance is through an opening on the cliff side. It leads into a practically perfect—and once civilized—chamber. I'll have to go inside to get a better look."

"That's fine. We're ready," Tanris said, picking up his pack.

"Tonight. I need some sleep. And I go alone. I only came back to tell you this is going to take a while. We cannot all go trooping around the place, knocking on doors and shouting for dear Uncle Enikar."

"We are not splitting up."

I looked askance at him. "You do know that in a typical situation this would require days—even weeks—to prepare."

"This isn't a typical situation."

"Not for you."

Senza and the others waited with packs in hand, heads swiveling between Tanris and me as they watched the debate. I was the only one sitting.

He leaned his head one way, then the other, cracking his neck. "The longer we camp out beneath Serhat's walls, the more likely we are to be discovered."

"Then go back up the mountain and camp. Better yet, go back to the ship."

"No."

"Yes."

"You've used the Ancestors to find people before. Use them now."

I thought about it, then shook my head. "I don't think so."

"Why not?"

"Because, as you keep pointing out, I cannot control them."

Senza took a step forward, her brow creased. *Not true, she signed. You seek foreigners. Find easy. Send them for Enikar.*

I had little confidence in what might happen, particularly after the debacle at sea. A knot formed in my throat at the thought. It didn't go down easily. "I have no way to describe him to them. I don't know the man, do you?"

Senza clearly did not, and Tanris shook his head. "What about the things you took from his office?" he asked. "Can they glean something from those?"

"Like a hound?" Even to me, I sounded affronted.

"Why not?"

Bilious reluctance crept through me.

"Well?" Tanris prodded when I didn't move.

I closed my eyes. If they could locate the old man, it would make our task easier. Easier than me prowling through the stronghold on my own. From my pack, I pulled out the leather tube with Enikar's notes and spread them out on the tree trunk, then closed my eyes again. They'd answered me once when I'd thought *at* them. (That was the only term that seemed to fit the occasion.)

[Ancestors?] I queried, then listed several of the names I knew.

As always—or nearly always—they ruffled my hair and clothes. Their dry, whispery voices assured me of their presence.

[Can you use these pages to find the man who wrote them?]

[Possibly… Posssssibly… It is a conceivable thing…]

The corners of the pages rippled.

Diti growled. Even with my eyes closed, I was aware of KipKap putting a hand on his brother's shoulder—of Tanris crouching opposite me, and Senza hugging herself.

[He will be in the stone keep on the bluff below. Not in the towers, but deeper. Perhaps underground.]

I had the impression of shadowy figures gathering beside me, stroking the papers, leaning down to smell them. The Ancestors murmured amongst themselves, and the cool energy of their presence expanded. They eddied in and away, back and forth, brushing against my companions as they did.

Senza shivered and rubbed her arms.

[Yes… yes…] came the answer at last. A score or more of affirmative responses overlapped and intertwined. *[If he is near, we can find… discover… uncover…]*

[Do it. Please,] I instructed. Politely. And they raced away, rustling branches and kicking up old leaves, dust, and a trio of hapless moths in their wake.

I touched the talisman beneath my shirt, then rolled the pages to stow them in the tube, in my pack. Tidy as you please. Useful work for occupying hands that wanted to shake. "They're going to look." Uneasy, I turned and sat on the log, elbows on my knees and one fist inside the other as I waited.

"Good." Tanris bobbed his head in an approving nod. "Can they guide him out?"

"If he's locked up?"

He grunted.

"He's unlikely to hear them," I pointed out, "but they can guide me in."

"If he's wounded, you're going to need help getting him out."

"I suppose so, yes. And if he's not, I won't."

Tanris said something under his breath about stubbornness. Before I could ask, he announced he was leaving to patrol the area, and if I left before he returned, he'd break my arm.

I didn't believe it. I doubted he did, either, and remembered how he had once told me to never make a threat I wasn't prepared to carry out. Maybe he *did* mean it...

Senza sat down on the opposite end of the tree trunk, near where the branches began. She looked sideways at me, but said nothing.

KipKap watched me for a long time, then asked, "Do Ancestors pain you?"

"What?" I blinked. "No. Not... exactly. At least they didn't before."

"Before?" His too-deep voice gave a hollow, ringing quality to the word that sent my imagination in unpleasant directions I refused to go.

"Do you sing?" I countered.

"Sing. Yes. Sometimes."

"I've never heard you. I imagine you have a—a talent. Don't you think, Girl?"

She stared at me as if I'd lost my mind, then nodded.

"I suppose now is not a good time to demonstrate." I sighed.

We fell quiet, and birds overhead took up a cheery song of their own, aided by the harmony of a pair of bullfrogs. Their deep, booming croaks carried through the trees better than one might expect. I did not remember seeing a pond nearby and closed my eyes, mentally retracing my steps. After a moment, I paused, *feeling* my way rather than thinking it.

The way the Ancestors had shown me...

That strange space that had opened inside me remained. I tried to decide if its temperature had changed. In focusing on it, I noticed that barely-banked fire. That... *anger.* No, it was more than that. It was—impatience? Need? Energy, certainly.

I veered away from it and back to the search for the pond. When we'd been in the moors early last spring, I'd found the little cabin where the seer lived. I hadn't even known he existed. But the Ancestors had. "One of them knew that place," I murmured to myself.

"Knew what place?" KipKap asked, something *round* and *mellow* about his voice.

I shook my head. The Ancestors did not know this place. Therefore, could I?

When I opened my eyes, I discovered Tanris crouching before me. Concern crooked his dark brows.

"I'm fine," I whispered.

"Are you? Then don't go drifting off like that again. At least not until we're back aboard the *Integrity.*"

"I was looking for the pond."

"Find it?"

"No. Maybe. I don't know."

He nodded. "You're extraordinarily unconvincing, which isn't like you. You have a talent for oozing self-confidence, even when you're panicking inside."

"Ah."

"Just for the fun of it, where do you think it lies from here?"

I squeezed my eyes shut and pointed.

Tanris grunted. "I guess you found it."

"I did?" Astonishment had my mouth hanging open. Not willing to invite bugs—or to look insecure—I snapped it closed.

Tanris stood. "Are your friends back?"

"Not yet."

And so we waited. I had never seen a group of people that could be so very still. I knew I could, but this was—eery. Or maybe I was spooked by the experiment with the strangeness inside myself. Annoyed, too, that Tanris insisted on going in the stronghold with me. Did he think I couldn't handle the job? Or...

A chill prickled up my spine. He thought I was mad. He'd said as much, hadn't he?

Terror swept through me. *No.* My hands curled into fists. I rejected the notion. It was not—could not—be possible. I got to my feet and started away. Somewhere. Anywhere. *Now.* Then I immediately forced myself to slow. To *wander* rather than bolt. I felt Tanris's gaze on my back. Curious. Worried.

Nonononono...

I stopped where I knew he could still make me out in the shadows under the trees. To keep my hands from shaking, I shoved my fists into my armpits, then stared across the field at Serhat's walls. The rising sun gilded the edges of stone and glinted off the armor of patrolling guards. Beyond the fortress, light danced on the waves of the strait. I focused on the memory of their endless surge, up and down, up and down—until some semblance of calm settled over me.

I found I'd taken out the little figurine Senza had given me—the twin to the one I stole and then returned. Over and over it turned in my heedless fingers. *Qarshan, god of merchants and thieves.* It was as if he said, *I am here, watching over you. Did you think I would forget you?*

"Thank you," I murmured.

I would be fine. This would be fine—whatever 'this' was.

Rather than panicking, I needed a plan. The current rough idea provided the beginning of a stable structure. I placed the information I'd learned thus far upon the broader map of the goal. Whatever Tanris thought about my mental instability, I was not so mad as to guide our little company across the open and over the wall in full daylight. Logic suggested the underground route would be more reasonable no matter the hour. Getting my companions from here to the cliff face unseen demanded the cover of darkness.

Would Tanris agree to wait until nightfall?

He *must.*

Even so, we would have considerable ground to travel—back down the slope by way of the woods, around the stronghold, down the cliff, and into the fortress. Retracing our steps would take too long and put us at the mercy of Serhat's men, which meant we'd have to descend the cliff and go around to the cove.

Too many variables.

I massaged my wound while I thought. There was a dull ache there, and it still burned as I'd told Tanris. It amazed me that Not-an-Egg had healed it so well. If I thought about it, the feat might scare me. What more could the little beast do?

No. Not going there. Going straight back to the Duke Dilemma. Even if we succeeded in trekking across the distance, found Enikar, and managed to lug him out of the fortress, could we do it before tomorrow's dawn? Being trapped inside throughout a full day was likely to be a death sentence.

"Why, oh why have you put me in this situation?" I muttered. Prayed. "I have felt your love through my entire life. Until now. Have you deserted me?"

Had the gods deserted me, or was this some crisis of faith? Perhaps I was being tried. It had happened before, and look—I proved myself every time and the gods *still* loved me after.

I drew a deep, slow breath, then let it out again. Once, twice, three times more. "I am called Crow, and I am a thief. I am not just any thief, mind, but the best and most famous in all the glittering empire."

The Ancestors returned in a rush, hissing, blowing, tumbling, exultant. *[Found the man... Found the prize! Come! Come! We will show you! Hurry! Must hasten! Hurt, he is...! Bleeding! Hunchinghuggingrockingdistressed!]*

"Dandy," I grumbled. There was no getting around it; I would need help, and where one of the others went, *everyone* went. Where was the version of me who walked away from an impossible job? The one that tended foremost to his own welfare—else how could I live to lift another day?

If I left now, like any sensible expert thief, Tanris would go on anyway. Senza would go with him. KipKap and Diti must follow as well, for they were unlikely to get off this island of slavers on their own.

"Calm yourselves, my friends." Yet it was me who trembled like a leaf. It was me breathing so fast my head swam. Bizarrely, inconceivably, I could not let these people march to certain failure and death.

They needed me.

And I was going to need magic…

—17—
The Choice

In the end, Tanris had no choice but to wait until dusk—which was the earliest time I would agree to. First, as I'd said, I required sleep. Second, some pointed questions to the Ancestors had assured me that Uncle Enikar was not actually on the very edge of expiration. Third, having *some* light by which to see might reduce the chances of injury and involuntary cliff-diving by the others in my group.

Moving five people through the woods and across the steep slope right beneath the fortress walls would have taken hours. Hours we couldn't afford. Instead, I relied on Tanris's ability to sneak entire troops of Eagles about the countryside. To my surprise, he opted for a longer route than the one I'd traveled the night before. Why? Because we could move faster if we needn't worry about making noise—not that he accepted anything but the greatest of stealth from us.

The woodland extended all the way up the headland from Bright Bay to Serhat's fortress. Not-an-Egg made a most excellent scout, helping us avoid two patrols. His first warning arrived in plenty of time to veer out of their path. The second was delivered in a rush from a branch overhead. We dropped to the ground where we were. More or less concealed by the bracken, we held our breaths while the guards passed within spitting distance.

"Did you even *see* the big one?" a distinctive rasping voice demanded. "Like a bull, but with arms and legs, eyah?"

"It was supposed to pull the main wagon," a calm tenor pointed out.

"It was *supposed* to be drugged," yet another complained. "Lucky it didn't kill more than trees and shrubs."

"And the cook fires. And stew."

"Don't forget the dog."

This beast sounded an awful lot like Gwurand, the avalanche creature.

"The dog's no loss, and the stew wasn't worth eating anyway," someone said with a laugh. "That thing saved lives."

The conversation about the cook's terrible—and frankly unbelievable—dishes dwindled in the distance. We walked on, stopping in the fringe of woodland right at the precipice. Now came the tricky part. We must climb down and traverse crevices and ledges more suited to cats than budding burglars. The rock formation here was in horizontal layers, making the going easier, though the 'paths' started and ended in strange places. Upheavals in the distant past had wrecked any sense of order. Great segments had tipped over sideways or fallen, leaving rubble behind.

Naturally, leadership for this part of the journey fell to me. What I would have undertaken in a matter of minutes turned into a slow crawl consuming half an age. Or it felt like one...

Owing to the size of some and the inexperience of all, our path included a lot of up-and-down to find the least traumatic passage for the most people. The darker it grew, the more treacherous the going became.

The little dragon had no difficulty crabbing sideways across the rock. While he waited for us, he helped himself to eggs from several bird nests. Twice he knocked protesting avian parents right out of the sky. His creaking blended into the susurrus of the waves below, but we learned in short order that he had an admirable whistle. It sounded much like the forest birds in the woods near Marketh. Also, he was not above throwing pebbles.

At my head...

Again, he helped us avoid gaining the attention of two more patrols.

The closer we came to the cave I'd discovered, the greater became my wish for silence, despite the concealing noise from the waves. I might as easily have wished for wings. When yet another stone clattered down into the blessed rumble of the surf, I leaned against the rock face and waited for disaster to strike. "Have none of you ever snuck silently *anywhere?*" I lamented under my breath.

KipKap touched my shoulder and gave me a quizzical look, to which I just shook my head.

At this point, the cliff extended outward overhead, protecting us somewhat from view. I craned my neck to watch the wall high above. Though difficult to believe, no stalwart, conscientious guard leaned over to investigate the racket we'd made. Not-an-Egg peered down at me. Hanging upside down, he stretched his wings out against his perch while he licked the remains of another snack from his snout. At least one of us was enjoying himself.

Tanris, who had brought up the rear, finally clambered past the others. Evidently, all the loose rocks had already been dislodged by that point. "Why did we stop?" he asked in a low voice near my ear. "Are you all right?"

His concern immediately, *tangibly* touched me. I'd have pulled away, but there was nowhere to go. The startling warmth conflicted with the chill mist of sea spray borne on a steady wind. I waved a hand as if that might diminish the sensation. It succeeded in driving Tanris back a cubit or so. "It's the increasingly intolerable intuition. There are too many of us."

The murmuring surf muffled his grunt, but he nodded understanding. "Which will be more dangerous—splitting up or staying together?"

"You want *me* to make that decision?"

"You are the one in charge."

It was my turn to grunt. "Except when I'm not." I leaned out to glance up at the wall again. A looming shadow against the encroaching night, it remained suspiciously empty.

"Not easy, is it?" he commiserated. Both of us kept our voices down.

"It is, however, an excellent argument for my practice of working alone." If I sent the brothers back, Senza would need to go too, to keep them from being claimed as slaves if someone should come across them whilst waiting for us.

Which would put her in danger...

But I couldn't trade her presence for Tanris's, hoping she could help me get Enikar to safety. I had every faith in her ability with her crossbow—as well as knives, blunt weapons, sewing needles, and sheer determination. But would she have the physical strength to lug an old man around? Even half an old man?

Bringing either of the brothers as a substitute was asking for trouble. A language barrier at the moment of crisis could have fatal consequences. I couldn't for the life of me remember why I'd wanted them along in the first place. But if they all came with me, numbers, noise, and even size might prove detrimental.

Great and glorious gods, this would be an appropriate time for you to offer suggestions...

"Can the Ancestors shield us somehow?" Tanris asked.

"I—don't know. Ancestors? Is it possible for you to do that?"

Tanris eyed me with skepticism and—Wait, what was that? Hope? Expectation? What a curious combination...

[Help you, yes... yes... we will...] The Ancestors rushed over me, pushing my hair in direct opposition to the wind. They plucked my clothes and gear, happily patting my cheeks. Such a strange sensation. I closed my eyes instinctively against it. Would I ever become used to this? Did I want to?

"How?" I asked. "Can you hide us when we go into the fortress?"

While they conferred among themselves, Tanris watched me. Uncomfortable, the others shifted on the narrow ledge we traversed. Not-an-Egg scraped out a complaint.

"Well?" Tanris was not always long on patience.

"They said yes."

[Yes... yes... yessss...] They echoed. *[Help you see. Show you the way. Easy magic. Easy to do. Easy for you.]*

"Wait, me?"

[Come... Come... Trust us... We are here... Always here... Helping... Guiding... Teaching... Come!]

"Now is not a good time for a lecture," I protested.

[Yesss... Yes... Come!]

"What are they saying?" Tanris looked up and all around, but he could not see the Ancestors any better than I could.

[Come! Come! The guards approach! They are here! Above! Searching! Ssssseeeeeing!] They tangled in a knot of alarm centered mere inches from my face. Half a heartbeat later, Not-an-Egg whistled.

Infected with their unease, I hastened along the ledge. "We need to move. Now. Stay close to the wall—and for all that's holy, be *quiet.*"

It took only a few minutes for me to outdistance them. The Ancestors hugged me, influencing every step and handhold. A fold in the rocks bent the scant trail back on itself, providing a view of Tanris and the others about ten paces across the gap. Tanris's mouth was tight as he inched along, his face three or four shades paler than usual. KipKap and Diti sidled behind. Their long limbs and extra digits made good use of nooks and crannies. Their bodies molded to the landscape, no matter which way it tested them.

"You're helping my friends, aren't you?" I whispered at the Ancestors.

[Help. Aid. Support. Yesyesyes...]

Senza strolled behind everyone else, pausing now and then to look out over the dark stretch of sea and the first stars appearing in the night sky. Apparently, she needed little assistance. A lone bird glided past us like a shadow. Absently, Senza pushed aside strands of hair tugged from her braid. Turning back to the task at hand, she saw me and smiled.

You are good at this, I signed.

Like home, she answered and shrugged. As always, Senza was full of surprises. I recalled the fierce terrain where we'd found her. It would have made for challenging climbing.

Shortly, there came a place where a section of the cliff had sheared off. Most of the trail had fallen away into the sea. The dark shape of a stunted evergreen sprouted from the rock twenty paces below. Beyond that, the sea frothed white amid jagged boulders gone black with moisture and nightfall. The turbulence sent up a salt-laden mist that clung to skin, clothes—and the surrounding rocks.

The gap itself spanned a space the length of two Tanrises. On the far side yawned the inky cave mouth. It was an easy distance, as I'd confirmed on my first visit. Swiftly, I shrugged out of my pack and dug out a small grapnel and lightweight rope. Now, the noise of a metal hook on stone is as good as sounding an alarm. I wrapped mine in cloth. It didn't interfere with their ability to bite, and reduced the sound of scraping, clanking steel.

"Crow…" came Tanris's growl, both warning and castigating. He had such a fine talent for mixing sentiments.

Out of habit, I checked my knots. Since I'd already done this once, it would have come as a surprise if they had loosened. In my line of work, however, one didn't trust assumptions. Satisfied, I slipped my pack on again, then let the rope slide through my hand. I gave the grapnel a few short turns before sending it flying over the breach. It caught exactly where I'd aimed it. Another tug proved the hook set, and I leaned my full weight on the rope. Perfect. Turning, I waggled my brows at my companion.

"We are not crossing this."

I shrugged and grasped the rope, surreptitiously favoring my uninjured side. "Suit yourself." Deliberately, I spun as I flew across the space, so Tanris would be sure to see my silent whoop of glee. I got the additional bonus of witnessing his expression of obvious apprehension. If only the distance had been farther! The rush of exultation ended too soon. I twirled back around in time to catch myself feet-first against the lip of the cave. Soon I was on solid ground again.

"Shall I go on?" I inquired and gestured ahead. Above me, I heard Not-an-Egg's talons scraping rock as he traversed the cliff, then glided down to the floor. With a muted croak, he trundled deeper into the darkness.

Tanris, meanwhile, glared down at the seething waters below, then back at me. "Throw me the confounded rope, you blooming mushroom."

Startled, I pressed my face into the crook of my arm, muffling a burst of unexpected laughter.

"Crow."

After a moment, I wiped my eyes and turned back to him. "Did you really call me a *mushroom*?" The accusation lost something when whispered.

"You're wasting time." If his glower grew any deeper, he risked breaking his face.

I rubbed my nose, nodded, snickered again, and tossed the rope across the shadowed chasm.

Tanris had no trouble catching it. He stretched his neck, let out a short sigh—and threw himself at me. I had just enough time to drop to a knee to catch him. It didn't prevent his crash into the rock and an explosive grunt, but at least there was no swinging back and forth nor sliding down the rope to certain death. Grabbing hold of his studded leather jerkin, I hauled him up over the edge and to the cave floor. He rolled onto his back—which had to be deuced uncomfortable, given the gear he wore and the torches I'd delegated to him. He rubbed his face with both hands, then gave me another incisive glare.

"Up with you, my intrepid squash."

He ignored my proffered hand and pushed himself to a sitting position, rubbing his chest—over his armor, mind.

"Are you injured?"

He shook his head.

"You're wasting time," I reminded, then pointed to the other side of the chasm. "KipKap is poised to pounce on you."

Fingers digging into Tanris's armor, I hauled him upward and shoved him further into the cavern. None too soon, either. Rejecting the scarce security of a mere rope, the foreigner launched himself easily over the void. He landed in a solid crouch, tipped his head to assess the cave, then immediately rose and moved further inside.

Diti was right behind him and no less agile. I considered jealousy. A jumping ability like theirs would come in quite handy in my occupation.

When I tossed the rope to Senza, Tanris materialized beside me.

"Tie the rope around yourself," he instructed her, signing at the same time.

She gave him a reproachful look and took hold of the rope the way she'd seen me do. Two running steps, and she soared through the air. Tanris might have cursed. I was too busy admiring her skill as she caught herself nimbly against the wall and immediately hauled herself up. I grinned as I helped her into the cave.

As if she risked losing her senses without warning and fall over backward into the sea, Tanris grabbed her arm and drew her further inside. "Well done," he managed gruffly. She kissed his cheek and patted him before moving on.

"Potato, potato, ginger," I said, smirking as I retrieved my hook and wound the rope.

"How do you figure?"

"Two solid but versatile; one unexpectedly spicy." Equipment stowed, I tested shoulder and hands for any sign of strain. Good so far... I swung my pack over my shoulder, then helped myself to a torch. When we'd first set out on our task of rounding up foreigners, Tanris had purchased new packs for all four of us. Clever devices they were, too, with pockets inside and out and lots of straps. There were so many ways to attach things that the sheer weight became a danger. Adding torches to his didn't seem to slow him down.

He rummaged for his flint. "So we've got mushrooms, squash, potatoes, and *ginger*? What kind of cook are you?"

"Now you know why I don't volunteer for dinner duty." Not volunteering didn't keep me from taking my turn when necessary. I wasn't a terrible cook. "Ancestors?" I still felt silly addressing invisible beings in front of the others. "Please lead us to Enikar."

With an eager rustle and the unexpected scent of autumn leaves scouring the salt-laden air, they rushed ahead. They whispered for me to follow. With the torch in hand, I led the way. Senza and I were the only ones who didn't have trouble pressing through the narrow spot.

"Watch your step," I warned, and held the light out over the crevasse I'd discovered earlier. "And keep your voices down. Sound carries here."

Senza merely nodded and made her way to the other end of the crevice. I followed her, while the Futha-fellows had gone on ahead. Tanris lingered near the edge, peering into the wreckage of the chamber.

"What has Prince Basi got down here?" he asked.

"You're welcome to go exploring," I suggested over one shoulder, "but I'm going to fetch the relic."

"Enikar or the idol?"

"Right, *two* relics. How could I forget?"

We had to descend into the crevice before ascending it like a mad, rubble-strewn staircase to the upper floors. KipKap and his brother kindly and conveniently helped us down.

"What is the name of your people again?" I asked, amused to watch KipKap handle Tanris as though he weighed no more than a child. Tanris found less amusement than indignation.

"Futharvyr." KipKap slid a too-long finger beneath the collar and tugged at it.

I wrinkled my nose in commiseration and resisted the urge to take the wretched thing off him. The pretense had to last until they were back aboard the ship. *FOO-thar-veer,* I repeated to myself twenty-seven times or more as I clambered up the incline. The word had a nice rhythm. I bounced to it as I sprang from boulder to boulder.

"Crow," Tanris growled a warning. "Quit your playing. It would be helpful if you avoided breaking your neck."

"Have you ever seen a bird fall off its perch?" He chose not to answer, and I reached the top soon after, with Diti a breath or two behind me. Tiled floors, grimy and worn, led left and right. The walls held iron brackets for torches, some empty and some not. None burned.

[This way, thisssss waaaay...] the Ancestors urged. I went left. Behind me, the others murmured as they crawled out of the gash.

"Quiet," I ordered.

From ahead came the moans and hoarse whispers I'd heard before. Other than those, only the sounds of footsteps and the crackling flame of the torch disturbed the silence. At one point, I climbed over a pile of rubble fallen from the ceiling. Oh, the joy that coursed through me at the thought of uncountable tons of rock waiting to collapse on my head... At least I needn't worry about the closeness of these particular quarters, and none of the others came close enough to see my white-knuckle grip on the torch. I confess, I am somewhat averse to dark, cramped places. It is a stupid anxiety for a thief to have. I kept it to myself.

Past the remains of the caved-in ceiling, tiles rippled outward in low, wide ridges. It slowed us, for we had only the one torch to light the way. Now and then someone behind me hissed complaints at stubbed toes and upset balance. Undeterred, the dragon trotted beside me through passages weathered by the ages. After a time, the impression we'd doubled back several times—or we were going in circles—crept up on me. The Ancestors did not hesitate, so I put it down to my overactive imagination.

What had this place once been, and who had built it? Doorways opened to either side, marked by carved pillars. Some of them had doors, most of which were closed. The light was poor, but I discerned intricate carvings and dark red plaques inscribed with neat symbols. Curious, I stopped to study a panel. I did not recognize the writing, and when I drew my finger down it, the figures remained undisturbed. "Red ochre," I murmured, "covered by a varnish to keep the words from smearing or fading."

A lump marred the top. I blew dust away and rubbed the surface underneath. "And what have we here?" The gem shone in the flickering light, which wasn't strong enough to reveal the color. I pried at one edge with my knife and it popped free.

"Can you go nowhere without thieving?" Tanris asked at my elbow.

"I am investigating. Researching." I tucked my blade away, then held the stone up to the flickering blaze. Its shape and size reminded me of a peach pit, and the interior gleamed warm and clear.

"Researching what?"

"The past, which I imagine Basi Serhat has found a way to use to his benefit."

"Is that a diamond?"

"Here? I've never heard of any diamond mines in the islands, have you?"

He gave a standard-style grunt that was no particular answer, but suggested that he knew little about the islands. Pocketing the stone, I tried the latch on the door, but untold centuries held it tight. The door opposite was no more forthcoming, and I lifted the torch to study them both. "They're red," I pointed out.

"So?"

"More ochre."

"Isn't ochre yellow or brown?"

"Unless it's mixed with hematite, which is widespread on Masni."

A momentary silence followed. "How do you know that?"

"I read Enikar's notes." I resisted the urge to be either critical or mocking, and started walking again. Where had the Ancestors got to? I didn't hear or feel them. This segment of the passage bore only doors, not intersections, so I expected we'd catch up with them. The prospect of dipping deeper into the pool of magic unsettled me, despite the choice I'd made to finish this job. Fretful, I pulled the amulet from beneath my clothes. I didn't question the fact that rubbing it calmed me.

As I approached a corner, I slowed warily. "Light ahead," I whispered. I heard Tanris check the looseness of several of his blades in their scabbards. We crept forward to an octagonal chamber about eight paces across. Three more passages opened from it. The walls between each bore niches with lifelike statues of men. Well-armed men, at that, garbed in black with brightly shining armor reminiscent of something I'd seen from the Asonian states.

Ax out and ready to use, Tanris held one hand out to stop the others. No one moved nor made a sound. Minutes slipped past before he eased closer to the statue on our left. "They look awfully real." He nudged the thing with his weapon. I'd have refused to touch it, too. It rocked back ever-so-slightly, but did not react.

A statue wouldn't, would it?

"Maybe is magic." KipKap's too-deep voice betrayed his uneasiness —an uneasiness that spread through all of us.

"Best leave well enough alone." I had no desire at all to wake magical creatures or to tempt the gods to test me. That made it easier to resist touching the figures or rifling through the pouches two of them wore. Instead, I turned my attention upward. Amber light gleamed from a glass box attached to the ceiling overhead. "Would you look at that… How do you suppose it works?"

"Is not fire," KipKap declared, peering at it between the fingers of an upraised hand. Preserving his vision, I imagined.

"Doesn't have the clarity of witchlights, either." Absently, I checked my pouch, where I'd stowed one for emergencies. For reasons I did not yet understand, the magic that made them—Mazhar magic—did not prickle or send spears of pain jabbing through me.

"Magic?" Diti asked. His head turned this way and that as he examined the room without actually entering.

What had him on edge? Did he dislike dark, narrow quarters, too? "Must be," I agreed with the Futharvyr. I wasn't sure I wanted to explore the peculiarity of a magical light. On the other hand, all those mysteriously marked doors made my curiosity itch unbearably. Torch lifted high, I walked around the chamber, peering down each passageway. They all looked the same. "It strikes me that the complex built under the fortress is considerably bigger inside than it looks from the outside."

The absence of the Ancestors made me itch as much as my curiosity did. I withdrew the talisman and pressed my lips against it. *[Where are you, my friends?]*

Nothing. The itch became a gnawing apprehension.

Not-an-Egg creaked anxiously and wound once around my shins before stopping to stare down one dark tunnel. Had he seen something? I ventured a few steps in without him, staring hard past the nimbus of torchlight. Wretched thing. Its flickering had me shuddering at shadows.

The others, meanwhile, milled about in the little chamber, looking at the magical light or squinting down the other passages. I noticed Tanris kept his ax in his hand and no one ventured near the eldritch statues.

"Something is wrong," I decided. "I can't hear or feel the Ancestors anymore."

"So which way do we go now?"

"I'm not sure," I said slowly. With the dragon sticking to me like dog hair on felt, I went a bit further.

"Can you—"

With no warning at all, an invisible force burst from the opposite passage, howling and rushing like the fiercest storm. Senza fell down on one knee. The others staggered against the blast, trying to stay upright.

I was plowed backward several lurching paces until the wall brought me up.

[Run! Run! Liiiiessss! Snare! Ruse! Fly, Friend Crow!]

"It's a trap!" I shouted, astonished to see the statues leaping into motion. Doors banged open within the corridors and more statues spilled out to surround us. *What magic was this?*

Not at all willing to be run over or stabbed full of holes, I swung the torch at the head of the nearest foe as a pair beset me. A dull *clang* and a very human-sounding grunt rewarded my effort. The thing kept coming. To discourage it, I feinted left and jabbed the business end of the torch into the T-shaped opening of its helm. The resulting scream shattered any illusion that our attackers were supernatural.

Not-an-Egg sank his fangs into the second fellow's leg, right at the knee joint. Dodging his victim's swinging sword, he slammed his knobby little head up between the legs. Then he twisted around to climb up the fighter's back, talons digging into armor. With a budding roar, he wrenched the helmet off and—

No, I did not want to see those gory details. Two more guards conveniently leaped forward to distract me. One grabbed my arm; the other swung a fist at my face. Judiciously, I dropped my weight to the floor, and the blow struck the arm-grabber. I helped his descent with a well-placed kick, rolled away, and scrambled to my feet. With the enemy filling the halls, I knew this was not a fight I could win. "Ancestors! *Ancestors!*" I shouted, battling panic. "Help me!"

I had little notion what they could do. Their indelible presence increased to a hurricane limited, evidently, to the passage in which I stood. One arm raised to protect my face, I could see just well enough to make out four black-clad figures tumbling like leaves. The Ancestors clutched at me, humming, chanting—spinning *energy*. Shadowy streamers drew across my vision. I tried to sweep them away.

My companions still struggled in the eight-sided chamber, surrounded on every side. Girl's pale face turned toward me, her shock and fury unmistakable.

Tanris used his ax to deadly effect. Three warriors laid at his feet, and one of the two facing him did so with an arm dangling uselessly at his side. "Crow!" he bellowed, sparing one glance in my direction. His mouth moved, but I could no longer hear him over the thrum and roar of the Ancestors.

Diti lay sprawled on the floor, his enormous eyes closed and blood staining one side of his face and neck.

KipKap had his mace. The weapon twisted through the air like a snake darting and biting. He, too, claimed three victories, though his tunic was slashed clear through to his skin.

"Help them!" I shouted over the tumult.

[No time... no time... Haaassste!]

"We have to do *something!*"

The fury of the storm wavered for an instant, then split in two. As it did, the streamers thickened and wound around me, muffling sound. A distinct vibration infiltrated the outrageous noise: rumbling like... like *an earthquake.*

"What have you done?" I screamed, flailing to free myself. I was an insect in a web.

Rocks and boulders crashed through the corridor like dice spilling from a cup. The space between me and the bloody, broken chamber stretched further and further until it snapped.

—18—
Scavenger Hunt

Blackness enveloped me as securely as any tomb and my ears rang like an entire bell tower gone mad. Fearing what I could not see, I pushed myself up on one elbow. Good so far...

"Tanris?" The darkness stifled my voice so much I barely heard myself. "Girl? KipKap? Egg? Are you here?"

Useless.

I licked dry lips and found them coated in tasteless, gritty dust. Venturing an exploration of the surrounding blackness, my fingers scraped smooth, dressed stone beneath me, then one wall. I hadn't fallen down some quake-created shaft, then.

Yet...

Recalling the crevice in the first chamber, I dared not indulge carelessness. I explored a goodly space around myself with arms and outstretched legs, then sat up and wriggled out of my pack. The movement reminded me of my wound. I rubbed it, then rotated my arm. It hurt, but the pain seemed... separate somehow. It didn't prevent using my arm at all, nor did it keep me from attempting some cautious stretches.

Water before anything else. I'd made such a habit of reaching for my waterskin that finding it in the dark presented no challenge at all. Thank the gods of preparedness. Untying my neckerchief, I dampened a corner to wipe my face. A sharp sting let me know I had a cut on one cheek. If that was the only damage, the gods were watching out for me indeed.

The oppressive darkness had me fumbling like a blind man, but I soon found my pouch of herbs, medicines, needles and thread, and such. My 'repair kit,' I called it, and worked hard not to put myself in situations that required its use. Placing it on the floor between my legs, I opened the flaps carefully. I didn't want to lose anything. Loops of leather held small brass tubes of various powders. With the tips of my fingers sliding over them, I tried to recall which held the powdered lemon balm for use on a headache. I closed my eyes —utter foolishness considering the circumstances—and went over in my head the order in which I'd packed them. It didn't help. I loathed thinking I was that rattled. Choosing at random, I uncorked it and sniffed.

No, and no again. It took three tries to find the right one and another eternity to calm my nerves. I washed a few pinches of the lemon balm down with a swig of tepid water. Put the case back together and into the larger pack. Rubbed the bridge of my nose between thumb and forefinger.

"Ancestors? Where am I?"

If they spoke to me, I could not hear over the incessant ringing in my ears. I'd lost the torch, but I still had my witchlights—courtesy of the erstwhile evil baron (and which my slow brain realized I could have used to unpack my herbs). Just as important, I still had my belt bag. I freed one little bottle from its protective wool wrapping. Delicate light illuminated the chamber. It didn't give off any heat at all, but the radiance was reassuring. Beautiful, even.

Witchlights, I was told, are an old magic. Old *Mazhar* magic. Mine, in other words. I hadn't a clue how they were contained, but they originated in the northern regions of, well, Mazhar. Country claimed by Emperor Gaziah, with little trace of my people left anywhere. I had no notion how I had come to be, never mind how I had ended up in the unfeeling arms of the Family. I didn't know my parents, not my countrymen—I hadn't even known my heritage until the Ancestors educated me.

The tiny creatures in the witchlights, rare and elusive, resemble amorphous bubbles no bigger than a thimble. If you hold them in your bare hand, you'll come away with a burn for your efforts. In the wilds, they have a sadly short lifespan, but magicked into a bottle they will live a long time. Longer if they are kept out of the light. The whole thing sounded backward to me, but what do you expect when magic is involved? Sense? Logic? Ha.

Witchlight in hand, I untied my shirt and examined my chest. The gash still looked bright pink, but there was no sign of tearing or bleeding.

"Thank you, gods, for your tender care." I paused. "And the dragon."

I held the witchlight in my palm and examined my surroundings. The windowless room had generous proportions. There was a long table buried with odds and ends. Several stools stood at the end. Opposite those was the door. A ragged carpet covered part of the floor—just not the part where I'd ended up. Two paintings hung askew on one wall, and a cracked, foggy mirror on another.

The door was shut, which begged the question about whether it had opened or closed during my arrival.

I was cautious getting to my feet, but aside from the unabated ringing, I suffered no dizziness, nausea, or any other discomfort. Booty lying about in the open always attracted my attention, but first things first. I needed to know what had happened to Tanris and the others. *Dead*, as far as I knew. Memory of the avalanche made me feel ill.

If they were lost, well...

I paced for a few minutes, mentally debating my course of action. Find Tanris or go after Enikar? Gaziah wanted him back; I wanted his brains.

Ew, no. I wanted the information he had stashed there.

One thing was certain: I wouldn't find either of them here. I tried the door. Not locked. Have I mentioned how the gods look out for me? I hid the brightness of the witchlight in my pocket and eased the slab open. Unsurprisingly, it was impossible to see anything at all, either up or down the corridor. I couldn't hear anything, though the ringing sensation had begun to fade.

"Tanris?" I whispered. No sense attracting more violent attention.

Impenetrable blackness swallowed the question. There was no answer, which left me at another decision-making point. I bounced on my toes a few times, then brought out the witchlight and spun back to the table.

Dust covered several small stacks of books, a box of glass tubes, more boxes and sacks, a collection of perfectly shaped iron balls, and a shallow dish filled with viscous copper-colored liquid that gave off a scent like lilacs when I stirred it with a feather lying nearby.

Curiosity begged me to take it.

Pragmatism suggested otherwise.

Experience pointed out that it looked wizard-ish, and now wasn't the time for foolish risks. For all I knew, moving it might kill me.

"Argh," I growled in frustration, and reluctantly moved on.

In a chest nearby, I found several tunics. There were also three woolen hats of curious workmanship, and a pair of leather slippers with shiny beadwork. I stashed the footwear in my pack, then picked through the oddments arrayed across the tabletop. Mindful of filling my pack to overflowing, I chose with care. A slender book bound in purple and worked with silver stitches. Two little carved pieces that looked like ivory. A goodly stack of coins the like of which I'd never seen, though I held them in my palm for a moment, considering the weight. *Worth it.* Six thumbnail-sized spheres—gems or glass? And a delightful wooden bird with wings that slipped a bit as if they might flap.

The pack needed rearranging to fit my new things. The shuffling brought Duzayan's dagger to the surface. Beautifully crafted with precious jewels set in the grip, it would have fetched a very generous price. Some would pay extra for the spells inlaid in the blade. Tanris had shocked me when he handed it over with apparent indifference.

"You keep it," I'd said, backing up a pace and keeping my hands well out of reach. It was the only way we knew to close the gates, but the last time I'd held it, it had given me an injury that still tormented me.

"You asked for it." Tanris followed my retreat, caught my wrist, and slapped the hilt in my hand. "You're the only one who can use it."

Thank all the gods paying attention, the spell lay dormant. That didn't keep me from wrapping the hilt in leather to avert another personal disaster. It had stayed hidden in my gear all this time. Truth to tell, I didn't even want to look at it. The Ancestors didn't either, and refused to acknowledge its presence.

Back into my pack it went. I glanced at the remaining books, heaved a sigh of regret, and shouldered my pack. Witchlight in hand, I returned to the door. "Ancestors?"

Still nothing. Not a whisper, not a rustle, not even an annoying brush of cool fingers through my hair.

"Ancestors, where are you? I need your help. Where have you put me? And where are the others?"

Impulsively, I reached for my talisman.

It was gone…

The shock froze me in my tracks. A block of ice formed in my belly, which was good for sudden swift thought.

The figure carved into it represented a doorway—

Which may or may not be figurative—

Had the Ancestors pulled me *through* the talisman?

All the nimble thinking slammed to a halt. The horrific notion of being squashed, reshaped, and jammed through a *picture* the size of an unshelled almond completely stopped my brain.

I may have whimpered.

That wouldn't help anything.

I cleared the horror from my throat. "Well, that was fun." If I repeated it enough, I might even believe it.

I sucked in a huge breath and expelled it along with all my agitation. My hand only shook a little when I lifted the witchlight and searched the entire room for the amulet. Twice.

"Son of a monkey."

The Ancestors had said I didn't—or wouldn't—need it. For a fact, I didn't actually need the Ancestors *or* the magic.

Except I had the latter, like it or not, and the Ancestors were the nearest thing I had to teachers. The best place to look for it would be where disaster had struck. Wonderful. Hide and seek in the dark with someone who had known we were coming and would no doubt be looking for me.

Facts, slim as they were, indicated wizardry.

"They don't call me Wizard Bane for nothing," I reminded myself. My voice lacked conviction, and with good reason. Crossing wizards *hurt*.

I bolstered my flagging resolve by reviewing how I'd once traversed the lair of several wizards and a dragon. As I walked the hallways of Basi Serhat's buried bastion, I made a map in my head. From time to time, I stopped to crouch and draw it out on the ground with a scrap of rock. Writing helped me commit it to memory, but the farther I went, the more maze-like the underground vaults became.

I removed Enikar's notes from my pack. What I needed were a pen and ink. What I came up with was a long sliver of wood carved from a door and colored water made from ochre scrapings.

I am not certain why it pained me to paint over the careful notations and drawings. On the bright side, I could still read the duke's writing through the new map.

With the help of the map, I eventually located the Chamber of False Statues. At least the Ancestors had transported me to a position on the same level. The entire way, I heard no sound but my own breathing and cautious footsteps. Even the ear-ringing dwindled away.

No one was there. The ceiling light still functioned, so I slipped the witchlight into my pocket. One niche had crumbled into oblivion. Blood stained the tiled floor. Had I noticed the tiles before? Rows of red bricks separated units of four square tiles. Each bore the symbol of a bird painted in white on a black background. *Red brick… ochre…* What did the birds symbolize?

A question for another day, alas. However, each of the niches held a trio of lovely polished gems set in an oblong metal plate on the wall. I didn't want the metal, but my knife proved unequal to the task of prying them free. Not to worry—I had a tool for that, and soon ownership of twelve shiny stones transferred to me. The first nine were easy, but the remaining three took some grubbing about, as they lay in the rubble of the blast. They made my fingers itch, which beat being burnt but signified non-druidic magic. Adding rocks to my person struck me as a possibly questionable idea, but if the gods were going to shower me with gems, who was I to refuse them?

The last one came free with an audible *pop* and a powerful jangling sensation. I shook my head, blinking my eyes and seeing everything through a greenish haze. Magic *and* guard-summoning clamor couldn't be good…

I hied myself off down the nearest hall and picked a room several doors down to wait for the guards to come running. I hadn't long to wait. Weapons out, three of them clattered into the cross-chamber. They passed by my hiding place without noticing the door set ajar. Further evidence of the adoration of the gods. Through the crack, I watched them poke through the fallen chunks of rock and masonry. They each had breastplates, but there the resemblance to the former statues ended. Island comfort won out—not that I blamed them, what with the heat and all. They wore their long hair braided and tied up, short-sleeved tunics, knee-length britches with wide legs, and sandals rather than boots.

"None here," the tallest grumbled.

"None wouldn't'a set the signal off," countered another, nimbly exercising his double negatives. Diagonal black tattoos marked his cheeks.

The third gestured down a corridor. "We check. Boss'll 'ave melons if we don'."

"Fine," Stripe-face bit out. "Split up. See five, six room down."

"I'm no' splittin'." Three shook his head and shifted the grip on his sword. His free hand fumbled to a collection of ornaments around his neck. He chose one by touch and held it tight.

"Nor I," the tall one agreed. "Don' like spirits."

Stripe-face glared at each of them. "S'no such thing's spirits."

"Tell that t'Maki and his. *Summat* throw down the lot."

They didn't notice, but I voted for them to stick together. The herd was easier to avoid.

"Fine." Stripe-face squared his shoulders and marched off with his friends in tow. They made quick work of investigating the rooms and started down another branch.

As soon as they turned their backs, I darted down the passage they'd just finished, slipping out of sight. I held my breath, but I needn't have worried they'd hear me; the trio were hardly subtle.

"Even he can't see everywhere." The tall one cast an uneasy look around the ruined chamber. "Magic or no."

Three lifted a pendant to press against his forehead while he muttered a prayer. "No good cumma magic."

"Unless it's your *hukun*." His sarcasm was sharp enough to cut through stone.

"*Hukun* no poison."

"So you say, but magic is magic." Stripe-face led them down the third passage.

"An' spirits is spirits."

Arguing comfortably, they popped in and out of several rooms, searched the hall they'd come from, then disappeared into the darkness. When I'd made certain the floor in the room I'd chosen was clear, I paced. It was no great leap to assume the spirits they'd mentioned were the Ancestors. That didn't worry me, but what did they mean about 'he' being able to see? Some variety of foresight or scrying explained how a trap had been laid for us.

"What is this?" I inquired of the darkened ceiling. "How is there *another* wizard for me to deal with? You know my opinion about them. What do you *want* from me?"

Experience told me that the gods never answered with mere words. They offered signs, but I must look for them, and generally I had to interpret on my own. It occurred to me that if I had come into the fortress alone, none of us would be in this situation. The Ancestors would have done whatever it is they'd done. I'd have been snatched out of the hands of the *wizard*. And the others would be safe in camp, chewing their nails while they waited for me to lug the old man out.

I had three choices: rescue my companions—supposing they were still alive—rescue the duke, or cut my losses and go home.

The last sounded eminently practical. Also easier than either of the other options. Safer, too, for I was no fighter and had no desire whatsoever to play the part of the hero.

Tanris could take care of himself. Senza, not so well, but she had Tanris. She *might* have Tanris. Not-an-Egg was his own peculiar story; I would not leave without him. KipKap and Diti had only come on this trip because of me.

I turned my face up to the ceiling again, arms akimbo. "Did I ask for a conscience? No, I did not. You can have it back now."

Silence answered me.

"Fine. It's not all bad, I suppose. I am *Wizard Bane*, you know." Or so Tanris called me. Mocking, as he never quite believed the woe I'd inflicted on the countless wizards of Hasiq jum'a Sahefal. And Duzayan, don't let's forget him.

That aside, I had a few new baubles as compensation for my trauma. However, with an all-seeing wizard lurking about, I couldn't afford to linger here. The passageway was empty and silent, so I trotted back to the cross-chamber to search for my talisman. I went over the entire floor. I tried not to think about how much blood had created the stains I stepped over. Though I found one of Tanris's daggers, the talisman remained lost. My heart sank a little further.

Hands on my hips again, I turned slow circles in a vain attempt to perceive the device the way I sometimes did Not-an-Egg. As it happened, I couldn't find him either. There were signs to follow, though, and I set off down one gruesomely streaked corridor. The streaking ended before very long, which came as both a relief and a problem. The body had stopped bleeding, but now I had only a general direction in which to proceed. Huzzah for scavenger hunts. But crows are expert scavengers, don't you know?

Eventually, I found my way to civilization. Lack of sleep and a nagging inner voice ruined my sociability. All good reasons to avoid collecting people. Backtracking a bit, I concealed myself in one of the thousand empty rooms beneath the fortress proper. In his wisdom, Tanris had doled out the food supply to each of us, so I had a cold meal of jerky, nuts, and hard cheese. It was a feast. I also had a blanket to keep me warm while I slept. A rock wedged under the door made a fair lock, too. I laid with my back against the panel, making it even harder for anyone poking about the weird warren to get inside.

I discovered the bounty of Basi's kitchens the next day. Shortly after, I located the laundry, which proved that pirates and pirate princes were not always filthy barbarians. It also provided me with a custom disguise. A handful of women of various size and disposition tended bubbling cauldrons. Fish-scented steam filled the room, which made it easier for me to slip through unnoticed. Unfortunately, the *clean* clothing hung outside through a single wide doorway. I did not doubt my laundry-filching skills, nor my ability to induce a woman to help me. The latter is the more satisfying route, and as tempting as liberating any fine piece of artwork or jewelry. However, circumstances required me to remain completely unseen. I could not risk having some delightful matron accidentally revealing my presence. Nor could I have her broadcasting the fact that I'd availed myself of the goods over which she was in charge.

The price for taking random items from this basket and the other was steep. I smelled like… dear gods who love me, what was that smell? Fish, without question. In one pocket, I discovered a bag of dried leaves that greatly contributed to the stench. I deposited it on a windowsill as I passed by. Whatever the stuff was, it made my eyes water and my nose burn. I took a moment to rub a bit of lemon balm on the end of my nose to disguise the odor. Perhaps when it faded, I would no longer notice my own stink.

Some well-spent time shadowing an actual pirate—mimicking his manner of walking, talking, and mocking—and I fit right in. The real challenge lay in not improving upon the model. I wanted to mingle in, not stand out. Tarsha and I had used to play a game in which I would don the costume and mannerisms of someone and she would guess who I was. She claimed I could have made a fine career as an actor, and I had to agree. The ability to hide in plain sight and blend in with one's marks are critical skills for a thief, and the gods had endowed me with an exceptional talent.

My medley of foreign clothing provided convenient spots to carry the most critical parts of my belongings so they'd be easy to access. The pack Tanris had acquired for me was too new and too conspicuous. So I redistributed the contents, flattened it as best I could, and stuffed it into the bottom of a plain canvas sack with a sturdy rope tie.

It, too, stank.

Head down and ears up, I passed through the more populated parts of the stronghold. Pirates predominated, but there were natives, too. The locals wore a plethora of amulets on beaded and braided necklaces or *paki*, sometimes stacked inches deep. There was also a goodly assortment of Bahsyri citizens of every stripe. I recognized a dozen cronies of the cultured classes—and a pattern of disaffection toward that Pinnacle of Princely Perfection, Gaziah the Second. How astonishing to find so many gathered in this precise place, far from sovereign sight.

The pool of suspects for the position of traitor shrank.

As blessings from the gods go, there were more pirates than tasks to keep them busy. One more skulker on the edges of conversations, games, plans, and sometimes-deadly fights went unnoticed. I took it as a sign I was interpreting the messages from the gods correctly. Not one to let opportunity or entertainment pass me by, I transferred small possessions from one person to another. Of course, I kept some of the most valuable for myself. Truly, I hadn't expected this visit to be so lucrative. Along the way,

I gathered a few pendants. After all, an islander without his *paki* might as well be naked. Nowhere among all the necklaces, knives, and knickknacks did I find my lost medallion.

I overheard Baron Mongar planning the transfer of iron for weapons into Basi's possession. And, lo! There was Agada Surriz, painter of the peerage and a man keen to thrust himself forward as often and loudly as possible. His mission was to gather financial aid and support to protest a tax levied by Gaziah. From what I understood, it was being used to pay for the invasion of some tiny country in the east. Vana Sarjin, an officer of the emperor's household, humbly explained—repeatedly—that he was a messenger of the gods sent to remove the 'tainted' emperor from power. He had a rather long list of transgressions committed by his Supreme Majesty. Some of them were actually true.

Eventually, one of the high-hatched snagged me to fetch him a fresh bottle of wine. This errand took me back to the kitchen regions and the gossip of the ordinary folk. Here, I learned that a local headman had been captured on the way to Asonia to garner aid against the invasion of Basi Serhat. One might note that Prince Basi was forbidden by treaty to take land from any native of the isles by force. Such a complaint would start a war and throw a club into the spokes of Prince Basi's machinations. The headman no longer had his head. Sympathetic Masni natives helping enslaved 'demons' with their revolt had closed a mine. A swiftly opening and closing gate had demolished a ship.

Listening to that conversation birthed the realization that I needed a map marking every gate in the islands. Hot on the heels of that was the comprehension that I could not close all the gates on Masni. They came and went like bolts of lightning. How could it be done, then? And how long would it take to clean up the ill-conceived scheme of the erstwhile Baron Duzayan? It looked like it was going to require another entire chapter of my life.

"You gotta problem, *cocho*?"

I had no idea what that word meant, but everyone at the table near where I stood had gone deadly silent.

"Me?" I asked, making wild assumptions based on the way they all stared as if I'd suddenly turned into a nice, shiny imperial officer. "Nah," I shrugged.

"You starin's gonna drive a hole through my head." The speaker curled both ham-sized fists on the edge of the table and leaned forward. His triple chins quivered. Tiny black eyes disappeared beneath a brow that inched from one side of his head to the other. A stack of necklaces rested between his chins and his chest.

Now that I actually looked at him, it was difficult *not* to stare. Another shrug and an awkward little shuffle knocked my possible threat level down several notches. "Jus' thought I saw summat," I muttered.

"Eyah? And what'd that be?"

"A—a shadow," I stammered, folding my arms tight and curling my shoulders in fearfully. "Summun said there was *spirits* about."

A rustle went around the table, some curious, some suspicious, some annoyed…

"Izzit true?" I dared a quick look up. "Spirits down below, shakin' and breakin' up the ways? And summuns *killed?*" I adopted an expression of terror.

Half the growing group of spectators made gestures against evil or touched protective amulets. One fellow spat over his shoulder and promptly got himself punched, which started a brawl. Ideal, to my way of thinking, for I preferred a smaller audience. Several of us backed out of the way.

Not the Big Fellow. He remained in his straining chair, drumming his fingers on the tabletop as if nothing else was happening. "Some *cocho* swag stalkers broke in," he said, finally deciding to share his knowledge.

Ah, now I had the gist of it. Staying in character, I laughed, looked around at those who'd elected to stay in Big Fellow's sphere, then laughed again. "Eyah, that's a good way to get dead. How many?"

He spared a glance at the skirmish. An invisible bulwark separated him from the fighting. "Seven, eight. Bahsyri and gate slaves."

I'd seen Tanris fight. The exaggeration in numbers was understandable.

"Brass-bold, that," commented another spectator. "As if th'prince'd stomach those *bibisut* in his house."

Didn't that word have something to do with bacon? I pinched my nose. "That'll teach 'em."

Big Fellow leaned forward, his chair creaking so loud I heard it over the scuffle. "'Cept the slys slipped away like snakes." Too bad his alliteration was accidental. I'd have been more impressed if he'd realized he'd done it. Still, he tilted his head and pinned me with cold black eyes, which wasn't nearly as amusing. "Were no spirits, only sly magic."

"Snake magic?" I asked—to qualify, of course.

Big Fellow's tiny eyes narrowed even more, on the verge of disappearing entirely between folds of skin. "Mebbe," he said at last. One of the scuffle's participants crashed into him. Unruffled, Big Fellow caught the man in one paw and tossed him back into the fray. Still looking at me, his single eyebrow bent down in the middle. "Dw'I know you?"

My shoulders slumped and I hung my head. "No one ever remembers me." Not strictly true, but I had a story to support here. I perked again before he could grill me. "So they's caught? The others?"

"Course they's caught."

The wave of relief that announcement brought astonished and unbalanced me. *Caught* was better than *dead.* "Huh," was all I could manage.

He picked up a long, leathery pod from a yellow bowl in front of him, broke the thing in half, and took a delicate bite. "Y'wanna see 'em."

"I do?" I could go with that, though it brushed the truth too closely for comfort. "Course I do. I mean… doesn't everyone?"

He spat small brown seeds into a separate bowl. How charming. "Better go hotfoot. Boss's movin' 'em."

"Where?"

"Depends."

I folded my arms and rocked back and forth in a show of indecision. "How much?"

His face split in a wide, surprisingly good smile. "Two bead."

With a deep glower, I finally removed a purloined *paki*. Taking a single dark red bead off the leather strand, I set it on the table.

Big Fellow glowered right back, contemplated it as if it were bird dung, then pinched it between two sausage-like fingers. "Now? Same's yestady. Den?" His massive shoulders heaved and he smiled again. "No'dee."

There is nothing like paying for non-information. Alas, he had no concept how fast or how steeply interest accrued. The ongoing brawl provided me a lucrative exit, and I timed it to perfection. As I slipped past Big Fellow, two scufflers crashed into me and we all staggered into him.

Mountain that he was, the collision didn't budge him more than an inch. He hollered his indignation. I pocketed a few of his *paki*. As someone who harbored a well-honed survival instinct, I didn't keep them. I immediately traded them both twice over for less conspicuous but equally valuable goods. The obstacle course created by the melee provided plenty of opportunity for escape. Soon I was out the door and safe on the other side.

What had I learned?

KipKap and Diti had escaped.

Tanris and Senza had not. Their location was common knowledge to everyone but me.

"Ancestors, I could use your help about now," I complained as I trotted down the busy corridor. I passed many storage rooms before I came into the keep's yard. Out of habit, I touched my chest to feel the outline of the talisman, but found only flesh and bone.

What did a man like Basi need with a pair of alleged thieves? He had an entire fortress full of them. He hadn't killed them yet, which was an element in their favor. Unless he'd decided to torture them for information. Either way, they faced mortal jeopardy and my people-stealing task had escalated from one to three.

I needed a vantage point, but first I must revisit the laundry.

—19—
The Liberties of Liquor

I am well known for taking surprises in stride, thinking fast on my feet. I could only imagine that the gods had decided I needed some very particular refining, for the surprises they piled upon me increased daily.

The squashed confines of decorative masonry provided a good view. I could see the yard, the doors to the great hall and to the barracks, and several other entrances. I'd been watching for some hint of the self-proclaimed prince moving his prisoners, and instead had the dubious opportunity of witnessing the arrival of a guest. It was a severe case of practicing open-mouthed astonishment. For who should alight from an elegant wicker coach but Tarsha. She wore scarlet-trimmed white silk that clung to every lovely curve. Her long dark hair curled over one shoulder. A magnificent red hibiscus tucked behind her ear complimented—well, everything about her. I would have heaved a wistful sigh if it had been any other woman, any other time.

She awarded the carriage driver with a pretty smile. The pair of guards outside the door were turned oafish by her mere presence. She had smiles for them, too. Then she swayed up the steps to give a smart knock.

I reclaimed the tongue hanging out of my mouth, tucked away the figurine I'd been playing with, scooted along the ledge, and popped back in through the window. My new disguise was a trifle unwieldy, chosen to conceal gear redistributed amongst smaller bags I strapped beneath a long canvas raincoat with enormous pockets.

It was a moment before I gained a position to peer over the low balcony wall to the entrance. A pirate posing as a servant opened the door for Tarsha, then stood there staring as if he'd never seen a woman before. I half expected his eyeballs to fall out of his head and plop on the floor. Tarsha had to explain twice that she had arrived to see her dear friend, Prince Basi, and would he please announce her arrival? There went the claim of the guard we'd met earlier, declaring Basi's schedule was full for weeks. While the man lurched off to fetch the master of the house, she waited with patient, perfect composure.

I fetched a stool from down the hall and settled in to stew. Er, to watch. My disguise yielded a regrettable stench of fish with undertones of ale, salt, and—something else. I could only pray to the gods of lurkers and saviors that it would go unnoticed by the pair below.

Boot heels clicked on a tile floor far too glorious for a military outpost. "Darling…" Tarsha crooned when someone—the prince, presumably—arrived.

"Well, well," he said, holding his hands out to her as he approached. Dark-haired and slender, he wore an emerald tunic embroidered nearly to oblivion in sparkling silver thread and beads. His single noteworthy feature were the bags under his eyes. If they were any indication, he had not slept in this lifetime. His expanding smile moved his mouth but seemed detached from the rest of his face. To my gratification, he was shorter than Tarsha. "You are a lovely surprise. How long has it been?" What he lacked in height, he made up for with a velvety voice. I'd so hoped he'd sound as small as he looked.

Tarsha took his hands and stepped close to kiss his cheek. "I'm hurt! You haven't been counting the days?"

Days? What was going on here? And why hadn't she mentioned she knew him? Very well, by appearances, the sly little minx. *That* ruffled my feathers—more for the fact that Tarsha had been playing games with me *again* while a part of me had wanted to give in to her sweet allure. Had *she* been responsible for the ambush in the fortress's lower reaches? She'd better hope I didn't get my hands around her lovely neck.

"I can't answer that. It'll make me look bad." Basi laughed softly, *knowingly*. "What's this?" He stroked her scarred cheek.

Her lashes lowered in ostensible self-consciousness. "I was in a rather awful accident."

Basi caught her chin and turned her back. "Unfortunate," he murmured, "but somehow inconsequential."

The scar or the accident? I wondered. What an oaf.

"You are too kind." She fluttered her lashes as she pulled her chin free.

"What brings you to my humble abode, my treasure?" He reclaimed her hand and tugged her closer.

Much to my disgust, she went without hesitation. She glanced up at him and smiled her knee-threatening smile. "Are we rushing straight to business?"

"Business with you is always a pleasure." Slick as oil.

Tarsha threw her head back and laughed.

Basi seized the opportunity to kiss her neck.

I had an unexpected desire to punch the wall, which would have hurt as well as giving away my presence. Sternly, I reminded myself that this was merely another unforeseen development to take in stride. It would be foolish to ruin my hands over the likes of Tarsha, who had more secrets than a priest and the morals of a cat. Tanris was going to regret not letting me put her over the side of the ship.

With careless grace, she lifted a shoulder to discourage his amorous intentions. Like the dancer she was, she pivoted and linked her arm through his. One could not fault her talent for rejection without alienation. "I see you're fine, Basi. How am I?" she teased.

"As perfect as always." He claimed her fingers for another kiss, as subtle as a starving man presented with a plump roast goose. "And as elusive."

Tarsha gave his nose a light, playful, and far too familiar tap. "You never were one for the genteel courtesies."

"They have their uses, but why squander time when you and I know each other so very well?"

"We did," she allowed, a coy tip to her head. The shameless flirt. "Once."

"You want something. I want something. We will come to an accommodation." His mouth created a smug smile; his eyes remained unmoved. "You wouldn't be here otherwise."

"Perhaps we could retire to your study to discuss our mutual needs over a glass of wine," she suggested.

"There are more comfortable rooms than my study." He had all the subtlety of an avalanche. What did she see in him?

Tarsha arched her neck, a swan courting a goat. One graceful finger traced a line down his shirt front. "As I recall," she said in a low, throaty voice that wafted to my little balcony and raised an unwelcome shiver up my spine, "*you* owe *me* a favor. I think we'll discuss that first."

"First," he repeated.

She smiled as she took two or three steps away from him. "As fascinating and talented as you are, darling, I've more important concerns."

Basi clasped his hands behind his back and walked a full circle around her. "Such as?"

"Do you always conduct your business on the doorstep?"

"Depends on what's in it for me."

From her bodice, Tarsha produced a small fan and snapped it open. Crimson flowers appeared like a magic bouquet. With thorns. I'd laughed at the idea of a fan as a weapon until she demonstrated. On me. She'd followed that with lessons on the use of scarves, hairpins, belts, quill pens, and sundry other items. Excellent skills to have when, on the rare occasion, a mere look didn't kill. With a desultory flap, she sighed and offered Basi a bored expression.

He snorted a laugh. "You drive a hard bargain."

"This is hardly a bargaining session. I am here to either collect a debt or—Well." Her serene smile might have curdled milk. "I've known you for a long time, haven't I? It would be such a shame to bring our friendship to an end."

I resisted the temptation to leap up and demand to know exactly how long and close their *friend*ship was. It wouldn't do to miss a single word of this revealing exchange.

Basi's superior stance melted into defensiveness as he folded his arms across his chest. Funny, but when Tanris did that, it usually signified an attempt to control his temper. People tended to retreat. "Pray tell, how can I be of service, lambkin?"

Still fanning herself, Tarsha studied her prey with an expression of adoration. If Basi knew her so well, he might wonder. Finally, she breathed a tremulous sigh. "My darling sister has gotten herself into an unfortunate predicament."

"And you want me to rescue her." Distaste dripped from every word.

"Good heavens, no. Rescue is hardly your specialty." She drifted further, letting her attention linger on an enormous picture. "How martial. Krysar's work?"

Basi bowed his head. "He is the foremost painter of war scenes."

"And domination." Her laugh was charming. "You've quite settled into your new guise, Basi—at least in your entrance hall."

"I suppose you want to see the rest," he remarked drily.

"I suppose you want to show it off," she shot back, glancing at him over her shoulder. A conspicuous tease marked the sway of her hips as she moved to another canvas.

This, I warned myself, *is what Tarsha does.*

Still, seeing her work her delightful wiles on another man made my mouth dry and my jaw hurt. I could well imagine the effect it had on Prince Basi. The man that didn't respond was carved of stone. And why did I react at all? That was exactly what had got me tossed into a cage and resulted in my figuratively clipped wings. I'd decided months ago that I was immune to her. *So be immune, Crow. Resist! There are other pearls in the ocean!*

I bent and pressed the crown of my head hard into the rock wall. Banging it in frustration would only garner attention I needed to avoid.

"Whatever is that *smell*?" Tarsha asked. "Offal?"

I stiffened, not even daring a peek.

If nothing else, I enjoyed picturing Basi's look of indignation. A lengthy silence fraught with sizzling energy followed, then he cleared his throat. "I detect only your sweet perfume and the flower in your hair. For all I know, you're making things up to distract me. And if that is the case, how can I help but admire your inventiveness and determination?"

"Indeed." It was far too easy to imagine the coy look to go along with that single sultry challenge.

That made him laugh. "Come, my lady, and I'll show you all the juicy bits of being the undisputed Prince of Masni."

Their voices followed them away into the prince's den. Left on my own, I did some quick debating about what to do next. What was Tarsha up to? The first and most obvious conclusion was another betrayal. There was also the minute possibility that she planned to help me. Us... But how? By getting herself imprisoned along with the others? Did the gods expect me to save her, too?

"Ancestors?" I muttered. "You can come back any moment. Sooner rather than later would be appreciated."

I had no time to waste waiting for them. The list of people and things needing rescue wasn't growing any shorter: Tanris, Senza, and our companions (for even if they'd escaped, they were in danger); Enikar; the idol; and now Tarsha, as likely as not. The gods must set real value by my skills. So, where to start?

It turned out that a drunk pirate could get away with a lot. And a drunk, incredibly *smelly* pirate had even more latitude. I blacked one eye with coal and berry juice, then rubbed ash into my hair and skin. With spoiled potatoes stuffed into a pocket, nobody wanted to get anywhere near me.

I sang—wildly off-key—and my adopted fellows cursed and gave me a wide berth. Who could blame them? I'd steer clear of me, too. Rotten potatoes smell worse than anything in the world. On the bright side, they prompted some genuine gagging. No one would doubt my otherwise superb performance.

With sloshing bottle in hand, I lurched up and down stairs and corridors. A woman with a broom dealt me a stern drubbing across the shoulders. A silk-clad dandy shouted and called for his guards when my clever calculations caused our collision. The guards, armed with spears, poked and prodded me on my way. Attempts to keep their elbows over their noses hampered their efforts.

It was a delicate game I played, measuring the amount of upset I created. Landing myself in a dungeon cell might lead me to my captured colleagues, but it would be easier to get them out if I remained free. My ability was not in question, but time was. The need for haste propelled my every step, and the occasional shudder of floors and walls only heightened the sense of urgency.

Locked doors presented personal challenges and rarely defeated me. Basi's were no different. One sealed up a stockpile of weapons. Another revealed a library with rows and rows of books and scrolls— and a librarian.

He turned a deep squint at me from a table piled head-high with ledgers. Light from a dozen candles gathered and reflected in the magnifying glass he gripped. "You can't be here," he croaked in alarm, and pointed menacingly with his quill pen.

"I can't?" I pressed both hands against my chest. "Am I dead?"

"No, fool. You can't enter through a locked door. It is impossible."

"That's what I thought. Something to do with science."

Doubt seeped into his expression.

"Let me explain. The door didn't open. And then it did. And look, here you are!" I clapped in delight.

"It was locked."

"You just said it wasn't. We couldn't be here, else."

"You must leave. Are you drunk?"

Such a question invited conversation rather than obedience. I smiled happily. "I am. Would you care to join me?" From the roomy pocket of my borrowed canvas raincoat, I fished a rotten potato. By now, my nose hardly recognized its offensiveness.

The librarian stared, caught his breath, then pursed his lips in rueful dismissal. "If that were a bottle, I might be tempted." He waved his feather. "Go away. I've work to do."

"Oh, sorry." I traded the potato for the wine and edged nearer with all meekness.

"Dear gods, you stink," he rasped. A cautious fellow, he gave serious study to the offering I made before slowly setting down his magnifying glass and snatching the liquor. Yanking the cork loose with more ferocity than any mild and meek clerk ever dared display in public, he took a hearty swig.

"Do I?" I took the opportunity to glance over the accounts before him.

"Like a cesspool." Cautious, as I'd noted, he put a hand over the papers.

"You can read all those squiggles?" I asked, picking up a loose page. I screwed up my eyes and turned it this way and that. It detailed cargo from the ship *Diamond* out of Brenath Port: wheat, cotton, iron ore… While that one-handed theatrical display occupied his attention, I slid a few more sheets into my ever-obliging pockets.

"Clearly." He snatched the *Diamond's* report away to safety.

"Got a headache from 'em already," I complained. "Whyever do you do it?" With thumb and forefinger, I massaged my allegedly aggrieved eyes.

"Unlike some, I like to make an honest living."

So did I. I was honestly very good at my trade. "Oh." I nodded. "Why?"

"I enjoy food and a roof over my head without the threat of having my neck stretched."

"Very sensible." Shaking one finger at him in appreciation, I turned my gaze about the room. I'd expected more dust. Mayhap he got his exercise cleaning. "You've read *all* this?"

"Indeed." He sniffed. It was a mistake covered by another hasty swallow of alcohol and the careful—and futile—placing of his feather over his nose.

Without further time to explore, I could see nothing to help find my friends or incriminate the prince. I whirled back to my host. "I can write my name. A friend—or someone—taught me once. Shall I show you?"

"As delightful as that sounds, I must return to my work." The man rose and came around the table, shooing me with his all-purpose feather. He gave my shoulder a push with an uncompromising finger, and shut the door firmly behind me. The lock clicked into place. "Thank you for the refreshment," he added, his voice muffled.

"A fine way to treat your friends!" I pretended to complain, then glanced down the corridor. I suspected Prince Pompous's office would be nearby. Indeed, a door sporting *two* locks neighbored the immaculate Hall of Records. I chewed on my tongue as I scrutinized them. The logic eluded me. Serhat employed *pirates* by the score, and he protected his—well, *anything*—with ordinary locks? Fully expecting a painful shock of energy, I scrunched my face and set a finger to one, then the other.

Nothing. No magic.

Hm. Perhaps they had to be opened simultaneously. I'd run into that trick a time or two. The consequences were usually extreme violence with an eye toward fatality. I checked the latch; just because a door boasted locks didn't always mean they were in use.

They were.

Another casual glance about reassured me I was still alone. The prince was either stupidly confident or this was a trap.

I bent low to peer into the keyholes. Diffused daylight waited beyond. With a shrug, I got out an extra pick to go with the one I'd used to introduce myself to the secretary next door and let myself in. A slow push against the wood revealed no unwelcome squeak, no trigger of death, and no occupant.

Further inspection showed no trip wires or other traps.

Perfect.

The prince's study was tastefully appointed. Pale panels lined the walls and made up both bookshelves and desk. Aquamarine draperies framed windows overlooking the ocean, and thick, expensive rugs padded the floor. The delightful scent of citrus filled the air. There were, of course, the usual items any thief would find attractive, but they'd been chosen with restraint and elegance. There was a stunning ivory diptych of a fellow with an enormous crown, riding his horse over the backs of the poor souls he'd vanquished. A round, lidded silver box inset with diamonds. A dragon as long as my forearm carved from amber (which I found acutely tempting). A human skull plated in gold (which decreased the tastefulness of the collection). A porcelain urn decorated with painted ships and filled with ashes. I've never understood the saving of ashes when they make such good fertilizer.

Behind the desk hung a painting of Serhat, complete with the tired-looking eyes. How unfortunate to be permanently saddled with the appearance of exhaustion—though it might be a useful way to deceive one's enemies. I recognized it as the work of the painter Surriz I'd seen in the parlor downstairs.

None of the aforementioned items would fit in my pocket or sack, but I contemplated the dragon. I could hide it somewhere within the fortress and return to retrieve it at a later date. The artist had cleverly captured the essence of scales with etching as delicate as a spider's web. Sleek wings tucked against the creature's sides had the look of fragile silk. Eyes of pearl were inscribed with inky black slits. Silver tipped its long, curling tail.

I was in love.

From the window, I scanned access to the roof and looked for a practical cranny to use as a hiding place. A chimney might do if I wrapped the dragon tightly, but I'd have to give up the coat. It was very handy for disguising things I couldn't afford to be questioned about.

Ah, but a panel from Princey-Poo's lovely silk drapes would also work, and silk was slow to ignite. I didn't want sparks from the fire to ruin the dragon, after all. As I turned about to search for a suitable binding, my gaze fell upon a crudely carved lump of rock on Basi's excruciatingly tidy desk. Such a desk said a lot about the man. Reed pens were assembled with military precision. A trio of ink pots marshaled the troops. A single stack of correspondence had every edge aligned, and dull marble bookends held a row of tomes captive. In the middle of all that, the rock resembled a turnip arrayed against jewels.

I edged around the desk with valid circumspection.

Squat and gray with over-rounded limbs, the carving cupped a delicious burnt orange gem in each bowl-like hand. The intense yellow-green eyes had to be niamedite—a gemstone named after the neighboring volcano island Niameda. Around the thing's neck (and clashing hideously with the other stones), was a string of bright red coral beads. Balls of tarnished silver interspersed them. I would have mistaken them for iron if someone had not gone to the effort of polishing a few to a brilliant sheen. It wasn't as big as I'd imagined; perhaps the size of a large grapefruit, but uglier by far.

The gods had led me right to the Masni Idol, but what did they want me to do with it?

I decided now was the perfect time to transfer my rotten, squishy potatoes into a desk drawer. This required removing a small coin purse and a slender book of poetry whose cover caught my eye. And while I was being efficient, I stashed the purloined papers from the other room into my boot where they'd be safe.

I rubbed my hands together, whispered a prayer, then gingerly touched the idol. A telltale tingle danced over my skin, but—to my wonder—I found the phenomenon pleasant. Bold now, I picked it up to ascertain its weight. The thing was too light to be solid. Turning it about, I could discover no opening where it had been hollowed. How curious…

"What do you make of this, oh great Ancestral Deserters?" I asked.

Peering into the idol's eyes, the queerest sensation came over me. My vision blurred. Shadows flitted back and forth. I was drawn *inside* and spun about like a child's toy. Then I was looking out into the world—or rather *a* world, as it was not the room in which I currently stood—through a haze of yellow-green.

I very nearly dropped the thing.

I thought I recognized the chamber where I'd bargained with the big fellow. Instantly, my vision cleared to reveal him sitting in the same chair, enthusiastically stuffing his face. He used fingers rather than utensils, and bits of white stuck to his layers of chins. Rice?

"Augh!" I jerked back, but shrewdly kept my grip, which was no small feat as my view spun like mad. I had to squeeze my eyes shut for a minute before I got sick. This thing would take some getting accustomed to.

"Very well," I told it. "Can you show me my friend Tanris?"

As I focused on an image of him in my mind, the idol whisked me through the halls at blinding, nauseating speed. I had the barest glimpse of Tanris standing before a wall of stone, head hanging low.

Keys clattering in the locks broke my focus.

Down went the idol, back to its place. I vaulted over the desk, grabbed a book off the shelf, and turned to a random page. Then I dropped into a casual lean against the windowsill. Smooth as butter.

The door opened, and several things came inside. Tarsha paused, wearing an air of surprise. Right behind her, Basi Serhat wore one of insufferable smugness. A black dog as big as a horse trailed at his heels. Then came half a dozen well-armed giants sporting enough *paki* to make normal men stoop under the weight.

Well, the giants waited outside in the hallway, or Basi's office would have become very crowded indeed.

Most notably, the Ancestors entered with a rustle of dried, faded leaves and the scent of earth.

Thank you, gods who love me, thank you...

"Crow..." Tarsha breathed.

"Who—" Basi's brow curled in irritation. "Do you know him?"

"What?" Recovering herself with enviable calm, she turned a confused look on Basi.

"You called him by name."

The confusion grew. "I said *oh*. I didn't expect—" She waved a hand up and down in my direction. "Blessed Goddess Tanju, what is that stench?" Of course she would call on the goddess of hearths, brooms, and cleanliness.

I did not know what game she played, or if it would help or hinder me to reveal our acquaintance, so I simply smiled. Meanwhile, the Ancestors petted and patted, reassuring themselves of my safety. Most troubling, I could barely hear them. Their eddying ruffled my hair and flipped the page of my book. Not helpful.

Basi couldn't decide whether to be angry, and the indecision contorted his features. He had a strange face—small eyes well cushioned in bags, and a small mouth with his upper lip more prominent than the lower. His chin was rather too pointed.

The dog, meanwhile, trotted up to me and began a very thorough acquaintance. Tail wagging, it was not at all troubled by my rotten-potato-induced miasma. A clear sign it had decreased markedly since abandoning the culprits in the drawer. My nose thanked me. My sense of physical self preservation did not. The dog didn't care.

"Er... hello?" Half expecting my hand to disappear in its maw, I offered it a pat on the head.

It licked my fingers.

"Spike!" Basi shouted. "Hold him!"

The Ancestors, sounding as distant as Bright Bay, hissed and fluttered their indignation. Evidently, Spike heard them quite well. He yelped and dashed out of the room, all but knocking Basi over. The waiting henchmen staggered like drunken pigeons as he crashed through them.

With the erstwhile guard dog gone, Basi turned to his guard humans. "Malu. Betsin. Get in here." He'd chosen the two tallest, no doubt for the intimidation factor. They filed in and when Basi gestured, they came to stand in front of me. One of them immediately took a step back. Who knew a stench could be such a useful weapon of defense? Not that they smelled so sweet themselves. I detected the reek of onions from the fellow in the red-striped vest. Between us, we overpowered the giant in the wonderful baggy coat. I do like baggy coats on my marks...

Basi glided between them, a delicate kerchief held over his nose and mouth. Sleepy eyes studied my features, my gear, settled on the *paki* hung round my neck, then drifted to the book. "You can read?"

"Some," I replied, and lifted the book.

"Oshada?"

"Not a word." I gave him a conspiratorial wink. "Can you?"

He took the tome and gently closed it before pressing it to his chest. "Who are you?"

"Bayram Blackfeather. Oh. I mean *Bayram Blackfeather, your Highness.*" I offered a deep bow.

"What are you doing here?"

When I straightened, I glanced Tarsha's direction. She gave a short, sharp inclination of her head toward the door. "Well… trying to read, m'lord." I waggled my fingers at the book.

"The truth," he demanded.

"It's a long story, shall we sit?"

"No."

I plopped myself down in one of the two chairs facing the desk anyway. *[Listen. Listen!]* I thought as hard as I could at the Ancestors. They whisked around me, runnels of chill against my skin, a flip of a strand of hair. Good. *[Make a little noise in the hall. A little, all right? And when I stand, turn this room upside down.]*

I wasn't certain, but I imagined they echoed *[upside down… upside down…]*

If they didn't hear or understand, I'd have to come up with another plan. Fast.

Meanwhile, I took my time yanking about my too-big coat until I was comfortable. Elbows on the arms of the chair, I steepled my fingers. No one had moved. "Well, I suppose I shouldn't have my back to my audience." I shifted about, which better suited me anyway.

"I am a finder," I announced. "I find things."

"He could find my fist in his face," one of the giants offered.

"In other words, you're a thief." Basi ignored him, brows lowering. He gave the book to the giant on the right, who set it down on a table with uncommon reverence.

The cover flapped open, drawing a lengthy stare from the guard.

Across the room, a picture *screeked* sideways on the wall. Murmurs bubbled in from the hall. As a marvelous bonus, Tarsha shrieked and grabbed for the hibiscus behind her ear. She missed. It tumbled to the ground and skipped away like a naughty child.

"By the stars." Basi's heated gaze shot to the doorway. "What is it *now?*"

Over and over, I repeated in my head the phrase—*prayed* the phrase—*[Chaos when I stand! Chaos when I stand!]*

Something—flowers?—fluttered past. A man shouted. Two giants hove into view, flailing at one another. When a hat cartwheeled past, I leaped to my feet.

"What in all the starry skies…!" I exclaimed, the perfect picture of innocence.

The Ancestors gusted into the room. I had to admit, when they did 'chaos,' they did a very thorough job. Books flew off the shelves. Paintings skewed, and a few joined the flying tomes. An ink pot shattered on the floor. Candles snapped into pieces. The neat column of carved pens leaped into the air. One after another, they stabbed into the nearest wall—barely missing me.

"Hey!" I protested the indignity.

While the others shouted, covered their heads, and held their windblown clothing down, I grabbed the idol with one hand and a giant with the other. The one with the coat. Into his pocket went the carving as I staggered against him and fished about the space. I came up with a stubby club to slide into my own pocket.

"Magic!" he cried in terror, trying to scrape me off himself.

But Tarsha was there to slap him. "Pull yourself together. Panic helps no one, least of all yourself." The Ancestors dragged her dark hair across her face. It did little to hide her blazing eyes.

"Bind him!" Basi pointed at me. "Take him to the secret chamber."

"Wait! Why?" I cried. "I didn't do anything!"

Stripe-Vest thrashed at the air, reeled our way, and caught me in a one-armed hug. "Come!" he shouted to his compatriot. "Hurry!"

The lovely painted urn streaked past, streaming ash in its wake. Coughing and hanging onto each other, the three of us lurched out the door and into the waiting arms of the remaining guards. Eager to be away from the frightening storm, the pirates closed in and shoved me down the corridor.

—20—
Secret Chamber

There is no fighting six giants, particularly if their determination is fortified by fear. A slight miscalculation, but acceptable if it got me where I needed to go. They prodded me all the way to the end of the hall and down twenty-nine dizzying flights of stairs. I may exaggerate. It was probably only about seven or so. One of the advantages of living atop a mountain was the considerable distance between your abode and the 'bottom,' wherever that might be. We left the knee-destroying stairs and journeyed through several twisting corridors, at last passing through an open doorway that was not secret at all.

Lights hung at regular intervals. They were strange things, the likes of which I'd never seen but immediately coveted. Clear, glowing stones filled glass bowls suspended from delicate golden ropes. They cast a light as bright as day. A good cubit wide, they were too big to carry off. At some point, I must talk to the Ancestors about creating a pocket that only I could access. One that would hold any size or shape of treasure, and was accessible no matter where it was. Oh, and if it went with me everywhere, it must be weightless, even when full. How big was 'full'?

The pirates interrupted my fantasizing. Three of them dragged me to the side and snapped a pair of manacles on my wrists. A chain of twelve miserly links connected one to the other, passing through an iron ring set in the wall. If the gods still loved me, I wouldn't develop an itch too low to scratch.

"Here now!" I complained. "Watch the hand. The hand! *Ow!*" My voice climbed three or four notches as I howled in false agony. If ever I retire from this career, I shall take up the theater. "You've broken it, *aaaggghhhh*, you've *broken* it!" I added to the horror of the scar I bore with an exaggerated twist of my fingers.

Kindly, the Pocket inspected the damage. "What happened to it?"

"A bloody-minded *wizard* like your master." I made a weak attempt to escape him, then dropped my head toward the opposite shoulder. Wrung out, I wilted against the wall in a theatrical pose. Did the discomfort come from actual pain of a still-healing wound, or was it in my head?

"Master's no wizard."

"Sure, he's not." The collar of my coat muffled my words. I still contrived to insert a note of despair. "I suppose that mess upstairs was your doing."

"Course not." He paused. "Maybe pretty lady."

"Great. Two of them."

"What's that?" another asked.

"Wizards. He says th'prince an' th'lady be wizards."

Silence fell. The six of them exchanged uneasy looks. Providently for the case, if not my health, the walls trembled and moaned. Dust sifted down from the ceiling.

Beyond my captors, I made out two figures at the far end of the room. The chamber's pale stone and tile reflected the clever lights. It hid not one detail of their miserable state. Bruised and bloodied, both of them, but I recognized Tanris's bald dome and Senza's unkempt ash blond locks.

I had not expected that. Didn't understand it, except they were thieves and trespassers in Basi's eyes. I knew well how thieves were treated when caught. Tanris raised his head a little, slowly, as if he feared moving too fast. What had the prince done to him? Darkness obscured his features—ruin rather than shadow.

Voices came from the hall, one masculine and one feminine, then Basi swept into the chamber with Tarsha at his side. The guards moved to clear the space around me, and the prince went to a shelf to gather several items into a sack.

Tarsha sauntered about, looking at this, touching that. There were plenty of things to admire: ropes and chains, manacles, a chair with nail-sharp spikes on the back and seat. A trio of spiked collars hung on the wall like gruesome picture frames. Pulleys dangled overhead. Half-a-dozen varieties of shears and pincers decorated the benches. Close by, a throne was fastened to the floor. Manacles and cuffs screwed into the woodwork suggested a less genteel purpose than seating royalty.

"Leisure pursuits?" I ventured, considering and discarding several ideas for escape, rescue, and possible destruction.

Basi turned a pleasant smile on me. "In a manner of speaking."

"I thought a secret chamber would be, oh, perhaps hidden?"

"You misunderstand. It is a chamber for *learning* secrets. Here." He handed the bundle to one of his men and grabbed another by the arm. "The two of you take this to my office. Don't get sidetracked. Stay and watch over it."

With them gone, I was left with four pirate giants, Basi, and the incomprehensible Tarsha to deal with.

Basi took a cloth from a stack beside a bowl on the table. He dipped it inside and wrung it out before he approached me. He washed the remnants of coal, juice, and ashes from my face with steady efficiency. "Ah, there you are," he murmured in satisfaction. "Malu, give him the rest of the bucket. See if we can wash some of the stench off."

Malu—or Stripe-Vest, as I'd thought of him—happily emptied the water over me. Coughing and spluttering, I shook my head to free my eyes of wet hair.

Basi wiped my face, but left the rest of me dripping. He sniffed. "Hmm, another, I think."

Another turned into four, with a heavy dose of vinegar added to the last. My eyes stung fiercely. I wanted to lick my lips, but spat instead. "Maybe one more of the water will finish the job?"

Basi studied me with narrowed eyes, but Malu had some genuine enthusiasm and obliged with joy.

"Thank you." I wiped my mouth with one hand, and gave him a grateful smile.

"Welcome." He bobbed his head—at which Basi rolled his eyes.

"Enough. What did you do with the idol, Blackfeather?"

A sound suspiciously like a cough came from Tanris's direction.

"The idol?"

"Don't play games with me; I'm not in the mood."

It would be imprudent to tell him I enjoyed games, and was good at them. Clapping my chest dragged the other hand toward the wall, thanks to the short chain. It also reminded me of the absence of my amulet. "I swear, I haven't seen the ugly thing since I was in your office."

"Search him."

Malu complied. Right away, he ran into the challenge of dealing with my hidden gear and padding. He opted to investigate my pockets before attempting anything more invasive. He found some sweets I'd taken from the kitchens and wrapped in a moderately clean cloth, a pair of bracelets provided by the general gathering in the great hall, and a feather pen that must have come from the good secretary. I only vaguely recalled putting it there.

In the other large pocket—the coat had six—he discovered the club I'd purloined from his friend. He paused and frowned before setting it in the pile he'd started at my feet. Then came the kerchief I'd used to keep the potatoes from seeping into the canvas.

He gagged and tossed it as far away as a damp, fragile piece of cloth could go—about the length of a horse from stem to stern.

"Dare I ask what died in there?" Basi inquired, nose wrinkled in distaste.

"Technically, I borrowed this coat, so I can't say what the previous wearer did with it. He should be firmly reprimanded." And blessed by the gods for aiding my cause.

Basi waved for Malu to go on. The big fellow added a collection of loose beads, a soggy bit of much-folded paper, a few coins, the Qarshan figurine, a sock, a folding knife with a bone handle, a chunk of cheese (a component to the stench I'd tried hard to ignore), and a tiny box with thread and needles.

Malu continued his task, patting down my legs and, perforce, running into my made-to-order greaves. He looked from me to Basi, who merely pursed his strange little mouth in annoyance. Malu loosed the greaves and massaged my boots to discover hidden weapons. I had to wonder if the shipping records tucked in there had suffered much from the bath. To my surprise, he buckled the leg armor back on when he finished.

"I need to take his coat off to finish," he told Basi.

"Obviously."

When Malu took the irons from my wrists, Pirate Pockets— Betsin, I supposed—picked up a spear from a barrel nearby. He shifted closer. Suspicious fellow. I was ordered to doff the coat and then keep my hands on my head. I waited for Betsin to recognize his weapon in the pile, but he merely watched the proceedings with a tight mouth and a tinge of green. Apparently, he was not an admirer of rotten potato, vinegar, and what-have-you.

Off came my bags, sacks, and padding. Removing all my gear and opening everything revealed rope, grappling hook, lock picks, a small flask of oil, a wedge, gloves, putty, pilfered trinkets, a utility knife, and so on. All the bits and bobs any good thief carried with him on a long job. But no idol. There were, however, two daggers besides the one I wore at my waist. Tanris's that I had found in the trap room, and Duzayan's...

Basi turned the latter over in his hands with a blend of fascination and discomposure. Eventually, he slid it free from the jeweled scabbard. The leather I'd wrapped around the hilt covered all the gems but the one in the pommel. Still, no man could deny the beauty of the thing. The weapon was well-crafted and perfectly balanced. It drew the eye in a manner that exceeded its physical attraction. *Witchy*, some would say, or *otherworldly*. They would be right. As much as looking at it provoked desire, holding it gave rise to an awfulness I had no words to describe.

Granted, recollection of my experience with it came in jumbled, disturbing pieces. What it had caused—and the wizard who had been responsible—would haunt me for a long time.

Behind Basi's shoulder, Tarsha stared at the blade. Slow recognition gave her skin a waxy hue. It was a weapon she knew intimately, painfully. After a moment, she hugged herself and shivered. Her thin silk gown did little to fend off the chill of the room, nor the breeze wafting through it. For a fact, I hadn't noticed either condition until I was dripping from head to toe. I decided to shiver, too. Must keep up appearances, though the act wasn't entirely feigned. While Basi contemplated me, I massaged my scarred hand and hunched miserably.

"So it's true," the prince said at last. He jammed the blade back into the scabbard and tucked it into his belt. Covertly, he rubbed his hands together as if trying to remove something unpleasant from his skin. "You're an assassin."

"Of character, occasionally; of people, no." Memory begged to differ. I'd sent one man tumbling into darkness and lit another up like a human torch. Wizards, both, and it had been in self-defense, but they were still dead because of me. It was bad enough those images troubled my dreams, I refused to go down that path while my eyes remained wide open. I nodded toward the dagger. "With that, you mean? It's ceremonial. Symbolic. Though I suppose it would suffice in a pinch, real knife work might ruin it."

"What ceremony?" He had the weapon, he could afford to venture closer.

I had to think fast, for I was not about to tell him it involved magic. "Coming of age," I lied. "It is a replica of a dagger used by one of my ancestors to kill a giant." One worked with the inspiration available.

"Seems impractical for such a sizable task." Funny, wasn't he?

One shoulder lifted in a shrug. "That's the story. The story is also that the jewels are real."

That information set him aback. "Why carry it if it is so useless?"

"G-good luck." I trembled involuntarily from head to toes. The cold wasn't an act anymore.

Basi gazed at our surroundings. "Is that so?"

Chattering teeth ruined my beam of assurance. "It's never let me d-d-down before."

"Well, it's mine now, but at this point I'm not sure I would trust it any more than I trust you."

"No, I suspect not." Pause. "H-h-highness," I added, weaving a thread of insult into a pretense of vulnerability whilst playing up my suffering. "C-can I have my coat back?"

In an unexpected show of consideration, he motioned for Malu to return the hideous thing. I wouldn't have bothered, but I needed the pockets. Silent, Basi continued to examine me after I'd shrugged it on. He examined me for so long that Malu had plenty of time to return everything to the packs, and he did a fair job of it, too. I could have left the club and the previous owner's cheap trinkets behind without tears, but they went in with the other things and I did not argue. When he was done, everything went into the big canvas sack. All thanks to the gods of packing things and (hopefully) speedy escapes.

"Where is the idol?"

I held my hands out to my sides, palm up, before hugging myself again, shivering dramatically. "I would tell you to search me, but you've already done that. If I had stolen it, wouldn't I have it on me?"

"The storm in my office. You caused it."

I snorted. "Magic, you mean? If I had used magic, both the idol *and* myself would be long gone."

"Unless you remained to rescue your friends."

"Wouldn't I have used the magic for that, too?" *If only…*

"*Where* did you put it?" he growled, catching my scarred hand in both of his and twisting it.

I found myself bent in half, pressed against the wall, gasping in pain. I heard the Ancestors then, their high-pitched wails scraping my eardrums. "Ancestors! Wait! *Wait!*" I shouted at them.

Betsin's spear tip hovered inches from my eye. More suspicion crimped his heavy brow. "What ancestors?"

Basi ignored him and eased his grip ever-so-slightly. "If you value your life, you will cooperate. Where is it?"

My position made it hard to look up. "I'd tell you if I could." Except that would mean he'd have it in his possession—and I'd have to steal it back again, along with the dagger. "I didn't have it when I left the office; I don't have it now. Twisting my arm off and beating me over the head with it won't change the answer."

Displeasure rolled off him in thick, heavy waves. He shoved me away and stepped back. "Ingas," he said over his shoulder. "Take a message to the steward. Tell him to lock down the fort."

"Eyah, lord." Ingas gave an awkward, hunched bow and ran out the door.

"I don't envy you." Unbending, I rubbed my abused wrist. Betsin eased back a fraction. A smart fellow, he kept the spear out of my reach. Not that I'd ever attempt to physically overpower an ogre half again as big as myself. "Having a wizard at large in your home. Fort. Castle."

"Is this the work of one of your demon slaves?" Basi pressed, more angry than worried. Normal people would worry; wizards would not.

I held up my fingers while I counted. "One, they can't do magic. Two, if they did, they wouldn't be slaves. Three, I imagine they'd all be slaughtered on sight; wizards aren't very popular in Bahsyr. Four, they aren't actually—"

"What is he paying you?"

I paused in theatrical bewilderment. "Who?"

"Gaziah." He might have been talking about a bag of peanuts for all the warmth in his tone.

"Gaziah?" I echoed. "The emperor of the Bahsyr Empire?" I inserted a hint of curiosity. "What would he be paying me *for*?"

"Do you think me a fool?"

"I don't know you well enough to judge, but I'm detecting shades of delusion."

Amusement concealed behind one hand, Tarsha resumed her casual stroll. "I thought you said he was a common thief." She pretended indifference to the surroundings, but I had an inkling she sought something.

"*What?*" A question that applied to her accusation and my suspicion.

"You do find things." Basi's expression turned mocking.

"He is entertaining," Tarsha said.

"Finding is hardly the same as stealing," I put in. "That requires taking."

"And subterfuge. For instance, is your true name *Blackfeather* or *Crow?*"

Did he know more about me than I supposed? I expected he hadn't missed Tarsha's blurt, and he certainly hadn't achieved his position by pure, dumb luck. "Crows do have black feathers. Though I've seen some with white," I mused. "And I've heard gray exists, too…"

"You're stalling. It won't help you. Walk with me." He started away abruptly.

Hands in my oversized, empty pockets, I trailed after him, and Betsin trailed after me. The array of torture instruments made me queasy. I reversed that trend by considering them as possible weapons—of self-defense, of course. I am a thief, not a fighter, remember?

The chamber was longer than it first appeared. At last we fetched up in front of the… *apparatus* that held my friends. Alarm at their condition brought the queasiness right back.

Two square iron rods the width of my hand and about three cubits long protruded from small openings in the wall behind them. Attached to the end of each was an iron platform barely large enough to stand on. Soaked and shivering, Tanris and Senza each balanced, ankles and hands bound. They could not lean back to rest. Even if they'd not been tied, it would have been a stretch to reach out their arms to touch hands. If I'd stretched out my own arm, I wouldn't quite reach them.

And below? Utter blackness muffled the drenched snarl of the sea. Crashing surges churned up a chill mist.

Another tremor shook the room and I caught my breath as the pair wobbled. Tanris kept his eyes on me; Senza kept her gaze on her feet. Somehow, they managed to remain upright.

When stillness reigned again, Basi gave a mock bow in Tanris's direction. Perhaps he thought the movement obscured his apprehension. "You've met Commander Corryth Tanris of Gaziah's colorfully named Eagles."

Of course Tanris had another name. Didn't everyone? His mother probably called him *Little Corry, darling*, as any soft-hearted mother would. Or I assumed they would. Not having one myself, I could only guess. "Commander." I gave a short, polite nod that didn't acknowledge any acquaintance.

"I expect you know his companion's name, as well, since the three of you arrived together."

"Did we." No one could match my expertise in *droll*, but it didn't sound right to me. Too much emotion tainted it.

"I have eyes."

He should have used the past tense. In fact, those magical eyes nestled comfortably in the pocket of the prince's baggy-coated underling. But Basi's smirk would have done the actors of Marketh's famous Grand Stair Theater proud, I had to admit. That the theater occupied the site of a former temple dedicated to the god of mischief, delusion, and folly befit the moment.

"If that's true," I said, trying to control my anger, "you should know that Girl is mute."

Head down and face hidden, blood dripped from her chin.

Fire burned in my chest.

"And her name?"

"Girl."

"*Girl?* That's what you call her? How... uncivilized."

I'd had to earn her name; why shouldn't he?

"Some men are oblivious to culture and sophistication. They've no idea how to respect a woman." Tarsha came to stand beside me, nose up in an expression of disdain. She'd acquired a coat. *The* coat. Absurdly huge on her delicate frame, the hem brushed her ankles, and the pockets hung level with her knees. Did she realize the idol hid there? She'd tucked her hands into opposite sleeves.

With an effort, I modulated my voice, giving it the tone of flippancy I reserved for the upper-crustiness. "Please explain the civility that prompts one to beat a mute girl. And surely you know *Corry* is far too noble and lofty to sneak about murdering people from the shadows."

"That brings us back to you."

"If I *were* an assassin, Your Luminescent Highness, I would have dispatched you in the entry while you were flirting with *her*." A slight tip of my head indicated Tarsha. "You should consider the timing of her arrival."

Tarsha glared at me as if I'd sprouted horns.

Basi laughed. "Lady Tarsha and I go back a long way. We are very dear friends and occasional lovers."

Lady, was it? Should I wonder that she'd never told me about this *dear friend*? And how could she have been intimate with someone so... oily? "Friends and lovers make the very best traitors." I felt her recoil in shock through that gift the Ancestors had given me. I didn't feel one whit of guilt.

"Indeed..." Basi echoed and rocked back on his heels, pursing his lips in reflection. It was not a flattering look.

"What do you want from me?"

"The truth."

"Do you? How will you recognize it? You won't accept the fact that we're here looking for someone. You think we're assassins, and nothing else will satisfy you. And *that* confession is a double-edged sword. If it's true, we die. If it's not, but we say so anyway because you torture us until we'll confess *anything* to be free of pain, we die." I threw one hand up in exasperation.

Tanris looked at me from the corners of his puffy eyes. It unnerved me that he continued to maintain his silence. Senza—well, she could hardly sign with her hands behind her back, but why did she not even glance my way? What malicious game was Basi playing?

"Tell me about this." I flicked my fingers toward the pair.

"Ah, this ingenious contraption is the work of previous residents." From a hook on the wall, Basi took an iron bar that looked very much like a key, but four cubits long. The bit was one piece, shaped like a blocky, squared zigzag, and well worn.

"The early natives left quite a legacy throughout the island. I'm not convinced their progeny inherited their intellect. Take this, for instance. The pedestals are balanced. If weight is taken off one, the other collapses. This key locks both of them in place for loading." Basi used it to point to a small hole in the wall between Tanris and Senza, on a level with the bars holding them up. "Or unloading, I suppose; I've never had the opportunity. I'm still learning to judge endurance."

"Have you had much practice?" Tarsha dared a cautious look over the edge, then swiftly pulled back.

"Enough." He followed her glance and his mouth twitched in a smile.

I had a mind to shove him into the space, and Tarsha with him, but I couldn't predict whether they'd go straight down or crash into one of my friends. And here, so close to the noisy churn of the sea below, I could not hear the mysteriously muted whisper of the Ancestors or even tell if the draft came from them or the opening. I didn't even know if they were still with me.

"I've offered them relief if they but confess." Basi rested the key against his shoulder and propped his hand on his hip, the very image of elegant disappointment.

"Confess to what, exactly?"

"The obvious. They—*you*—are here to rid Gaziah of his inconvenient, interfering uncle."

I took a step sideways, which brought me directly in front of Tanris. "You look hideous. Are you all right?"

He grunted. Though I knew him and his grunts well, this time I couldn't interpret, but it was impossible to miss the pain he suffered. A fierce beating had mangled Tanris's face, leaving it swollen and bleeding. No visible gag or contraption prevented him from speaking. Another thought occurred to me, too horrifying to contemplate.

Gods give me strength…

I forced myself to go on, forced myself to show no concern. "Did you have a murder plan you didn't tell me about?"

Another grunt accompanied a minute shake of his head.

He must think me unforgivably cavalier.

"I will confess to one thing, your Highness" I said, directing my words to the self-named prince. "I know Commander Tanris fairly well. And here's something about him: he would never lie. Not ever." It might have been my imagination, but Tanris's eyes seemed to thaw slightly from icy outrage to gratitude. "Why do you need a confession if you're going to kill us anyway?"

"I am not a monster!" Basi growled, mouth curling in a most unattractive manner. "I have principles."

Tanris growled back, broad shoulders hunched and abused face livid. I feared his emotions would tumble him into the abyss.

I couldn't watch, so I considered the ceiling. "What principle are you exercising here? I don't recall these particular lessons in any of the books I've read about nobility and chivalry and—"

"Stop."

I gave him a sideways glance. He'd lowered his hands to his sides, one fisted and the other still gripping the key. He actually *trembled*. Next to him, Tarsha rubbed his arm, conciliating.

"Your Duke Enikar—" Basi's smooth voice deserted him, coming out in a rasp. "It's him you're looking for. He's the traitor. He came to ask for my help."

False, but not completely so… "Yes, petitioning a man long a thorn in his nephew's side seems like a logical move for him to make."

"Gaziah has unpopular plans to expand his borders."

"To Corunn and Uburrh?" Who'd want them? But the north countries were the only bit of unconquered land on the continent, so I supposed it made sense to any empire-building sovereign.

"Oh, Corunn is already accomplished. Gaziah's daughter will wed Prince Dheki in three weeks. With the alliance of the powerful Bahsyri Empire sealed, his father will take Uburrh, whether or not they cooperate. The other kingdoms will fall like dominos. It may very well be the first bloodless integration in centuries. And once the north is his, Gaziah will turn his eyes westward."

All true. Or he believed it true, anyway. "Taking the islands would provoke a war with the Confederacy."

"Oh…" Tarsha breathed, all delicate alarm and dismay.

"You're thinking too small."

"You think he wants to—what? Conquer the world?" I could not hide my astonishment.

"Are you familiar with the Yetajat?"

"Of course." Corunn's southern neighbors across the Gulf of Kalju, Yetaja owed its fame to wondrous ship-building skills. And access to an enormous forest. They were also firmly controlled by the empire.

Basi turned his gaze upon Tanris, who glared back. "They're already making ships for him."

Tanris grunted again, and I imagined a sour expression beneath the blood.

"How does Enikar fit into this?" I asked.

"Enikar and several other foreword thinking *citizens* devised a way to stall Gaziah until they can move to stop his attempt at world domination. Enikar would foolishly venture into my grasp by seeking ancient artifacts here on the island. I'd pretend to hold him hostage. Demands for an exorbitant amount of gold would paralyze Gaziah's war funds. Whatever Gaziah feels about his uncle, I truly cannot say, but the empire loves him. Gaziah would be forced to step in, and I could see no harm in accepting boatloads of treasure from Gaziah, war or not." He swung the key to and fro—the *fro* bit putting it out over the chasm. "Imagine my surprise when the *Silver Hind* and Enikar's confederates never set sail. Instead, *Gaziah's* delegation snuck in through my back door. Not long after your arrival I realized that he actually planned to murder Enikar rather than buy his life." His mouth pursed in feigned regret. "Too late."

Cold crept over me, and it had nothing to do with the temperature spilling out of the crevice. "What do you mean?"

"Do you really believe I will let Gaziah cheat me again?" His arms swept outward; the key nearly clipped Tarsha's temple. A lithe dip-

and-step saved her. "He won't accept any fault in our quarrel. He won't negotiate a settlement with me. In fact, he refuses to have anything to do with me. It's time he pays for what he's done."

"With the lives of innocent people?" The tendons in my neck stood out, tight as bow-strings.

"You don't understand. Gaziah didn't care what it took to bring about my downfall. I don't care what it takes to bring about his—and he *will* fall. Enikar's little band is not composed entirely of saintly benefactors. They are powerful men more concerned with their purses than their peasants."

"Wouldn't it have been easier to hire an assassin?" He had to have plans that ran deeper than ruining one man.

"So much less satisfactory."

"How will this war benefit you?"

"Spectacular riches, from which comes spectacular power." A smile that oily might baste an entire goat.

I rubbed my forehead, then gave Tarsha a critical look. "This is a new depth of betrayal, even for you. What do you get out of this arrangement?"

She flinched, though not enough to draw Serhat's attention. What self-control she had… "I imagine you'll find out soon."

"Well." I turned back to my friends, arms akimbo. "You don't need us for this affair. Let us go."

"What I don't need is you trying to stop me or foolishly attempting to arrest me."

A low, ugly roar built up around us, and the entire room shook. Lamps swayed and danced. One fell as a crack raced across the ceiling. A shelf tumbled, spewing its contents across the floor.

Automatically, I widened my stance and put a hand out toward Tanris. He was so far!

"Ghiir'!" he cried.

I didn't understand. Panic constricted my lungs. Then it came to me. "Girl!" That same panic drove me to snatch the spear from Betsin's hand and jab him in the belly with the butt. The shaking floor assisted his fall.

Whirling, I pressed it against Girl's chest, hoping to give her enough support to stay upright. She wobbled. I tried to follow the motion, fear stabbing me. There were too many variables. The floor or the rods would dip. My strength would give out. I'd make a wrong move. Or I'd overcompensate and push her off. She'd fall, and Tanris would plummet after.

The earth's movement stopped, but the muffled, angry rumble remained.

I let out my breath. "Are you all right?"

Senza lifted her head. Her nose was broken, her mouth bloodied, and both eyes blackened. She gave a jerky nod.

What I felt then was as foreign as virtue to the nobility. Hot and cold all at once. Edges sharp as razors. "Let them go." I enunciated each word as I turned slowly on Basi.

"No." He retreated a step. Dust dulled the silver embroidery of his tunic and flecked his dark hair. "Betsin."

Tarsha screamed.

I spun, swinging with every ounce of strength I owned. Wood met the pirate's skull. Shattered. The giant tipped over sideways and crashed to the floor. Blood flowed from his temple.

I whirled back to Basi, flipping the broken weapon in my hand. It still had the pointy bit. "Give me the key."

"Not possible." He hurled it into the chasm, grabbed Tarsha's hand, and ran.

—21—
If I Coulda, Woulda, Shoulda

An entirely new level of panic—bristling with sheer horror—sliced through me. I was powerless to stop their dash toward a second door. *How could he do such a thing? And did Tarsha actually hate me?*

I hurled the broken spear after them. "Come back, you viperous cowards!"

I'm an excellent shot and my aim did not *quite* desert me. The spear sliced across Basi Serhat's back, eliciting a shout as it clattered into the far wall. It slowed him down not a bit. Tarsha flung a frightened look at me and disappeared.

With a cry of frustration, I whirled to Tanris and Senza. If I stayed to help them, there was a spectacular chance we'd all die, smashed in the rubble of Basi's crumbling fortress. The best, smartest option was to flee—to go after Basi, the dagger, and the idol.

Another alternative was to forget the baubles and the pardon, and instead escape to the health and safety of the Asonian coast.

Tanris watched me as if he knew every thought careening through my mind. I hated that he didn't yell at me, threaten me, or call me abusive names. He just stood there, calm and stoic and *Tanris*.

What I wouldn't do for a dollop of real magic right now... I couldn't even hear the Ancestors over the constant rumble, and what would I do with them if I did? They were *there*, though, contributing to the furor. Icy fingers scraped over me, pushing and pulling at me. Ragged motion filled the air with the scent of dirt and stone and old things. They might as well be in Marketh for all the good they did.

Except they could *move* me if I told them to. Would they wait for that?

Tanris motioned with his head toward Senza.

"No." Dashing a hand across my mouth, I searched for another key, clambering over fallen furniture and debris. There had to be another key. The walls, tables, and shelves turned up nothing.

"Crow." The word was badly mangled, but I recognized my name. Tanris gestured to Senza again.

The walls shuddered, dropping tiles, lights, dust, rocks... How long until it collapsed entirely?

Senza made an awful, quivering, moaning sound. One look at her, shaking like a leaf, and I knew she wouldn't be able to keep her balance much longer. She had to expect she'd die here.

"Gods who love me, there has to be *something* I can do!" I shouted. *I* didn't want to die; I didn't want my friends to, either. Frantic with desperate energy, I went through the room again, looking for a solution. There was no one else there. I'd laid Betsin right out, and I doubted he'd ever get up again. Where had the other two guards got off to? Not that I blamed them for making a hasty escape the instant their master turned his back.

I scooped up my sack, hitching it up over my shoulder, and spun in place.

There! The barrel of spears!

As fast as I could, I dragged it to the infernal contraption holding Tanris and Senza. Too many times, I had to stop to push debris out of the way. Every vibration, every tremor made me grind my teeth. They'd be nubs by the time we got out.

If we got out.

I settled my sack more securely, grabbed a spear, and dropped to my knees to shove the point beneath the rod holding Tanris up.

The very tip slid in, then jammed, not nearly deep enough in to accomplish anything. Stupid, useless thing! If only I could reach the lock!

Swearing, praying, I crawled along the chasm on my knees. One spear, two, then three, I wedged into the opening beneath Tanris. I repeated the maneuver for Senza.

"Hold," I ordered them. *Hold, hold, hold!*

I spied a pile of chains. Could I use those to tie them to something? Keep them from falling? Three cubits of space stood between the floor and my friends. Three cubits too far. Throw the chains around them? No, that invited disaster. Put them around their necks? Horrendous idea. Counterproductive, too.

"Ccggrow," Tanris tried again, half the word stuck in the back of his throat. He didn't move his mouth when he spoke. "You have to help Ggghir'. I 'e fine."

There was no possible way he'd be fine. "No."

"Zhoo it. You musht."

"I can't."

"Who elshe is der?" Remarkably intelligible. Far too calm.

I snatched another spear and shoved it beneath Senza. The metal wedges didn't quite fill the space. Rags might close the gaps and keep the bar from dropping. Leather would work better.

A high-pitched whine joined the steady grumbling of the earth. Further down the room the floor bulged up… and up. Fierce violet light stabbed my eyes, and squeezed them shut, yanking my head aside.

A *gate!* Gods no, not a gate!

The entire floor broke, skewing away from the eruption. Barrels, crates, books, boxes, shelves, papers, buckets, and *everything* slid toward us. The ground dropped once, twice, hard, plunging below the level of the blocks. The wall tipped. I had no time to brace myself before Senza toppled toward me, eyes wide and mouth open in a soundless scream.

Still on my knees, I reached up to seize the front of her shirt with both hands, hoisting her up and to the side. My legs fervently protested the wrenching. So did my back. Rolling over a sack of solid, oddly shaped things is painful.

Senza scarcely managed to tuck her shoulder as she crashed into the floor. I rolled on top of her, protecting her from the rubble raining down on us. Dust set us both to coughing.

Tanris was barely visible, sprawled crookedly across the spears whose ends had caught on the floor. A fresh line of blood scored his forehead where he'd struck. He didn't move. Couldn't if he'd wanted.

I dragged Senza against a tumbled cabinet for the scant protection it offered and staggered upright. A chunk of masonry bounced off my shoulder, sending me stumbling toward the brink of the chasm. I jerked away, fell to one knee, fought back up.

Fine particles choked the air. Purple light throbbed, distorting perception, blinding the eyes. The gate had formed *in* the floor, the top edge jutting upward about a yard. Joists and tiles cracked upward like a shell before the exit of a chick.

If any foreigners came through, they did so in the room below us.

If they survived at all.

Launching Senza to safety had widened the distance between me and Tanris. Small things—books and hammers and rocks—skittered past and fell into the chasm. I slung the sack down next to Senza and took an unsteady step forward. Then another. The urge for haste contended with the need for caution. Crow I may be, but my flying skills were severely limited, and no good would come of joining the items disappearing over the brink.

Amid the chaotic uproar, a fresh note of destruction demanded my attention. A slab freed by the gate hurtled my way.

Of a length and breadth as myself, but far heavier, I had no illusions about which of us would best survive the encounter. The peril of becoming Crushed Crow propelled me out of its path and back toward Girl's scanty shelter. The cupboard had a serious fault: there was space for only one person to huddle against the staved in doors. Well, that and its fragility.

On hands and knees, I grabbed the end and hauled myself to safety. I wasn't fast enough. A rough edge of the slab snagged my foot and tore, dragging me back, then shoving me away. Dirt and grit scraped bare skin. I scrambled further and curled in a tight ball, praying to reduce my size sufficiently to avoid getting caught, dragged, and mutilated. Head buried in my arms, I shouted—at the gods, the Ancestors, Tanris, Basi Serhat.

The slab blasted by, a reckless avalanche in its wake. Flying across the chasm, it rammed into the wall, shuddered, then the far end shrieked, stone dragging on stone before it plunged into the darkness. Stark terror paralyzed me.

Smaller rocks pelted me, reminding me of the danger of sitting still, like a chunk of salt in a grinder.

Warily, I lifted my head. The pall of dust obscured my view, but I knew where the doorway was. Or had been. A glance at Senza showed wide eyes in a smudge of pale face. I pulled myself together, forced myself up, and ran to where I'd last seen Tanris.

"Tanris!" I cried, getting a mouthful of grit for my effort. Mindful of debris that continued to bombard me, I crept forward. It was too far. It had to be too far… I inched a little further, squinting against the dust and against the awful violet light.

Finally, I made out a darker square against the far wall that had to mark the hole the support bar had fit into. And there was the keyhole.

And no Tanris.

"Gods of miracles and fortunes, please say you've caught him on some convenient pointy rock. Something. Anything…" Down on my knees again, I searched the murky darkness. "Tanris? *Tanris!*"

Stones from the lights I'd admired bounced past and into the depths. I grabbed a handful, hoping that several together would provide more concentrated light than a bunch of them skipping by. They inspired a painful burning sensation and the additional glow of green sparks. The gods are helpful in their way, but even with that illumination I saw nothing and no one below me, nor to either side.

The stones disappeared into a pocket. Fist against my mouth, I sat back on my heels. My head pounded and a vice squeezed my chest. This was *not* the time for my vivid imagination to supply images of Tanris, bound and helpless, crashing into the walls. Into the water.

I staggered to my feet, forcing myself to go to Girl. Malu hadn't put everything back the way I'd done, and it made finding Tanris's blade difficult. As soon as I had it I sawed at Girl's—*Senza's*, blast it! —bindings. Her wrists were raw, but the leather of her boots had saved her ankles.

"Can you walk?" I demanded.

Where is Tanris? she signed.

"We can't stay here." I got up, slung the bulky sack on, and dragged her upright. Every word I spoke sounded as if it came from underwater.

She shoved at me. *Where is Tanris?*

"Gone." A knot of horror clutched at my throat. I caught Senza's arm and pushed her toward the doorway. She fought, digging in her heels and slapping at me. "He's *gone!*" I shouted, giving her a hard shake and a glare she didn't deserve.

Her head moved back and forth vehemently.

"You want to die here?" I demanded aloud and with my hands at the same time.

She kept shaking her head.

I grabbed her wrist and hauled her after me.

Hope, I've discovered, is a curious thing. For instance, it gave us a reason to embark on the insane endeavor of trying to outrun a magic-fueled earthquake.

Underground.

In the dark.

Through unfamiliar territory.

Thank the gods, Senza didn't balk for long. We followed passages lit by torches for a short distance. A corridor crumbling before our very eyes quickly put that to an end, dowsing us in darkness. I pressed the stinging, shining stones into her hand. *Glowstones.*

"You'll have to go ahead."

She shook her head and tried to push the stones back at me.

"These are magic. I can't hold them. Now *go*."

Even as I gave her a little push of encouragement, a *crack!* deafened me. Apparently, I was not completely bereft of hearing, for right after that, a booming growl rocked the hill upon which the fortress stood. The entire island, for all I knew.

The gate had failed.

The resulting quake knocked us off our feet.

The earth screamed and popped and quivered—a surreal thing, given the loss of hearing. Muffled as it was, it sounded far away, but the rocks and broken bits of tile and plaster from the walls pelting us were real and immediate.

It was impossible to get up for what seemed like eternity. Even then, the ground continued to shift violently as we bounced and staggered down the passage. Senza took the lead at a lurching run.

The path forced upon us led further down. I resolved not to dwell on things like tombs and—How long would the light of those stones last?

Little by little, the shaking settled. All the many gods be thanked. We still had to navigate the rubble and squeeze through partially destroyed corridors. After walking for about a hundred miles, Senza stopped. She set the stones side by side in a niche, then slid down, back against the wall, hands over her face.

Now that sheer terror had distilled down to unrelenting dread, I slung my sack to the ground and joined her. It would probably be a wise idea to rest a little. Malu had put my water flask back in its place after he'd inspected it for dangerous weapons. A good fellow, all in all. I hoped he'd made it out of the fortress. I freed the cork and handed the flask to Senza.

"It's not quite full," I cautioned. My hearing was still muffled. Did she hear me, or merely read my lips?

She gulped two deep swallows and gave it back.

I wanted to wet a cloth and wash her battered face, but I didn't know how long the water would have to last. Instead, I took a sip and stowed it away again, then pulled everything out of the unwieldy canvas bag. I belted on the pouch that held repair items and such, then set about restoring order. I'd learned a thing or two from watching Tanris's extreme talent with bag-packing.

Tanris...

My throat closed. My chest knotted. I might have loaded things with more vigor than they deserved.

Senza made no move to help.

I gave her some dried fruit. "When did you eat last?"

She just frowned, so I signed the question.

She shrugged. Understandable. Lack of sunlight made it hard to estimate the passage of time. Her rope-burned wrists caught my attention.

I found my little vessel of salve. When I removed the lid, the scent of thyme and gentle green things filled the air. Tenderly, I took Senza's elbow.

She pulled away.

"Let me help you."

She scooted off a bit and drew her knees up. Since she hadn't turned down the water or the fruit, I placed the open jar next to her and leaned against the wall.

The last time I'd sat in a cave like this, *waiting*, the Ancestors had come and claimed me. Where were they now? I stretched my legs out. The stone-light exposed some significant dents and scrapes in one greave. Courtesy of the rock slab, no doubt. A seam in my boot had sprung and the boot heel looked ready to come off, but I could walk. I breathed. The gods still loved me.

And if the gods loved me, my story had not yet finished.

I heaved myself up and walked a little away, out of the light. "What is it you need from me?" I whispered, lifting my face. Blind. Confused. Lost—certainly lost.

The Ancestors flowed around me, spectral in the silence left behind after the quakes. Instinct made me rub my chest. The absence of the medallion hurt like a physical wound. They'd told me I didn't need it—then *why* was I impervious to their voices?

"You won't leave me, will you?" I asked.

They answered. I knew they had, however deaf my ears.

"I can't hear you. My ears are damaged."

Alarm and *concern* wrapped around me. The gods loved me, I reminded myself, and returned to Senza.

She stood where I'd left her, turned toward me, hugging herself. Waiting, frightened, silent.

"Have you—" I started, then worked the muscles in my jaw for a moment. *Do you know what happened to Not-an-Egg?* I signed.

She stared at me, then gave a terse shake of her head.

Did you see him during the attack?

Another head shake.

I rubbed my nose. Propped my hands on my hips. Turned blind eyes down the passage the way we'd come. Everything in me wanted to shout *NO*, a hundred times *no*.

"Let's go." I picked up my pack while Senza gathered the stones. She handed the salve jar back to me, then moved off down the tunnel. She limped a little. I hadn't noticed before.

I caught her arm and signed. *I can give you something to help with whatever pain you're feeling.*

She pulled away.

We walked. I worked my jaw, trying to pop my eardrums. I rubbed my ears. Grumbled at the inscrutable working of the gods. Even prodded what basically amounted to a new scar on my chest. Yes, it still hurt, but no, it didn't seem to prevent me from using my arm.

"The stonework here is plain, not like that in the tunnels we came up through." Inane to talk about walls in the face of our tragedy, but I thought it helped judge the slow return of sound. "Older, do you think? I can't imagine what people need with all these underground passages and rooms. Who would *live* here?"

Even if she were so inclined, she couldn't walk and sign whilst carrying our light. So I chattered away, telling her about some of the sights I'd seen while looking for—for *you*. I could say that. Singular or inclusive. Every time we came to a cross tunnel, Senza debated silently, then made her choice.

I decided not to offer my opinion.

After a time, I ran out of things to talk about. Never was one to talk to myself, really. Not aloud, anyway. But I didn't like the silence. Not *this* silence, so fraught with tension and uncertainty.

"You're angry with me."

Senza stopped and spun to face me. Evidently, her ears worked well enough. In a quick movement, she set the glowing stones at her feet and straightened. *Yes*, she signed. A small symbol, but passionate. *Why didn't you save him?* The hard, fast motion of her hands was almost violent.

"Senza, I tried. The quake and the rock—"

No. You have the Ancestors. You have magic. You saved yourself. Twice! Why wouldn't you save him?

"You know it doesn't work that way."

Is he dead?

I opened my mouth, then shut it again, unable to voice the question: *How can he be?*

Ask your Ancestors, she demanded.

"I—I can't." Whatever their response, I couldn't bear the thought of them confirming his death.

Everything she'd bottled inside blazed free. Fury and pain. Grief and utter disappointment. Betrayal.

The weight of it staggered me like a punch to the chest.

She grabbed the stones and stalked away, but she'd hardly gone a dozen steps before turning back. She made a show of pinching her nose and pointing at me. *You stink.* That said, she whirled on her heel and marched off.

While she moved on, I put a hand to the wall to keep myself upright. Have you ever come face to face with a view that simply stopped your brain? My view included too much: my terror, Tanris's loss, Senza's pain and disgust, the knowledge that this weakness—this awful ability to know the emotions of others—would destroy me.

Unless I learned how to control it.

I didn't go after her until the light had almost disappeared.

She stayed ahead, even when the way sloped upward. If I increased to a trot to close the gap, she quickened her pace. My dread of confined spaces shredded me. It had me looking repeatedly over my shoulder. Rubbing my aching chest. Jumping at every skittering stone for fear the cavern would fall apart and bury me.

When Senza stopped abruptly, a new jolt of panic rushed through me. Breathing hard, I came up beside her.

"What is it?" My nose and lips tingled.

She pointed. A light shone ahead.

"Could be Basi Serhat."

Her mouth tightened, her shoulders straightened—and she marched on.

As it turned out, it was no one. Far overhead, sweet, beautiful daylight streamed through a sloping fissure. I had never been so relieved in my life. This, I guessed, was the seaward side of Serhat's little mountain. The passage widened into a chamber, and a new series of tunnels opened up like a hand with fingers pointing. Five different directions, five different choices.

"I propose we go left." The obvious choice. I glanced at Senza. She headed into the left-most tunnel, and I found myself following her again. Or following her anger, which had actually taken the lead.

"How do you suppose we've come so far without running into another single person?" I asked. I might as easily have inquired of the wall. After a few minutes, a sound came to my ears, distant, but rushing.

When she stopped again a few minutes later, it was upon a landing with stairs curving downward. Underground. Against my prediction. She didn't offer either her opinion or a rebuke. After a moment or two, I descended several steps and through one complete turn, then paused. Chill air blew gently against my face, carrying a salty dampness. The rushing sound had become a distant roar.

"The sea," I said, addressing the obvious with agility. "If it can get in, maybe there's a way for us to get out."

Right behind me, Senza shrugged—an improvement over the strict, no-communication stance she'd adopted. She stared down into the gloom, then pushed past me to lead again.

I didn't know what to make of this version of her. Since she'd first come into our lives on our mission for Baron Duzayan, it had been her habit to cry. She cried about nearly everything—which was understandable. Her family had died tragically at the hand of robbers. While she watched. Her future had gone from predictable to unknowable in a matter of minutes. To our constant amazement, she always persisted anyway, tears or not. Good, bad, or ugly, Senza did what needed doing. The crying had diminished as time passed, but the fact that she hadn't cried at all yet worried me. It was not like her.

Not that I wanted to deal with a flood of tears…

Not hers.

Not mine.

I may have stomped a little in my descent, for she turned to glare at me.

Only two more levels, and a large chamber opened before us. We now had the questionable blessing of choosing between continuing our descent or opting for flat ground. Down was water. Flat was, well, *out*, one could hope.

Senza must have felt the same about the stairs. She ventured out into the chamber, where we left the roaring behind. Was that good or bad?

Torches—some lit and some not—dotted the circumference. Together with the light spilling through rents high overhead, they revealed a floor constructed of huge dressed tiles, each as big as a door. Smooth walls—miraculously intact—with stone benches placed at regular intervals displayed cunning stonework. The space seemed positively civilized but for the piles of rubble strewn from one end to the other.

A quick glance around didn't reveal any pirates waiting to assault us, so I turned my gaze upward. Hands on hips, I surveyed the blessed cracks and splits through which sunlight spilled. None of them were large enough to admit an adult body, even if I somehow sprouted wings.

"Looks like morning, doesn't it?" I inquired.

Senza pointed upward, then made a clawing sign with two fingers.

"Grapnel?" I shook my head. "I don't trust the rock. The gashes are too new. We can't test loose edges without either falling or pulling the ceiling down on us."

Her mouth crimped. Pushing the glowing stones into a pocket, she walked a slow circle around me.

"Ancestors, are you here?" I no longer cared what Senza thought about this one-sided conversation. Aside from casting a curious glance my way, she continued her own inspection. A telltale ruffle of hair and clothes revealed their presence. Still, their voices remained muffled and indistinct. Beneath my coat, I rubbed my chest where the amulet had once rested. I had never wanted it, but now I missed it. I'd never wanted Tanris, either, and now…

For a heartbeat or ten, I experienced the vision of him tumbling helplessly into the awful depths. My imagination was trying to run away with me again.

Ancestors? Senza asked. When I nodded, she glared. *Tell them to find Tanris.*

I licked parched lips and hoped she failed to notice the tremble in my jaw. My hands. My *body*. "I still can't hear them."

She turned both palms up. *So? Tell them!*

"What good is that if I can't hear their report?" Helplessness and fear made my voice sound funny.

Her mouth pinched in anger. She stared past me for a long time, then gave me a none-too-gentle punch to the shoulder, pointing. Shadows swallowed the chamber's far reaches, but an even darker gash huddled within the murky edges. More or less in the middle of that, two posts stuck up like signs with the tops lopped off.

"Gods above, you know I love you, but if that is the entrance to another set of stairs, I will scream. And I promise, it will hurt your ears."

With that dangerous threat lingering in the air, Senza rolled her eyes and trekked across the space. This taking-the-lead thing had worked a wonder on her confidence.

The gash was wide, though the far side disappeared into darkness. Unnatural darkness, if anyone cared to ask me. Between the posts hung a bridge, uneven wooden planks suspended in a framework of rope. I didn't trust it. Who knew how long it had dangled there, or if rot ate at it?

The noise of the sea returned here. How far down?

When I peered over the edge, I could not make out the churning water below, but it was angry and hungry as any wolf in the old tales. And it had already eaten one of us. I gripped a post to give it a shake, testing its sturdiness. It didn't budge, so I gave the other a kick and was rewarded with a hollow thud. Still, it held as firm as its mate.

Something besides my audacity felt off. I bent to rearrange a few things in my pack, putting the rope and hook at the top, and digging my gloves out. As I tugged them on, I narrowed my eyes, trying to penetrate the dense dark.

"What is that?" I asked, pointing. "Do you see it? There's a line. Fuzzy, but—amber colored." A narrow smudge of gold might be anything, though only one or two ideas came to mind. Light, yes. A strange subterranean growth of lichen? Hope suggested a doorway or—more likely—a crack in the mountainside.

At my shoulder, Senza sighted down my arm. She stood still and quiet for so long I lowered my hand. Then, just when I'd decided I was a fool and she'd merely humored me, she bobbed in a short nod.

As I hefted my pack, Senza grabbed me, her brows deeply furrowed.

"What? If that's a way out, I don't want to miss it. Do you?"

Her lower lip disappeared between her teeth, then she shook her head.

I rolled my shoulders and neck, stretched, and started across. Cool, damp air swirled up to meet me. Not knowing how decayed the structure might be, I opted to tread on each plank as close to the outside edge as I could manage. In places, the mist from below made the boards slick. I grasped the rope on one side, then the other, never completely letting go.

"Feels strong enough," I called back. "Wait till I'm across, then step on the outside exactly like I'm doing. Take your time."

I heard a tearing sound behind me. Senza had a glowstone tucked under her chin while she wrapped cloth from her shirt around her hands. Clever Girl…

I had no way to gauge the halfway point in my progress, which I found unnerving. Shadow cloaked the distance. The bridge swayed under my weight and from the push of cold air from below. A *thrumming* sensation filled ropes and boards. I focused hard on them, trying to feel the slightest change.

A change came, all right—A violent *thud* rent the air and the bridge rocked. Then another and another. The entire bridge shuddered and bucked beneath me. I grabbed onto the ropes with both hands and a shout. Another quake threatened to cast us both into the fissure. "Get back!"

A rock hurtled past me—across, not down—and I dared a look at the far end. A dim figure floated in the darkness, half bathed in shadow.

Basi Serhat! With a length of wood, he swung at the anchoring post. The impact vibrated through the bridge.

Another rock zipped by. Senza was every bit as good with fist-sized rocks as she was with the pebbles she'd lobbed at Tanris. The time we'd spent practicing whilst we'd tromped about the wilds in search of foreigners had clearly not gone to waste. She didn't miss.

Basi reeled backward with a grunt, then came around again. He slammed his weapon into the pole with a *crack!*

"Are you crazy?" I hollered.

"You were supposed to die!" he yelled back and swung.

I launched myself across the planks, hoping to get to him before the post—and the entire bridge—collapsed.

He glanced up, faint light gleaming in his bulging eyes, face a pale blob. Another rock struck him, right between the eyes. Grunting, he grabbed his head and staggered back.

I did not slow.

When Basi straightened, a black smear marred his brow, but Senza's throws from such a distance didn't have the power to do him serious injury. He snarled something I didn't catch and hammered at the post again.

One side of the bridge jerked downward. It seemed an opportune time to wrap both arms around the rope attached to the unmolested post.

Basi's next blow took the other post out.

The top rope went slack, then the bottom.

I got my feet planted, then hurried onward, hand over hand. "Multiple murders aren't going to do your reputation any good."

"Not murders." *Thud! Thud!* "An unfortunate result of a natural disaster."

If it had been Tanris hammering at the posts, they'd have turned to kindling by the second or third strike. Lucky for me, Basi wasn't a very big fellow, and *brawn* didn't fit into his daily activities.

Twelve yards to go.

"You should know the gods love me."

Nine.

He straightened and gave the post a vicious kick. The ropes jolted once, twice… then the tension went out of them completely.

—22—
New Depths

Falling was such a thrill.

The unknowable height and the rope's dubious reliability increased the stakes exponentially. It would have been a logical time to panic, and yet—A dozen realizations and possibilities flew through my head even faster than I fell.

How far up the rope could I climb before I struck?

How much difference would it make?

Lights dotted the approaching rock face like the brightly lit windows in the Kumeti Palace in Marketh. Fewer perhaps, but surprising in number nevertheless. *What were they for? What did people do down here?* Questions for another time. I repositioned one arm for better security and kicked my feet free. Given the arc of the fall, predicting which direction I wanted to face came as easy as breathing. Unlike leaping the gap with Tanris and the others, this impact promised pain. The wall approached too fast to do much more than pray. With fervor.

"Gods and Ancestors, help me now—I'll do almost anything you ask!" Making unconditional promises under duress was a stupid plan. Sticking to the plan always turned out to be another story altogether.

But really, what wouldn't I do to keep from smashing every bone against the unforgiving barrier of rock rushing at me? "Fine! I'll do anything! Don't let me break, don't let me break, *don'tletmebreeeeaaak!*"

The wind buffeted me, damp and cold. I lifted my feet, knees bent to absorb the impact. Research, science—even experience crashing into walls from lesser heights—promised surpassing agony. I was not disappointed.

I bounced off the wall like a tortured squirrel, twisted sideways, and returned for another pounding. This time the fates spun me toward one of the lighted openings. I rebounded again, grunted, and took a hitching slide downward. The next arc aimed me beneath an outcropping. I ducked and squeezed my eyes shut, but smashed my head anyway. The jerky drop became an alarming glide down, down...

Then the gods wrapped me in their embrace, drawing me into darkness.

Someone ran gentle fingers through my hair over and over. Mesmerizing at first, it grew more terrifying with each breath that brought me closer to the memory of where I was. I shot straight from lazy recognition to full-scale alarm and wide eyes. A fragile glow of amber gilded surroundings of dressed stone. A blurry figure loomed over me and I blinked, trying to clear the image of—

"Tarsha?" I croaked.

"Thank the gods of miracles and fortunes," she breathed with obvious relief. My habits had worn off on her. When I moved to sit up, she stopped me. "Slow down. You've—You had an accident. Do you remember?"

I'd last seen her ducking out of a crumbling chamber with her old sweetheart. "You left me to die."

She winced. "And after that?"

Fuzzy bits and pieces looped through my memory. "Ugh." I lifted a hand and Tarsha caught my wrist.

"Careful. You're a mess. You only had a bit of water, and I used it to help you take some willow oil."

Willow oil was for pain and rashes. I'd administered it to her a time or three in the past. A few of the fuzzy bits cleared, including an image of a breaking bridge post. "You are frightened," I observed.

She nodded. "You've been unconscious for a while. I couldn't find any obviously broken bones." Her voice went up on the last word, almost a question. A hope? She licked her lips. "You need to move carefully. Test the—the damage."

Movement was a mistake. Pain clutched the entire right side of my skull and partially blurred my vision. "My eye?"

"Swollen shut. And your face—" Tarsha gestured at her own. "It's all scraped up."

"But I ducked." Frowning hurt, too.

"You remember." Relief shaded her voice. "You hit the wall a few times; your arm was tangled in the rope or you'd have fallen. I pulled you in."

"By yourself?"

She glanced around the chamber uneasily. "I don't think so. Exactly…"

"What do you mean?" A more searching examination relieved me of the burden of anymore unwanted companions. "Basi didn't help you." I recalled he'd been on the other side of the rift. I stretched my arms out, one at a time. My right shoulder and ribs protested.

"No." She hesitated. "I couldn't lift you by myself. You were below the edge. I tried, but you were too heavy. I couldn't leave you hanging there, and I dared not cut you down. And you were—"

"Girl!" I sat up with a shock. "Where is Senza? Is she still up on the top?"

"I-I imagine," Tarsha stammered. She looked a fright. Tousled hair had fallen free of its clip. Dirt and blood smudged her face. Her lovely white silk gown was smeared and torn. "I'm sure Tanris will take care of her."

I lurched up to my feet, shoving her hands off when she would have stopped me. "Tanris is gone," I growled. I didn't say *dead*. The word refused to form. Denial at its finest.

"Oh."

One could cover a surprising amount of territory with such a small sound. Spurning it, I hobbled to the opening. My legs still worked. Praise the gods. Mist washed my face, salty on my lips, and the crash of waves splashed me. Only a little, but we were that close to the water... I gripped the rock edge and looked upward. A thrust of stone obstructed the view. I called out anyway. "Girl?"

The thunder of the sea obscured any answer.

"Why do you keep calling her that? She has a name."

Indeed she did. "Habit," I said flippantly, and immediately had a vision of Tanris giving me a sour look.

"Sure," he'd say, arms folded as he often did, *"but how about 'laziness'? How about holding her at arm's distance? Would saying her name unravel the illusion that you don't care?"*

"I don't need a lecture," I snapped. There was more truth to that than I wanted to face right now, and I definitely didn't want Dead Tanris haunting me.

"All right," Tarsha whispered.

Maybe Tanris was right, and I really was losing my mind.

The end of the rope curled on the floor near the brink, so I took hold and gave a tug. It held firm, so I grabbed on with both hands and leaned back into the chamber.

Still steady, but with the protest of muscle and sinew, I wondered if my battered body would endure. I had a considerable distance to climb. And Tarsha to consider. Her silk dress and—

"Where are your shoes?" I asked.

"Shredded." She shrugged. "Can you believe I didn't prepare for an earthquake?" Her lower lip trembled and she avoided my eyes.

"You have my pack?"

She nodded to where she'd propped it against the wall. The witchlight sat atop it, imparting its delicate gleam. How foolish that I hadn't noticed it...

On my knees, I rummaged through the pack for an idea. When I encountered Tanris's dagger, I stilled. As an occasion for a flood of memories, this one reeked.

"Crow?" Tarsha's hand on my shoulder saved me from tumbling over that mad brink.

"I'm fine." I shrugged away, and tossed her the only clean shirt I had, and the jerkin I'd abandoned because of the heat. Then came the antique slippers. "I'm not sure how long these will hold up…" I was also not sure I wanted to surrender such a prize. Brighter light might suggest they weren't worth much, but a pastry is still a pastry.

Tarsha grasped the shoes.

I didn't let go.

She tugged them away and examined them in the glow of the fading witchlight. "They're beautiful," she decided, slipping them on her feet.

Without washing first. "How do they fit?" My voice didn't sound strangled, did it?

"They're a little big."

"Easy enough to fix." I pulled my coat off and cut two strips from the bottom. "Try this."

"They stink," she objected.

"Stink or bleed; your choice." I dragged the coat on again. The scrapes, bruises, and the gods knew what else—physical and emotional—made it a challenge that left me lightheaded and my cheek nearly bit through. The price of manly pride. That accomplished, I strapped my knife—mine, not Tanris's—around my waist. To my exasperation, I couldn't simply swing the pack onto my shoulders. I had to wriggle it on. It hurt enough to make my eyes sting and my breath catch all over again.

"Let me help…"

"I'm *fine*."

"You're not. You *smashed* into the rocks. Several times." One hand whisked up and down, indicating my entire person with patent dismay. And worry. Why was she worried about me now? Too little too late, if you ask me.

"What do you suggest?"

"Rest."

"Impossible."

"Where are we going?"

"To find Senza, then get out of here."

"This place is a maze! You don't know where she's gone. We'll never find her!" A wild look displaced the concern.

"And you plan to sit here and wait for divine deliverance? I hate to tell you the gods don't work that way, which leaves you with a choice to make: come with me, or—don't." With that, I headed for the doorway. Darkness lay beyond. I held the witchlight up, regarded it solemnly for a moment, then pressed a kiss to the cool glass. "Stay with me. I fear we have a long way to go."

I knew the layout of the level where I'd left Senza and I could make a guess at the length of the bridge. Did the circular stairs we'd traversed reach this deep, or was this level accessed by another means? Banking on the former, I sought corridors that aimed me the right way—back into the mountain. The path involved several twists and turns, a wagonload of doubt, and instances where I simply stopped and waited for the direction to come to me.

You may think that absurd, but when we'd traveled the wilds on Duzayan's idiotic quest, that's exactly what had happened. Visions, memories, hints, whispers… The latter stemmed from the Ancestors. I didn't know about the others. Were they a result of general Mazhar magic, or also part of whatever the Ancestors did?

Did I still have the magic? Were these *hunches* true? My head throbbed and my stupid heart ached. Thoughts and emotions came at me from angles. I should never have stayed with him. He was my best, stupidest, most stubborn and annoying friend. *I didn't have best friends.* Current circumstances provided a marvelous example of why I'd worked alone for so long. Why I avoided getting attached to anyone. By all the excellent and terrible gods, I *would* find Senza and I *would* get her out of this place. Then leave her someplace safe.

Safe for her. Safe for me.

And what about the dragon? The fool creature trusted me. *Loved* me. I refused to think about what he'd come to mean to me. Not on top of all the other dreadful feelings.

"Crow, slow down. Please."

I whirled around, grabbed Tarsha by the shoulders, and pressed her backward. She banged into a niche in the rock with a startled squeak. She didn't even have time to open her mouth to protest before the mountain shook, growling and shrieking.

Maybe the shrieking was her.

Or it might have been the Ancestors... I *prayed* it was the Ancestors.

Tarsha clung to me. I ducked as rubble beat my shoulders and dust set us both to coughing. It only lasted a moment or two, then eerie silence settled in. The occasional punctuation of rocks falling from overhead was too loud. Too unsettling.

"Are you hurt?" I asked through clenched teeth. No more coughing. Gods help me.

"No." She trembled, but let go of me to wrap her arms around her belly. "H-How did you know?"

"The Ancestors." The knowledge was like a weight lifting from me. Now, if only I could hear their voices...

I crouched to dig my neckerchief out of my pack, which involved letting Tarsha help me, despite my inclinations. A gentleman would give it to her. But then another idea occurred, and I opted to keep it for myself. I tied it on and lifted it to cover my nose and mouth, while she watched me with suspicion and growing hurt.

"Your skirt," I said, unsheathing my knife and offering it to her. In short order, Tarsha had her own kerchief and we set off again.

We came at last to stairs. They wound both upward and further down. Winding was a good sign. Ours had done that. I started up. After two levels, I had to stop and rest. Each breath stabbed my ribs and threatened my resolve. When I began again, I took the steps at a slower pace.

"Crow, please stop. You need to rest. You're in no shape to do this."

"You're right, but I prefer it to the alternative. Chances of survival increase once we're out of these tunnels." Neither ribs nor skull agreed with me, and the pain made focusing on the *spirit guides* arduous. "Ancestors," I muttered under my breath. "I need you to be a little more obvious. Ah… Forgive me, I can't think straight. Loud. Pushy." The opposite of everything I'd demanded thus far.

"If you want me to hear you, you'll have to talk louder." Worry colored Tarsha's voice.

"I'll do that."

After three levels, I exited to look around. The witchlight didn't reach far, but I recalled in detail the floor Senza and I had come out on. Not this one.

Not the next, either.

The fifth opened out as I remembered. The large chamber gathered and strengthened the sound of the sea below. "Senza?" I hollered. Torches still flickered on the walls, though their light didn't reach all the way to the chasm.

"Wait here," I instructed Tarsha, pointing to one of the stone benches and heading for the faraway edge.

There was no sign of Senza anywhere in the vast chamber.

Disheartened, I returned to Tarsha, dropping on the bench beside her.

"Now what?" she ventured.

"Rest for a minute."

"I could use a drink."

I grunted. That went without saying.

She was quiet for a few heartbeats. "I'd like a weapon. I know we haven't seen anyone, but I'd feel better. Could I have yours, and you take this?" She drew something from one of the enormous pockets and held it out to me.

Duzayan's dagger…

A new shaft of relief ran through me. I took it before she changed her mind. Was it my imagination, or did my fingers tingle even through the leather wrap? "How considerate…"

"I want to help you." She shrugged and reached into another pocket. "And there's this." She offered the Masni idol, cradled carefully in both hands.

I straightened.

"Since Basi wanted it so badly, I figured it must be worth something—though I've rarely seen anything so ugly."

Laying the dagger in my lap, I accepted the idol, careful to avoid its eyes. Until I realized I *couldn't*. What better way to find—well, Senza? I couldn't bear the notion of actually seeing Tanris broken on the rocks, or dragged about by the current. I had to take a deep, steadying breath. Possibly five. Then I concentrated on Senza; what she looked like, how she moved, how she *felt* to the magic within me.

My surroundings blurred, then disappeared. The corridors upon which I gazed through the idol's eyes bore a distinct, sickly green tinge. Images raced at dizzying speed, then came to an abrupt halt where Senza sat on the floor. Back to the wall, tears made glistening tracks through the grime on her pale face. I could see her so clearly!

"Good, good," I murmured. "How do I get there from here?"

"Crow?"

Again, the walls and doorways rushed past. Stairs. Columns. A bulky carved figure at what might have been a doorway. A broad swath of silver, then a stretch of darkness. *There.* The sense of movement stopped when I recognized the entry to the five tunnels.

"Crow."

I lifted my head. The chamber gave a dizzying lurch. "I'm fine. It's fine." I set the idol and the dagger down next to me, then pitched sideways to retch.

"You're not fine!" Tarsha exclaimed, leaping up. "What happened? Didn't I tell you? You have *got* to rest!"

The queasiness subsided, though the room kept tilting. "I just need to lie down a minute." Horizontal, I clutched my skull to keep it from slipping from my shoulders.

Tarsha hovered, uncharacteristically wringing her hands.

"Stop," I said. "Please." And closed my eyes.

"I'm sorry." Cloth rustled against stone as she sat near my feet. "I don't know what to do. You need water. We have none. You're sick. It's this place, this—this poisonous *place*."

"Are you sick?"

"No!" She paused for a beat, then repeated in a softer voice, "No."

She got up to pace. I rested. Neither of us spoke. In the quiet, I pondered the color through which I'd viewed the labyrinth. Was that normal idol behavior, or a product of incompatible Mazhar magic?

After a time, I sat up. My body protested, but it pleased me no end to find the chamber had settled back on an even keel. The experience had left me exhausted, but beneath that, the need to locate Senza continued to burn. Removal of food and clothing had created space for the idol in my pack. I started to place the dagger in beside it, then —didn't. Instead, I buckled it onto my belt and got to my feet. The room stayed still.

Tarsha watched with a critical eye.

I stretched my neck this way, then the other. "Coming?" The idea of confronting the magically endless stairs held about as much appeal as swimming back to Marketh. Up we climbed, and up... and up...

The whole 'uphill' thing brought unpleasant memories of toiling through another such setting. Worse, the beating—and the lack of water and actual food—threatened to end me. Every agonizing, monotonous step announced my mortality. My side hurt. My muscles shook.

I took a step that wasn't there and promptly tumbled in an inelegant heap. The witchlight bounced away. With a groan, I got to my knees. "No more stairs. Thank all the bounteous gods of flatness."

Tarsha sat beside me, breathing hard. Pale. "So you fell down in worship?"

I breathed a painful laugh. "Exactly. You know, Duzayan's little excursion bore a striking resemblance to this. All kinds of climbing. Did you know dragons like to live near the tops of mountains?" At least those we'd tracked down had...

"I can imagine that would provide a good vantage point. Good for taking off, too."

Stupid dragons. Stupid Not-an-Egg for getting separated. Stupid Ancestors for letting him.

"What happened to your, ah, little companion?" she asked, as if reading my mind. "And the Futharvyr?" *She* remembered what KipKap and his kin were called.

"I don't know." My trembling muscles wanted to stay right there; my fretful brain did not. I crawled to the witchlight. Clenched teeth held back another groan as I stood, then shuffled around the corner into the next tunnel. At least the level ground made forward motion achievable. I contemplated what I'd be willing to trade for a length of cloth to wrap my ribs.

No, I had to stop. Had to lean against the wall.

Tarsha opted to sit.

As the shakiness faded, I rummaged through my pockets, and discovered the handful of sweets I'd swiped from the kitchen. "Hungry?" I asked. "I have a fine selection of slightly dusty honeyed nuts and marchpane. They're not as pretty as when they started this journey."

She made a face, then sighed. "Neither are we."

We sat on the stair to share them. Wished for a drink to wash them down. Silently resumed our trek.

"How did you end up so deep in this infernal maze?" The question was all about distraction. It didn't calculate the cost of answers.

"Cabs, I suppose you'd call them. Raised and lifted on ropes." Eagerness and relief colored her reply.

Vexation shaded mine and brought me to a standstill. "Why didn't you say so?"

Surprise, now. "They're broken." She waved at our surrounds. "Earthquake. Collapsed shafts. Runaway slaves."

I grunted and resumed my awkward pace. Punishment, or another learning opportunity? It felt like the former.

"The fortress sits on a mine of some kind. Basi didn't tell me what. He was in a hurry to leave."

"And slaves be damned," I muttered. That explained the lights, though. And the lack of people. "Why this way? Why so deep?"

"Earthquake, remember? He said we had to go all the way down to get across—I imagine he was talking about the canyon you tried to cross? There was another tremor. The cave roof collapsed and we got separated." Her throat tightened on her words. "He was unhurt."

"Left you to save his own skin, eh?"

"Eh," she agreed sourly.

Did I want to ask about her history with him? No, actually. "Why did you go with him?"

She didn't answer right away. A web of remorse coiled around her. "I was scared. He knew the way out."

"Cowardice, you mean." Bitter. Angry.

"Yes. And hope. If he got me out, there was a chance I could help you."

"Supposing I wasn't crushed like a grape in a winepress."

Her shudder rippled against my senses. Uncomfortable and unwelcome.

"How could you be? The gods love you." Now who was bitter?

—23—
So Loved By the Gods

Darkness mutates time. Weightless, it crushes the soul. We trudged on through the next decade, our only source of illumination the slowly dimming witchlight. Logic insisted the distance wasn't as far as it felt, while discouragement loudly argued the opposite. The view the idol had shown suggested a straight path, but it curved as it followed incomprehensible folds in the mountain. Openings loomed, announcing other chambers and tunnels. Again, I wondered about the purpose. Not a mine—had people actually lived here? Miners, would, I supposed.

A sound crept up on us. Like rain. Like—

"Water!"

The witchlight glimmered across a broad section of rock sheathed in moisture. The trickle disappeared beneath an unexpected grate. Sudden primitives, we both leaned against the wall to lap the stuff up like dogs. Never had water tasted sweeter or been more welcome.

I set the witchlight on a narrow ledge and filled my flask.

Tarsha used a strip torn from her skirt to wash my bloodied face. I let her and studied her dirty face, red-rimmed eyes, fluttering fear, and all. When she finished, I took the cloth and returned the favor. She gave me a rueful smile.

While she rinsed the rag and wrung it out, I collected the light. Surreptitiously, I looked down my shirt to inspect the wound Diti had inflicted. Pink, puckered skin showed advanced healing. I approved of that, but an uncomfortable burning ache remained to trouble me. As Tarsha turned back to me, I straightened, rolling my shoulder to ease the pang—then the other, too, for good measure.

"Did you hurt your arm?"

Was there a place that didn't hurt after getting clobbered by the mountain? I chose to trade the criticism that rose to my lips for a more characteristic quip. "This could be your last chance for a bath for the foreseeable future." Waggling my brows was a painful idea, but I did it anyway.

She blinked, then looked sideways at the trickling water. The light sparkled off it like diamonds against black velvet. "Tempting as that is, I crave sunlight more than soaking."

"Perhaps you'll better enjoy the upcoming stop on our luxury tour."

"Which is?"

"A surprise."

Not long after that, we came to the carving of a stout man. Face to face, I beheld much more detail than the idol had provided. There were, in fact, two such statues. Sculpted from the wall, they faced one another. "I'd have gone for muscular rather than paunchy."

"Maybe paunchy was fashionable."

"Expensive to keep up." They each showed off a pair of gems for eyes. Something yellow. Pry them free or leave them for the next explorer? A streak of generosity overcame me and I turned away. "Senza is close."

When we rounded the corner, the happy glow of flickering torches lit the way. They also revealed an empty corridor. I quickened my pace.

"GIRL!" I shouted. "Senza!"

"She's not here," Tarsha protested from some distance.

Annoyed, I spun around. Or toddled to face her. Take your pick. The sharp words hovering on my lips should have cut me. Or perhaps that was the result of too little food, sleep, and clear sky. Whatever the case, they died a brittle death when I saw Tarsha limping.

"You're hurt…"

"Thanks to Duzayan." Exasperation peeled off her—a strange sensation, but not unfamiliar. Sensitivity to the magic was not only returning, it was sharpening.

"And?"

The exasperation increased. "I may have fallen."

"Did you get some of the willow oil?"

She shook her head.

"Will you?"

"I'm fine."

If looks could lance, I'd be lacerated. The images and impressions, gone for so long *(hours!)*, prompted a buzzing in my temples and a band of pressure around my skull. Or did that herald the return of the warning I'd had when I pushed Tarsha into the cranny earlier?

The thought birthed a knot of dread in my chest, but the sensation itself lacked fullness and urgency, so I pretended to ignore it. "Will you let me look at your ankle?"

"Will looking mend it?"

I scrunched my nose, but only for a second. Such facial exercise hurt. "Nnnnot likely."

She'd caught up with me and gestured ahead. "Then we'd best keep going."

"Are you angry with me?" I walked alongside her.

"Not yet."

"Good." I cupped my hands to my mouth and hollered again. "Senza!"

"How do you know she was here?" Tarsha wiped a hand across her brow, then drew it down her coat.

Oh, the fun of discussing a crazy man's visions… "I just know."

"If she's gone on ahead, she could have turned down any of these passages."

"Except that they're dark." Curious, that. And never mind that Senza had the glowing stones.

A little farther, and I caught her elbow. "Look."

A figure appeared in front of us, light leaking from its hand. The spill of torchlight shone on dirty blond hair.

"Senza!" I hurried toward her, only to come to a standstill as *that* sensation enveloped me. "Stop! Go back!" I waved frantically, and she slowed, hesitating.

The ground beneath us gave way between us with a tearing sound. Tarsha and I fell straight down, then slammed to a halt that pitched us both face downward. She screamed. I flailed to keep from sliding as our section of floor tilted.

Tarsha grabbed hold of my coat. Instinctively, I wrapped an arm around her. The grinding continued as an avalanche of rock crashed around us. The floor jolted, shrieked like a demon, then dropped again. Rocks of every size pummeled us, inflicting new agonies. I dared a glance up, clutched Tarsha tighter to me, and rolled to the side—not an easy feat wearing a pack on my back. A slight overhang protected us somewhat. Or it might collapse and crush us.

I prayed.

The gods listened.

The awful grinding stopped as suddenly as it started.

A patter of falling rocks and dirt continued, then abated like rain. After a brief surge or two, it was done.

"Tarsha?"

She whimpered into my chest. Still breathing, then.

Sitting up required dislodging debris and set me to coughing, which came with sharp pains in my side. A narrow boulder as big as a goat pinned one leg. I flexed my foot, and was immediately reassured I hadn't broken it. The burning pain it elicited came as no surprise. Did my metal greave now bear a new shape? And if so, what did that mean for my leg?

I helped Tarsha get herself free of the rubble. Blood trickled down her temple. She explored the wound gingerly.

"How bad is it?" I asked.

"I expect I'll have a headache." She winced as she stretched each limb. Everything seemed to be in working order. "I can move. Are you all right?"

"I will be." I craned my neck, but nowhere did I see any sign of Girl. "Senza!" I hallooed once, then several more times, but there was not the smallest sound, nor did she show herself.

I fell quiet, a new dread seeping through me.

Tarsha looked at me for a long time, then hitched close to help me out of my pack. Her poking and prodding revealed no new broken ribs. The gods must have had a hand in preserving me from further damage. Together, our best efforts against the boulder made no impact whatsoever. I surrendered with a gusty sigh and collapsed back to the ground. The exercise warmed our bodies, if nothing else.

Tarsha took her coat off, rolled it up, and pressed it under my head.

"Thank you. Hey. Look up."

Shafts of sunlight pierced through lingering clouds of dust. If we'd remained on the same level where we'd been walking a minute ago, it would have been reachable.

I wanted to weep.

Tarsha stared at the gap—*two* gaps—then wiped her face, hiding her tears.

I saw them anyway. *Felt* them. "We'll rest a bit, then we'll try something else."

"What? There's nothing to try, nobody to help us." A hitching breath left her as she folded over, one leg crooked beneath the other. She might not dance anymore, but she'd lost none of her grace and flexibility.

"When did you sleep last?"

She had to turn her head to crook a brow at me. "That depends on what day it is."

I considered the sun again. "I think it's tomorrow, which means we're both behind."

"What about Senza?"

Would that I could sprout wings and fly out of this miserable tomb full of miserable grief. I gathered up my fractured equilibrium and pointed at the rock trap. "First things first. Minus all the fuss of getting a bath and—" I squinted at the gaps overhead, "dinner, I am now free to nap. Napping will restore my strength and clear my head." One could hope, anyway.

"How can you sleep at a time like this?"

I squirmed to settle myself more comfortably on my nest of rocks. If I had wings, feathers would go a considerable way to making my bed more cozy. "Dearth of options?"

She let me close my eyes. Let me take a few deep, relaxing breaths, then—

"Aren't you afraid?" she whispered.

"Mm-mh. The gods love me. Go to sleep."

CLICK...

Click...

Thump!

"Hey..."

A hiss came from above me. It sounded a lot like Girl.

I rubbed my eyes, trying to open them. Mistake. The right eye felt the size of an orange, but far more tender and squishy. How unsettling. It was a terrible thing to wake up to after a pleasant dream of sprawling in the bottom of a giant nest with the warm sun shining down on me. Being *pelted* awake was especially irritating. But—

"Girl?"

Thump. A piece of gravel bounced off my chest. Because I wasn't conscious enough yet.

Overhead, Senza perched on a slab of rock, peering down. I hadn't felt so much relief in—well, a long time. *Why are you sleeping?* she signed. She must have found the water, too, for her face was reasonably clean.

Tired, I replied. *Stuck.*

She held out a handful of light to shine down upon me and my boulder, then made a mournful face. *Hurt?*

Not bad. I am glad to see you, I told her. *Are you all right?*

She waggled her free hand back and forth, then set the stones down to sign. *Quake broke roof. Made pile. In is out.* The glow illuminated her hands from beneath, eerie and strangely beautiful. It also gave away her reddened eyes and nose.

Half distracted, it took me a minute to decipher what she meant. We were close to freedom—and the pile suggested a way out, a slope of debris. *Walk or climb?*

Walk.

I had a dozen questions, none of which meant a thing if I remained prisoned by stone. "Do you happen to have an iron crow?" I whispered.

Curiosity peaked her brows. *Only wood.* She tapped her head and pointed to me.

"Ha. Ha. It's a bar for lifting things."

Beside me, Tarsha stirred, asleep in spite of herself. By the appearance of the sky beyond Senza, dusk was settling in. I refused to dwell on the time spent in and below Fort Serhat. Or whatever he called it.

Not-an-Egg? I dreaded her answer, but she shrugged and made a sad face.

I will look for a branch. Back soon. She vanished.

"Wait..."

When she didn't reappear, I assessed what the nap had done for me, then embarked on the unsavory process of thinking. The gods have blessed me with a clear head and quick wit, and on most occasions I enjoy using it. This time I needed to think about the Ancestors and their magic—*my* magic. Much to my dismay, magic might be the only thing to get me out of this place before the entire mountain caved in.

Or it might precipitate the collapse.

As if to underscore my predicament, the earth rumbled. One or two more rocks fell. While it was a definite improvement over the earlier tremors, it meant little with Gates winking in and out of existence.

It was a chore to sit up. I wiggled my toes again to make sure the circulation hadn't cut off, then made another vain attempt to shove the boulder off my leg. It didn't shift so much as a fraction. I sucked on my teeth and thought uncomplimentary things about—well, nearly everything. Wizards, emperors, caves, thirst, magic, earthquakes, loss…

No, I would not think about Tanris disappearing from view.

How long had I known him? *Years* before Duzayan had bound us together as partners for his own benefit. I collected pretty baubles. Tanris chased me. I flew away. From time to time, we shouted witty banter across a safe distance. Tanris threatened. I taunted.

I picked up a stone to roll between my fingers. Circumstance limited my options. Fear didn't make it to the list. The gods loved me and would give me a way out of this predicament. "Any time, now," I murmured.

Nothing happened.

I huffed a sigh in irritation, glanced at the stone—and froze. It looked for all the world like a lump of rough glass. Still not moving, I surveyed the rocks scattered around me and saw several more like it. Hardly daring to breathe, I drew out my knife and the witchlight. I dragged the tip of my blade across the surface of the stone. Once, then twice more. I held it as close to the witchlight as I could and scraped a fingernail over it in search of the scratch I had just made.

Or not.

Oh, how the gods do love me…

Not that a handful of diamonds would do me any good in my current bind. But if the gods gave me gems, they must mean for me to do something with them. I set about collecting those within reach, plotting all the while. It turned out that diamonds could fuel a lot of brain activity as well as mindless, happy humming.

I didn't have the amulet, but it didn't matter, did it? The Ancestors had told me I was mostly, completely, practically magic.

"Ancestors?" I whispered, lest I disturb Tarsha's sleep. I tucked the witchlight away and secured my little treasure, wrapping it in my scarf and putting it in my pocket. *Deep* in my pocket.

The Ancestors whirled around me, caressing, reassuring.

"I cannot hear you." Melodramatic as they were, they'd either be insulted or horrified. "I'm sorry. I've lost the amulet, and—" I chewed on my lip. "We'll deal with that later, but I need your help now. I can feel you when you touch me, so I'm going to ask questions. Only touch me if the answer is *yes*. Got it?"

My hair ruffled. Tightness in my chest I hadn't realized was there eased.

"Good." I blew out a breath and asked: Could they move the boulder? Did I have the power to move it myself? Did it require the carved horn disk? Could they exert any influence to help me summon the magic? Control it? Keep from hurting myself or triggering another quake?

When I ran out of questions, I stared at the rock, gathering my courage. The Ancestors twisted around me, keeping their distance, but not their emotions. I understood anticipation, concern, a sense of *more*. Of urgency.

The last worried me. Try as I might, though, I couldn't entirely dispel the horrible butterflies in my belly. Cleansing breaths—but not enough to make myself dizzy. Calm thoughts. Self-belief.

And trust in the gods, who had never—mostly—let me down.

I stroked the surface of the rock, and the Ancestors drew close, touching now, whispering words I could not hear. Their whispers became suggestions, much like the visions I'd seen. Mouth dry, I *pretended* I could split the stone into pieces. I refused to worry about it exploding and killing me (and Tarsha) with the shards. Something about the moment reminded me of the time the Ancestors had—What *had* they done? I hadn't gone anywhere, but time had passed. And during that occasion, the Ancestors had taught me. *Awareness* swelled.

I knew things… Things that hovered beyond my grasp.

Into that space, the Ancestors slipped as if I'd opened a door. Suddenly I was in two places at once: one watching, the other acting. Most extraordinary, I saw myself overlapped by a trio of insubstantial figures.

They drew energy up within me, warm but not unpleasant. It lit me like the pale green of celery, but smelling of grass and sunlight. *How astonishing!*

I let their knowledge fill me, and when they reached for the boulder, I reached for it as well. One tap of my finger, and the entire thing shattered into a hundred pieces, slithering into piles on either side of my leg.

"Dear, *dear* gods." I didn't know whether to laugh or cry. I did a little of both, rubbing my jaw in incredulity.

A tiny stone struck me.

Senza smiled from her roost overhead. *Very good*, she signed. *I found no branch. Short bushes here. Trees far. You climb up?*

Experimentally, I rotated my arm. Or started to, anyway. With a wince, I shook my head. "Can't. Is there another way out of this trench?"

Think yes. Maybe, in other words. *Wait for moon.*

Waiting for anything seemed like a bad idea, but unless I wanted to test the resilience of my injury, I had no choice. Experience told me I could not climb such a distance in this condition, but the probability of more aftershocks inspired me to take flight.

Except there was Tarsha. She could neither fly nor, I imagined, climb.

"Toss down a couple of your shiny rocks."

One after another, two motes of light arced through the growing darkness and landed at my feet. They revealed solid wall to either side and extending into an unknown distance.

"Can you walk alongside this cleft?"

A nod.

"Tarsha." I shook her shoulder. "Time to wake up. We're getting out of here."

—24—
Duke Magpie

"How did you break free?" Tarsha's nap had not mended her limp. She held the stone lights, so she chose the pace.

"Employment of charm." I had a limp of my own. The boulder had bent my greave into my shin. I'd had to take it off to walk, and a bandage kept the resulting cuts from making a mess.

"Hammering on that rock would have woke me up."

"No doubt," I agreed.

"You had nothing for a lever."

"True."

"Crow."

"Tarsha."

She turned around, halting our progression. "Why is it a secret?"

"You want the truth?" I stopped, toe-to-toe. "I tapped it with my finger."

Outrage boiled up in her and transformed her aura to crimson. "You expect me to believe that?"

"I expect nothing at all from you, Tarsha." I gestured for her to continue up the rubble-strewn fissure. So narrow I could touch either side with my hands, it didn't invite walking side by side, which suited me perfectly.

"After all I've done for you?"

Dubious was one of my finer affectations.

She stabbed my chest with her finger, provoking a wince. No apology. "If it wasn't for me, how do you suppose things would have turned out?"

They didn't seem terrific now, but I didn't want to argue with her. "You're right. Thank you."

Her eyes narrowed, and her tone challenged. "Do you even know what you're thankful for?"

How much more did she need? My jaw worked. "For saving me from the embarrassment of dangling head-first over certain death."

"For saving your life."

Suspension over a yawning cavern surrendered some of its danger when one was firmly moored to a rope. Unconsciousness notwithstanding. Also damaged shoulders. I realized I could have lost my arm entirely. "Probably, yes."

"What about saving you from that man's spear?"

"Excuse my skepticism. You screamed."

"I warned you in time to keep from getting skewered." Her chin came up.

"Very well then, that, too."

"And getting your knife."

"It's a dagger, but fine."

"And the idol? Don't tell me you didn't put it in the guard's pocket." The woman's hackles were definitely up.

"Where is this going, Tarsha?"

KipKap couldn't have given an icier glare. "I've never seen anyone make such blinders out of pride before. A word of advice? Someone in your position cannot afford to be blind." She spun about and marched away. An admirable feat considering the condition of her feet.

"Blindness happened when I fell—" No, confessing love would only give her a weapon to use against me. "Fell in with you."

She snorted. Very unladylike.

"Everything after that has been a wreck." I may have harbored a small portion of bitterness. "You single-handedly destroyed my life."

"Is that so? From what I see, association with me has benefitted you. You've grown—some, anyway. You've learned new skills. Your natural talents have been put to good use. You have friends. A pet."

"*Had* friends." Again, that awful hollow gaped inside. My steps wavered, and I slowed to keep from stumbling.

"I'm pretty sure Senza is still walking with us." She waved one stone-lit hand upward.

My gaze followed. Senza pinched her face in a grimace, the exaggerated depth proof of her hurt. *I will go*, she signed.

No! I shook my head vehemently. Foolishly, for it made my brain slosh in my abused skull. *Sorry. Sorry. Stay. Please.* Before all this had happened, I'd never found myself in emotionally awkward positions.

Why? she asked.

Not you, too.

Stupid man, she signed, then formed a shape I didn't recognize.

Someone shouted from somewhere nearby. We all froze.

A second later, that same someone launched into a tongue-lashing. I made out words like *uncooperative, blasted,* and *foolhardy.*

Tarsha moved onward, then paused. "I think it's coming from here."

The lopsided top of a doorway and lintel lay at her feet. Only a portion about an arm's length high protruded from the rubble. The space beyond it seemed open, and faint light leaked from it, as well as continued grumbling.

I bent closer, listened for a moment, then called out. "Hello?"

No reply came, but the rambling went on at a decreasing volume.

"Help me out of my pack." I turned my back to Tarsha.

"Say please."

A glance over my shoulder showed a harridan in Tarsha's place. "Please."

She harrumphed and helped pull my pack off with cruel and unnecessary vigor.

"Thank you." I laced the words with saccharine sweetness. Then—in a graceless minute—I was on my belly, shimmying down feet first.

At the bottom, what had once been a wall crooked at a close angle. It made a fantastic prop where I could lean and catch my breath, which was possibly on fire.

Once around that, an entire room opened, broken and misshapen. Another doorway on the opposite wall had buckled in half and a pile of rubble spilled through from the other side. Fallen, shattered tiles lay in lines at the base of the walls, and dust dulled red—*ochre*—paint on the walls. A lamp sat on the floor, square in the center of a single undamaged tile. Its steady flame illuminated the man sitting cross-legged next to it, his carping reduced to a mutter. His grizzled head bent to examine something in his hand where he held a disk slightly smaller than his palm.

Even from a distance, cloaked in gloom, I connected to it instantly. My heart lurched up into my throat and sharp emotion flooded me.

"That's mine, old man." I stood on the knife edge of murder, held back only by the fragile wings of relief. The Ancestors, so long distant, breathed out. Not all at once, but here and there, tiny wisps and zephyrs flitted over me. They curled in green-edged energy to wrap around the stranger. I forced myself to loosen my fists. Don a small smile. Pick my way across the debris-strewn floor. "I'm glad you found it. I feared it was lost."

"It's Mazhar. Timolar period, if I'm not mistaken. Marvelous." He dragged his study from it, and blinked at me owlishly. "You're a druid?"

I pasted my smile in place, and wondered what the Ancestors knew about Timolar. "A druid? Me?"

The fellow's head bobbed in what might have been a nod. "This *is* yours, you say?"

"I do."

"Where did you get it?" There wasn't a trace of accusation in his voice or his posture. Only curiosity. Nevertheless, I found myself aggravated.

"It was given to me." The Ancestors had found it, and insisted I take it. The old man's expression remained expectant. I gave him an evasive explanation, subject to interpretation. "By my family."

"Your father, I assume?"

"Assume anything you like."

"Ah." A certain lack of conviction weighted the sound. And then, "Ah," he said again, as if he'd resolved something important. He held the talisman out. "Then you can work it."

I managed not to tear it from his grasp, knock him over, and kick him into insensibility. A tingle rippled through me as my fingers tightened on it, and the combination of rage and hysteria eased. Familiar warmth stole over me. I turned a sob into a cough.

"What do you mean?" I asked, knotting the cord to slip it over my head. It would need a new length of leather. Or a chain might be less likely to break. All the while, invisible fingers ruffled my hair and my clothes, a sense of desperation in each pluck and flick. I rubbed my chest, struggling to avoid being overcome.

[Hush! Wait!] I thought at them. Loudly. Could they hear me, or was the deafness entirely mine?

The fellow huffed a laugh. "I've been studying these for a long time, young man. Your pretended ignorance won't work on me."

I wasn't willing to admit to my real ignorance, so I merely crooked a questioning brow.

"It's a *joziba*," he continued helpfully, as I'd suspected he would. Scholars enjoy making a display of their abilities and knowledge. "A type of key. This one works as a metaphysical door of sorts, a connection allowing—Well, many things, as you know."

I didn't. *Like what?* I wanted to demand, and, *There are others like mine?* But that would ruin my bluff. "Right," I nodded, inserting bored annoyance into my voice and stepping away. "You're Enikar?"

His eyes rounded. "Have we met?"

"I'll take that as a yes. Gaziah sent me." See How the gods love me?

On second inspection, he looked rather worse for the wear. His baggy tunic had lost a sleeve and was wrinkled around the middle as if he'd once worn a belt. Both tunic and breeches had stains and tears. His knee-high boots, though dusty, were well-cared-for. Worn. Comfortable, I imagined. Whatever jewelry or decorations he might have owned were long gone. His clothing didn't exactly scream *royalty*.

"And you are…?"

"Crow. Shall we go?"

"Just *Crow*? No surname or ancestral name? Epithet?"

Wretched social custom forbade me from smacking him. "It gets the job done." I gestured to the exit with my thumb. "I'm leaving. Are you coming?"

Enikar rocked himself once, twice, then up to his feet. Wincing, he brushed dust from his clothes.

"Can you walk?"

"I believe so." Hesitating, he touched the side of his head. The side I couldn't see. His fingers came away bloody. "I'm not as good at dodging as I used to be."

The wound was a shallow gash and it bled more than it was worth. I cut a strip off the hem of Enikar's tunic and wet it. He screwed up his face as I dabbed at the mess.

"My, were you dragged through a latrine?" He made a face.

"More or less. Hold still."

"Sorry about this," he apologized.

"For only getting clobbered when it was raining rocks?"

That made him smile. When I tied the cloth around his head, he fished a kerchief out of his pocket. It had seen better days. He passed it to me wordlessly, and I soon fashioned a decent makeshift bandage. "Now you look more like a native and less like an invalid."

"I just need a necklace or twenty to complete the style." To my surprise, he struck a pose.

"Here." I don't know why I handed my small collection over. They might be worth something, at least to the people of Masni. "We should go."

For emphasis, a rumble stirred the earth. Dust sifted down over us like fine-ground salt. I touched the talisman where it lay safely under my shirt again.

"Why thank you, how kind. The natives use these for barter and sometimes as a form of promissory note. What did you say you were here for?"

"You." I seized one skinny arm and pulled him around the corner to the half-buried door through which I'd come.

"How did Gaziah know I needed rescuing? He didn't have the idol. Have you seen Basi Serhat?"

I put an impulsive hand to my battered face. "Indeed."

"Where is he? You look as bad as I do, young man. You should get that looked at. Did he do it? He's got a temper, that one."

May the gods of garrulous magpies protect me...

"Tarsha?" I called. "We need some help." Without pomp or even permission, I propelled Enikar toward the opening. "Up with you. Hurry." He was tall and broad-shouldered, but thin as the patience of a skeptic— which thought immediately reminded me of Tanris. Skeptical, brooding Tanris. *Perished* Tanris. Wasn't that a poetic way to describe his death?

Tarsha took hold of Enikar's wrists. "Watch your head, m'lord," she murmured, pulling while I pushed. Pain stabbed. He'd better be worth the effort.

"Oh, aren't you considerate... And pretty."

"And untrustworthy," I muttered, teeth clenched against the strain. I thought my arm would give out, but Tarsha got the old goat up and out of the way. If only the exercise ended there. Teeth gritted, relying as much as possible on my left arm (and therefore my weaker hand), I inched upward.

A firm grip on the back of my coat hauled me out of the hole.

"Thanks."

"You're welcome." Tarsha kept pulling, forcing me to my feet. "Go. Go!"

Please let me rest, I didn't beg. *And please hold the world still.*

Ah, what a quartet we made, limping, bloodied, and weary.

Senza guided us to a spot where rubble poured down onto our level. I misliked it, unsettled as it was, but lack of other options gave us no choice. Slipping, sliding, and dodging bouncing rocks, we worked our way up. My wrenched arm handicapped me, but the gods have blessed me with nimble feet and an excellent sense of balance. Another dozen paces beyond the top edge, moonlight beckoned, and never had it been so beautiful.

"I am never going into another cave as long as I live."

Senza shook her head. *Stupid oath.*

"I know. Nevertheless, I am moved to swear it. May the gods forgive and protect me."

She shook her head again, then threw her arms around me and buried her face in my shoulder.

I stiffened, just trying to keep breathing. "Easy," I croaked. She didn't let go, so I patted her gently, which produced a strange trembling and muffled noises. It took a heartbeat or two to realize she was crying.

Dear, sweet, predictable Girl.

Er... Senza.

Telling her everything would be all right didn't seem quite truthful, so I held her and looked out at the scene spread before me. We'd come out next to the sea. Moonlight transformed the water into a lyrical silver, and a warm breeze blew some of the dust off us. Maybe some of the stink, as well.

In her own time, Senza straightened, turned away, and wiped her face with a sleeve.

"Am I forgiven?" I asked.

One arm lashed out to clobber me in the chest. Since the gods loved me, the blow was high and avoided my ribs. She marched off, leaving me to rub my abused but adored self.

Tarsha appeared at my side, a questioning look going from me to Senza, then back again.

I ignored her to follow Senza.

There were rocks and boulders to climb to get to the water itself. Senza found a fish trapped in a tidal pool, and Enikar discovered a handful of wrinkly figs in a patch of scrub. A true vagabond feast.

While the others sat around our tiny fire talking, I went down to the water. I took off my pack, coat, boots, and belt inch by painful inch, then walked right in, clothes and all. With any luck, the sea would pickle the unwashed laundry scent and leave me permanently stinky. After the initial sting of salt in my wounds, the water felt good. Sweet goddess of sea, it felt good...

I didn't go too far from the shore; couldn't swim in my current condition. So I found a pair of boulders to serve as a miniature harbor and floated for a while. As the water rocked me, I worshipped the stars I had feared I'd never view again.

How different this stretch of water was from the waves thundering through the caves beneath us… I had a vision of Tanris's face as he fell, which is foolish, because I hadn't actually seen him. It didn't stop a pit of horror from opening in my belly.

Heaving upward, I sloshed back to the shore.

Enikar awaited me. "Did it help?"

"Almost." I peeled off my drenched shirt and hung it around my neck. I didn't want company, except perhaps the Ancestors, and I *needed* to hear them. But Enikar held Duzayan's dagger, idly dragging the point through the sand. With a sigh, I dropped down next to him, ignoring the way he looked over my bruised torso.

"I hope my nephew is paying you an outrageous sum. What did he really send you here to do?"

"Fetch you home." I looped my arms around my knees. "While he was quite persuasive, I didn't come on his account, and I haven't decided whether I will take you back." If Gaziah knew what his uncle had planned—or if any of Basi's guests returned to Marketh to throw him under the cabbage wagon—Enikar would lose his head and all the knowledge I needed.

The duke cast me an oblique glance. It slid to the wildly colorful bruising and ended in a worried knot of his brow.

"Does he know what you were here to do?" I asked. And then, to forestall beating around lifeless bushes, "I saw Mongar. Surriz. A few others. Vana Sarjin, of all people. Heard them making plans. And then there was Basi Serhat. He had an interesting story to tell. Something about a false hostage situation—and suddenly the presence of his house guests made sense to me. Not *good* sense, mind."

He let out a noise like a laugh, but without humor. "Gaziah is a smart man, and he has a web of agents to carry tales."

"He's really planning on a more, ah, *global* expansion?"

"Mmhm."

"What proof have you got?"

"You're aware of the war being waged in the east." A statement, not a question. *Everyone* was aware. "It is not an actual war. Gaziah is collecting conscripts to fight in his armies."

Slaves? Oh. *That* explained why he'd agreed not to kill all the foreigners on sight. "And you think you can stop him."

"I have to try."

"What's the idol got to do with that?" I had my own ideas, but I wanted to hear what Enikar knew.

"Nothing." *Lie.* "Not at first," he relented with uncertain reluctance. *Truth.* He picked up a stone and lobbed it into the surf. "It's a trinket in a petty war against Serhat." *Lie.*

"Don't," I snapped. "I'm relying on a corrupt emperor—who may or may not be removed from the throne—for a pardon that may or may not be delivered. I do not like the unmistakable political turn my involvement has taken, so don't lie to me."

"Pardon me?"

"No, it's *my* pardon. What does Gaziah plan to use the idol for?"

The bare, pointed end of the dagger hovered over the sand while Enikar deliberated. I held my hand out in a silent command, palm up. The old man stared at it for a few heartbeats, then placed the blade there with reverence.

"It's magic. But you know that."

"The idol? You suggested as much." I re-sheathed the dagger and set it on the ground between my legs.

"No, the dagger. Magical items have a peculiar energy."

"You're a wizard."

He laughed. "Not at all. I've had a long and varied experience." Absent the dagger, he picked sand up and sifted it through his fingers.

"Either way, you're avoiding an answer."

The Ancestors skipped about, making runnels in the sand, tousling my hair, tugging at a clump of grass near my knee. Did Enikar sense their energy?

"I've known you for a handful of hours, young man." The Ancestors zipped through a stream of falling sand, scattering it in all directions. He crooked a brow, startled and curious. "I've no druidic power to discern truth or lie in you. Even if I did, I could not divine your intentions. And gratitude does not equate trust."

A standoff loomed between us. I lifted the talisman and turned it this way and that, letting it catch the light of the moon.

"You said you were undecided about my fate." Enikar continued playing with the sand. "Why is that?"

Reluctance tried to sew my lips shut. Logic understood I wouldn't get information without confessing at least a few things. I rubbed my thumb across the smooth horn, reassuring myself yet again of its presence. At the back of my mind, the *need* for that presence raised a host of philosophical questions. "You may be able to help me with a dilemma or two."

"What is the first?"

First suggested greater importance. Funny how gravity could compete with urgency. I felt an *urgent* need to rectify the issue with the gate, but the wider and more personal issue was my identity. "You know something about the Mazhar."

"I do." Humor danced off him. "I assume that's not dangerous, or you'd have made sure I stayed underground."

"I need to learn about them."

The Ancestral loons whispered, enthusiasm wrecking our agreement for them to only speak one at a time. My short hairs stood up. I rubbed my neck to ease the sensation.

"May I ask why? I wouldn't, after all, wish to become an inadvertent detriment to them."

My mouth tightened and my brows lowered. "I don't want to kill them. I want to find them. I'm an orphan."

"Oh. Oh, I'm—That must be very difficult. They are a fascinating people."

I swung my frown on him. "They still exist?"

"Of course. You are proof of that, if nothing else. Also fascinating."

I employed one of Tanris's deep glares, and Enikar hurried on.

"What is the second problem?"

"Returning the foreigners to their home."

"Foreigners?"

"The people coming through the gates."

"Oh, the demons." He nodded. "That is a serious problem, beyond a doubt."

"They're not demons." Annoyance crabbed through me. "If you fell through a hole into their world, would you be a demon?"

"Excellent point, young man!" He rocked back, mirth glittering around him. It was an awareness first denied me, then muted in the caves. I'd yet to figure out why or how—unless it had something to do with the Chamber of False Statues where disaster had originally struck. Or, I realized with a sinking sensation, my vacillating attitude toward magic.

"You're the one!" he exclaimed with a snap of his fingers. "The fellow who closed Duzayan's gate. It was incredibly foolish to open the thing, by the way. What was he thinking?"

I grunted. "World domination."

"Also foolish. Can you imagine the logistics? What was it like?"

"Painful. What can you tell me about the gates here in the islands?"

"Oh." He rubbed his hands together. "It's not localized. I've deduced that they fall into two categories: primary and secondary. The primaries follow a lengthening, arcing pattern. That is, the sites of the appearances follow a growing curve." He drew one in the sand. "I've been away from my charts and any new reports, but I believe it will eventually create a full circle. The secondaries scatter along that trajectory like sparks from the fall of a burning log. They wink in and out of existence at various rates." Here, he poked dots to either side of his arc.

"And the others… stay?" How horrific.

"Indeed. I heard a rumor that one collapsed, but I suspect it was actually a powerful secondary that occurred on the principle route. Probability for that increases with each new primary."

Paint my mind boggled. With every piece of information, the sensation of the ground disintegrating beneath me grew. "Two questions. No, three." I held up a finger for each. "What happens when—if—a primary gate is closed or destroyed?"

"No idea."

Comforting. "And when the circle closes?"

"Same answer." He paused, weathered features scrunching. "Given the fact that only sentient creatures come through each, one might assume that either nothing at all will happen, or every sentient creature in their world will fall into ours. You may have noticed that their numbers don't equate with the space the gates occupy. The power of the gate seems to draw demons—I'm sorry, people—from a broad area."

"The places they come from are different, too."

"You've spoken with them?"

"Yes." I waggled two fingers, not about to let him distract me from the third question. "Do foreigners keep, ah, *draining* out of the primary gates?"

"No, which suggests the pull has a limited reach."

Thank the gods of small blessings.

"Are you acquainted with any Mazhar druids?"

"That's four questions," he grinned, "but no, you're the first I've met. Very exciting. How long have—"

"You're enjoying this, aren't you?" Did insanity run in the family?

"From an academic point of view, certainly. There is another possible outcome to the closure of the circle. It may initiate a concentration of energy that changes or expands the original intention."

I must have looked blank.

"Think of the way a protective spell works." I had a vague idea about the principles and didn't protest when he continued. "A series of anchors are created around a specific space. Say, a floor—which most closely resembles our current concern." He stabbed holes in the sand again. "Walking across any one of them may result in trauma, but when they are connected, the entire space they encircle is closed. A unique plane of energy occurs. Anything within that plane is affected.

"If that turns out to be the case, all bets are off. The new construct may siphon every last soul from there through to here. It may draw *everything* through, smashing our world in the process."

"Gods," I murmured, half epithet and all supplication.

Enikar tapped his index finger against his lips several times. "Or the entire thing may simply explode. Same result, I imagine."

I tipped over backwards into the sand. My head hurt. My *brain* hurt. The injuries I'd taken earlier faded before this new onslaught. "In other words, we're doomed."

"On the contrary, our chances of survival are merely minuscule. Barring more information."

Careful of the aforementioned injuries, I massaged the bridge of my nose. "Well, that's encouraging."

"Indeed." I didn't need to see him to sense a wide grin crossing his face. It was in his voice. In the air. "*You* can close the gates, young man."

He left when I stopped talking to him. I simply could not process another detail, idea, or assumption—particularly those involving me as the Official Dispatcher of Gates. Solitude with my thoughts didn't appeal, either, but the Ancestors happily filled the space. They sped back and forth, whispering unintelligible nonsense in my ears.

"Why can't I hear you? I have the talisman again." Let's pile misery on top of misery, shall we? And when did I start believing it was miserable to be without my invisible guardians?

They had a fix for that.

A miniature hurricane surrounded me. I remained untouched at its center, but steady pressure built. I worked my jaw to pop my ears. "What are you doing?" I didn't like it; not one bit.

But I *heard* them. Soft voices, not whispers. Someone—Keshava— sat cross-legged in front of me. I don't know how I recognized him, I just *did*. Everyone else quieted, and he lectured gently about *will, strength, purpose, focus,* and *energy.*

"Crow?"

I watched the word approach like a feather drifting on the wind. When it brushed my skin, I blinked. "What?"

"You're scaring me." Tarsha knelt in front of me, hands tucked into the sleeves of her too-big coat.

The temperature had dropped, but I wasn't cold. I touched my face to see if my fingers agreed with my assessment. Short scruff reminded me of what had happened over the past several days. "What's wrong?"

"You. You haven't moved in hours, and you kept—whispering. I don't even know what language you were speaking!"

"It was me," I murmured. It had started with the trap in the eight-sided room. Something there had separated me from the Ancestors. But afterward? My fears and insecurities had put a barrier between myself and them. "It was me all along."

"What are you talking about?" Tears edged her voice.

"Nothing. I'm fine." Fine, but tutored. And so tired I could sleep for days. "Has anything else happened?"

"No, the others are asleep." She wiped the corner of her eye.

"As you should be."

"We decided to keep a watch."

A sound choice, given the pirates, foreigners, and rebels on the loose. I nodded and glanced around. A fine boulder nearby offered a backrest, and I crawled to it.

Tarsha followed, bringing my discarded things. She sat down beside me, somehow looking graceful in her ugly coat and torn gown. Moonlight bathed her face in silver. The lack of civilized living arrangements did nothing to diminish her beauty. The scar was a strange thing to me, even now. On the one hand, it didn't belong to her, and its existence awoke gloomy guilt. At the same time, it added to her sense of character. She had been somewhere awful and survived something terrible. More, she had grown in ways I still didn't recognize.

"Do you mind if I sit with you?"

Too late for that, but I ignored the obvious. "Are you all right?"

"I don't know." She turned her gaze to the sea. "I've been thinking. I can't *stop* thinking, even before we left Marketh. Before I came to see you. I wish I had known—or better understood—the consequences of the choices I made." She closed her eyes and leaned her head back against the stone. "Seeing the future would have prevented so much hurt."

"That may be true," I allowed, "but always knowing how things will turn out would ruin the sense of adventure. Don't you think?" What would I have done differently? Knowing she would ultimately betray me, could I have avoided giving her my heart?

"I mean it, Crow."

"Why?"

Her mouth turned down as she considered. "I would have killed him."

"Duzayan? If he knew his future, he'd have stopped you." And likely killed her before she could lift so much as a finger against him. He had not been the sort to leave enemies living.

"Not everyone can see their future in this different world." She sniffed and tossed her head, sending silver moonlight rippling through her hair.

"How would you have done it?" I asked, curious.

"A stake through his cruel heart," she said without hesitation. "You know the cellar under my apartment? The floor is dirt. Easy to plant stakes in."

"And the floor of your apartment?"

"Rigged to collapse beneath him. That's what I should have done instead of letting him use me the way he did. Use you." She clenched her teeth and the muscle in her jaw quivered, a shadow in the pale light. The space around her quivered, too, stirred by her anger.

"I see you've given this some thought."

"Is it true that you burned him?"

"If burning would have stopped him, Tanris wouldn't have had such a glorious opportunity to be heroic."

"And Senza."

Tanris must have told her the whole sordid story. "You'd best count the dragon, too."

Tarsha rolled her head toward me as she opened her eyes. So dark. So sad. "I have not thanked you properly for saving my life back then."

"That is true, though you did give me a reward." The mysterious, prickle-inducing Gandil. If I renamed it, would the epithet stick? "What is the proper way?"

She studied me until I wanted to squirm, but refused to surrender to the urge. Neither would I be the first to break eye contact.

"Thank you," she said, soft words chasing an impossible shiver through me.

I hid the reaction with a shift, pulling up a knee.

"You could have let me die. I know—" Her lips tightened, and she gave a little shake of her head. A thick strand of hair slipped from her shoulder, drawing my gaze. "I know saving me wasn't your first concern. Not after what I did to you. And though you could have pulled me away from—from the wizard's spell and just left me there, you didn't."

Her observation surprised me. Had there been more to what I did than breaking Duzayan's spell-casting and making sure he couldn't use her further?

"You might even," Tarsha went on, her voice quivering, "have killed me. It would have stopped Duzayan's plan."

Ah, a safer subject to grasp like a lifeline. I took it. "I doubt it. Dead or alive, your blood would have fueled his spell. He already had enough to open his gate."

"But you didn't kill me. You didn't let me die."

She had me there.

"Crow? Hold me."

And her a married woman… And with such desolate eyes, how could I refuse? Wisdom demanded it. Wisdom crumpled like an old leaf as half-a-dozen other emotions I had no desire to examine bowled it over. I lifted my arm in silent invitation. Tarsha scooted close and tucked her head against my shoulder. Curled into a small, miserable ball, she trembled against me.

This had escalated quickly. Only a moment ago, she'd confided her secret bloodthirsty plan to slay Baron Duzayan in her own home. What was I to believe of her? Was she the vengeful, manipulative witch or the wronged lover?

—25—
Raining Pirates

*W*hat is the plan? Senza asked.

We stood at the opening of a narrow, jagged, newly minted canyon. It seemed level, but the rise of the mountain increased the depth the farther it went. It was one of four ways off the section of beach upon which we'd stumbled in the night. The others? A steep climb, return through the caverns, or a lengthy swim.

Enikar, oblivious to her question, came up beside me and surveyed the path ahead. "How did you do it, by the way? Close the gate, that is."

I answered Senza. *I'm working on it. First, secure the idol and the uncle. Then close the gate. Zakkis is waiting in*—I didn't know the word, so I spelled out the word—*cove.*

Maybe. Only one gate? she questioned.

My head bobbed in a nod, then tipped toward Enikar. *He drew a map. I close the gate, the others stop. We hope.*

She chewed on her lip. *We must hurry. Captain won't wait long.*

I struck my palm with the other fist several times. *He'd better.*

She snorted her amusement and started into the canyon.

"What was all that about?" Enikar leaned on a twisted branch that served as a walking stick. I was learning that *intense curiosity* was his predominant emotion.

"Just explaining the best way to tenderize rats."

A surprised laugh squeaked out of Tarsha. "You can't be serious."

I gave her a fake smile. "Or I might. How are your new slippers holding up?" Her coat was shorter now—another sacrifice to protect her feet. The gods, in their infinite wisdom, had provided the fortuitous miniature sewing kit to make the strips more secure.

She held up one foot. "I'm not sure they will catch on in Marketh."

"Pfft. Tasteless heathens."

"I still think you could have donated some of those beads."

For a marvel, they'd survived the first leg of her trek. I'd picked them off the slippers to keep them safe. "Out of the question. If they were lost, I wouldn't be able to use them to fashion keepsake bracelets." With a broad wink, I started after Senza.

Warm and sunny, the only thing to mar the morning came from the occasional trembles under our feet. Well, that and a sad lack of food. Look out *Integrity,* here we come. I would eat octopus stew with fierce relish.

As we pressed on, the stripe of sky overhead grew more narrow, and the passage ever cooler. The canyon traveled in the general direction we needed to go, but I calculated it would bring us too far north. The Ancestors assured me it had an open end overlooking a tiny bay. That sounded promising, if vague.

Was there a ship in it?

Yes, and a second kept its distance out to sea.

It was enough information to give me hope. Either one of the ships was the *Integrity* waiting for us, or we would appropriate a vessel for our use. How? I'd worry about those details later.

Our various states of disability kept us to a sedate pace. The floor of the canyon not only wove up and down, but it was littered with rubble we had to maneuver through. The more breaks we had to take, the more impatient I grew. My occasional attempts to see if I could sense Not-an-Egg did nothing to help my mood.

An hour before midday, Enikar came to walk beside me.

"I've got a question for you," I said. "Is our barren-spirited prince a wizard?"

"Basi?" Surprise flickered from him. "Not that I've heard. If he is, his skill is abysmal."

I liked his answer. It sorted out a few puzzles, though it made the idol—what? Too convenient? If anyone at all could use it, having it fall into greedy, amoral hands might lead to catastrophe. But the Masnians had kept it safe for centuries... How? And why?

We walked for a while without talking. Once we'd got past a particularly challenging stretch, the duke recovered his ability to jabber. I was divided—did I tell him to hush and save his breath, or let him share what he knew? His choice of history lesson encouraged me to listen.

"The Mazhar people disappeared so long ago," he mused. "During the rule of Dimir the Great, I believe, so your *joziba* couldn't have been made after that. Well... unless some of the druids survived The Purge."

Is that what outsiders called it? The Purge? *We must flush the entire area, Olive, the way hazelwort is administered to rid the body of ill humors.* And what was so great about a monarch who obliterated an entire people?

"The thing is, I'm certain that is not sheep horn, but *zukara*."

I'd never heard the word.

Enikar had an explanation at the ready. "They're like a big deer. Rough red coats with a dark line down their spine. The brow tines are short and the—what do you call them?" Pointer fingers waggled over his head. "The main antlers fork at the tips." He spoke as if they still roamed the countryside. "After the Purge, the Nahzym hunted them. They tried to obliterate the Mazhar and everything to do with them." His expression turned pensive.

"Antlers?" I echoed, settling on the least sensitive item of information. The source of such vicious enmity was the subject for some other time. Enikar stumbled, and I helped him over another rough patch.

"Thank you, young man. If you got this from your—What? Your grandfather? Great-grandfather?" Enikar's voice vibrated with enthusiasm despite his breathlessness. "I've heard myths and rumors that small pockets evaded the extermination. Are there more of you?" He made the Mazhar sound like peculiar relics.

"Obviously. The question is, are there more talismans?"

We'd come to a bend, and on the other side, the way was fairly clear, though darker than our current position. The slice of sky narrowed. I halted to let Enikar rest. My gaze went to Senza and Tarsha. The former lagged behind, keeping a reserved distance. Daylight revealed all too well the mistreatment she'd received at Basi's hands. It didn't seem to slow her, but then, our pace wasn't exactly *blistering*. Tarsha still favored one leg; the frequent rests did her good. For a truth, I needed them, too. The ache in my shoulder and ribs worried me. Not that I wouldn't recover—the injuries weren't severe—but that the damage was a liability.

"More talismans? Certainly, there are!" Seated on a low boulder, Enikar scratched his stubbled chin. "I have two, but they are broken. A third specimen is merely half," he apologized. "Gaziah has a couple in the Imperial Museum. Private collectors are interested in such items. Mind, they are all distinct."

So many? "You are familiar with the Mazhar runes, then?"

"Only marginally, I'm afraid."

"Why's that?" I glanced up. Shadows disguised the walls, one of which slanted inward, narrowing the opening above. I guessed the distance from the floor to the upper edge about the height of three men. Something about the space ahead made me uneasy.

"There are some extant scrolls in the museum," Enikar continued. "I consulted them to learn more about my own pieces. The Nahzym were pretty thorough, but they had no control over things that had already left the country. Or the country as it was then, you understand. There's a historian at Smokewood College in Halim City, though. What is his name?" One finger tapped his lips as he racked his brains.

Curiosity often crossed the path of my occupation, and learning about an item's history could provide ideas for liberating it from its current location to transport to another. So yes, I was acquainted with a few academics.

"I'll write to my friend and see what he can tell us. I am certain he has several manuscripts. The author professed to have copied down original Mazhar correspondence."

The Ancestors would confirm their authenticity. My heart missed a beat. I would give much to get my hands on those... "You didn't make copies of your own?"

"Well, no, my studies at the time were directed more to the, ahm, Nahzym." He cleared his throat.

Perhaps a man long familiar with his own background and loyal to his history might have found the situation irksome. But I'd only recently come into the knowledge and, aside from the Ancestors, I had no kinsmen to be loyal *to*. I hadn't yet worked up a boiling outrage at the Nahzym for destroying the Mazhar. "No doubt the articles they left behind were more plentiful and easier to find."

"Just so. Shall we go on?"

I turned to our companions. "Ladies?"

Tarsha stood, pressing her hands against her lower back to stretch. "How long is this going to take?"

"A couple of hours." I touched my amulet and felt the thrill of relief shoot through me again.

"You said that a couple hours ago." Her delicate brow drew down with a pretty pout.

"I grossly miscalculated the speed of invalids." With a shrug, I resettled my pack and resumed the trek.

"You mean you miscalculated and you're blaming us."

Her sympathy hadn't lasted long. I clamped down on a scathing retort. "We're all tired, sore, and hungry."

"Why would we be hungry?" She had less restraint in her snap. "We ate a few days ago."

"Last night," Enikar corrected, either deaf to her shrewish tone or gently reprimanding. Brave of him, if that were the case. "What sort of fish was that?"

"Barely cooked." I kept scanning the top of the canyon, waiting for my uneasiness to turn into an actual problem. When a shadow flickered across the space, I stopped, only to have Enikar run right into me. He grabbed my shirt to keep from going down, apologizing profusely. Out of habit, I checked my person to make sure my belongings remained where they ought, but a deft pickpocket he was not.

"So sorry." He patted me contritely.

"How are you feeling, old man?" I inquired in a quiet voice. "Steady?"

"I'm fine, fine."

"Hang on to the back of my shirt." Hopefully, Enikar wouldn't trip and pull me down. Tarsha and I had long ago taken our coats off to tie around our waists. The canyon's cool temperature didn't keep exercise from heating us.

"What's the matter?" Tarsha whispered behind us.

"I saw something up there—" I glanced up, then pointed in the direction our path took us, "and down there."

Running at an oblique angle, a crack split the canyon floor. From the rushing sound emanating from it, we'd get wet. Or drown. The fissure was wider than I thought I could safely jump on a good day. We'd need to use the grapnel, but imagining Enikar swinging over the space made my hands clammy.

As I examined our woefully limited options, a trio of shadows fell across the opening and I glanced up again. Topside, silhouetted figures moved along the crack.

"Stay here," I whispered to Enikar. "All of you tuck in against the wall there, and keep quiet." Without waiting for his acknowledgement, I crept toward the rift, where the sound of the surf below would cover my voice. "Beloved Ancestors," I murmured. "Would you be so kind as to see who is up there?"

[Yes! Yes! Yes!] Their whispers harmonized with the burble of the water far below. *[We can look... Discover... Determine...]* They whisked around the tunnel and up, stirring dust and gravel from along the edges of the split. It was uniquely marvelous to listen to their foolish chattering again.

"Young man?" Enikar's voice quavered.

"Hush!" I hissed, craning my neck as if I might see whatever the Ancestors saw. Sometimes they did that—sharing images or reflections of what they viewed or what they understood. They did not this time, but they came rushing and shrieking back in an instant.

[Grim! Grim! Grimfist! And others! Yes, others! Soldiers! Warriors! Fighters and swords and axes and speeeeaarrs!]

"What?" Dumfounded, I reeled backward two steps, tripped, and sat down hard. The impact made my eyes water and my ribs scream. *"Tanris?"*

[Tanris! Tanristanristanris...] they echoed.

How was that possible? Was his spirit watching over me? I didn't know if I could bear the idea of him joining the ranks of invisible, insane parrots.

"Crow?" Tarsha hissed.

"Hush." I put a hand against my chest as if that might slow my hammering heart. I swallowed a dozen lumps in my throat, then slowly got to my feet. There was only one way to find out. I cupped my hands around my mouth, calling, *"Tanris! Hello! Tanris!"*

In no time at all, Tanris's face peered down at us. Glaring, as usual. Mangled and lumpy. Maybe it was a shapeshifter with poor aptitude. He signaled for us to be quiet. A shapeshifter wouldn't have the knowledge to do that. Would it? Besides, shapeshifters were folktales. Weren't they?

"Is that Commander Tanris?" Enikar asked.

Tanris held a finger to his lips, then pointed at something out of sight. *Wait*, he signed, then vanished.

You know what intensifies tension and really gets the heart racing? An immeasurable silence, ignorance, and a sudden explosion of yelling, whacking, metal-on-metal battle.

I gasped and took another involuntary step back.

A body dropped onto the floor in front of me, which frightened the spit right out of my mouth and made Tarsha scream. A sword clattered down next to him like an exclamation point of alarm. Pirate, by his clothing. Sensibility called for retreat. We eased away from the open area. I waited and wondered if Tanris would win the day or if I should shepherd my little flock at speed back up the canyon.

Still having trouble with my racing heart. And breath. And ribs…

The noise upstairs quieted. Unfortunately, that did nothing to calm my nerves. Then Tanris reappeared.

Of course he did… How could I have doubted?

"You all right? Enikar with you?" He didn't open his mouth when he talked, which gave him a peculiar lisp.

"I'm here!" Enikar waved, but Tanris just squinted. The old man was too far in the shadows to make out.

"We're fine," I called as loud as I dared. "And he is. Is it really you?"

"Yesh, feather brain." Definitely Tanris. He glanced up. "Be right back."

"Splendid!" Enikar said, coming out into the light to beam. "I always liked the commander. A man with a mind of his own, but plenty of respect."

Senza came to join me, gripping my arm. We both stared up at the gash—until she shook me. I went from one startlement to another as she threw her arms around my neck and burst into Girl-like sobbing.

What was I to do but embrace her in return? My wrenched shoulder protested and my ribs screamed yet again. I ignored them, at least for a minute or two, then moved away.

She followed.

We were far enough from the others that I could speak to my invisible companions again without anyone overhearing. "Ancestors, please help my friends. Keep them safe. Please."

[Grimfist! Daaaaangerous.]

"Keep him *out* of danger," I urged.

"What's that?" Enikar asked.

"What?" I echoed as the spirits shot up through the narrow opening, hissing and shrieking like an entire flock of geese under attack.

"And th-th-that," he stammered, white as one of the aforementioned geese.

Tarsha, eyes wide and her own face pale, put her arm around the old man's waist. She kept her gaze on me, fearful, disbelieving.

Before I had to provide an answer, the shrieking turned into another full-scale battle. I made it a point to avoid the completely illogical pastime, but in this case I wished I could see the results of the Ancestors pitching in.

Another body crashed down across the crack in the floor, then a third. Perhaps *pitch* hadn't been a wise choice of wording. Both instances induced gasps and moans. Senza dug new bruises into my arm. I had to turn from the sight; my stomach was never cut out to be a warrior or an assassin.

The noise died down, and for the second time, we had to wait to learn the outcome. I did not like it one bit. We heard voices, saw shadows and brief glimpses of men. The longer we waited, the tighter our nerves wound. When a rope slithered down over the edge, we all jumped.

A dark, curly head came into view. Not Tanris. "Can you climb, sir?"

I glanced at my companions, then shook my head. "Better not risk it."

He spoke to someone out of sight, then turned back to us. "No trouble. We'll pull you up if you'll make the line secure on your end."

Enikar insisted the ladies go first, and when his turn came, he grinned like a boy all the way. When the rope returned, I looped it in the same pattern I'd used on the others, putting the weight on my backside. Up I went, like a sack of water. No, a sack of fine wine. Helping hands grabbed hold of my pack and shoulders at the top, then deposited me on the ground. My unintentional warble of pain drew looks of alarm.

"I'm fine," I choked. "Fine, *fine.*"

"You don't look fine." The strange way of speaking didn't disguise the timbre of Tanris's voice.

Shedding my pack and pushing off the rope, I got up as fast as I could. Swayed a fraction. Tanris watched me, one hip cocked and fists on his hips. I laughed at the familiar pose and grabbed him in a hard embrace. "Bless the gods of miracles, you look *good* for a dead man!"

He grunted as he always did and thumped me on the back. I didn't even mind the pain. "You, too."

"Me? I'm not dead." I thumped him, too.

"Me neither."

I wanted to hold on to him, but that got awkward in a hurry. Hands on his shoulders, I stepped back to look him over. I could only shake my head in incredulity. In relief.

Amusement and *pleasure* made his eyes shine. "You stink so bad."

I laughed again and let him go. "Fish paste: it's not just a seasoning anymore."

"How old was the stuff?"

I plucked at the coat tied around my waist. "Got it from the fortress laundry. The stench kept people away, and I found some interesting things in the pockets."

"You would."

Another shriek split the air and a shadow speared straight at us. I ducked. Tanris stepped back—and Not-an-Egg plowed me over.

"Egg!" I hollered, flat on the ground, laughing and wondering how to hug a dragon. I didn't even mind the jarring of my wounds. His wings enveloped me, his claws pricked my skin, and he licked my face with unrestrained enthusiasm. Prying him off took some effort.

While I struggled with that, Tanris folded his arms and looked smug. "Found him after we left the ship again. Crying. He came along for a while, then perked up all of a sudden. Started pushing me and had a tantrum when I ignored him. Figured he knew something I didn't, so here we are."

The dragon gave a final lick, then sat back proudly. On my belly.

"You've got to move, Brute. I hurt."

Alarmed, he leaped off, then peered at me with intense worry. From two inches away.

"I'll be fine," I assured him, rubbing his knobby head before I stood. He promptly wrapped himself around one leg. "So you came back to look for Senza." My attention returned to Tanris.

He nodded. "Long shot. Half the fortress is gone. The ridge behind it collapsed. The harbor's on fire."

"It is?" I twisted to scan the sky. Four funnels of smoke curled upward. When we'd come from under the fort itself and gone straight into the canyon, we'd missed it. "Starry nights… I can't believe you took the risk. Wait—Yes, I can. You would."

He smiled a little. It clearly hurt.

I gestured with my chin. "What happened to your face?" Compounding the bruises, lumps, and a days-old beard, he had bloodshot, glassy eyes. Pain, yes, and medication unless I missed my guess.

He opted to sign, and I didn't blame him. *Broken jaw. Side, too.* He must not know the sign for *rib*. Come to think of it, neither did I. With his thumb, he motioned to where the others had gathered. Food, water, and bandages drew me like a lodestone. Tanris sat down with us, and when we'd all got the attention we needed, he heard our story, then told his own. Mostly, he signed; I translated.

He'd seen me catch Senza and throw her to safety, and hoped she might have escaped. But he'd also seen the slab of rock—impossible to miss—barrel toward me. It had obscured everything. He thought I'd been killed. Knocked off the bar when the slab struck, he'd thought *he* was dead, but something uncanny had happened. At this, he looked anywhere but at me.

Even Not-an-Egg paused his chewing to wait with bated breath. He could make out sign language? I'd have to find out. Later.

With one hand, Tanris illustrated the gentle downward drift of a feather. *He fell in slow motion.*

My fingers drifted to my talisman. A space opened inside me, charged with shock, relief, realization, possibility…

He'd landed hard on a rocky shelf—hard enough to knock him out, but he didn't know for how long. It took awhile to get the ropes off his wrists and ankles, then he'd dragged himself out of the caves before making his way to the *Integrity*.

"Zakkis did wait!" I exclaimed and pointed at Senza.

"Forced," Tanris declared. "He wanted to sail because of the quakes. The sea was choppy." An understatement, no doubt. "The Eagles persuaded him to stay."

Tarsha covered her mouth.

Enikar nodded sharply. "Bully for them! Good men, those Eagles. You Eagles," he amended.

"We'll rest for an hour," Tanris said, getting to his feet.

"A whole hour! How extravagant." I stretched out on the ground, tucking my coat of many pockets under my head. Not-an-Egg pushed it out of the way, wriggling into its place.

"There's a gate to close."

"Blah, blah, blah," I retorted, suppressing a stupid smile and closing my eyes.

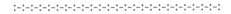

A tap on my shoulder woke me. I opened my eyes to see Tanris crouched at my side, holding a folded cloth. Impulsively, I bumped my fist against his knee. "You're still real."

He snorted. "Miss me, did you?" His mouth twitched in the faintest of smiles.

"Did you miss me, too, darling?" I batted my lashes.

The smile widened a fraction. "It's been quiet. Doesn't sit well anymore."

I flicked the cloth with one finger. "So you brought a gift for me?"

"Yes. Shirt." He handed it over and switched to signing. *Stream that way. First see healer.* He pointed across the grassy, flat-topped knoll. There stood the green-garbed Ishramite dragged along on the journey for occasions like this. Curiously, he, Senza, and two Eagles were the only ones in sight.

"Perfect." Stars, I was stiff. "And then is there more food?"

He made a shooing motion. *Go. Talk after.*

"Maybe you should try drawing pictures instead."

All I got was a droll look. Then he left to pretend to speak to one of the Eagles.

With my pack in hand, I hobbled over to the healer, who stood when he saw me coming. "Brother... Josni, isn't it?"

Black-haired and dark-eyed as myself, we might have been related, except he wasn't nearly as good looking. "Yes, sir."

"Walk with me." I took us to the far side of the hillock, where a jumble of smooth boulders marked one edge. They gave us protection from view, as well as taking us out of hearing range. "The commander says you're to tend my bumps and bruises."

"Yes, sir." Inky brows crooked in question.

I dropped the clean shirt on a rock and peeled myself out of the old, smelly one. Happily wadding it into a ball, I tossed it away. "Listen. I know what you are and what you can do, so I need you to do it. Completely."

The brows dove downward. "I'm sure I don't—"

"You are perfectly aware what I mean. We have no time for tender sensibilities, modesty, or awkward evasions. You use that magic of yours to make me whole again, and do it quick." I pointed to the ground. "Today. No dragging your feet."

The brothers of Ishram must have lengthy workshops on facial neutrality. They are experts.

I heaved an exasperated sigh. "If you don't, I won't be able to do what I need to, and that will be a problem. For you. Probably permanently."

He wasn't convinced.

"Sweet mother-of-*pearl*, man! I will not tell anyone your secret. I never have. Please don't let's do this the hard way."

His mouth crimped, but he finally nodded. "You'll want to sit." When I had, he explored my head, shoulder, elbow, and ribs. Then he took my wrist in one hand and the opposite shoulder in the other and made me wish I'd never heard of Ishramites. Never having been conscious during such attentions before, I couldn't say how much of his efforts fell into the category of vengeance.

Unaware how I'd ended up there, I laid on the ground until the stars faded, my breathing steadied, and a brisk breeze dried the clammy sweat. "Thank you," I rasped.

Josni merely pursed his lips and nodded. He stiffened as Not-an-Egg flap-ran to my side, his croaky voice raised in alarm that only eased when I rubbed his head and told him to be still.

My muscles still twitched as I dragged myself upright. The dragon pushed under my arm and helped. How endearing. "Now you need to do the same thing for Commander Tanris. And Senza."

I loved watching Josni's mouth flap soundlessly. "But he doesn't— He can't—"

Fist on hip, I massaged my eyeballs. "I realize this is difficult. It is necessary. The situation is grave beyond your wildest imagination. And if you can trust anyone in the entire glittering empire, it's Commander Tanris, and Senza can't speak. Just do it."

I may have reeled like a drunkard as I trekked to the stream Tanris had promised. He'd exaggerated, but what the trickle lacked in volume it made up for in cleanliness. Not-an-Egg gamboled up and down the alleged stream, splashing with delight. I washed, shaved, and traded my smelly borrowed pants for the clean ones. Transferred my little bundle of shiny rocks from the old pocket to a new one. Donned my clean shirt. By the time I strolled back to the others, I was nearly human. Sleep would do the rest.

Tanris sat cross-legged by a tiny fire, his head in one hand and a steaming cup in the other.

"Feel better?" I asked, setting the pack down and taking a seat beside him. The dragon sat next to me, leaning against my hip as if he might keep me from wandering off and getting lost again.

"You knew about him?"

"Mmm, yes. All of them. And you know about this." I tapped my pack where the lumpy idol pushed up against the leather.

"About what?"

"Don't play innocent with me. You only brought me a shirt, so you must have known I had pants in here, which means you looked, which means you saw. Also, you took your dagger back. That was a little obvious."

"I was only looking for clean clothes. You—"

"Smelled. I know. And now I think my sniffer is broken forever. Don't worry about it, I'm not upset."

Tanris rubbed his bristly chin, rightfully cautious. A healer's magic, aside from being more violent than I ever expected, didn't merely mend the injury. It did that to a limited extent, but it also started a process. I could *feel* it working in my bones. Tanris's jaw was going to be painful and tender for some time.

My ribs sympathized, but they hadn't taken as serious an abuse. My shoulder—I shifted it in an exploratory circle. It ached fiercely, but I could deal with it.

"Enikar thinks Serhat still has the idol," Tanris said. "He's worried about it falling into Gaziah's hands."

"If the story about Gaziah is true, he's not wrong."

"You've used it?"

I nodded. "The first time when I picked it up in Serhat's office. It was unintentional, but I used it to find you. It reacted to my thoughts. Does Enikar intend to keep it himself?"

"No." Tanris shifted. "He thinks it should be destroyed."

"I'm not sure he does, but that's a fine way to deal with priceless artifacts that don't belong to him," I sniffed.

Tanris quirked a brow. "Are you really taking that route?"

I peeked into the pot nestled in the coals. The piquant scent of herbs met my nose. A healer's tea. A pile of dented tin cups next to the fire ring invited me to help myself, so I did.

"Serhat thought I had it, but he couldn't find it on me," I said as I emptied the liquid into my cup. Tanris nodded. He'd seen the guard search me. "It was in the guard's coat pocket."

"And Tarsha got cold and took the coat." A faint smile tugged at the corner of his mouth. "Did she know it was there?"

"Not until after the two of them fled the chamber."

"So she brought you the idol *and* the dagger. Clever woman. How do you feel about that?"

I snorted and sipped the tea. The heat made me blink my eyes. "Where is she?"

"On the way back to the ship with Enikar and a pair of Eagles." He emptied his own cup and set it aside. "Is it too early to ask if you have a plan for taking care of the gate? I suspect it's not as simple as just stabbing it."

He knew me well. I always had a plan, but sometimes it required time to perfect. And sometimes circumstances ripened it in the blink of an eye. "Did Enikar explain his theory about how the gates work?" He shook his head, so I took a drink and sketched out the same arc the duke had and told him what I knew. "I've been thinking about the Marketh gate and putting together bits and pieces I've learned since then. You know this is all mostly..." My voice tapered off. It was *mostly insane.*

"Guesswork? Because this has never happened before in all of history?"

"Exactly. I don't have the training of a six-week pup, Tanris. I don't think I can do this."

Lips in a thin line, he let out a slow sigh. "I don't think you *can't.*"

"Well." I tossed back the rest of my tea. "The gods do love me. If I fail, a legion of chariots will come to escort me to paradise."

"And if you succeed, you'll be even more insufferable."

"Ye takes yer chances, fren'!" So saying, I leaped to my feet and dusted my backside. "Let's go stab a gate."

—26—
Crow of No Other Name

The gate lay inland, north of the fortress and behind the mine. Enikar's map led straight to it, not that we needed it. Once headed in the right direction, the noise guided us, and then the twisted energy it gave off. Even from half a mile away, it made my teeth hurt. Made me feel that I might fall apart like so many pieces of a puzzle.

The closer we got, the lower to the ground Not-an-Egg went, until his walk turned into a slink. I reminded him for the fourth time that I would bear him no ill will if he wanted to return to the ship. In fact, I would worry very much less. I had to admit, the sight of a small, indignant dragon stalking off like a crab held its share of amusement. However inappropriate, I'd take humor where I could get it.

We all fell silent as we approached the portal. The pair of Eagles accompanying us spread out to either side, weapons already drawn. Their eyes shifted nervously from the gate to the surrounding trees. Josni hovered at my elbow, more agitated by the yard. Did the magic of the construction affect him the same way it did me?

The pale purple arch soared skyward and stretched as wide as two Tanrises end to end. The edges hissed and sputtered, though the flames resembled liquid more than fire. They roiled into a surface unlike what I recalled of that night in Marketh or the gate in the strait. Rather than a black, opaque center, we beheld a window. Filmy and churned by random ripples, it allowed a vision of what lay beyond. A broad sand waste footed low, craggy hills topped by stunted trees. A peculiar smell emanated from it: vegetables roasted in the oven too long and coated liberally with dust. Nothing, as far as I could tell, moved within that landscape.

The lower edge hovered at waist height, and the ground beneath it cracked and withered for twenty or thirty feet in every direction. One side aligned on the perpendicular with a cliff. How many foreigners had hurtled off that as they burst through, all unsuspecting?

While we stared, the gate threw out a deep, wavering whine. How strange to see it pale and empty...

"Well, that's somewhat bigger than I expected." Tanris rested either hand on a weapon at his waist. His own sword and ax lost, he'd reclaimed new ones from the dead pirates. A few extra knives, too.

"It's huge," I agreed. "Though the lack of foreigners flying out strikes me as an advantage." Even presuming the gate had already dumped as many as possible into this side, and friendliness might not be their strong point. "Do you suppose it grows?"

Senza ventured closer, a stark expression on her face. Each of us had our own memories of the first time we'd seen such a gate. Baron Duzayan had called it into being, determined to bring through it an army he would command. How, I did not know. Not-an-Egg was meant to play a vital part in that event, but he had already bonded with me—a fact that enraged Duzayan beyond sanity. The story reminded me of my own fallibility and the necessity of being prepared to shift my plans. I survived because I was flexible; Duzayan died because he refused to be wrong.

I could sense Not-an-Egg nearby. He'd chosen a good hiding place; invisible. What I wouldn't have given to join him... Instead, nerves had me fiddling with some item I'd unconsciously picked up along our trek. I glanced down at it—and discovered the figurine

Senza had given me in Bright Bay. A duplicate of my offering to the god of thieves.

A powerful shiver went through me. I shoved the thing into my pocket, still gripping it.

"Duzayan's gate was much brighter. More substantial." I had intimate, sparkling clear memories. "The one over the water, too."

"True," Tanris agreed. "Maybe it has something to do with its age."

"Most things die when they get old."

He grunted. "You think we should wait?"

"No, I suppose not." A generous sigh left me. "Well, it's been a good run, eh?"

"I'm not going anywhere."

I grinned as I dumped my pack at his feet. "Then you know more about this monstrosity than I do." Mustering my swagger, I proceeded to the gate. All the short hairs on my body stood on end. My belly flopped back and forth like a snared fish.

I tried to muster my old motto: *I choose not to live in panic, but to face each situation sensibly and with faith. What I lack in knowledge or skill, the gods make up for, and the gods love me.*

"The gods love me," I repeated.

The Ancestors came along, hushed but on edge. They created a bulwark on every side, as they'd done before. What good it might serve eluded me—though I noticed the effect of the whining diminished.

Mouth dry, I took off the talisman—the *joziba*—and wrapped the cord around my wrist; I refused to lose it again. The etching on it resembled the gate somewhat. A key, the duke had named it. That made sense. And if it was a key, would it work without the wretched dagger? It hadn't before.

I pressed the *joziba* against the frame.

A shock ran through me and green sparks erupted from my hand, then chased up my arm. I jerked back with a yelp.

Nothing happened.

[Two... Twain... A pair...] The voices of the Ancestors shivered over me.

"I didn't have two medallions before. Oh. Of course." *The dagger.* My desire to use it again was about as strong as my desire to shove my hand into a blacksmith's fire. My palm ached, and I hadn't even begun. I took a few deep breaths, stretched my neck, then walked myself through the memory of closing Duzayan's gate.

It had pulled me closer and closer. The dagger had changed shape. My hand had welded to it and I'd lost both skin and blood. Blood that had flowed through the markings on the talisman. The Ancestors had poured into me, much as they'd done when my leg was trapped.

I was missing something here...

"Crow."

Dear gods of untimely demises, didn't Tanris see I was busy?

"Crow."

His insistent tone demanded attention. I turned to find the entire scene changed. Not only had the sun drastically shifted its position in the sky, but a small army of Basi Serhat's men stood in a semicircle around the gate. The two Eagles and the healer lay on their bellies, each with a booted foot on their shoulders and a sword at their necks. On his knees, Tanris had one arm bent up behind him by none other than Basi himself, though two companions flanked him. They must have muscled Tanris to his knees, for Basi couldn't have done it on his own.

Tanris looked battered. Again. Blood oozed from the edge of the self-proclaimed prince's knife where it pressed against his throat.

As a testament to the prowess of the Eagles, several pirates were strewn on the ground. They either didn't move at all, or groaned and held onto various bleeding body parts.

I saw nothing of Senza or Not-an-Egg.

Curiously, my pack now lay at my feet, though I remembered surrendering it to Tanris.

"Toss me the bag," Basi ordered. He had a wicked bruise in the middle of his forehead. The gift from Senza in the tunnels.

Don't, Tanris mouthed.

From off to one side, within the trees surrounding the little clearing, came a thud. A grunt and hiss followed, then a shower of leaves and twigs. Then another thud, harder than before. Squishy.

Basi smiled, smug as a cat. "That'll be your girl. Oops." Tanris must have moved, for Basi yanked more forcefully on his arm, eliciting a snarl of pain from my stalwart friend. "The bag. Now."

Opposing needs divided my thinking. As much as I may have wanted to focus on Tanris and his predicament, images and thoughts about the gate crowded my head. Magic intensified them. "The bag," I echoed, trying to wrap one strand of lucidity around that thought. "Because… you actually liked my reeking clothes? You want the beads? They can't be worth enough for you to go to all this trouble. The—"

"The idol, fool."

"You already looked through my things and did not find your ugly rock thing."

"Then you won't mind if I look again. Or are you willing to trade this man's life for your insolence?"

Tanris had a remarkable way of looking stubborn and stoic. "Close the gate." His mouth jerked as Basi's knife opened more of his skin.

"Stop!" I hollered.

But, *[Close the gate. Close the gate! Cloooosethegate…!]* hammered at me from all sides. The wind, thick with the scent of burnt things and damp earth, kicked up. Dust swirled in violent little eddies. Pressure on my ears and head muffled sound, and I was so very tired of not being able to hear.

The whites showed around Basi Serhat's bulging eyes as his gaze darted. His companions, too, flinched. Ashen faces, fearful looks, and white knuckles gripping swords suggested they would fight or flee any moment. Possibly both.

Into that gale of need and tension strode a tall figure. KipKap! He paused on the edge of the thicket, swung a mace up onto his shoulder, then pinned Basi Serhat with a glacial glare that actually froze the man in place. He'd done the same to me once. I didn't like it.

Tanris didn't waste one second of his surprise deliverance. He twisted free and punched his captor in the chest. Basi's stagger broke the strange hold KipKap had on him, but left him at Tanris's mercy.

In a blink, the prince was on the ground. "Close that infernal gate!" he bellowed, swinging a fist at the nearest pirate.

Not-an-Egg burst from the bushes with a rasping scream. In a heartbeat, he wrapped himself around the head of one of our foes, teeth and talons bared. KipKap waded into the re-erupting melee. Senza stepped out of the trees brandishing a bow and not at all shy about using it. More surprising, foreigners swarmed from behind me —*behind the gate*—to attack the pirate force with alarming ferocity.

The Ancestors did not let me gape for long. *[Now! Now! Now!]* they shrieked.

I spun back to the gate. To my consternation, the faded purple had deepened, the licking liquid flames lengthened. As it stirred, the buzzing energy it emitted increased. The sound drilled into my eardrums and threatened to cleave my head in two.

"What do I do? Help me!"

The shield they'd formed stilled instantly. *[Hush... hush... Find your self... your center... your strength. Let us in.]*

Instinct encouraged me strongly to refuse. At the same time, logic reminded me they'd been *inside* before, and they had never hurt me. "Do it," I said. "Just do it!"

Coolness pressed against me, then slipped past the fragile barrier of my skin. I shuddered in reflex. Layers of competing images dizzied me: This fight, the fight in Marketh. This instant of possession, the possession in Marketh. *This* moment. *This* need.

On my knees between the pillars, I laid the talisman down as I'd done before. I had to free the cord from my wrist. With Duzayan's dagger, I made a cut in the fatty part of my thumb. Blood dripped from it and into the channels on the talisman. I felt threads of myself following. It *burned* in my veins. Whoever had devised the practice of blood magic had been completely, stark raving mad.

"Where are the words?" I demanded of the Ancestors, and stabbed the dagger into the desiccated soil. "What are they?"

[The dagger... uncover the dagger.]

"What?" My voice climbed twenty alarmed notches. "It will cripple me!" Why did they *think* I'd wrapped the hilt in layers of leather?

[Hands... hands... hold out hands...]

Belly quivering, ears throbbing, I did as they said.

Two figures coalesced, each bending over one hand. The gate's purple radiance shone right through them, but I saw their faces, their eyes, their mouths. It was like looking into a mirror except their hair was long where mine was short. Silken locks floated gently around them in direct opposition to the escalating maelstrom.

Indistinct fingers created icy patterns on my skin that glowed brilliant green. Then, from the center of my hands, they drew lines down each finger. Each stroke accompanied a word or phrase. I do not know what they said, but the words pulled at more strings within me.

When they finished and withdrew, I knew exactly what I had to do. Purpose and terror filled me in equal measure. I snatched my own knife from my waist to slice through the strands of leather wrapped around the dagger's hilt. They fell away, baring the jewels embedded there. Jewels that gleamed as brightly as miniature suns, and tinted with the base color of each gem. I dropped my knife, then held my cut hand out. I had to massage it to encourage a few drops of blood.

More threads of my self passed into the weapon, only the dagger was not a sympathetic receptacle like the talisman. It ripped pieces of me away.

[Now,] the Ancestors whispered. *[You can do this. We are here. Always here...]*

I wrapped both hands around the hilt, drew it out of the soil—and felt the Ancestors' words spilling out of me. Just as had transpired before, cool, gleaming green light edged every syllable. So bewitching and so frightening... With one swift move, I plunged the blade back into the earth.

Time stopped.

The air froze. Tiny fissures laced it. Beautiful, like ice over a lake.

And yet... something was different from my previous experience. I didn't know what to look for, so I let the familiar voices flow over, around, and within me. When I lifted my gaze to the semi-transparent surface of the gate, I saw movement—a reversal of motion.

Focus intensified.

My breath caught.

Still gripping Duzayan's terrible dagger, I pulled it from the ground ever-so-slightly.

The gate stilled, though the eardrum-shredding hum remained.

"KipKap!" I shouted, and hoped he heard me. It seemed he did not, and I called out again and again until six spindly fingers clasped my shoulder.

"Here am I." His too-deep voice bounced like a gong in the strange middle ground provided by the Ancestors.

"It's open. Hurry. I don't know how long I can hold it."

His amazement shone all around him, too bright to see. I had to close my eyes, but I knew the moment he bounded away. Seconds later, I felt myself surrounded.

"Easy, easy," I whispered to the Ancestors. To myself. "Let them pass."

The crushing sensation abated fraction by fraction. The foreigners —so eager to return home that they dared to brave both the Ancestors and the awful magic of the gate—pressed close. I could not imagine the courage it took for the first to step through the throbbing magic. I could not even watch for fear of losing my tenuous hold.

"Help me," I whispered, lips dry, veins burning, muscles quivering under the strain.

A shout went up.

I squeezed my eyes tighter and relied on other senses to tell me when one figure after another filed past and *home*. Some of them balked and shouted and swore. I ignored them and held tight, tight— until the dagger sank slowly back into the earth. "I can't hold it!" The tumult swallowed my voice.

Did anyone hear me?

I knew what was coming. It had happened before.

I bled. My very essence oozed out of me to weave a closure. There were no words to describe the agony. None of the wounds I'd ever taken over my sometimes insane life compared. Still, it did not blot out the awareness of the way I fit into this instant, this world, this *existence*. I was part of the pattern; the pattern was part of me. The pattern was wounded, and I must mend it.

Me.

Crow of no other name.

That knowledge, that *mission,* touched me in the exact instant the last thread was woven and sealed. A welcome nothingness cocooned me. I existed outside of any thought, feeling, or sensation, divorced from the torment of my body and my heart.

Then the gate winked out of existence, and I fell.

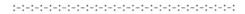

The marks on my hands didn't go away. *It might be early still,* I tried to convince myself. And, *really, what harm is a pair of exotic tattoos?* Better those than losing skin and gaining scars.

I sat studying them, warm sunshine melting across my head and shoulders. A cool breeze—from the sea rather than the Ancestors—ruffled my hair. It bore the persistent odor of smoke. Toes buried in the sand, waves purling up and down the beach, clean body and clothes, food in my belly... What more could a man want?

I pinched the bridge of my nose, then surged to my feet to walk down into the surf. A little way out, Not-an-Egg dove and splashed, chasing fish. It was the farthest he'd been from my side since I woke. Tanris had not been able to pry him away. Hands shoved into the pockets of my baggy islander pants, my fingers closed around a rough stone and I rubbed the surface with my thumb. Farther out, the *Integrity* bobbed on gentle swells.

"Hey!" a voice called out from behind, and I twisted to watch Tanris trot down the incline to join me. "I thought I'd find you here."

He looked better, the healer's reservations notwithstanding.

"We should bring Josni with us," I said.

"Where are we going?"

"The next gate, I suppose."

He took off his boots and rolled up his pant legs, then waded into the water with me. I'd never seen him so... casual. "You want to adopt him into our little crew? We hardly know him."

"He might like to stay away from the company of Eagles for a while after his, ah, outing."

"Are you saying Eagles aren't to be trusted?" He slanted me a look of chastisement.

"I trust exactly one Eagle."

"Oh, do you? And who would that be?"

I ignored him. Together, we wandered down the beach. "Does Josni have another name? Is that his first or his last?"

"Last. His first name is Timon."

"Mmm. And your name, Corryth... Where does that come from?"

"My mother's father."

"Do you know your grandparents?" I asked, striving for a casual tone. It was always good to have something to occupy one's hands during vulnerable moments like this, so I fiddled with the stone.

"Yes."

"They're still alive?"

"Yes."

"Mmm."

"Why?"

I held the stone up to examine in the sunlight, focusing on it intently lest he think I was getting maudlin. We'd done that before. It was best saved for special occasions. "What are grandparents like?"

Tanris favored me with a well-worn expression of exasperation. "They're like shirts," he said after an uncomfortable space. "Some of them do the job better than others."

I could not help myself. I snorted a laugh.

It was his turn to ignore me. He gestured with his chin toward the object of my attention. "What's that?"

"A rock, I think." A lump like pale colored glass with a hint of pink I hadn't been able to see underground, its surface had an oily appearance. Duke Enikar hadn't mentioned diamonds in his notes, and nothing I'd ever heard about the islands suggested such wealth.

"The only rocks you're interested in come with visions of gold dancing around them."

"That's poetic. I like that about you. All tough on the outside, warm and fuzzy on the inside."

"So what kind of rock is it?"

"Are you asking as my friend or as the emperor's lackey?"

Tanris's jaw slid forward, but he let the insult slide and glanced about. "We're on a protected island in the strait. I have no jurisdiction here."

"Except to take Basi Serhat into custody. Right?"

"Didn't I tell you? He escaped."

"He what?" I stopped sharply.

"Mmhm. All that chaos at the gate. The earthquake. The fires…" He shrugged.

My eyes narrowed. "I'm still trying to decide how much I resent three and a half days of unconsciousness. I mean, I *deserved* to see how things worked out, and I'm already tired of the way our adventures end."

"Oh, the end hasn't come yet, and you didn't miss out on everything. Not that I understand why you'd want to go through another earthquake. Or the disaster it set off."

We still contended with aftershocks and uncontrolled fires continued to burn on the other side of the island.

I added suspicion to my already narrow gaze. "What are you not telling me?"

"My middle name."

"You have *another* name?"

"Wouldn't you like to know." He resumed our stroll, *mischief* dancing around him like little fireflies. Intriguing, if unexpected. Tanris rarely teased.

"You're trying to distract me. What are you hiding?"

"Nothing!" He held up a hand in defense. "I only wanted to see how you're doing."

"You saw how I was doing this morning. I daresay there's a reason for this second assessment." I tucked the diamond back in my pocket.

"Very well. How do you feel about meeting with some locals and your foreigners?"

It did not escape me that he'd taken pains to refrain from calling them demons. A handful of those with us at the gate, including KipKap and his brother, had not made it through before it closed. Many others were trapped here on the island.

"Me? Why?"

"Why don't we sit down…" He veered. I followed, and Not-an-Egg followed me, striving to look like he wasn't. He plopped down to crunch away at—something. Maybe it had been a crab once.

"That bad, eh?"

Dropping himself onto a broad bench of rock, Tanris stretched his feet out and braced his arms to either side. He waited until I sat before he spoke. "A lot happened after the gate closed."

"So you said: another earthquake, fires…" I waved a *get on with it* hand.

"Bright Bay is a wreck. Half the town is now, well, *gone*. What the quakes didn't break, the fire took, and then it started on the forest. Foreigners are trying to put it out." He stopped my question with an upraised finger. "We're still working on a body count. It's harder with them because no one knows how many were killed or trapped when the mine caved in. Natives are leaving by the score. Their families are destroyed, homes and livelihoods lost, crops ruined, the whole shape of the island changed…" He let out a long, worried sigh.

"And they're blaming me."

"Not at all. I cannot tell you how greatly it pains me to say this, but you are now the hero of both natives and foreigners." He wrinkled his nose as if he'd smelled something bad.

I liked that appointment far better than scapegoat. "Oh?"

He chewed on that for a minute, then nodded. "From what I gather, the pirates have been a fixture here for some years. Their numbers were much smaller before Basi Serhat's appearance. They and the locals had worked out a truce of sorts. Then Serhat came along and stole the idol. He ousted the former governor, took over the mine, and began collecting slaves to work them. Villagers were the targets. I mean, he had a whole island full of ignorant, helpless fools. And he had pirates patrolling the waters to keep the fools from going for help." The skin around his eyes and mouth tightened.

"And the hero part?"

"I'm getting to it. Serhat's presence had already set the pattern for death and destruction. Then the gates happened. Things got worse." Talking about Basi Serhat chased away Tanris's rare humor.

I worked to intervene. "Can we skip to the good part?" I whined and put on a pleading face.

It did not go unappreciated. Tension eased in his shoulders and he gave me a rueful smile. "Yes, why bother with all the tiresome details?"

"Right! We only need the *engaging* details."

"You are such a child." He shook his head. "Very well. You closed the gate, saving a score of foreigners, giving the rest hope, and stopping the damage it was causing."

"All that," I breathed, and fanned myself with both hands.

"That was a neat trick KipKap pulled, by the way."

I scrunched my nose, struggling to remember what he'd done, besides come out of nowhere at the perfect moment.

"The freezing thing?" Tanris reminded. "At any rate, the mine collapsed. The foreigners turned on their overseers—and on any pirate they ran into. Some of the locals fled the island. Others remained, but their commitment is currently questionable. Earthquakes, fires, and demons being what they are... We brought you here. Basi escaped. Basi got caught again. The locals and—"

"*What?*" I leaped to my feet and whirled on him, planting fists on my hips. "You told me he escaped just to vex me, didn't you?"

He pulled a face, attempting innocence. He needed practice. "Yyyes?"

I tossed my hands up, then plunked down again. "Consider me vexed."

"Happily. To continue the short version of the story, everyone wants Serhat's head."

"And welcome to it," I grumbled.

"As tempting as that is, we're going to trade him for Enikar's freedom."

"We are?" I muddled through a puddle of confusion, then sat up straighter. "We are! Sometimes you are more brilliant than I give you credit for. We need Enikar to chart the gates, and he can't do that without his head. But... how are you dealing with the whole treason side of things?"

He crooked a brow and shrugged. "Is it treasonous for a man to protect his dear nephew? The empire he loves? He wants to distract and divert, not destroy. Prince Basi, being a Bahsyri citizen—"

"Former citizen," I clarified, though I liked the turn his mind had taken.

"—tried to start a war by claiming neutral territory *and* kidnapping Uncle Beloved. Such a citizen is bound straight for the chopping block. I suppose you could ask Gaziah nicely if you can send his head to the natives," he mused.

I snorted. My excellent wit was rubbing off on him. "In the meantime, what are we going to do to keep the natives and the foreigners from killing each other?"

"I haven't figured that out yet." He leaned forward to brace his elbows on his knees, fingers interlaced. "Maybe we can leverage the idol."

"Buy peace with it?" That thought set the wheels in my head into motion down another path.

"I know that look. You're planning something."

"Mmm... I have an idea. Where is Enikar?"

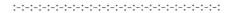

Getting the information I wanted from the duke was a delicate exercise in burglary. I had two reasons for not asking for the details outright. First, I didn't want him involved, being so closely related to the emperor and the government. Second, I delighted in picking his brain like a pocket.

And for both those reasons, I didn't invite Tanris.

Enikar loved to share what he knew. It took little prompting to get him started, and a few judicious questions shepherded him in the most useful directions. Namely, the existence of natural diamonds on Masni. Mind, I never *said* the word *diamond*. He was easily distracted, and told me more than I dreamed possible about our location: the idol; the local customs and belief systems; economy; care and cultivation of crops and resources; and traditional arts and crafts.

I regretted not bringing KipKap along. He'd have been intrigued, though his language skills would have collapsed under the deluge of information.

Enikar eventually brought the conversation around to my ancestry. I minded that not at all, despite the advent of a headache. Such was the price of having my skull cram-packed full of thousands of details.

Dinner saved me. The cook from aboard the *Integrity* knew how to prepare sea bass perfectly in wine and olives. He also managed a fine dish of broad beans, green beans, onions, garlic, and tomatoes. There was bread aplenty to soak up all the lovely juices. Being docked allowed him more culinary freedom than he had when sailing. I considered hiring him on as my personal cook...

Stuffed full of information and good food, I leaned against a clever rest Tanris had fashioned of branches and rope. The man had unexpected depths. Idly, I took out the figurine. After a brief examination, I rolled it over my fingers. It hadn't the same easy flow as a coin, but the extra focus reminded me about how I needed to pay attention to the gifts of the gods. Not take them for granted. Eyes closed, light from the fire danced across my lids. Someone played a flute, another sang. Not-an-Egg snored lightly behind me. It was easy to pretend we were safe here.

Somebody planted themselves next to me.

I opened one eye to see Tarsha, but she didn't look at me. In a red blouse and a gold-striped skirt, she wrapped her arms around upraised knees. I noticed she'd changed her footwear and the beaded slippers sat beside her. After a minute or two, she rested her cheek on her knees and watched the flames dance.

Soon Senza came and settled on my other side. She crossed her legs and sat with her back straight. Only her head bent as she applied a small knife to a piece of wood with zeal. I wasn't sure if she planned to carve it or demolish it. The air around her was decidedly prickly.

I opted to say nothing, but waited for sparks from more than the fire.

—27—
Bread, Wine, and Sour Truth

"Kaffa?" asked a deep voice wrapped in wool.

I swam up from the cozy depths of sleep. Someone had put a blanket over me. They'd also slid the backrest from behind me. Should such manhandling alarm or please me?

"Yes." I struggled upright and scrubbed my face. I needed a shave. "I suppose it's morning?"

"I suppose you're right. Here." Tanris pressed the warm cup into my hands and I finally got my eyes open. Fog blanketed the cove, hindering vision and muffling sound. The tang of smoke permeated everything. The hazy shapes of Eagles drifted in a semi-circle, watching for the trouble that might come from any of the three factions on the island. Senza bent over the fire, stirring a pot of something delicious-smelling. Tarsha stood several paces away. With a scarf wrapped around her shoulders, she stared into the mist. Beyond her, the ghostlike *Integrity* floated.

It occurred to me that I'd slept through whatever tension had simmered between the ladies. How disappointing. On the bright side, the slippers had moved to a place by my pack.

Tanris got himself a cup, then sat down beside me. He deposited a bowl of tiny, speckled boiled eggs and damp flatbread between us.

"What about what Senza's cooking?" I asked.

"Dinner." He arranged himself until he was comfortable, then pulled a book out from beneath his leather jerkin.

"The cook run off?"

"Hardly. She's helping him out. Bored, I expect."

She shot him a grin, set her spoon on a rock near the fire, and turned away. At a whistle, Not-an-Egg trotted out of the undergrowth to join her, nuzzling at her pockets and evidently finding a treat.

"Bribery will get you everywhere." I helped myself to the morning's plain fare.

"You find out what you needed from the duke that way?"

"Mmhm." I wished vainly for honey.

"What was the reward?"

"A book from my collection."

He stared, nonplussed. "It was that easy?"

I shrugged. My attention settled on Tarsha. After our interlude in the caves, I'd expected further interactions to be awkward. Instead, she treated me much the same as she treated anyone else.

A comfortable silence fell as we broke our fast, and Tanris began reading. I thought him engrossed until he said, "Are you going to help her?"

I cast a glance at him, but the book shielded his face. *Mysteries of the Phoenix Circle*. At least he'd elected not to study tricks for hunting criminals while I looked on.

"You think I should."

Tanris marked his place with one finger. It took me back to our trip up the Zenn River on the *Nightingale*. As it had been then, his expression was serious. "I think people are often more complicated than we give them credit for. We can't always understand what drives them to do the things they do. And no, I'm not taking her side, especially. I just don't want you to miss something important to you."

"Such as?"

"I couldn't say. You still have feelings for her."

"Feelings of annoyance. She betrayed me. Deeply." It made my chest tight, made my heart beat fast and my blood simmer.

"Yes, she did. Do you know why?"

To my wonder, the knot of emotions enveloping all things Tarsha had loosened. The cords no longer threatened strangulation. I remembered telling her I didn't hate her; that I wouldn't waste my energy on hatred. Evidently, that hadn't been entirely true, but I had at last reached a place where it had *become* true. At the same time, I was unwilling to take the next step. Not yet. Perhaps not ever. "I don't care why, Tanris. I want her out of my life. Forever."

Silence lingered for a long moment. Then, "You protest too much."

"And you're a few loops short of a knot." I kept my voice even, my expression neutral. "Are *you* going to go to her aid?"

"She asked you, my friend." He took a drink and returned to his book.

Just to be obnoxious, I pushed it up so I could read the title aloud. "This sounds more interesting than your last read. What was it? *Stalked and Chalked?* Where do you get all these?"

"Oh, this?" He pulled the book free to regard the cover, his thumb still marking his place. "Found it in your apartment."

"Point to you." I gave my head a rueful shake. He certainly hadn't found the *hunting* manual there, though it might be judicious to read it. Know your enemy and all that.

"You're keeping score?"

"Of course."

"Ah. Am I ahead?"

"In your dreams."

"That's good." He nodded and started reading again.

"It is? How?"

"Establishing and fostering overconfidence in one's quarry."

"You got that from the other book, didn't you?" It made me smile to slip into our old routine of badgering one another. "Still chasing me?"

"Weaving a web of false security."

The arrival of an Eagle interrupted our verbal sparring. "Dasamu Kabir has agreed to meet with you, sir," he said. To me.

Dasamu was the leader of the locals, barring the next political or physical upheaval.

"Good," Tanris answered. "Have you heard from KipKap yet?"

"No, sir."

He returned to his book. "Let me know when he shows."

KipKap did his best to act as an intermediary between us and the other foreigners. His witness of twenty-two of his people returning home through the gate had given him some authority, but trust was hard won. And who could blame them? Terror, servitude, and death did not make convincing motivations for cooperation.

We had it in mind to change that. To this end, we'd arranged a meeting between the foreigner leaders, the local leaders, and ourselves. Given my popularity, Tanris suggested I take the lead. I could only imagine how that must have pained him.

The messenger disappeared into the mist. I finished the last egg, got to my feet, and headed off for my morning ablutions. Predictably, Not-an-Egg appeared out of nowhere to accompany me.

"Be careful out there. The pirates are grumpy and stabby."

I gave Tanris a mock salute and a grin. He really was starting to sound like me. I passed a watchful guard and found the stream with no trouble. The dismal gray cloak of fog looked colder than it felt, and the water was, well, let's call it *brisk*. A quick splash for face and torso seemed sufficient. I sat back on my haunches to let my fingers dangle in the water and gratitude wash through me.

"My thanks to the gods of light and air," I murmured. "I cannot measure my relief at being out of those dark, miserable caves, though I allow they were not *entirely* miserable. There are the diamonds, after all, for which I am overjoyed." Were they a consolation for what I'd had to face? I'd like to know what the gods thought, but the idea of sitting down for a chat with them was frankly terrifying.

"Ancestors?" I breathed the word out, and they gently stirred the mist around me. "Thank you for your help. I realize I haven't—That I push and pull at you. It doesn't make sense. I'm sorry."

Invisible fingers caressed my cheeks. *[We see. We know. It is a valuable thing.]*

"How's that?"

[You do not seek power... dominion...]

What would it be like to get what I wanted whenever I wanted it? Boring, to begin with. And after a while, people would hate me for it. I'd suffered enough disgust and contempt for far less significant things; I had no need to look for more.

"If I ever do—if I start to use this magic for the wrong reasons, will you stop me?"

Their voices rose as they conferred among themselves, words slipping over and past me, just out of reach. It reminded me of my childhood, crouched by the fire while the adults talked over me in terms I didn't understand. At least the Ancestors didn't shout, nor did they seem to fight amongst themselves. Disagree, yes, but I couldn't recall a single instant that their disputes had erupted in violence.

[We will try,] they offered at last. *[Purpose is complicated... tangled... elaborate. Reasons and choices are individual. Answers are not definitive.]*

Their words were like dry leaves scraping together and echoing. Such a strange thing... The more I listened, the better I became at separating the sounds and discovering their meanings.

"Then will you keep watch? You know what I am feeling—and if I become past feeling, if I fall into the footsteps of people like Duzayan Metin, I must be stopped."

Their touches on my cheeks, head, and shoulders firmed in reassurance. *[That we can do, Friend Crow. We are Guardians. Counselors. Here always... always...]*

"And if I should panic and stop hearing you again, is there a way I can..." My chest constricted at the thought of—what? Doing something wrong. Insulting these beings who cared about me and for me as no one had ever done in my life.

[The key... You are the Way...]

"Me? The whole me? I mean—"

A blood-curdling scream heralded a figure leaping out of the shrubs and over the stream, straight at me. He bowled me over backward. Praise the gods, the Ancestors, and years of training, I automatically went with the motion. With legs and momentum, I tossed him over my head.

A chorus of cries arose from every side. *Pirates.* We were under attack.

I rolled up to a crouch, prepared to do my least favorite thing: fight. The Ancestors surged, enclosing me in a sheath. I fisted my hands; they filled them with energy.

The pirate rose to my right. Far too close! I pushed him as hard as I could. The energy burst from me, shocking us both.

He somersaulted backward and landed in a boneless heap. More, the force I released didn't stop with him. It knocked down two pairs of grappling fighters, sent others staggering, and completely cleared the fog. Pots, branches, clothing, and blankets flew every which way. Some of them thwacked into people.

One big *whoosh* and it was done.

Tanris was up again in a heartbeat, and his soldiers followed his lead. In the thick murk, the pirates might have bested us, for they had greater numbers. With the element of surprise turned on them, they didn't have a chance. Not against the emperor's Eagles.

Tanris divested them of their weapons and slapped two of them upside the head when they got cheeky. They wanted our food. He elected not to share. Instead, he gave them marching orders. That is to say, he told them on no uncertain terms not to show their ugly faces again or he'd forget he'd been in a good mood the first time he saw them. If they ever returned to the island, they'd be killed on sight.

Very decisive of him, and it displayed his usual generosity and nobility. They should thank the gods they still drew breath.

During the commotion, I took a roundabout circuit back into camp, hoping to throw off any suspicion that I'd been the source of the wind. It gave me time to pull my shirt on, as well. Not-an-Egg put on a show of snapping sharp little teeth at the pirates as we passed. One more surprise to pile on them.

"Thanks." Tanris was not fooled in the least. "That was brilliant, if a trifle excessive. How are you?"

I nodded. Several times. "Surprised," I managed. "Can we not— make this a thing?"

He crooked a brow. "It is a thing, but we can keep it between us, if that's what you're asking. It won't stay a secret for long," he warned.

I kept nodding. I felt as though that energy had come all the way from my toes, and its going left me—not *hollow*, exactly. Hands turned up, I looked at my palms. The lines on them glowed. A strangled noise scraped out of me and I hid them in my armpits.

Tanris squeezed my shoulder and remained at my side while he gave the men orders to pack up the camp and get ready for battle. Battle was the last thing I wanted. KipKap stood out of the way, watching me with curiosity and sympathy. Evidently, he'd arrived during the melee. Senza, bless her, strode up and handed me a cup of water.

I gulped it down and backhanded my mouth. Restoring my poise never used to take so long. "Are you all right?"

She gave a sharp nod, but her eyes were awfully bright.

"What happened?"

Her hands flew. *Hit a pirate in the head with the pot lid. Burned him. He jumped on me, but your wind carried a blanket over his head.* At this, she started giggling helplessly. Her giggles turned into tears. She buried her face in my shoulder while I patted her and said nonsense soothing words.

Across the smothered campfire, Tarsha regarded me with pursed lips. Still clutching a spear in her hands, she looked quite fierce.

"Finish getting dressed." Tanris clapped my back. "We've got a meeting to go to."

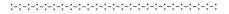

Dasamu Kabir had chosen a wide bluff north of the crippled mine. The craggy, tree-covered hillside that had once bordered the east side was now a valley some fifteen or twenty feet lower than the cliff top. Access was fairly easy, and hiding places nonexistent.

Not-an-Egg found one anyway, much aggrieved at my orders. "Stay quiet and invisible unless you *see* me getting attacked." The possibility of defending me mollified him slightly.

The governor sat at the center of a long, narrow table. An assortment of cups and goblets clustered around several large ceramic amphoras. I assumed they were filled with *perhayan* wine. It was a local beverage used strictly for celebrations, according to Enikar. Rumor claimed it was potent in the extreme. Random chairs, benches, and stools provided seating for other guests. What had it taken to carry all this from the wreckage of their villages and homes?

Also thanks to Enikar, we'd known to bring an offering of bread. A pair of Eagles toted a basketful between them, setting it on the table to the governor's right, then backing away. They each offered a polite bow before retreating.

Tanris hadn't convinced me that parading the emperor's elite guards was a wise move, but I hadn't convinced him to leave them behind, either. With the numbers the locals and the foreigners boasted, I confess I felt easier knowing the Eagles stood close at hand. And the dauntless KipKap. Not that any of them were armed. In accordance with meeting rules, weapons were forbidden. I found that only mildly reassuring, as I'd seen what people were willing to do with their bare hands when provoked.

"I don't like this," Tanris muttered, waiting for his men to take their places.

He wasn't the only one. KipKap resented being kept from the conference table, and was only slightly appeased when I pointed out that the only reason for my own presence there was him.

"I told you, you can't be a part of this." I hiked the strap of my pack more comfortably on my shoulder.

"Because I'm a commander in the Eagles, I know. I just wish I knew what *this* is."

"I'm not even sure it will work, so don't get your britches in a twist."

Senza backhanded my belly. *Will we survive?* she signed.

"I would say yes, but you should be prepared to run."

"Crow—"

That tone from Tanris always meant I was about to be in trouble. Luckily, the governor stood and motioned for us to approach. I strode confidently to join him. He gestured to a place across the table from him. I eased my pack down and offered him my free hand, marked palm tilted downward.

He still stared at it with obvious unease. "You are the wizard who closed the doorway."

As much as I longed to correct him, I resisted. While I knew the word *wizard* kindled fear, I couldn't depend on the same reaction for a druid. Their anxiety could be manipulated. "I am Crow."

He continued to stare.

"And you're Dasamu Kabir, yes?" At his nod I pressed on: "I believe it's customary for two men meeting over the *mejal vela iriwan* to shake hands?"

Kabir's mouth turned down. With obvious apprehension, he put his hand in mine. I shook it firmly enough that he couldn't jerk away when our palms touched. I smiled. He didn't. We both sat.

"You are also the doorway opener."

"Me?" I pressed a hand to my chest. "No. That ill favor belongs to the late Duzayan Metin, may his shroud be wound too tight."

"He is dead?"

"Quite." I still had nightmares of the way his—no, never mind. It did no good to dwell on that horror.

"Why did he open the cursed thing here? What have we done to deserve this savagery?"

"No one deserves it, Master Kabir, and he has paid the ultimate price. He will never do such terrible things again."

Kabir leaned forward. "He *ruined* our country! Our lives, our homes, our crops, our—"

"Yes, he did. I am sorry for that." I pursed my lips and looked about. Off to the east the forest burned, and there was no telling if the wind would remain in the favor of the firefighters. What a waste... I coughed raggedly, dramatically, and took a drink.

A few enterprising souls amongst my followers took my lead and coughed, too. I saw a few foreigners hold cloths over their faces. Was the smoke really that hard on them?

"How—Hm. There is no discreet way to put this. How much would you say your island is worth now?"

Kabir glared at me, then turned his head and spat. So much for the high regard I'd earned among his people.

I kept my own gaze steady and drummed my fingers on the table as though deep in thought. It probably wouldn't do to think too long about how Tanris had hoodwinked me with his story of my alleged heroism. "I wonder if we could help each other."

"Can you make our island new?"

"No, but I have a proposal." I set a single gem down and turned it in a little circle. Then I pushed it across the table. Kabir picked it up to examine with obvious curiosity. "It's a diamond."

He leaned close again, suspicion not easing a whit. "A real diamond?"

I nodded.

Kabir hollered over his shoulder, and a gangly youth sped off. "Supposing it is real—why would you offer it?"

I folded my arms and took a turn with the leaning. "The foreigners that have come through the gate—"

"Demons!"

"Foreigners," I repeated with exaggerated calm. "They need someplace to live until we can find a safe way for them to return to their lands."

Kabir's expression turned to outrage. "You think you can buy our home?"

"Buy it?" I feigned shock, quite accurately, too, I'll tell you. "That is—well, I suppose that is an option…" I scratched my chin as I dragged the sentence out, letting the seeds of possibility fall.

"You *wizards* wrecked our land so you could trade it for a stupid shiny rock?" He shook the diamond at me. Spittle stuck to his mustache. His other fist curled against the tabletop.

Diamonds are not fragile, but there should be laws against treating them like gravel. Especially the rare varieties. "If we actually wanted you gone from this land, do you think you'd be sitting here right now?"

Kabir stood so fast I had to catch the edge of the table to stop it from plowing into me. "This *iriwan* is finished." The locals gathered behind him moved forward as one, faces fierce, a few of them shouting. The governor picked up his goblet and slammed it upside down with an air that could only be interpreted as insulting.

This was not going quite the way I'd hoped. "Is this what you want?" I lifted my voice for the crowd to hear me. "You choose conflict and suffering over survival? Over prosperity?"

"Your words are worthless." Kabir banged the goblet twice on the table for emphasis—but his comrades muttered among themselves and a handful edged closer.

"What's he got to say?" a tall, dark-haired man asked.

"He can help us? How?" came another.

"We won't sell our souls to these devils. Not that…"

With both hands lifted, I requested quiet. "I want to help all of you—people of Masni and people from the gates. I think I have a way." Altruism rested strange and precarious on my shoulders. I did not much like the fit of it, but I liked uncontrolled violence even less. Particularly when I sat in the middle of the battlefield. "Can we discuss a few ideas and work together to make the best of what's happened here?"

"By stealing from us!" Kabir's voice trembled with emotion.

"No." I shook my head and dropped my hands to the table. Where were the gods when I need them to unstopper deaf ears?

"What are you saying?" The tall man who'd first spoken speared me with a fierce frown.

I'd suffered far worse from Tanris. "I have three ideas. Will you hear me out? And are you willing to discuss them—improve upon them, perhaps—until we can come to an agreement?"

"No." When Kabir made up his mind about something, he stuck to it.

"Yes," the other man contradicted. A dozen voices from the crowd supported him. He approached the table and turned the goblet over. "Another seat," he instructed, and soon he sat on a folding stool beside Kabir's empty chair. "I am Jova Cayani. Begin."

I feared the crowd of natives would turn the meeting into a fight, but they quieted, listening. Apparently this sort of thing was permissible at their *iriwan*. I gave Cayani a brief nod of appreciation and waited until Kabir sank into his seat. "First, I want it known that I do not in any way represent the empire or the confederacy. I speak to you only as an independent mediator." Cayani nodded his understanding. He should. That was the easy part. "My proposals are these: One, you sell the island outright and leave. Two, you lease the island to the foreigners, with me acting as their agent. The lease remains in place until both parties come to a mutual agreement to end it. Three, you lease out half the island and agree to live peacefully and amicably with the foreigners until after their departure."

My suggestions raised indignation and fear among the natives. Jova Cayani lifted one fist and silence fell with startling speed. His gaze never left mine. "And if we refuse?"

"First, you'll get no recompense. Second, you'll face the foreigners, who have no place to go and nothing to lose."

"They would remain here?" If the idea affected him at all, he didn't show it.

"As I said, they've nowhere to go, and I must leave to search for a way to help them."

Cayani looked away then, turning his attention to the mob of foreigners behind Tanris and the Eagles. KipKap stood at the forefront of the group. How he kept them quiet and patient eluded me. I suspected they outnumbered the natives who'd come to watch this event. While this situation was not in the plans I'd devised, he gave a wonderful performance as the commander of his people.

Where was Diti?

"I hear you," Cayani said at last, softly. "We will discuss this and meet again tomorrow. Kabir, please return the stone."

The muscles in Kabir's jaw worked, but he did not contradict his companion, and he didn't voice either doubts or threats. He put the diamond on the table, then flexed his hand as if letting the thing go physically pained him.

"That is all I ask. Thank you." Enikar's lessons had not deserted me. I stood, placed my fingertips together in a rounded shape, and bowed.

Cayani and Kabir did the same.

"On a separate matter, I would speak to your highest-ranking *hukun*, if that is permitted." Both men stared at me. "Your... shaman? Priest?"

They had not expected that, and hadn't the freedom to discuss it amongst themselves before answering. Eventually, Cayani nodded. "We will carry your request."

"Thank you," I said again, and gave another humble bow.

As the islanders departed, Tanris, Senza, and KipKap joined me.

"That looked more like a standoff than an agreement." Tanris watched the stragglers, hand caressing the hilt of his sword.

"Not at all. This is a recess." I retrieved the diamond, hefted my pack, and leveled my best Evil Eye. "You said the natives revered me."

His nod was suspicious, but not the least sliver of dishonesty—or even amusement—touched him.

I snorted. "Their reverence needs practice." I started off. "We meet again tomorrow, and the haggling will begin."

"What haggling, exactly?" Tanris feigned mild interest tolerably well, but he didn't fool me.

KipKap sat with me on the beach, legs folded and long fingers interlaced in his lap. The movement of the waves entranced him, even though he'd had time to get used to the spectacle. The sinking sun painted the horizon in brilliant shades of yellow, orange, and fuchsia. A procession of birds drew a stark line, then faded into the distance.

"Is much beautiful, this place," his voice low and his expression musing.

"Is that why you stayed? You could have gone through the gate with the others."

He did not answer right away, likely trying to figure out which of his limited words to use. "Because of you, my people have hope. My people are—" He hesitated, tipping his head and rubbing one finger up and down the length of his strange nose. "Many. Frightened. Angered."

"I imagine they're also having trouble adjusting to a forced truce. Ah, no fighting. Peace. Cooperation." What I gained with the first explanation, I lost with the final word. "Friends."

"Yes or no." Humor flickered around him. "Maybe."

"Allies. Working together." I drew in the sand with a stick, nonsense figures that came and went as one overlapped the next. "It would be grand if you found peace here and took it home with you. No more fighting."

"Grand, yes. What is word for big amazing thing?"

"Miracle."

"Miracle," he repeated dutifully, and I knew he would not forget. "Is interesting problem: stay in your world and make peace, or go home and fight more."

"Let us aim for peace *and* home." I clasped his forearm and squeezed, genuinely wishing he could have both.

"You find home miracle. I find peace miracle." He patted my arm in return, his touch light as leaves.

"KipKap?" I bit my lip, doubting the wisdom of poking possible wounds. "Where is your brother? Did he make it out of the prince's trap?"

"Ah, Diti. He breathes." Too-long fingers brushed the air in slow motion, up and down, up and down...

Breathing was good. Unless it meant that he was badly injured and breathing was the best he could do.

"How—How bad was it? His—" I gestured vaguely at my head.

"Head crash." His fingers kept moving. I wondered if he used them like a bug uses its antenna, or perhaps a cat's whiskers. "Difficult," he said at last. "I carry him from trap. You leave us. Leave your friends."

I didn't want to admit my selfishness, so I said nothing. My gut spoke for me, roiling and unhappy. Not that KipKap could hear it.

"Diti wanted to kill you. Kill all your kind."

"Because of something I did?" I shouldn't be surprised. Humans throughout history did the same. To each other, never mind unfamiliar races. I scratched my ear, focused on my knee.

"Young Diti has fire in head. Fire in heart. Did not see past flames."

"See... what?"

"See Friend Crow struggle at fight. Call out." His fingers closed as if he'd captured some fragile, undefinable spark. More interesting by far than my knee, but I wasn't certain I wanted to see disappointment in those great blue eyes, so kept my eyes on that imaginary light.

"Crow want safe for Crow and for friends. Spirits fail."

I had to pinch the bridge of my nose. How like him to assume the best of me, even if I didn't deserve it. "They did not. There was a lot more pain than I wished, but the Ancestors saved Tanris. They saved me and Tarsha. Senza, too, I think. Then all of us again after we got free of the mountain."

"Hmm," he mused in his deep, tranquil voice, stretching out the sound. "Maybe KipKap and Diti, too."

If so, that meant they'd listened to me. Done what I, well, *demanded*. "I hope yes."

He loosed the imaginary spark he'd held and formed a steeple with his hands to press against his lips. "KipKap thanks you."

"For dragging you into catastrophe?"

"I know not this word." He repeated it carefully. Perfectly.

"It means ruin and woe. Loss. Pain."

"Not this." He stroked my forearm, where my up-rolled sleeve exposed skin. One finger at a time descending, brushing, reassuring. "For trust. Hope. Friending."

"Friendship." I swallowed a knot in my throat.

"Ah."

"Can we save the grammar lesson for later?" I was still trying to fathom his willingness—no, his natural tendency—to look past my initial instinct to save myself. *Crow first and always...*

"I like ship of friend." He wove his long fingers together and brought them close to his heart.

I opened my mouth, though words eluded me.

"Sir?" From a safe, polite distance, a voice intruded. An Eagle stood on the bank behind us, half hiding another figure. "This fellow says you asked to see him?"

I jumped up, putting myself between the new arrivals and my pack. "The shaman? Er... *hukun?*"

The fellow stepped forward, and I stifled a scream. Gray hair pulled back severely bore streaks of red ochre. More of the stuff encircled his eyes, outlined in white dots and bisected by a stripe of black. Black stripes decorated his forehead and the rest of his face. Beneath an enviable collection of necklaces, he wore a curious item. Was it ornamental or defensive? Wide concentric plates hung from throat to belly, adorned with engraving around the edges. His bare arms were red with black stripes and white dots. He—or was it a she?—was dressed in a multi-layered skirt. Red, of course. No hint of an aura or flicker of emotion could I detect. Admirable... Not that I was an expert, by any means.

"You are chaos." Definitely a woman.

How rude. "I am actually Crow. And you are?"

"Here at your request."

"How kind." A minimal nod of gratitude was all she got. "I would have come to you. I did not mean to inconvenience you."

"You are strange."

"I might say the same about you." An unexpected bubble of humor rose inside me. Thankfully, I didn't need to negotiate with this most forthright and unimpressed person.

"What do you want?" There was a complete lack of inflection in her voice. Not bored, but not quite interested. Not angry, but not pleased, either.

I motioned for KipKap and the Eagle to leave us. While they made their departures, the *hukun* and I had a staring contest. After the initial shock of seeing her unusual appearance, I enjoyed the game. I maintained a placid air under her unwavering inspection—which the Ancestors broke. They flitted about her, full of curiosity and caution.

A little flip of the woman's skirt in opposition to the direction of the wind made her eyes narrow.

"You are impertinent." She turned to leave.

"I am, I confess, but I have done naught but stand here, politely waiting for you to join me."

She spun back, expression sharp and disbelieving. After a still, knife-edged moment, she stepped down the incline to walk a full circle around me. "You do not lie," she murmured.

Currently, no, and I thought it best not to point out that I *might*. "I have something for you."

She stopped in front of me, tall and straight, metal-bedecked hands relaxed at her sides. "Another bargain?"

The question offered so many possibilities… I shrugged them off and gestured to my pack. "May I?"

She took two steps back and turned her palms toward me, revealing curious jewelry. A small stone set in gold fit into each palm, held in place by a circlet around her wrist and delicate chains on each finger. The stones, patterned in shades of green and polished to perfection, piqued my interest.

Caution prompted me to lift the bag rather than make myself vulnerable crouching beside it. I made no sudden moves as I opened it and removed the idol.

The *hukun* finally reacted, painted eyes widening as she came up even straighter. Still, she stayed where she was.

With the eyes facing away from both of us, I held the thing out. I doubted the choice a hundred times over, yet I wanted to be rid of it. It was dangerous in the wrong hands, and the islanders had taken good care of it for unknown centuries. There'd been nary a sign of aggression against their neighbors on either side of the strait. "I don't imagine I need to caution you to keep this well hidden and guarded."

Disbelief, astonishment, and relief leaked through her wards like rain through a leaky roof. She hesitated, as if expecting me to snatch it back and run away cackling. "Why do you not hold it for yourself?"

"I have a finely honed sense of self-preservation. Besides, it makes me queasy. Sick."

She made a noise in her nose and took the thing to wrap in a layer of her skirt.

"I plan to avoid it zealously, but should a dire need arise, may I use it?"

She darted a look at me. "Perhaps."

"That's fair." Over her shoulder, I glimpsed Tanris approaching and let out a sigh. "You'd best go."

One more long, searching stare, and the *hukun* made her way up the embankment to disappear from view.

—28—
Unexpected Consequences

"New girlfriend?" Tanris squinted after her in the growing gloom.

"Custodian."

"Of what?" He drew the question out with practiced suspicion.

I slung my pack over my shoulder and set out for the camp and dinner. "Cultural treasure."

"You gave her the idol?"

I castigated myself for beginning my trek too soon. I missed his incredulous expression. "Have you ever heard of anyone stealing it before? Enikar hasn't."

"What about trading it for cooperation between the locals and the foreigners?"

"Won't work." I shook my head. "If they made proper use of the thing, there is no reason at all that Masni wouldn't have become a genuine power in the area. Prevented Serhat's takeover, I imagine. I suspect there's more to it than we realize. A curse. The wrath of the gods. I don't know, but I don't trust it."

Silence followed until we approached the camp. "You realize you just threw away your pardon."

"As if Gaziah ever intended to give it to me."

He exhaled a long breath. "What do you expect me to tell him?"

"Tell him it was taken from us. It's true." I smelled food. Pork, unless I missed my guess. That meant the cook had returned to shore. "Did you bring Enikar off the ship?"

"And Tarsha. It's Serhat everyone wants, not them, and I thought they'd be safer away from him. Chains and a cage will not keep his enemies from trying to collect his head."

I suspected the rumor of a wizard would make them think twice. "Speaking of heads, I wonder if Enikar can help figure out how to get rid of the gates."

"You did fine."

"I did *accidental.* Knowledge and logic will improve the likelihood of my survival, which, incidentally, will keep the empire from evaporating. Then you'll only have to worry about Gaziah's plan for becoming emperor of the entire world."

"I suppose you want me to tell him the duke was taken, too?"

I snorted. "Now you're being silly." My pack hit the ground with a satisfying thump. I sat myself down in the trampled grass near the fire and the delicious aromas wafting from it. "That smells insanely good. I may have died and gone to paradise. Is it time for dinner?"

Stuffed to the gills with roast pork, wild asparagus, figs, olives, some sort of tuber, and an unexpectedly fine wine, I had no trouble at all falling asleep. Tanris had sent most of the soldiers to the ship to guard our prisoner, but I knew the Ancestors would alert me if anything disturbed the camp. It turned out that Enikar had a passably good voice. A melancholy mood had him crooning tunes perfect for drifting off to dreamland.

"Crow."

With consciousness came awareness of the sun shining on my face. Why must Tanris always be so keen to wake me at the crack of dawn? I hid behind one arm. "Is the apartment on fire?"

"What is this?"

I scrunched my nose. "Morning, most likely. And far earlier than I requested."

"I'm going to open it." He plonked himself down beside me and a dragging noise followed. It created a strange, cool space against my thigh.

"You can't open morning," I grumbled. "You can open curtains, locks, pockets, bottles of wine—"

"Mysterious boxes?"

"Yes, of course. Wait. What?" He had my attention now. I pushed up on one elbow. Something slid off my chest as I did, and I groped my shirt absently. Latches clattered on a dark red lacquered casket about two feet long, and a foot deep and wide. "Where did that come from?"

"You tell me." Tanris frowned and tapped a circular inset in the middle, between the latches. "It's locked."

I patted my chest, then searched about in the blankets underneath me. "Aha." A shiny silver key promised to fix the problem. The bow —the bit one grips to turn it—was a hollowed circle with a raised pattern on it. Three plain loops encircled that. The bit was intriguingly intricate. As Enikar would say, *fascinating*...

Nobody but me was interested in the ornate details of a key. While Tanris pushed the chest sideways, I scooted around, and a moment later had the key in the lock. I paused. "I'm just going to point out the obvious here. This was left for me."

"Do you think so?" His brows furrowed. I noticed that he'd already shaved both chin and pate. He had a terrible habit of rising with the sun and getting things done. "Right up against your side the way it was? Your arm over it and the key on your chest? Are you sure it wasn't meant for me? Or Senza. She deserves a reward."

I pointed at him threateningly. "No one should have full access to sarcasm before they've broken their fast."

One brow hooked upward, dragging mockery with it.

"Figures. Did you save anything for me?"

"Depends on what's in the chest."

Senza came to stand over us, brimming with curiosity. She held a steaming cup in her hands. She also blocked the sun in my eyes.

"Could be feathers," I retorted.

"Too heavy."

"Worms."

Senza snickered. I turned the key and eased the lid open.

"What've you got there, young man?" Enikar was quick to join the party, bringing along a curious Eagle.

A treasure lay within the box, but something was wrong with it. It looked... faded, as if viewed through a film, and the edges seemed to ripple.

We all stared in astonishment. Tanris was the first to reach out. His fingers hovered against the odd surface, then he pushed slowly against it—only to jerk back with a hiss.

"What? What happened?" I caught his wrist. The fingertips were pale and cold as ice.

He pulled his hand free to tuck into his armpit. "Cursed?"

"Curses are usually spells," Enikar murmured, crouching down with a stick next to Tanris. He poked at the trove. The stick turned white. After a minute or two, the end simply disintegrated, the pieces drifting away like snow. "Look at this." He stabbed the stick in a little further, and succeeded in tapping against a blurry disk before more of the wood disappeared.

Tanris shifted, cocking his head. "Is that a Mazhar talisman?"

"It is." Enikar gave me a significant look.

"What is it?" I whispered to the Ancestors.

[Guard... block... defend... protect...] The Ancestors swirled around us, rumpling clothes and hair.

"A warding of some sort." Enikar's chin jutted forward at an angle that had to be uncomfortable. "Fascinating."

"Aside from the obvious question of what it's doing here so far from the mainland, why do you say that?" Tanris asked.

"It's in pristine condition. It's active. There's a druid here who can unlock it."

I grunted, trying to disguise my surprise at his blurt. "The duke decided if my talisman actually belongs to me, I must be a druid."

"Fascinating," Tanris echoed drily.

"Well, it can't hurt for him to try." Enikar sniffed.

Can we drag the old man to the water and dunk him? I signed.

Senza bit her lip and ducked her head.

"Much." Tanris looked at his fingers, then at me. "It *is* a nice collection of baubles."

I got to my feet. "I need a drink."

Senza pushed her mug into my hand, offering a far too sweet smile.

"Traitor," I grumbled. Tea wasn't exactly what I had in mind, but it cured my dry mouth. I set the empty mug in the pile by the fire and paced away, then back.

The others watched and waited.

The Eagle ventured a closer look at the contents, and his brows shot up. "Maybe we should leave it alone…"

"Why's that?" Enikar scrunched his nose as he peered up at him.

"Wasn't here when we went to sleep, m'lord, and the sentries didn't see anyone. What if it's poisoned? A trap of some kind?"

Tanris rubbed his chin. "Take a turn around the perimeter. Talk to the others. Keep a close eye out for anything strange."

"Yessir." With a sharp salute, the man trotted away.

Tanris gave me an expectant look. "Well?"

"Yes. Well." I was the one who had experience with things like poison and traps. *Mundane* experience. Lips pressed together so tight it hurt, I dragged my talisman free of my shirt. I could do this, whatever *this* was. I drew a few deep, steadying breaths, then knelt before the chest. What had I done before? *Focused.* I could feel things, discern them around me. I'd sensed the rock I'd shattered. This was different, so I didn't rush. At last, a familiar awareness seeped through me. *A scent of green. A pale color filling me. Time and energy and matter sliding into place like pieces of a puzzle…*

The Ancestors recognized the new talisman and hung back with even more expectancy than Tanris.

Instinctively, I stretched one finger out to trace the line carved through the center of the new talisman. Once, twice, three times. With each stroke, I heard a different word. A Mazhar word. My vision quivered. I felt my breathing stop. A sigh left the bone, taking with it a sense of chill.

Tanris's voice came down a tube from about a mile away. His hand on my shoulder brought me abruptly back to the camp. "Are you all right?"

"Yes." I swallowed. "I'm… fine." My fingers closed around the disk and I drew it free.

The Ancestors scampered in circles, delight and pride cascading in their wake.

"Fascinating…"

A perfect round hole near one edge matched the one on my own. A leather cord or chain had once threaded it. Age and care had worn the surface smooth as glass, but for the indentation of the figures carved in it. A vertical line with three shorter horizontal lines. Around that, a square.

Peripherally, I was aware of Enikar poking his stick into the chest again. "I knew it! I knew it!" He reached for a necklace.

Tanris's hand closed on his wrist. With his head, he gestured toward me. "It's his."

"Ah. Yes, indeed it is."

Senza knelt beside me to cup my jaw. She looked me right in the eye, holding my gaze until my breathing finally evened out. Then she gave a nod and drew away.

This, of all the things I'd done, evidenced my use of the magic. Accidental and haphazard before, purposeful now. I'd *used* the power. I couldn't go back from that and say it wasn't me. With thumb and forefinger I lifted a string of pearls, draped it over the lid, then added several more necklaces. Chains, mostly, with an assortment of pendants. Some with gems, some without. None of them sparked any magical reaction.

"It's all right," I said. "Go ahead…"

Senza and Tanris removed more items from the chest. There was a beautiful pair of white ceramic cups. A trio of heavily ornamented wooden boxes. Embroidered cloth bags holding small polished stones, beads, shells, metal fittings and such. Several leather tubes, bracelets, and collars…

Enikar appropriated a tube, turned it over in his hands in appreciation, then worked the cap off.

Senza opened a little box and poured a handful of square coins of various metals into her cupped palm. Her mouth shaped an *oh* of delight and curiosity.

A low whistle drew my attention to Enikar. He'd removed a parchment scroll from the tube, and he wore the expression of a child with an entire basket of sweets. "Fascinating... *Fascinating!* Do you know what these are? Mazhar documents." He shook them at us gleefully.

"What are they about?" I asked.

"No idea." His grin didn't diminish in the slightest. "I recognize the alphabet, though. You recall I've seen the scrolls in the Imperial Museum, yes? Discussed them with colleagues? I may be able to decipher a few words..." And just like that, they captivated him. Bent over them, he muttered and blinked repeatedly as he tried to make sense of what he saw.

"What are we going to do with this?" Tanris asked. "It's a lot of temptation."

"Corryth Tanris tempted by antique treasure? I never thought I'd see the day."

"Not me, feather-head. You've already foisted a house in the city on me—why would I want this stuff?"

"Oh, you poor thing." I began putting the jewels back in the box. Tanris and Senza helped. I had to get cross with the old man.

"What would it hurt if I kept one tube apart?" he complained.

"What's good for one is good for all, isn't that what they say? And trusty, dependable Eagles aside, there's an entire ship's crew to consider."

Ignoring his crestfallen face, I tucked the last bits in place, then set the talisman atop the lot. Did the words I'd heard work to fix the ward again, or should they be in reverse? "*Baturi... ra'zindi... ax'serbati...*" I whispered.

Nothing happened. Did I say it wrong?

Three pairs of watching eyes unnerved me, so I closed mine and focused on the talisman, the little quaver of energy in it, and the memory of working the magic. One finger moved up and down the vertical carving. When I touched it like that, I could *almost* hear the concept I needed—which sounded ridiculous.

Since I was the only one in my head, I shrugged aside the sense of foolishness. Relax. Focus—until instinct froze me in mid-motion.

[Splendid... Very good... Nearly there...] the Ancestors whispered. *[The words... the words... Repeat the words, let them flow!]*

"Baturi ra'zindi ax'serbati." Each one poured like water from my lips. A chill spread outward from where I touched the talisman. I hardly dared look.

"Nicely done," Tanris murmured.

I jerked in reaction to his nearness. He sat beside me, a lidded pot by his knee. Enikar had disappeared. The Eagles had packed up the camp. I saw Senza striding to greet Tarsha, who had been swimming or bathing, for her damp hair hung long and loose around her shoulders. Not-an-Egg crouched across from me, watching intently.

Tanris closed the coffer and pushed the pot into my unresisting hands. "Eat up," he murmured. "It's time to get to your meeting."

"Thank you." My head felt swimmy, and my belly hollow. Removing the pot lid revived me considerably. Pork from the night before smelled heavenly.

He grunted. "You were at that for nearly half an hour."

"That long?" I paused with a piece of meat halfway to my mouth.

Tarsha interrupted. "Whatever is that?" she asked. Senza hadn't slowed her much. "I don't remember seeing it before. What's in it?"

"It's locked." Tanris held his hand out in an invitation she quickly accepted.

"What do you mean? Crow can open anything."

He gave her the key and crooked a brow.

I busied myself with the pork and watched.

"For goodness' sake." Tarsha inserted the key and lifted the lid. "Ooh!"

Tanris caught her wrist as she reached for the gold. "Careful."

He earned a frown for his trouble. She yanked free, then carefully touched the filmy surface. With a shriek of surprise, she tottered backward.

"Did I mention it was locked?" Tanris asked with syrupy sweetness.

"You didn't tell me it had a spell on it!"

"What it really needs," I mused, licking my fingers, "is one of those nice, screechy guard demons."

"That spell seems to work pretty well, to my way of thinking."

"We could break the wood." Tarsha sat up again, frowning as she looked the thing over.

"That might be worth a try," I agreed, "but not now. We've got more important things to do."

As if my words had summoned him, KipKap appeared on what was becoming a worn path inland. Two score foreigners in all shapes and sizes swelled behind him.

"Well, that's a little alarming."

Half a dozen Eagles drawing swiftly around us was a chivalrous gesture, but in reality, how long would they last if the foreigners attacked? Armed with clubs, shovels, picks, and disgruntled faces, they were ready to exact all kinds of vengeance.

Undaunted, Tanris stood and lifted a hand. It might have been a greeting or a warning. "Morning. We'll be with you shortly."

In the meantime, Tarsha got herself behind the Eagles in a hurry. Senza planted herself to the side and back only a step. She looked frightened, but determined. The Ancestors met this volatile state of affairs with their usual leap to agitation and self-defense. Or rather Crow-defense. They whistled through the air, thankfully overhead and not sending up clouds of dust and sand. Yet.

KipKap swept one arm out, two fingers raised. The group halted, but he kept coming. "We have anger."

"So I see. What happened?"

"Fight in dawn."

"Pirates?"

"All look same." KipKap's usually gentle eyes glinted with an unfamiliar chill. "Short. Pale. Much hair."

Self-consciously, I rubbed my unshaven chin. "But some of us are better looking." Speaking of appearances, I realized he no longer wore the slave collar. When had that happened? Come to think of it, none of his companions had them either… In their place, getting them off would have been my first order of business, too. Well, that and incidental things like *survival*.

"How many were killed?" Tanris asked.

"Them all. Us some."

He winced. "I'm sorry to hear that, KipKap. You do know there are two groups of humans we're dealing with, yes?"

KipKap's head lowered suddenly, putting his eyes on a level with Tanris's. To his credit, Tanris didn't flinch. I did. "Yes. Know also we are pestverminrodent in this place."

"You are not," I protested, a flare of indignation warming my belly.

He swiveled his gaze in my direction. "Hunted. Killed or slaved."

"Wrongly. I am trying to fix that, KipKap, but if your people attack the locals, I won't be able to stop the reprisals." He didn't know that word. "You kill islanders and *everyone* will turn against you."

He blew out a harsh, reverberating breath through his strange nose and straightened. "Yes."

"Help me help you, my friend," I urged, daring to put a hand on his arm.

His expression gentled a fraction. "You are good."

Tanris snorted.

"We need food. Shelter. Others want—what you say. Repies."

"I don't blame them, but the man responsible for hurting them is in chains. This has to stop, or all is lost. *You* will be lost." There was no accounting for how that grieved me. "Give me this day to talk with the islanders."

"We see." He stalked back to his companions. As soon as he reached them, a heated discussion broke out. Angry, desperate sparks flared and gleamed.

The sight made me uneasy. This arrangement with the islanders would be difficult enough without the foreigners going off their tethers. Pain, fear, and fury were not at all conducive to rational discourse.

"Ancestors," I bid under my breath, "if you can soothe them you will prevent the spilling of much blood…"

The Ancestors spiraled around me, then swept toward the foreigners. Despite that, several remained behind. I reached out a cautious hand and discerned a *thickening* of the air. Like when they'd protected me at the gate. *Gates.* My palm tingled, and I beheld a faint green glow emanating from the marks.

Tanris observed with pursed lips, then abruptly rounded to summon a soldier. "Get the duke and Tarsha to the ship. Take the chest, too. Split the squad—half stay with them, half with me."

"Yes, sir."

"I'll be staying ashore," Enikar announced, rubbing his hands together with enthusiasm. "This isn't my first diplomatic mission, and I've no intention of missing this historic event. I do wish I had writing materials."

"It's too dangerous." Tanris stepped in front of him, effectively blocking progress.

Enikar lifted his chin. "And I outrank you considerably, young fellow." The ocean breeze tossed his white hair back and forth without regard for station.

"You do, but the emperor outranks *you*, and he's the one I take orders from."

Eye to eye and nose to nose, they stared each other down for a considerable time. Then Enikar harrumphed. "I do admire your loyalty, Commander. Your integrity as well. Not every officer in the emperor's Eagles would stay to make and keep peace here in a place where he's no authority. It's a ticklish situation, beyond question, but of great consequence if we're to—" He glanced about, but the nearest Eagle stood a polite distance away, waiting to escort the duke the ship. "If we're to avoid inadvertently setting off a crisis between nations."

Though they were the same height, Tanris leaned forward, looming. "This commander out of his jurisdiction *does* have the authority to protect the empire's citizens. Which is why I will do everything in my power to see that Crow's scheme succeeds."

Enikar's gaze narrowed on me.

I shrugged one shoulder and rocked back on my heels, innocent as the dawn.

"Interesting," was all he said about that. "Very well. I wish you the best of luck and the favor of the gods." He gave a curt nod and turned away. "I'll expect a full report from both of you when this is done!" he hollered.

Tanris only grunted.

"A *scheme* sounds rather dastardly," I commented.

"Be glad I didn't call it a feather-brained scheme."

"I know that must have been difficult to resist." Sunlight behind him made me squint. "Between that stoicism and going so far as to credit me for the plan, I'm all teary."

He wasn't even looking at me when he cuffed the back of my head. "Let's get moving."

"Ow." I winced. "You didn't have to say anything, and it would have been fine."

Tanris walked away.

I stood for a moment to watch as the Eagles loaded the duke and Tarsha into the skiff. When she'd taken her seat, Tarsha looked to the camp, and her eyes found me. Worry shadowed her features. *Be careful*, she mouthed.

I gave her an elaborate bow.

A stiff wind blew across the bluff, flapping the row of banners the islanders had erected to divide the space. The *iriwan* table sat in the middle of that stark line. The area for the locals was larger than for the foreigners. No doubt a choice calculated to establish their superiority.

Unfortunately for them, such tactics impressed me not at all. I'd face too many situations in which I'd been meant to feel intimidated.

Unfortunately for me, the foreigners bridled at the perceived insult. Or possibly the red standards didn't suit their taste.

I did an about-face and strode right up to them. They'd stopped when they'd crested the bluff, more of them now than those KipKap had brought to the camp. They milled about, grumbling amongst themselves, howling, barking, waving their makeshift weapons…

"KipKap, I need you to translate for me. Please."

The tall foreigner didn't answer right away, but played with the untidy bits of skin that made up his ear as if to distract me from the lethal mace propped against the opposite shoulder. "Yes," he agreed at last.

"Thank you." I drew in a deep breath and let it out by degrees. The Ancestors alerted me to their presence, skipping up and down my person and whirling about. KipKap took heed and straightened, wary.

After a slow nod, he turned to his companions and gave an uncanny whistle that shuddered my very bones. It also stilled the group. "Calm yourselves," he said, and then something lengthy I didn't comprehend.

I had to calm *myself* after that. Lacking time for any such indulgence, I adopted a severe expression and thanked the gods for my acting skills. "I am disappointed in this—this anger and threat of violence. The islanders haven't given you as much space as they gave themselves. *What of it?* Do you believe you are weaker or less important than they are?"

A keen glint came into KipKap's enormous eyes. Dutifully, he translated. Low voices echoed him, passing his words along.

The foreigners stilled even further. A few slowly lowered their weapons. One of the immense avalanche creatures towered in the midst of the group. Not terrifying at all. I stifled the urge to slink away and hide, and prayed KipKap could keep the fellow from losing his temper.

Next to the monstrosity was none other than Diti, sporting a crimson bandage around his head and a necklace of unidentifiable ivory carvings. Hopefully not bones.

"Show them your courage. Show them you are not afraid." In that moment, I recognized the blessing of the gods upon me. With the necessity of speaking through a translator, I only needed KipKap to hear me—not the entire assembly. I could rally the foreigners and instruct them without including the islanders.

"Do not show your thinking and feeling to them at all," I went on. Choosing words that KipKap would understand made the endeavor challenging. Alas, it robbed me of eloquence, too. Good thing Enikar was not on hand to record my speech. "Be calm. Put your weapons down—they break the truce. The, er, agreement to stop fighting while we bargain. Spread out, but stay back from their banners. This respect will please them and keep you safe."

I waited for KipKap to interpret, and when a shadow of disgruntlement surged around them, I continued. "What they deserve is not important. If they feel threatened, they will fight. If they fight, your cause is lost—here and across the sea."

KipKap relayed my words, then more. When he finished, the foreigners talked among themselves for a moment. Then they fanned out, which allowed more of their people to join them atop the bluff. And when they settled down, still and silent, they presented an intimidating front.

"What did you promise them?" Tanris asked as I rejoined him.

"Dinner with the emperor. Or the emperor for dinner. It's up in the air." I waved one hand.

He ground his teeth. "Your sense of humor leaves something to be desired." He cast them a probing glance, then fell in beside me as I walked toward the islanders. "I'm coming with you."

"Not necessary, but thank you."

He nodded at the table. "They have two negotiators. Now you do, too."

"*Really* not necessary."

"Too bad."

I stopped in my tracks. "Look. This *discussion* might veer into pathways you are forbidden to tread. You—"

"Are you stealing from them?" The fierceness of his narrowed gaze surprised me.

Our confrontation reminded me of the earlier scene with Enikar, but Tanris would never win a glaring contest with me. "If I must."

He grunted, which was neither acceptance nor surrender. "I admit, I'm curious. I don't see how you can steal an entire island, never mind doing it without coming under censure from the powers that be."

"Is that a challenge?"

He wagged his index finger beneath my nose. "Don't even go there, Crow. Curiosity is not endorsement. Or support."

"But maybe it's worth a little wager?" I bobbed my brows.

He drew his down. *"No."*

"You're no fun at all." I resumed my trek to the meeting table.

"Only you would think this is *fun*," he grumbled.

"Just promise you'll keep your opinions, outrage, warnings, and curses to yourself. If you say anything, we'll likely end up with fun slit throats."

I knew without seeing that his fist tightened at his side. Likewise, it did not escape me that his presence beside me expressed trust. In me. A thief he'd hunted for years... I kept my smile to myself.

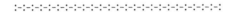

Dasamu Kabir and Jova Cayani awaited us, both seated in proper chairs with the proper wine and the proper bread displayed on the table before them. They had also brought parchment, pen, ink, a candle, and what looked like seals. To further intimidate us, they had substantially more reinforcements than yesterday. Mimicking the foreigners, they arrayed themselves around the edge of the bluff, but left a wide space between themselves and the boundary indicated by the banners—which appeared to be mounted on spears. How cozy...

The leaders stood and bowed.

We bowed in return. Like ducks bobbing at each other. If they bowed again, I would laugh out loud.

"Let the *iriwan* begin," Cayani intoned. He took his seat, signaling that we do the same. He wore resignation and exhaustion like a millstone. Likely, he'd been up all night debating with his people. "The gods have turned their backs on us. Our lands are broken and burning. Our people—" He looked down at the table, clearly struggling with emotion. "Our people are ruined."

His opening remarks directly contradicted the assertive placement of the banners. Had I misinterpreted?

Kabir cleared his throat. "It is decided that foreigners—that is you —cannot be trusted to honor a lease. We mean no offense." So stiff was his voice that it clearly conveyed the opposite. "If you refuse payment, we have no way to enforce it and no way to remove the, ah… tenants. Before we go on, we have one demand: we want the one called Basi Serhat."

Tanris gritted his teeth. It was a miracle they weren't nubs.

As I tapped my fingers on the sturdy wood surface, I pretended to think about something I'd already considered and decided. "Not possible. I wish I could hand him over, but he is needed elsewhere." I gestured to the sky.

The two of them fixated on my palm.

I would have to start wearing gloves. Perhaps the fingerless variety… "Basi Serhat is going to buy our way closer to a solution for shutting down the gates. *All* the gates."

"There are more than what was here?" Cayani asked, startled. Concern knit his brows.

"Yes. From what we've worked out, they are linked in an expanding arc." I drew a circle on the table. "They've caused damage on other islands and the mainland, too. Given the destruction already inflicted, there's no telling what will happen when that arc closes."

Kabir sat back with a short, guttural explosion of breath. "This is bad."

Understatement of the year.

"Extraordinary," Cayani agreed in a strained murmur. "Do you believe it could erase the islands altogether?"

"The islands. The empire. The world. I do not know. I'm sorry I can't tell you more than that."

His dark-eye study was so intense I wondered if he, too, held magic. "How will you use Serhat?"

"There is a man who has the education, skill, and associations necessary to help. He's in trouble with Gaziah." At their blank looks, I clarified. "Gaziah will likely kill him. We will trade Serhat for this man's freedom."

The two exchanged a long, fraught look.

A groan filled the air, then grew. Beneath us, the earth shook for the space of thirty or forty terrifying heartbeats, then quieted. I so love when the gods smile upon me…

Scraping my aplomb back into place, I leaned forward. "Let me help you with your decision."

Murmuring voices and restless movement marked the uneasiness in our onlookers. More swiftly than I'd have believed possible, the foreigners recovered from their alarm and resumed their stoic waiting.

Kabir made a curt motion, fist up, then fingers extended. I didn't know what it meant.

"Go on," Cayani supplied.

"I will lease the entire island for the next three years and pay you now." There went Tanris's teeth again. "I will also pay twenty of your people to remain here to work with the foreigners. They can teach how to manage these lands, and the foreigners will begin rebuilding. At the end of three years, we will meet here to decide whether to continue the arrangement. If I do not return, the lease ends and the island reverts to you."

"If the island is still here."

I shrugged.

"And these?" Cayani pointed at the foreigners.

"Pray to the gods that we can restore them to their homes. If not, remember what it is like to lose your own homes and families. That's exactly what's happened to them, and worse."

Kabir spoke, looking like he had a mouth full of worms. "We do not trust you. How much do you offer to purchase the island?"

From my jerkin, I withdrew a small cloth bag, and loosed the ties. I shook four glittering stones the size of my thumbnail onto the table. Raw, they were worth somewhat less than their cut and polished peers. Their value lay in their potential. How much did the locals know about diamonds?

Kabir's breath caught and I thought he would choke. He turned to gesture to someone in the crowd, then breathed again. Noisily.

Tanris worked hard to conceal a strangled noise in his throat—which, of course, did not go unremarked. The gods, in their generous wisdom, blessed me.

A tidy little man appeared, garbed in what had once been finery but had suffered through the quakes. He produced a glass magnifier sphere and bent to examine the stones.

I confess to some anxiety. While I was familiar with uncut gems and had often strategically transported them, there existed the minuscule chance that I might be wrong. Embarrassing, but not the end of the world; I still had a chest full of treasure to offer instead.

The little man straightened after a small eternity. Wonder rounded his eyes. "They're real."

I grinned.

Tanris silently performed some breathing exercises.

Kabir picked up a diamond and stared at it. "This will do."

"This will do," Cayani echoed, incredulous.

I laid the carved figurine from the temple beside the stones.

"What—what is this?" he asked.

"The gods always provide." They loved me. And I could afford to be cryptic.

Kabir shook his head and hollered for the scribe.

−29−
The Tidiest of Bows

The papers were solemnly signed, witnessed, and sealed. We exchanged them for the diamonds. And, at long last, we partook of the *really* strong *viyan vela perhayan*—the tribute wine—and bread. Our hosts gave their reluctant permission to invite KipKap to join us. He cried. It might have been the wine.

Soon after, a select group of foreigners was assigned to help the islanders prepare to set sail in a ragtag fleet. Part of the cargo consisted of prisoners. Several of Basi Serhat's guests had found themselves captured and detained. We had no way of telling how many had escaped the island already.

Joint efforts began to make headway against the wildfires encroaching on the town. Locals and foreigners alike worked to dig survivors out of the destruction. The crew of the *Integrity* pitched in to help. Tanris stationed the Eagles on board to ensure Basi Serhat's safety. Three at a time came ashore, working in shifts. Enikar arranged a small group to salvage Serhat's library and whatever other valuables he could discover. The food stores proved invaluable.

The pirate situation got a little sticky, but Tanris and I let the new allies work that out.

The island continued to tremble from time to time, but nowhere did we find evidence of a gate.

"I can see why you'd want to live here." Tanris walked beside me, the edges of the surf washing up over our bare feet.

It was an altogether perfect day. Afternoon sun shone down warmly. A tangy breeze blew in from the sea. Gulls and a handful of other birds wheeled overhead. Senza trailed behind us, picking up seashells she toted in an increasingly heavy bag.

Not-an-Egg, too, had come along. He chased the waves or galloped right into them, diving underneath. Now and then he emerged with a fish in his jaws. He wasn't *with* us, exactly, but we were never out of his sight.

"I like it better without earthquakes."

"I'd be happy never to experience another in this lifetime," he agreed. Picking up a flat stone, he skipped it across the water. The waves were gentle today. Peaceful, even. Tanris spent as much time examining the tree line as he did the surf. Stray pirates were always a possibility.

"Hey. How are your fingers?"

He showed me, wiggling to prove they worked. "Good as new."

"That's a relief."

"Indeed." He bent down for a shell. "I've got to ask—where did you get the diamonds?"

"You should *not* ask," I advised.

"Are they from the coffer? I don't recall seeing them."

I pressed my lips tight and pretended to turn a key.

"Would I have to arrest you if I knew?"

I ignored him and kicked my feet through the foam as I walked.

"Speaking of the coffer, how did that woman know you were Mazhar? Because with a Mazhar talisman protecting it, only someone like you could work the ward. Which begs the question about how a Mazhar hoard ended up here, of all places. And is she Mazhar?"

"You are full of questions today, Friend Tanris. Are you nervous about something? Nobody will pin any illegal activities on you, I swear."

"That's good to know." He didn't look like he believed me.

"Maybe the *hukun* saw my talisman. Or maybe she figured only a wizard could open the box—and she's not one." Those disks in her hands suggested she might have access to magic of some kind, though. Tanris hadn't been close enough to see them, and there was no need to add to his list of things to fret about. "You're also assuming she furnished it, and not someone else."

He gave a good old-fashioned grunt. "Because I don't want any more puzzles to untangle. And it *is* convenient. You give her the idol, and the coffer mysteriously shows up the next morning with a key laying on your chest..."

"Hmm. Mazhar chest and Mazhar chest. I love the symmetry."

A feeling of relief came over him, and I lifted my head from my inspection of the sand and surf to see why. We'd come to a narrow inlet between two low, wooded hills. The dark blue center suggested a depth we likely couldn't walk across. Tanris turned to follow the edge, and I went along, too.

"Symmetry, yes," he said. "All these wretched gates pop up, and it happens that a Mazhar druid can work them. It also happens that I know a Mazhar druid. It's like poetry."

It was my turn to grunt. "I suppose I might not mind becoming the hero of an epic ode."

"Of course you wouldn't. Have you decided what your heroic self will do with the maiden in distress?"

"What maiden?"

I should have known that would earn me another cuff.

"Tarsha, fool."

I rubbed my abused shoulder. "I don't know what I *can* do. The situation with the gates feels a little pressing. Should I save the world or the girl?" And who would ever have expected me to do either?

"Both, naturally. That's what heroes do."

I groaned. "As one hero to another, how will we accomplish that?"

His sideways glance brimmed with an odd mixture of amusement and foreboding. This gift of magic had me learning more every day about the complicated thoughts and emotions of my fellow humans. "First, we have to get Enikar's situation figured out."

"That's easy enough. You're the one who said we would trade Basi Serhat for the old man's freedom."

"Gaziah won't like it."

"Poor him," I said without sympathy. "He wanted us to rescue Enikar. We did." One might expect disbelief from His Most Lofty Magnificence. "Enikar must write him a letter, and I imagine he's got some insignia or jewelry you can offer as proof. And the Eagles. They've seen what's happening."

"You're not going with me?"

"I've gates to puzzle out." And imperial wrath to avoid. "In fact, Enikar's letter should describe the enormity of the problem we face, and the dearth of druids with the ability to influence the outcome."

Tanris still kept scanning our surroundings. It made me nervous, and *nervous* made me latch on to the Ancestors. Figuratively, that is. Grasping incorporeal figures would be quite an accomplishment. "And when Basi Serhat confesses his knowledge about the plot against Gaziah?"

"Enikar will be out of reach—and how believable is a man so bent on vengeance? He'll twist any fact that presents itself."

"If Gaziah knows about it—and he very well might—he won't accept anything at face value. If he has hard evidence against the duke and I hide him…" His voice trailed off and he frowned at the landscape ahead.

"You could always leave his employ and take up transporting goods."

"Thievery?"

Despite our lengthening association and familiarity, it was still delightfully easy to provoke a growl out of him. I gaped with theatrical finesse. "Well, that's unexpected… You'd do that?"

"*No.*"

I patted his shoulder. "Perhaps just shipping, then. I have a perfectly suitable vessel you could start with."

That earned another sideways look, at which he also was skilled. No one could deliver glancing suspicion like Corryth Tanris. "I don't like it," he said after a momentary silence.

"The *Integrity* or shipping?"

"This… *rumor* Serhat is cooking." He rubbed his bare pate hard.

"Considering the assembly he was entertaining, I think more than a rumor is afoot, but is it a strategy to curb the emperor or depose him?"

"You're not helping, Crow."

"Sorry." To my astonishment, I really was. "Let me think about it. I'll come up with a plan to keep you out of trouble." I'd already thought of one, and I didn't like it. It involved me going to the emperor in Tanris's stead. With trusty Eagles in tow, I could turn Basi Serhat over to him, explain what the gates were doing, and tell His Supreme Migraine that the good commander had stayed behind to guard his uncle the duke. It might even work, but it would require a substantial serving of selflessness. And dealing with false-hearted aristocrats. *And…* layers upon layers of contingency strategies.

"Your plans usually include criminal activities and dubious morals."

"Don't forget wizards." I gave him a bright smile.

"Never a dull moment." He pointed ahead. "We're here."

His hand on my shoulder turned me away from the shore. Tucked against the curve of the hill sat a stone house with a tile roof. A fence of woven driftwood separated a garden from the sward. Colorful flowers peeked through, and a stream rushed along one side, emptying into the inlet. It was comfy and quaint and—abandoned.

"Where is here? Does someone live here? Is this where we're setting up Enikar?"

"Now who's full of questions?" Tanris steered me closer, and Senza ran up. Her smile was far more radiant than gathering shells would inspire. "Jova Cayani's aunt used to live here. She passed a few years ago."

"It's haunted? What am I supposed to do about that?" My voice went up an octave. I had plenty of spirits following me around, thank you very much.

"Enjoy it, I suppose. It's yours."

"Mine? Why?"

From his jerkin, Tanris withdrew an oiled and bound packet. He drew in an exaggerated breath and let it out with a gust before handing it over. "This is going to make you insufferable, but he told me he has no use for it, and you deserve a small reward." His voice adopted a stern timbre. "For your bravery in closing the gate, dealing with the, er, demons, and your patience and generosity toward all."

"A house." I was seldom dumbfounded. Unfastening the packet, I looked over the contents. I had the deed to my apartment in Marketh and, well, others, but this was different. This touched hopes and dreams I blathered about, but rarely believed in.

"Some considerable property, too. It's set out there in the papers."

"A house," I repeated, wonder and delight brimming. "I'd have bought it."

"As one would expect. Never mind the source of your funds. But I believe that would have defeated the purpose."

"A house! In the islands!" Shoving the packet into my shirt, I caught Tanris's arms and swung him around, then abandoned him for Senza, who was a much more willing partner. "Come on, then," I directed, hurrying up the overgrown path. "Let's clear it out and clean it up. We've plotting to do!"

"Insufferable," Tanris complained.

Senza grinned, dropped her bag by the gatepost, and followed me.

I paused in the doorway to bow extravagantly. "Welcome to Crow's Nest!"

— THE END

FROM THE AUTHOR

If you enjoyed this story, I encourage you to take a few minutes to leave a review. These positive reviews help other readers discover my books (and keep me writing). Even better, your review encourages me to write more!

Thank you!

Connect with Robin online:
Website: http://www.robinlythgoe.com

Printed in Great Britain
by Amazon

75386251R00241